THE TAOIST EMPEROR

LIU HEPING

Translated by
Wen Huang

SINOIST

ACA Publishing Ltd
University House
11-13 Lower Grosvenor Place,
London SW1W 0EX, UK
Tel: +44 20 3289 3885
E-mail: info@alaincharlesasia.com
Web: www.alaincharlesasia.com

Beijing Office
Tel: +86(0)10 8472 1250

Author: Liu Heping
Translator: Wen Huang

Published by Sinoist Books (an imprint of ACA Publishing Ltd) in arrangement with Guangdong Flower City Publishing House co., Ltd.

Original Chinese Text © 大明王朝 1566 (Dà Míng Wáng Cháo 1566) 2016, Guangdong Flower City Publishing House co., Ltd, Guangdong, China

English Translation text © 2020 ACA Publishing Ltd, London, UK

ALL RIGHTS RESERVED. NO PART OF THIS PUBLICATION MAY BE REPRODUCED IN MATERIAL FORM, BY ANY MEANS, WHETHER GRAPHIC, ELECTRONIC, MECHANICAL OR OTHER, INCLUDING PHOTOCOPYING OR INFORMATION STORAGE, IN WHOLE OR IN PART, AND MAY NOT BE USED TO PREPARE OTHER PUBLICATIONS WITHOUT WRITTEN PERMISSION FROM THE PUBLISHER.

This novel is entirely a work of fiction. The names, characters and incidents portrayed in it are the work of the author's imagination. Any resemblance to actual persons, living or dead, events or localities is entirely coincidental.

Paperback ISBN: 978-1-910760-59-8
eBook ISBN: 978-1-910760-60-4

A catalogue record for *The 1566 Series (Book One): The Taoist Emperor* is available from the National Bibliographic Service of the British Library.

THE TAOIST EMPEROR

Book One of the 1 5 6 6 series

LIU HEPING

Translated by
WEN HUANG

Sinoist Books

CHIEF CHARACTERS

The Imperial Family

- **Emperor Jiajing:** 12th emperor of the Ming dynasty
- **Prince of Yu:** son of Emperor Jiajing
- **Princess Li:** consort of the Prince of Yu

The Imperial Court

- **Lu Fang:** chief of the interior ministry, Emperor Jiajing's most senior eunuch
- **Yan Song:** grand secretary of the Privy Council
- **Yan Shifan:** son of Yan Song
- **Xu Jie:** deputy grand secretary of the Privy Council and head of the Imperial Treasury
- **Tan Lun:** the Prince of Yu's chief of staff
- **Zhang Juzheng:** head of the Ministry of Defence
- **Gao Gong:** deputy minister of the Imperial Treasury
- **Mao Qing:** deputy minister of justice
- **Feng Bao:** commander of the Imperial Secret Police
- **Zhou Yunyi:** imperial astronomer
- **Luo Wenlong:** director of the Imperial Post Office and Yan Song's confidante

The Zhejiang Provincial Government

- **Hu Zongxian:** governor of Zhejiang Province
- **Zheng Bichang:** chief administrator and second in command of Zhejiang Province
- **Ho Maocai:** head of the Zhejiang Provincial Justice Department
- **Ma Ningyuan:** mayor of Hangzhou City
- **Gao Hanwen:** successor to Ma Ningyuan as mayor of Hangzhou City
- **Wang Yongji:** magistrate of Jiande County
- **Hai Rui:** magistrate of Chun'an County
- **Tian Youlou:** deputy magistrate of Chun'an County

Other Characters

- **Yang Jinshui:** head of the South China Textile Bureau and the Zhejiang Provincial Maritime Affairs Department
- **Shen Yishi:** silk mill owner and Zhejiang's wealthiest businessman
- **Chee Dazhu:** leader of rebel farmers in Chun'an County
- **General Qi Jiguang:** regional military commissioner responsible for fighting Japanese pirates in southeast China
- **Dr Li Shizhen:** legendary doctor, considered to be the founder of Chinese medicine
- **Zhao Zhenji:** governor and imperial inspector of Nanjing
- **Li Xuan:** protégé of Yang Jinshui and manager of the Xin'an River Flood Control Commission
- **Inoue Toushirou:** Japanese pirate
- **Warden Wang:** warden of Chun'an County prison
- **Officer Xu:** squad leader of troops in Chun'an County
- **Officer Jiang:** police officer in Hangzhou City

PROLOGUE

ON THE BRINK OF CHINESE NEW YEAR'S EVE IN 1560, NO ONE IN the capital city of Beijing seemed to be in the mood to engage in their usual frenzy of preparations. Since the winter solstice, no snow or rain had graced the city and neighbouring provinces. It was widely feared that a dry, barren winter would lead to drought and spawn large-scale locust infestations. Famine would follow, and the heavenly god soon would descend to earth to conscript his lost people back into the fold.

The public shuddered at the dire situation, which had no parallel in the long history of the Ming dynasty. Ten emperors had ruled, and they had all received their expected annual precipitation. Crops routinely flourished, and business continued apace. Surely this bizarre long-lasting absence of snow and rain was the manifestation of heavenly condemnation. For a while, the rumour mill went wild. Who, exactly, had incurred the wrath of heaven?

That same year – the 39th under Emperor Jiajing's reign – the state coffers suffered a similar dry spell, running so low that officials working for the imperial ministries in Beijing went months without pay. One could only imagine the predicament of ordinary folks who lived hand-to-mouth in the best of days. Eager for scapegoats, the public soon targeted Grand Secretary Yan Song, who had controlled the Privy Council for nearly two decades, and his son,

Yan Shifan, nicknamed "Grand Secretary Junior". To add insult to injury, a fire in November on the lunar calendar destroyed the Longevity Palace, Emperor Jiajing's haven for meditation and other Taoist practices.

Gradually, the gossip and rumours reached Emperor Jiajing's ears. The disturbing weather had induced a political power struggle.

The day before New Year's Eve, pale winter sun shone on the capital city, and the latest batch of weather reports brought further distressing news when they arrived that morning: no snowfall in the provinces of Shandong and Shanxi, nor in districts under the direct jurisdiction of the capital!

Emperor Jiajing, who had presided over a series of Taoist worshipping ceremonies to pray for snowfalls, finally lost patience. A devout believer in the predictions of a Taoist priest, he seldom trusted the analyses of the imperial astronomer. But in late morning, he hastily summoned Zhou Yunyi, his weather official, to the Yuxi Palace in the west wing of the Forbidden City. Emperor Jiajing requested that Zhou research the weather conditions under the reigns of his three predecessors and produce an analysis that portrayed snowless winters as common occurrences even during times of prosperity. The current abnormal weather, then, would not be linked to the emperor's rule.

The meeting was a disaster that bright, dry morning. Zhou refused to alter his analysis of the situation, which did not reflect well on the scruples of the Imperial Court. The emperor became so enraged at Zhou that he smashed a jade pestle into pieces and ordered the removal of all Zhou's imperial titles. Staffed by court eunuchs, the Imperial Police escorted the stunned astronomer to the Meridian Gate, the southern entrance to the Forbidden City.

At noon sharp, the police tied Zhou to a stake on the central pathway. Looking up at the unusually bright sun, he waited calmly for his *zhang*, a brutal punishment that involved beatings with a large thick wooden stick on the back, buttocks or legs.

"On behalf of His Majesty, I want to question you one last time," a voice bellowed from the Meridian Tower behind Zhou. "Why hasn't it snowed this winter?"

"I've already stated to His Majesty – the Imperial Court spends with no restraint, and officials at all levels are corrupt. Consequently, the treasury is being emptied out, and ordinary folks are becoming destitute," Zhou replied, his eyes blinking in the glare. "A snowless winter serves as a dire warning from heaven."

"Aiya," the eunuch who questioned Zhou uttered with a disappointed sigh, so soft that it was barely audible, but Zhou could detect the underlying terror in the tone. Before long, the four executioners standing around Zhou began the dreaded ritual: the first two straightened his upper body by inserting their wooden sticks under his armpits while the other two smacked him on the back of his kneecaps. Helpless, the astronomer dropped to his knees. As the police yanked the sticks from under his armpits, Zhou collapsed and fell spreadeagled on the dry brick pathway. The four executioners pinned him squarely down and proceeded to stamp their feet on his hands and ankles. Eventually, they looked up from their crumpled victim to the head eunuch for further instructions.

Feng Bao, the eunuch who commanded the Imperial Secret Police, did not issue his final order right away. Looking hesitant, he strolled over to the imperial astronomer and bent over. "It's New Year's Eve tomorrow, and your family members are waiting for you at home," he whispered in a pitying voice. "Could you for heaven's sake change your statement?"

Imploring Zhou "for heaven's sake" felt cruelly ironic to an official known for his outspoken righteousness. Zhou could not respond. Closing his eyes, he pressed his wobbly forehead close to the ground. A few tears leaked from the corners of his eyes. Zhou's muteness soon exasperated Feng, who sprang to his feet. "I want to ask you one more question," he raised his voice. "Who instructed you to deliver the blasphemous statement to His Majesty?"

"I was an official of the Imperial Government, and my job was to observe the astronomical phenomena," Zhou finally spoke, with his eyes closed. "I faithfully interpreted the heavenly signals, and with honesty I conveyed the messages to His Majesty, the son of heaven. Nobody could tell me what to do, except our heavenly father."

The short but bulky Feng stepped back and turned his gaze away from the heretical astronomer. With his feet turning inward, he muttered through his teeth, "Start the *zhang*."

The four executioners looked at each other knowingly – an inward turn of Feng's feet signalled the death penalty. Moments later, four thick wooden sticks struck hard on Zhou's lower back, just above his kidneys. Each horrific stroke landed silently. But the astronomer did not moan or show quick evidence of any external injuries, even as his internal organs shattered. Finally, blood spewed out of Zhou's mouth and nose.

Twenty strokes later, two eunuchs lifted Zhou from the ground. Re-inserting their wooden sticks under his armpits, they propped him up. Zhou's upper body wilted, his once-wise head now drooping onto his shoulder like an idiot doll's. Feng walked over and cupped Zhou's head in his hands like a scientific specimen. There was no sign of life. To certify Zhou's death, Feng plucked off a long hair from the astronomer's head and placed it under the dead man's nose. The hair did not move.

With a long sigh, Feng stood up. "Notify his family," he ordered. "Tell them to come and collect the body."

The white sun hung stubbornly over the Forbidden City, bathing the empty palace with lukewarm light. With the day's activity and quick crescendo to brutality, it was hard to believe that Emperor Jiajing had deserted this imperial complex for 21 years.

1

CONSIDERING THE PROMISE OF ITS NAME, LONGEVITY PALACE SHOULD never have burned down, forcing Emperor Jiajing to relocate to the outlying Yuxi Palace. Disillusioned, he spent most of his waking moments sequestered in the Taoist Alchemy Room which he christened "Cultivation, Discipline and Prudence". Once again, however, the emperor's isolated existence and devout faith could not attain the heavenly blessings that his kingdom sorely needed. When a worrisome drought plagued the surrounding land, he felt obligated to reappear in public and address the crisis by issuing a rare edict of self-criticism:

> Due to my negligence and insufficient reverence for the heavenly god, a nourishing snowfall has failed to bless us. If any of you in the myriad regions have committed offences, they must rest on me alone. In recompense, I hereby vow to fast and pray with all my heart for snowfall from the first to the fifteenth of January 1561. Hopefully, my sincerity and piousness at Yuxi Palace will draw the favour of the heavenly god to honour the Ming empire with an auspicious snowfall.

Emperor Jiajing would not remain alone for long in his self-imposed austerity. Other officials soon rushed to mimic his example; Privy Council members from Grand Secretary Yan Song on down. Lu Fang, the eunuch who headed the Interior Ministry, also expressed remorse and assumed blame for the bone-dry winter. A notice jointly issued by the Privy Council and the Interior Ministry appeared on the walls of the Meridian Gate: "In solidarity with His Majesty, all imperial officials in Beijing will eschew lavish cooking and refrain from eating meat or fish during the New Year holidays."

Publicly, officials unanimously supported the austerity measures, going about their business with fear and sobriety, but in private many stealthily celebrated the holiday with contraband meat and intoxicating drinks in their deep courtyard mansions. Regardless of how the public chose to celebrate the New Year, if the Emperor's prayers and fasting produced no snow by the fifteenth of January, the first full moon, the results could be calamitous for the entire empire. It was hard to predict who would incur the wrath of the famously capricious emperor and become the next scapegoat. Politics was becoming as unpredictable as the weather.

After two weeks of fervent prayers and sacrifice, snow still eluded the parched kingdom. Now the fifteenth of January, in the wee morning hours, dark heavy clouds gathered over the west wing and blotted out the stars, but there was still no sign of ice crystals. When daylight broke, Emperor Jiajing was to convene the much-dreaded annual treasury meeting at his residence. Exhausted and thin, the emperor was incredulous that he had not been able to generate a single six-sided flake. He wondered how he would face his subjects, much less his Privy Council members and the five eunuchs controlling the Interior Ministry. Fierce arguments over blame for the abnormally punishing weather promised to intensify the power struggle between the Yan clan and the "Clear Stream" faction led by the Prince of Yu. Countless lives could be lost.

Even without the life-giving snow, fireworks on New Year's Eve went ahead as usual. For the Lantern Festival, which fell on the fifteenth of January on the lunar calendar, tradition dictated that the palace lit up red lanterns a day earlier than ordinary households. Before three o'clock that morning, the eunuchs and maids had arisen even earlier than usual. For a few hours, shadows of servants and officials reflected busy preparations according to custom. When the lanterns under the eaves lit up one after another, they formed streams of crimson in the vast expanse of darkness. The lanterns' long beams silhouetted the intricate palace rooftops against the sky as if the buildings were floating in mid-air.

Two young eunuchs were tasked with finishing up the remaining lanterns. The tall, stronger one hoisted a shorter, thin colleague up in the air by his legs. "This damn weather," whined the eunuch on the top as he tried repeatedly to ignite a tinder by striking a flint with his cold, numb hands. "Even without the snow, it sure feels cold as hell."

"Shut your filthy mouth," cursed the fellow beneath, who was hoisting him up by the legs. "If anyone hears you, our hides could be tanned for jinxing it, especially if we still don't get any snow today."

Muttering more epithets, the eunuch balanced on top finally procured the sparks he needed, and the lantern lit up. As he slowly pulled a red muslin cover over the lantern, his body suddenly froze. The eunuch's hands stopped in mid-air, and his eyes gazed at the lantern cover.

A big feathery snowflake had landed on the left corner of the red cover. After one, he saw another.

The yeoman shut his tired eyes in disbelief and opened them again to see another snowflake followed by another.

"What's taking you so long?" grumbled the eunuch beneath him. "Did you see the face of the Zhu Yuanzhang or something in the flame?"

"Snow!" he yelped in his high-pitched voice, shattering the quiet solitude of the dark empty palace.

The eunuch beneath him stiffened, and for a moment the screamer feared he had hallucinated the powdery boon.

Fortunately, white flurries danced silently in the air, glistening in the red light before merging into the darkness.

"It's snowing!" the second eunuch affirmed and became so exuberant that he nearly lost his grip on the fellow lamplighter.

Soon, screams of shrill confirmation sounded in various corners. A high-pitched chorus penetrated the thick cold air.

"Who's that screaming?" A stern voice put a brake on the excitement. The courtyard quietened down momentarily as Feng Bao emerged, along with several other members of the Imperial Police. The grim-faced officers paused under the eaves of a palace on the left side of the space rumoured to be the emperor's residence.

Slowly, Feng inspected the early-morning sky. Reaching out his fingers as though expecting a bird to come and perch, he caught a few lacy flakes. Feng's eyes sparkled for the first time in months, and he announced, "The heavenly god has finally answered our prayers and granted his blessings." He blabbered, "I'm going to report the good tidings to His Majesty first and then run over to the Interior Ministry. Take those screaming boys to the House of Honours for punishment later. Before I bring the happy tidings to His Majesty, I want everyone to keep their mouths shut. Otherwise, I'm going to have the shrill ninnies beaten to death." The director's firm practical side quickly countered his uncharacteristic euphoria.

"Yes, sir!" His taller and stronger subordinates bowed to him before scattering to capture the disobedient eunuchs. Feng turned on his heel and hurried over to Yuxi Palace, walking with long strides.

明

Two bronze braziers warmed the Interior Ministry's duty room. Filled to the brim with silver charcoals, the braziers glowed like two red eyes. But the warm air and red festival lights failed to lift the spirits of five senior eunuchs who were sitting on a row of fragrant rosewood chairs against the north wall. All looked sullen, and a few young eunuchs fussed around them. Some knelt in front of their feet, replacing their warm slippers with boots, while others stood behind their seats, trying to wrap their necks with white fox fur mufflers. The five patriarchal figures were preparing for that morning's Privy Council meeting.

Suddenly, the thick curtain lifted, and a bitter cold wind gusted in. A eunuch on duty in the courtyard burst in, his face flushed. "Congratulations," he exclaimed, dropping to his knees before the group. "Congratulations to all my papas here. The heavenly god has bestowed snow upon us, at last. It's becoming quite heavy."

Both the senior and junior eunuchs in the room rose simultaneously. Even though some were eager to step out and examine the brilliant phenomena for themselves, they resisted the urge. Instead, everyone turned to the eunuch sitting in the middle. Named Lu Fang, he was known to the outside world as the interior minister and within the imperial compound as "Daddy". Excitement glimmered in Lu's eyes, but he quickly composed himself. Rather than dashing out into the courtyard, he simply shot a casual glance at the curtain. It was as if he could see the snow through the big thick fabric with his deep sharp eyes.

"Kudos to His Majesty," he praised. As chief of the Interior Ministry who commanded a staff of ten thousand strong, Lu supplied the right words for every occasion. "Let's take a look," he said before stepping towards the door.

Whiteness carpeted the ground, which glistened under the red lanterns. The snowfall had intensified. What an auspicious scene!

"His Majesty must be meditating at the moment," Lu Fang told his deputy Huang Jin.

"I assume so," Huang answered.

"Since it's almost time for the treasury meeting, why don't we walk over to His Majesty's residence together," Fang suggested to the rest of his deputies. "Then, we can report the good tidings in person and offer our congratulations."

As the group was about to leave, the fellow who first reported sightings of the snowfall crept up to Lu. "I hear that Feng Gong-gong[1] forbids anyone from talking about the snow because he's on his way to report the good news to His Majesty," he whispered.

"Are you sure?" Lu asked, his long thick eyebrows quivering slightly. "Who told you this?"

"Feng Bao is quite fast on his feet," quipped Chen Hong, Lu's executive deputy, in his cold shrill voice. "His Majesty might be so pleased that he would invite Feng to join the Privy Council and send all the rest of us packing."

"If Feng Bao has already done the reporting on our behalf, why don't we wait for a few more moments," Lu decided. "Once he's done relaying the good tidings to His Majesty, I assume he should at least make an appearance here."

Before Lu even finished his sentence, a junior eunuch carrying a lantern ushered Feng into the courtyard through a moon-shaped entrance.

"Oh, Daddy and my brothers, I'm glad you've seen the snow," he said, kneeling on the snow-covered stairs in front of Lu. "Your son is here to offer his sincere congratulations! This heavy snowfall will put His Majesty in a good mood, making things easier for Daddy and my brothers."

Lu did not meet his eyes. Feng kowtowed again before springing to his feet. Once more, he tried to ingratiate himself with Lu.

"So His Majesty is aware of the snowfall, I assume," Lu finally spoke with a fake smile.

"Yes, Your Highness," Feng replied. "Your humble son has already reported the amazing news to His Majesty on your behalf."

"What did His Majesty say when he heard of the miracle?"

"Ah… well, I didn't exactly get to see His Majesty," Feng said. "I knelt outside the palace and relayed the news. I heard the bell chime once. So I assume His Majesty knew about it."

"I thought the emperor would have been so pleased that he would grant you a promotion at the Interior Ministry," Lu interrupted him with a sardonic laugh.

The four deputies glared at Feng. A startled look spread across his face.

"That's true," Cheng Hong, who had just badmouthed Feng a few minutes before, mocked in his icy tone. "It's time for us to make room for you."

Fear distorted Feng's face. He quickly plopped to the slippery white ground, slapping both sides of his face fiercely. "I deserve to die, I deserve to die," he pleaded. "All I did was to bring good tidings to His Majesty on Daddy's behalf. Other than that, I harboured no selfish intentions."

Lu ignored his pleading. "The other council members are probably there already," he said to his deputies. "Let's get going."

The junior eunuchs put the cloaks on the patriarchs and handed them white fox fur hand muffs. Sedan carriers removed the tarpaulins over the parked two-wheeled vehicles in the courtyard, flinging off the snow. Lu and his deputies stepped down the stairs, and each climbed into his litter. Before departing, their porters handed each of them a leather blanket to cover their knees. Bundled up and fussed over like children, they were ready for the happy errand. A few minutes later, five sedans left the Interior Ministry's courtyard in the accumulating snow.

Those employees who were supposed to stay and staff the night duty room also slipped out briefly to watch the stunning weather. Soon, the courtyard became deserted. Feng remained alone, a pitiful figure kneeling on cold, immaculate ground.

Daylight broke when the procession of sedans left the Interior Ministry complex. The ubiquitous red lanterns cast their faint and grey light on the snow. It was hard to believe that in merely half an hour, the ground had been completely transformed into an expanse of whiteness. The snowfall was supposedly a "heavenly" event worth celebrating, but Feng's earlier ban dampened the enthusiasm. Except for the occasional snow shovelling, a dead silence reigned.

Seeing that the procession of sedans approached, the eunuchs who were busily shovelling the pathway, quickly dropped to their knees. Soon, palace maids and eunuchs who were running errands in the vicinity followed suit – the blanketed pathways, stairs and corridors were packed with Imperial Court staff on their knees and with their eyes cast downward as signs of respect.

Scanning the obsequious, quiet crowd, Lu had an idea. "Feng has really made these kids scared," he said to an assistant who escorted his sedan. "The snow heralds auspice for our Ming empire. Let them stop shovelling. Ask them to rise and go to celebrate the good tidings. The louder they shout, the better."

"Yes, sir," the eunuch answered before commencing to scream at the top of his lungs. "I have words from Lu Gonggong. The snow heralds the auspices of our Ming empire. Stop shovelling. Get up and relay the good news – the louder the better."

After a pregnant pause, one eunuch rose. Tossing his broom into the air, he released a pent-up holler. "Snowfall!"

"Snow is falling!" Others began to cheer. "The heavenly god is blessing us with snow. The heavenly god has bestowed auspicious snow on our Ming empire."

As the sedan carriers moved forward through the ecstatic crowd, a benevolent smile illuminated Lu's face.

Before approaching the Yuxi Palace, Lu suddenly halted his sedan and the others behind him quickly. In the distance, Lu could see several cloaked figures passing through a moon gate and coming towards them.

"They are arriving as well," Lu said to his deputies as he disembarked from his sedan. "Why don't we walk over to greet them?"

The four deputies complied, descending from their sedans and following Lu.

Despite the intense snowfall, the morning sky began to brighten up. A small entourage quickly came into clear view: they were members of the Privy Council, donning red robes and thick cloaks with white fur earmuffs, outfits specifically reserved for top-ranking imperial officials.

Grand Secretary Yan Song, who rested in a big sedan chair, led the group. Deputy Grand Secretary Xu Jie and council members Yan Shifan and Li Chunfang walked behind. The previous December, the emperor had specifically designated Gao Gong from the Ministry of Treasury and Zhang Juzheng from the Ministry of Defence as observers of council meetings. Both were known opponents of the notorious Yan clan. The emperor's pointed invitation to the council's most important finance meeting came at the height of public frustration over the government's budget problems. Additionally, the ominous implications from the disobedient weather had added a sense of foreboding and unpredictability.

Yan Song assumed his poker face. In contrast, his son, Yan Shifan, projected confidence and preparation. As head of the Ministry of Construction and Personnel, he was responsible for most of the previous year's budget deficit. Could it be that the emperor had invited these two provisional members to restrict him and his father? Or perhaps His Majesty had intended to determine if members of the Clear Stream faction instigated the latest round of criticism against him and the Imperial Government. Both possibilities were chilling.

Fortunately, the magnificent snowfall would ease much of the tension: if those two dared attack him, Yan Shifan would resort to a sabre that never failed him before – accusing Gao and Zhang of conspiring with the convicted imperial astronomer against the emperor. If things were to go Yan's way, the charges could no doubt cost the newcomers their lives.

Yan Song's sedan lurched to a stop. The ageing grand secretary, with his grey hair and long grey beard, realised that the man walking towards him was Lu Fang and hastily whispered to his son, "Quick, help me get out."

Yan Shifan raised his arms to help his father alight from the sedan. The father-son duo walked over to greet Lu. Other council members, including Gao and Zhang, followed the Yans but kept their distance.

"Congratulations," Lu offered the fist and palm salute while they were still a dozen feet apart.

"Likewise, likewise," Yan Song returned the greetings, his smiling face blooming like a chrysanthemum.

"Grand Secretary," Lu held Yan's other arm and complimented the octogenarian with equally feigned enthusiasm. "The big snowfall is truly age-reversing. If you were eighty last year, you would turn seventy-nine this year."

"Lu Gonggong, are you making fun of my old age?" Yan Song teased in his signature Jiangxi accent. "The snowfall is life-saving, but if it had rained silver dollars I would have been happier because I would no longer need to worry about our budget and could retire with ease."

"We cannot allow you to retire," Lu joked, tightening his grip over Yan's right arm as they slowly climbed the stairs that led to the Yuxi Palace. "If His Majesty lives ten thousand years, you should live at least one hundred years. Don't forget you have twenty more years to serve His Majesty."

"Twenty more years?" blurted Yan Shifan in his usual acrimonious tone as he walked beside his father and Lu. "I'm sure that would make some people really upset."

Yan Shifan was only in his early fifties. Having lived in the capital city for more than two decades, he had largely lost his accent and spoke like a local Beijinger.

"How could that be?" Lu said with an awkward laugh while

glancing sideways at other council members behind them. Pretending that they hadn't heard it, the other council members simply shifted their gazes elsewhere.

"We're crossing the river in the same boat, and collaboration is key," Lu said, still smiling.

As the group ascended the stairs, a plaque inscribed *Yuxi Palace* towered over them. Yan had personally written the calligraphy, which conveyed vigour and strength.

In front of the entrance, silence fell. The junior eunuchs guarding the palace stepped up to greet members of the emperor's inner circle. They helped untie the guests' cloaks and shook them vigorously to clear the snowflakes. Every single move was done briskly and quietly as if even a decibel of noise could disrupt the solemnity of the palace.

Once inside, Lu quickly took on a sombre expression. "I assume you are well aware of the incident involving Zhou Yunyi, the imperial astronomer, the day before New Year's Eve." He slowly scanned the faces of each colleague and reminded them. "His Majesty has been staying here to pray for snow since New Year's Day. The heavenly god has manifested his mercy today, but, with the looming budget deficit, I'm not so certain if even the auspicious snow alone can truly buoy the spirit of His Majesty. I beseech each one of you to show some flexibility and, if possible, let certain items pass without making too much of an issue. We can figure out other ways to resolve it next year. I'm sticking with what I just said – we're crossing a river in the same boat. Regardless of what happens, collaboration is key."

Yan Song nodded in agreement, but Yan Shifan shot a few nasty glances at certain council members standing behind him. Once again, they simply ignored him by gazing at the ground.

Two junior eunuchs proceeded to open the gate to the emperor's inner chamber – since pushing the iron gate could produce loud squeaks, the young eunuchs relied on their strong arms to give the heavy double doors a small, strategic lift before easing it inside slowly. Once the doors slid open, the group marched in like geese in a V-shaped formation – eunuchs from the Interior Ministry on the left and members of the Privy Council on the right.

The emperor's new residence looked spacious, but nothing like a palace hall. At the centre sat a simple rosewood horseshoe chair with a round back, rather than the usual Sumeru platform. The customary design in other palaces symbolised Mount Sumeru as the centre of the earth and universe. An enormous three-legged incense burner with a lid, hollow-carved with the Taoist trigram symbol, stood behind the chair.

Light smoke swirled out of the hollow top of the burner, sending a faint fragrance of incense wafting in the air. Behind a wall on the north side hung a plain white scroll, on which appeared a few lines by Lao Tse, the founder of Taoism. The elegant calligraphy proclaimed, *I have three precious things which I hold fast and prize. The first is gentleness; the second is frugality; the third is humility, which keeps me from putting myself before others.*

Four square columns supported the soaring ceiling; two on each side and seven metres apart. Between each set of columns lay two long rosewood desks, piled up with stacks of documents, books, empty letterheads, writing brushes and ink boxes. Strangely, no chairs sat behind the long desks. A lone embroidered drum stool sat at the end of the table on the right side. Besides, the bronze ink box on the left desk contained red ink while its twins on the right desk held black ink.

In the corners, slightly behind the columns, rested four gigantic bronze heating stoves. Four puppet-like eunuchs closely monitored the burning silver charcoal inside. This simple but effective heating device, with bluish red flames flickering inside, warmed up the palace like a spring breeze – without a single wisp of smoke.

Lu and his four deputies lined up on the left while Yan Song and his fellow Privy Council members moved to the right. Simultaneously, they knelt and kowtowed three times to the empty throne in the middle of the palace. When the meeting commenced, the eunuchs moved over and stood behind the long desk on the left while Deputy Grand Secretary Xu Jie and four other council members stood behind the right desk. Grand Secretary Yan Song hobbled over to the front and sat on the embroidered drum stool next to the desk on the right.

Thus, the 1561 AD treasury meeting officially opened in front of the emperor's empty throne.

Cabinet members held their breath as Lu turned his eyes towards the passageway curtained gracefully by white veils on the east side of the palace. Soon, everyone else looked in the same direction. The opening led to the palace's outer wall on the south end, with paned windows that were left open. The emperor's Alchemy Room, where he had lived in isolation for two weeks, stood on the north end. Now the emperor kept the inner chamber door wide open, allowing flurries of snowflakes to twirl into the room. The cold air did not seem to bother the emperor. In fact, the snowflakes obviously delighted him.

A few moments later, a chime sounded from a brass singing bowl. The bright sound, which signified that the emperor was ready, echoed in the hall.

"I call this meeting to order," Lu declared.

The four puppet-like eunuchs who were tending the stoves quietly covered the heating devices with bronze lids. Duty done for now, the eunuchs silently scampered away, like cats.

As usual, Lu presided over the proceedings and moved directly to business. "We'll follow our usual routine – the council will review last year's actual expenditures from all the ministries, the north and south capitals, and the governments of thirteen provinces. Then, we will decide which items to settle and which ones to deny." He paused but hardly glanced up before barrelling into his next item. "Regardless, every item needs a detailed explanation. At the same time, we will deliberate over next year's budget. The Ministry of Revenue will compile a list of major spending items and come up with a total number. The council will review each item with comments. Let's approve as many as possible. What do you think?"

Yan Song spoke in his usual measured tone to set the theme for the meeting. "Thanks to His Majesty's heavenly virtue and everyone's hard work, the most difficult days are finally behind us. Last year, two provinces suffered severe drought, three provinces were struck with extensive flooding, wars broke out in the north and southeast, and we also had that damaging fire inside the palace here. To tell you the truth, I didn't know how we would get through these trying times. With His Majesty diligently tending state affairs, toiling away for our Ming empire was the least we could do. It just so happened that several provinces suffered snow deprivation this winter, and some people took advantage of the dire situation, attempting to attack our Imperial Court. If it hadn't snowed today, we would have had to submit our resignation. Anyway, none of these dire prognostications matter. The most important thing is how well the crops will fare this year. Fortunately, we are having snow today, and it's substantial. We also shouldn't forget the fact that His Majesty has been fasting since New Year's Day to pay homage to heaven. His prayers have secured this snow because the heavenly god has been deeply moved by His Majesty's piety. We now have the continued blessings of the heavenly god. As long as we, the stewards of our empire, continue to work tirelessly, our country will be able to maintain its power and prosperity."

Yan Song then paused for a few seconds – not for the applause or recognition of his peers, but rather to wait for the emperor next door to savour his words. Meanwhile, the Privy Council members standing behind the two tables looked on solemnly, seemingly oblivious to Yan's obviously flattering remarks.

If one took the passageway and walked north into the emperor's Alchemy Room, the first thing in sight was an altar, with the statues of Three Divine Taoist Masters. Underneath the altar stood a platform in the shape of the Taoist eight trigrams, with a yellow meditation cushion on top. Since no one was sitting on the platform, the brass singing bowl with brass mallet placed diagonally inside looked conspicuous on the rosewood shelf, reminding one of the crisp chiming that filled the hall before a meeting commenced.

A row of gigantic rosewood bookcases lined the wall adjacent to the palace hall. Zhu Houcong – Emperor Jiajing – a tall thin man with long hair tied into a bun on top, sauntered back and forth in front of the bookcases. Dressed in a light loose silk robe, he seemed to be in his early fifties. If this had been elsewhere, nobody would have guessed that he was the most powerful man in the Middle Kingdom.

Since moving into this mansion the previous November,

Emperor Jiajing had converted it into an alchemy room, doubling it as his living quarters, where he reviewed Imperial Court documents and reports. A special place certainly deserved a special name. To illustrate the virtue of self-reflection, he christened it "Cultivation, Discipline and Prudence". The emperor's emphasis on "self- discipline" also served as a cautionary message and reminder for his council members sitting in the hall and for tens of thousands of officials governing the provinces.

The accumulating snow outside obviously pleased the emperor, and he appeared somewhat relaxed. Despite fifteen days of fasting and non-stop meditation, he showed no palpable sign of fatigue. Pausing in front of a bookcase marked with the label "Ministry of Revenue", he pulled out a stack of ledgers. Instead of opening them, however, he tilted his head, staring at the gap in the bookcase where the ledgers used to sit – the back of the bookcase was not sealed, and standing in front of the bookcase accorded the emperor a more advantageous position than his usual seat on the eight-trigram platform. From here, he could privately observe the discussions more clearly. Having heard the first half of Grand Secretary Yan Song's opening remarks, he was waiting for him to continue.

At the same time, Yan Song knew perfectly well how his words would be received. Having served His Majesty for twenty years, he felt smug about his special bond with his ruler. In fact, he knew exactly where the emperor was standing at that very moment. So he took a pause and measured his tone before continuing. "Over the past month, everyone has been working hard to itemise and review last year's expenditure," he stated. "At the same time, all of the council members have already attached their comments and suggestions. If the Interior Ministry signs off on them, we'll be able to settle last year's bills and move on to this year's budget."

Yan paused again and turned to his deputy, Xu Jie, who also headed the Ministry of Revenue. "You and Zhang Juzheng are in charge of the Ministry of Revenue, which reviews all of the treasury reports," Yan Song continued. "I assume you have gathered the comments from other council members. Please give us a report before we submit them to Lu Gonggong's Interior Ministry for approval."

"The Ministry of Revenue did not receive the reports and council members' comments from Yan Shifan until yesterday," Xu said slowly – he was as calm and calculated as Yan Song but did not have the grand secretary's overarching authoritative air. "My colleague Gao Gong and I spent the whole night perusing the reports. We have signed off on some but left some unsigned because we wouldn't dare without further discussions with all of you."

"What?" Yan Shifan, the son of the grand secretary, reacted first. "Do you mean to say that you didn't sign off on some of my budgeted items? Which ones?"

Lu and his four deputies at the Interior Ministry were also taken aback by Xu's statement. They looked to Xu for explanations.

"We approved the defence budget," Xu continued, maintaining his composure. "But if we approve the budgets of the Ministry of Personnel and the Ministry of Public Works, we could incur a huge deficit in the coming year. So we did not sign off on them because we don't have the authority to do so."

Yan Shifan repeated his question. "Are you saying that you object to budgets prepared by the Ministry of Personnel and Ministry of Public Works?" Even though he had considered the possibility of opposition at the meeting, he did not anticipate that Xu, known for his prudence and acquiescence, would be the one to raise tough questions. Shocked, Yan Shifan's eyes widened. In fact, other council members and eunuchs also looked on in disbelief. The air seemed to have frozen along with the weather outdoors.

Xu's words also caught the attention of Emperor Jiajing. He raised his head abruptly and stared at the ceiling. Once again, the voice of his former astronomer, Zhou Yunyi, reverberated in his ear – it sounded so distant and yet so close. "The Imperial Court spends without restraint... the heavenly god is sending a warning... heaven's warning." The emperor's dismal eyes focused on the cover of a treasury report he held in front of him.

Back in the hall, Deputy Grand Secretary Xu Jie closed his eyes as usual after his short remarks. Yan Shifan faced Gao Gong, the deputy minister of revenue. Despite his visible efforts to contain his anger, his rejoinders sounded like howling. "You were all there when the ministries presented their budgets, and now you authorise some while denying others. What in the name of the heavenly god is your Ministry of Revenue trying to do?"

His angry voice vibrated in the otherwise-quiet palace.

Gao pushed forward a pile of ledgers and reports on his desk and coughed slightly to clear his throat. "Your Highness, the Department of Revenue is part of our Imperial Government," he said in a low voice that exuded arrogance. "Please do not refer to it as ours. The Ministry of Personnel and the Ministry of Public Works also belong to the Imperial Government, and they shouldn't be called yours either. If the Ministry of Revenue must follow everything that the Ministry of Personnel and Ministry of Public Works dictate, why don't you take it over? In this way, there is no need for us to discuss the issues here."

The bold and blunt remarks made everyone nervous. The assembled council members looked from Gao Gong to Yan Shifan, who was slightly taken aback by what he had just heard. But he quickly recovered from his shock. "One of you is the minister of revenue and the other the deputy minister. What's wrong with calling it 'your Ministry of Revenue'? Of course, the Ministry of Personnel and the Ministry of Works are not my family business. The council has attached their support for the budgets of these two ministries. If you are unwilling or unable to handle these tasks, please feel free to let us know. But you threaten the Imperial Court by refusing to sign off on the budget. Do you know the consequences of delaying big government projects?"

"Yes, if you want to remove me from my post, please go ahead," Gao Gong replied, refusing to budge. "After reviewing the budget report you submitted yesterday, both Minister Xu and I are prepared for this eventuality. If you don't think we can handle the revenue, feel free to appoint anyone you see fit."

"Gao Gong!" Yan Shifan raised his fist, but before it landed on the table, his father, Yan Song, stopped him with a stern warning.

"This is His Majesty's council meeting," he reminded.

Inside the Alchemy Room, Emperor Jiajing, who was flipping through the budget book, paused and glanced at the hall through the gap in the bookcase.

"Father," Yan Shifan sounded wounded by the reprimand.

"Do not call me 'Father' here," Yan Song could be heard saying to his son. "We're at the council meeting, and you are addressing an official of the Ming. At meetings like this, everyone is entitled to his opinions. Gao Gong, why didn't the Ministry of Revenue sign off on the budget approved by the council? If you have run into any problems, please share them with the council."

Emperor Jiajing pricked his ears and listened.

"Just a reminder, everyone," Lu's voice said. "Let's limit our discussions to issues only – there's no need to throw around things like 'dismiss me from my title'. It is up to His Majesty to decide who should and should not take on certain tasks. He has a steel yardstick in his hand, and I hope everyone understands that."

The Emperor looked on silently.

"If that's the case, let me focus on a few numbers in last year's expenditure," Gao Gong stated.

Emperor Jiajing flipped open the national treasury report and put one of his forefingers on page one.

Inside the hall, Gao Gong also held up a copy of the national treasury report, identical to the one Emperor Jiajing was reading, and began. "The revenue collected from the two capital cities and thirteen provinces totalled forty-five million, three hundred and sixty-seven thousand taels of silver dollars. At the beginning of last year, we budgeted thirty-nine million and eight hundred thousand taels, but when the expenditure reports came in yesterday, we noticed that total spending reached fifty-three million and eight hundred thousand taels. If we balance the spending against the revenue, the deficit climbed to more than eight million and four hundred and thirteen thousand."

Inside the Alchemy Room, Emperor Jiajing appeared to be perusing the national treasury report but was actually listening to the debate outside.

"But when we carefully reviewed last year's total spending against last year's budget, we realised that the operating deficit has actually exceeded fourteen million taels," Gao continued.

Emperor Jiajing closed the treasury report and tossed it on a rosewood desk in front of him. Then, he strolled over to a cushion near the incense burners and sat cross-legged, with his eyes closed.

Gao Gong's presentation outside went on. "If we look at a breakdown of the figures, the Ministry of Defence outspent by three million, and the remaining eleven million taels of deficit came from the Ministry of Personnel and the Ministry of Public Works. Many are wondering why we refuse to authorise the defence spending. This is because the extra three million taels allocated for the Ministry of Defence were used by the Ministry of Works. In other words, all of the fourteen-million-tael deficit was incurred by the two ministries."

To illustrate his point, Gao pulled out an invoice. "Let me show you the three-million deficit originally budgeted for the Ministry of War," he said. "Since the Ministry of War never saw their money last year, how do you expect us to sign off on the spending?"

Upon hearing Gao Gong's accusatory remarks, Emperor Jiajing's eyebrows shook a bit, but his eyes remained closed.

In the hall, everyone now turned to Yan Shifan, who looked visibly exasperated. "When we presented the spending report, both of you were there and saw it, but none of you said anything," Yan retorted. "Now you have shifted all the blame to the Ministry of Public Works."

Nobody responded. Yan Shifan skipped Gao Gong and confronted Deputy Grand Secretary Xu Jie. "What on earth do you intend to do?" he asked.

"We did see it, but it didn't mean that we reviewed it," Deputy Xu replied calmly. "Last night, upon checking with officials at the Ministry of War, we noticed the discrepancy. I think Zhang Juzheng can better explain this."

Zhang, the youngest provisional council member who headed the Ministry of Defence, stood at the far end of the table.

"Yes, sir," he began. "We submitted the Department of Defence's budget to the Ministry of Revenue for authorisation on the twenty-seventh of December last year. Our total spending fell well within the budget. But when the Ministry of Revenue invited me over to check a few items in our report yesterday, I was surprised to learn that we had a deficit of three million taels. When I examined the details, I noticed that the spending was related to thirty gunboats that the Ministry of War had ordered. According to the explanation, the gunboats were built at the requests of Generals Qi Jiguang and Yu Dayou to use in their fight against Japanese pirates in the southeast. But, as of now, we at the Ministry of Defence haven't seen a single gunboat."

Zhang finished his statement in one breath, and those who had not been briefed on the issue began looking at each other in confusion and hostility.

In the Alchemy Room, Emperor Jiajing sat motionless on top of his cushion, looking totally immersed in his meditation. It had been twenty years since he moved out of the Forbidden City, following an attempted coup by a group of palace maids who had conspired to strangle him during his sleep. Over the past two decades, he no longer held court, and neither did he summon or meet with his cabinet members for meetings. Instead, he spent his days meditating, and he ostentatiously described his way of governing as "ruling by doing nothing that is against nature" or "non-interference governing".

However, few had realised that he had long grasped the Taoist truth of "great polarity" politics – a monarch could not monopolise power and make all the decisions by himself. One needed to delegate decision-making to one's subordinates, allowing them to fight over it. If they did it right, he took credit. If something went wrong, his ministers and eunuchs would inevitably take the blame. As the saying goes, one moment of silence is more eloquent than ten thousand beautiful and appropriate remarks. For each remark, you are its master before you utter it. Once you let it out of your mouth, you become its slave. Let the council members speak. Let the interior ministers debate it. Let them speculate what was going through his mind. At meetings like this, he had to make it clear that he had the final say in every decision and that every decision would be implemented according to his will.

But he never showed his face. Instead, he would chime his singing bowl next door to approve or deny each item. If any errors occurred, he would hold the cabinet or the eunuchs accountable.

As the budget meeting was turning boisterous, the emperor felt calmer and more immersed. While they were arguing fiercely, he simply listened. Very soon, both sides were deadlocked. Without him to mediate in person, Lu took up the task on his behalf.

"Could anyone elaborate on that?" he asked, referring to Zhang's allegation relating to the gunboats. While he launched his questioning, Lu fixed his eyes on the red ink boxes in front of him.

"You try to make my job difficult, and it doesn't work," Yan Shifan said, glaring at Gao Gong and Zhang before turning to Lu. "Allow me to explain. It is true that we ordered thirty gunboats which cost three million silver taels. They were built simultaneously at two shipyards – one in Zhejiang and the other in Fujian. It is true that those gunboats were initially commissioned for the navy to fight the pirates, but we had to temporarily allocate ten boats to the Department of Public Works, which used the boats to ship a large quantity of lumber when we were rebuilding several palace halls damaged by fire. The other twenty boats were leased to the Maritime Affairs Department, which should have reported this arrangement to the Privy Council."

"Is that true?" Lu asked his deputies at the Interior Ministry. It was obvious that Lu knew the answer, but he deliberately deferred it to his deputies, who glanced at each other knowingly.

"Yes, we are aware of this," responded Chen Hong, Lu's executive deputy. "The Maritime Affairs Department employed those boats to export silk, tea and china to Persia and India. Since they were short of boats, they used those newly built gunboats. Subsequently, however, due to the rampant piracy along the coastal region, we couldn't cobble together enough military personnel to escort the commercial boats. Eventually, they were transported back to the capital via the Hangzhou-Beijing canal."

Lu uttered a dramatic sigh of relief.

"Now, we have a better idea," he said. "Ten gunboats were used to transport lumber for the palace repair and the other twenty for Maritime Affairs. Even though the Ministry of Defence never saw the boats, the money that they budgeted has been put to good use. Several of the damaged halls have been restored to their previous splendour. There are still a few left, but they can wait. Minister Yan, the Ministry of Public Works should return the ten gunboats to the

Ministry of Defence. I'll notify Maritime Affairs, urging them to do the same. If they need extra boats, they could apply for funding – there is no need for them to take gunboats from the Ministry of Defence. Once the thirty gunboats go back to the Ministry of War, the three-million-tael deficit can be justified."

Lu's remarks met total silence. Gao Gong froze, holding the three-million-tael invoice. Everyone was waiting for the chime next door, which signified the emperor's approval or denial.

Inside the Alchemy Room, Emperor Jiajing was sitting on the cushion with his eyes closed and his crossed fingers resting on his knees. He waited for quite some time before raising his hands to grab the pestle inside the singing bowl. Haltingly, he hit the brass bowl. The sound rang inside the hall.

"The Ministry of Revenue can authorise the three-million-tael spending," Lu declared in his high-pitched voice.

Yan Shifan looked visibly relieved and peered at Gao smugly. It was obvious that Gao and his allies had lost this round. In frustration, Gao held the invoice in his hand and stood there sulking.

"Please sign it," said Xu Jie, his superior at the Ministry of Revenue, who grabbed the invoice from Gao's hand and carefully wrote his name on it. When he handed it back to Gao, Xu jerked his hand slightly in mid-air. Gao understood the signal. Even though he tried to control his emotions while signing his name, his hand shook slightly. As a result, his signature looked a bit rougher than usual.

Once again, Lu's voice raised a few octaves. "Red ink authorisation," he intoned. One of his deputies standing next to him left his desk, walked to Gao and took the invoice from him. When he returned, he handed it over to Lu reverentially, with both hands. Picking up a paintbrush, Lu soaked it in red ink and carefully wrote "Approved" on the invoice.

"Do we have any other invoices that the Ministry of Revenue has not signed?" Lu asked with a touch of iciness in his voice.

"Yes," Gao growled. "We have several items budgeted for river repairs. One of them involves the repair of Xijiang River, which was initially budgeted one million taels but the actual spending ran up to two million."

"The fact that Zhejiang Province is one of our key tax bases certainly justifies the extra money spent on river repairs," Yan Shifan argued. "The Water Management yamen has kept each expense in detail, so feel free to check their books. Besides, the Water Management yamen is staffed by officials at the Interior Ministry. When you refuse to sign off on it, are you targeting anyone else, besides the Ministry of Public Works?"

"Let's move on," Lu said, his tone revealing a touch of impatience with Gao.

"The amount of loan that the palace had taken out for repairs after the fire," Gao continued. "The Ministry of Public Works budgeted three million taels, but the actual invoice reached as high as seven million – four million over budget."

"So, after you go around attacking everyone, you're going to make His Majesty your target," Yan Shifan accused, revealing his invisible sword.

As expected, Emperor Jiajing, who sat on his cushion with his eyes closed, tightened the grip on the pestle.

In the hall, Gao felt he had to defend himself and stand up to his opponent. "I'm merely talking about the four-million-tael deficit incurred by the Ministry of Public Works," he said sternly. "I didn't say we shouldn't repair the palace. Grand Secretary Junior, if you want to kill me, why don't you just do it now, rather than trumping up these arbitrary charges?"

"Please stop," Xu Jie interrupted Gao's tirade. "This is a public debate. Nobody here is trying to trump up charges against you. Neither is His Majesty. When the Ministry of Revenue raises a question, it is important for the Ministry of Public Works to respond to any queries. It shouldn't be considered a criminal act, don't you agree?"

Xu turned to Yan Shifan. "Grand Secretary Junior, when the invoices don't match the budget, it is our job to question the discrepancy," he said. "There is no need to be upset."

Xu Jie's impromptu remarks, irrefutable at best, subtly protected Gao while helping defuse Yan Shifan's bloodthirsty anger. Unable to formulate the appropriate rebuttal, Yan Shifan swallowed his pride and looked to his father for cues.

Yan Song, who kept his eyes slightly shut, remained expressionless. Yan Shifan then turned to Lu, who ignored him and picked up where Xu left. "Deputy Grand Secretary Xu is absolutely right," he said to Yan Shifan. "Why don't you explain to us why your ministry exceeded the budget for this project?"

Yan Shifan looked reluctant. "There isn't much to explain because everybody here already knows about it," he mumbled. "The original budget for palace repair was based on the price of lumber in the southwestern provinces of Yunnan and Guizhou. However, when we sent people over there for site investigation, they reported that the mountains were too high and the forests were too dense. There were no decent roads for us to transport the lumber out. So we ended up purchasing lumber from Southeast Asia. We were given one year to complete the repair work, and the fact that domestic lumber was not available aggravated the challenges. Workers at the Ministry of Public Works had put in many extra hours, trying to find an alternative source. Several boats were capsized when transporting the lumber from Southeast Asia to Beijing. Despite the difficulties, we were able to finish most of the sections before year's end. We don't mind the troubles and the hard work because we are rewarded by serving His Majesty. But why are you picking over the bones? Why won't you let everything go?"

"If that's the case, I would recommend that the Ministry of Revenue authorise the expenditure," Lu said in an apparent attempt to exculpate Yan Shifan. Once again, all eyes were on Xu and Gao, both of whom kept their thoughts to themselves.

Emperor Jiajing rose from his cushioned seat, pacing up and down impatiently. His long wide sleeves fluttered in the air. He enjoyed the heated arguments outside as much as their silence, which bred action. Thunder and rain were normally preceded by silence.

Zhang, who sat at the end of the long table, broke the silence. "While Minister Xu and Deputy Minister Gao might not feel a bit restrained, let me say a few words first."

"Please go ahead," Lu permitted.

"I'll only focus on the Ministry of Defence," Zhang enunciated each word slowly. "We spent most of our resources last year defending our northern borders. Due to the increase in troops and personnel, we were able to ward off several invasions by Altan Khan, ruler of the Tümed Mongols. We have just received intelligence from the border region that he is planning more large-scale attacks this year. While more troops are needed in the region, we also need to repair and reinforce the Great Wall that connected the northeast and northwestern regions. This item alone would require an increase of two million taels in our military budget this year. Besides, we also need to bolster our military along the coastal regions in the southeast. In Zhejiang and Fujian Provinces, we relied solely on the twenty thousand strong troops commanded by General Qi Jiguang and Yu Dayou to fight against the Japanese pirates whose frequent raids are preventing commercial boats from transporting silk, tea and china overseas. These losses alone amount to millions of taels. To guarantee the safe passage of commercial boats in the southeast region, it is imperative that we recruit more troops in Zhejiang, Fujian and Guangdong. The recruitment drive will no doubt add another two million taels to our budget. If we follow last year's example and use up all the funds in the treasury in one year, the Imperial Government will have to raise taxes. Before this meeting, I heard that some provinces have started collecting advance taxes for 1566. If we allow the situation to continue, how are we supposed to sustain it? It is a tremendous challenge to run the Ministry of Revenue. I don't think this is something for which Minister Xu Jie and Gao Gong should be held accountable."

"Then who should be held accountable?" Yan Shifan questioned.

"I'm not in any position to assign blame now," Zhang continued eloquently. "In all things, success lies in preparedness, and lack of preparation leads to failure. Forearmed is forewarned. If we follow last year's example and outspend our budget, we'll always end up borrowing money from next year's. What will happen if next year's money runs out? I don't know how our empire can survive in its present form if we do not deal with these issues carefully."

"Are you saying that repairing the palace and fixing the rivers have exhausted our government's resources?" Yan Shifan interrogated.

"No, that's not what I meant," Zhang contended.

"What did you mean?" Yan Shifan began to press Gao aggressively.

"Given that you don't agree with Zhang's statement, are you saying that we should continue our deficit spending like last year?" Gao interjected.

"Lu Gonggong, the traitorous and the disloyal are clawing out of their dens," Yan Shifan yelled, realising that the argument had escalated into a life-and-death battle. "Gao and Zhang are teaming up to attack us."

The thunder finally rolled. Emperor Jiajing returned to his seat but was in no mood to sit down. He stood there quietly, watching for the rainstorm to arrive.

With his life hanging by a thread, Gao remained undeterred. His response showed both his grit and wisdom. "How do you write the character *traitorous*? This character happens to be made up of three components, each of which means 'female'. Everyone here knows that I have only one humble wife. Grand Secretary Junior has just taken another woman as his concubine. Now that he has nine wives and concubines, it's probably a bit far-fetched to use the word *traitorous* on me."

"This is totally irrelevant," Yan Shifan lost control and banged on the desk. "You and a handful of your cohorts are secret supporters of Zhou Yunyi, who defamed His Majesty on the twenty-ninth of December. Zhou was a mere astronomer, so how could he know so much about our spending report last year? It puzzled me for quite some time, and now I finally understand. Some people sitting in this room must have disclosed our spending details. Who is this snake? Why are you afraid to admit your role in this and take responsibility for what you have done?"

Gao Gong didn't answer. Neither did Zhang. Once again, silence fell. Even Lu found it hard to intervene on behalf of His Majesty. Unconsciously, Lu cast a glance at the passageway that led to the Alchemy Room. Time seemed to have stalled.

Finally, a murmur sounded in the passage. Emperor Jiajing emerged in his flowing robe, reciting a Tang dynasty poem. "Cultivating the body, detached and free like a crane…"

Instead of hailing him "Wansui" or "Wish you live ten thousand years", council members knelt on the floor silently, waiting for His Majesty to complete the poem.

"Under a pine tree inside a grove lay two sets of scriptures," the emperor intoned. "I come to enquire about the Way, but the master simply stated, like the clouds in the blue sky and the water inside a bottle."

The emperor moved towards the throne in the middle of the hall, and instead of taking the seat, he stood quietly. Resting an arm on the side of the platform, he looked with disdain at the people kneeling in front of him.

Realising that the emperor had finished his chant, Yan Song waited for a few seconds before offering his greetings. "We, the servants of our Ming empire, wish His Majesty…"

"A long life, a long long life," the other council members chimed in unison and offered three kowtows in reverence.

"Grand Secretary Yan, your son just claimed that astronomer Zhou Yunyi had a few co-conspirators and they might be hiding in this council," the emperor demanded. "Tell me who these traitors are."

"Your Majesty, I do not believe that any of our council members are supporters of Zhou Yunyi," Yan Song responded with his head down.

"Then how on earth did he manage to obtain so many intimate details of last year's spending?"

"How could he not? Those figures are public knowledge and accessible to all ministries! For example, a directive distributed to all ministries itemised the money we allocated for riverbed repairs in Jiangsu and Zhejiang Provinces, and for drought relief in Henan and Shaanxi Provinces."

Emperor Jiajing raised his voice and continued. "Then how did he know so much about the privately brokered fund that we had budgeted for the palace repair?"

"It merely shows that the Ministry of Public Works also publicised it as a measure of transparency," Yan Song answered calmly.

Nobody expected Yan Song to offer such a conciliatory response in the face of a new wave of political power struggle.

Regardless of whether the council members understood his intention, many looked visibly relaxed; a few glanced at Emperor Jiajing furtively to see his reaction.

Emperor Jiajing's face loosened up. Seating himself on the throne, he ordered his cabinet members to rise from their kneeling positions. "Please continue with your fights," he teased, with a smile.

His cabinet members kowtowed one more time before standing up.

Yan Shifan gaped at his father, looking a bit perplexed that the old man would fail to come to his defence.

"Don't look at your father like that," Emperor Jiajing chastised. "Learn something from him."

"Yes, Your Majesty," Yan Shifan answered quickly, with his eyes cast on the floor.

"The piece I chanted just now is called *The Poem of Seeking the Way*," Emperor Jiajing said in a cheerful tone. "Maybe some of you know it – Li Ao of the Tang dynasty composed it. The last stanza was my favourite – 'The clouds in the blue sky and water inside the bottle.' There is nothing mystical about truth. It lies in things around you, in different forms – the clouds and the water," he said, pointing around the tense room. "Everyone here is my cloud and water, and each person performs different duties. Regardless, you're my loyal ministers, and no one is traitorous."

Puckering up enough courage, Yan Shifan looked up at the emperor and repeated his allegation. "Your Majesty, I have to air my suspicions of Gao and Zhang because their tirades sounded similar to Zhou Yunyi's incendiary remarks on the twenty-ninth of December."

"It is not a bad thing if they do sound similar, is it?" Emperor Jiajing retorted. His unexpected reply held everyone in suspense.

"Looking back, I feel somewhat regretful about Zhou Yunyi's death," the emperor added with a sigh. "He harboured no ill or selfish intentions even though his words could cause disruptions to the Imperial Court. I merely ordered twenty strokes as a warning to him, but little did I know that he would have been killed... Lu Fang, it's about time you instilled some discipline in the Imperial

Police Force. Go and find out which viper took charge of Zhou Yunyi's execution on the twenty-ninth of December."

"Yes, sir," Lu Fang replied nervously. "I'll look into it right away."

Emperor Jiajing then softened his icy tone. "I'm told that Zhou Yunyi left a large brood, with an ailing mother," he said. "Let's allocate some money to help take care of them. The money can come straight from the treasury."

"Yes, sir, I'll do accordingly," Lu answered.

"Running a country is equally as hard as running a family," the emperor began to wax sentimental. "They operate on similar principles."

Many nodded, unsure if the leader's sudden shift in tone would continue.

Then, Emperor Jiajing suddenly turned to Yan Shifan. "I just heard Gao Gong mentioning your taking in a new concubine. Wife Number Nine, yesterday?" he asked. "What is that about?"

Taken aback by the emperor's question, Yan Shifan dropped to his knees. "When I get home today, I'll have the marriage annulled and send her home," he vowed.

"A true manly man can afford to have nine wives," the emperor joked. "What would she do if you send her home? Just keep her and the other of your concubines. It's OK with me as long as you focus more on your duties as an imperial official. Please rise."

"Yes, Your Majesty," Yan Shifan said in a barely audible voice.

After a few minutes of bantering, Emperor Jiajing brought up a serious topic. "We just had an extraordinarily difficult year, so what are we planning to do differently this year?" he asked Yan Song. "We need a strategy – to battle over the things that are worth battling for. As head of the Privy Council, you're the housekeeper. What's your plan?"

"Regardless of the situation, the well-being of a family's finance always depends on either cutting costs or increasing profits," Yan Song said with sincerity. "Even though every expense we incurred last year was justifiable, we must ask ourselves if we really needed to spend that much. Zhang Juzheng was right when he quoted the saying that success lies in preparedness, and lack of preparation leads to failure. Take the palace repair as an example. Why did the

Ministry of Public Works purchase lumber from southeast Asia and ship it all the way to Beijing? Why couldn't we take lumber from Yunnan and Guizhou Provinces? There's a sad but simple reason – we couldn't access them due to shoddy road conditions. I remember we discussed building roads in those two provinces a few years ago. Such improved roads would not only make it easier for the national government to manage the resources better inside the mountains but also benefit the locals, who could finally move their products out and sell them. All told, if this project had been implemented, we would have saved three million taels."

Emperor Jiajing nodded with approval and directed a questioning gaze at Yan Shifan.

"The Ministry of Public Works was partially to blame, and I should take full responsibility," Yan Shifan admitted reluctantly.

The emperor nodded again, his face brightening up.

"When we discuss this year's spending, we need to focus more on savings," Yan Song continued.

"Zhang Juzheng," Emperor Jiajing interrupted Yan Song and directly addressed his young minister of defence "Did the grand secretary sum up your views correctly?" he asked.

"Yes, Your Majesty," Zhang replied. "The grand secretary expanded it, making it more succinct."

"You're pretty good with figures," the emperor said, looking at Zhang appreciatively. "While I was inside, I heard you talk eloquently about the benefits of protecting the sea routes. In this way, our country's commercial fleets can ferry goods to India and Persia, bringing back more than ten million taels of silver a year. I want to hear more about this idea."

"Yes, Your Majesty," said Zhang, who looked visibly flustered but excited. "Actually, this is not my own idea. Back in 1405, Emperor Chengzu sent Zheng He, a fleet admiral on an expedition. Between 1405 to 1433, Zheng commanded several expeditional voyages to Southeast Asia, South Asia, Western Asia and East Africa, dispensing and receiving goods along the way, promoting trade and spreading the influence of our Ming empire. Since then, the sea routes became crowded with commercial fleets. But about thirty years ago, Japanese pirates disrupted the passageway, deterring commercial fleets from trade missions. Given that I'm with the Ministry of War, however, I see things differently. My belief is that we should increase our military budget and bolster troops guarding the coastal regions in Zhejiang and Fujian Provinces. We should encourage Generals Qi Jiguang and Yu Dayou to recruit more soldiers and build more gunboats. In this way, we can hunt down the pirates, defeat them and reopen the trade routes."

"Zhang Juzheng has discussed this idea with me," Yan Song added.

Both Deputy Xu Jie and Gao Gong cast a subtle but quizzical glance at Zhang, who was apparently surprised by Yan Song's assertion. Shaking his head slightly, he signalled to Deputy Xu and Gao Gong that Yan Song's claim was false.

Growing bolder, Yan Song continued to hijack the idea and shamelessly took credit for it. "When our trade route reopens, we can decide what sorts of products to export," he continued. "For example, we can increase the profit on silk produced in Zhejiang Province. A bolt of high-quality silk can sell for six taels of silver here, but if we can transport it to a foreign country, we can get at least ten taels per bolt. At present, we have about ten thousand weaving machines in the southern capital of Nanjing and eight thousand in Zhejiang Province. Do you think we can add more weaving machines to increase production?"

"Of course we can," Emperor Jiajing jumped into the conversation. "The key is to expand mulberry farms and increase silk production."

"Your Majesty's wisdom will guide us," Yan Song complimented. "Historically, farmers in Zhejiang provided raw silk for weavers in Nanjing because the climate conditions there are perfect for mulberry trees and silkworms. The council thinks it is feasible to convert half of the farmland in Zhejiang into mulberry fields. In this way, they can produce ten million taels of raw silk, which can translate into two million bolts of silk."

"But if peasants convert all their farmland into mulberry fields, how are they going to feed themselves?" the emperor reasonably enquired.

"We can move grain there from other provinces," Yan Song said.

"In the past, Zhejiang has received about sixty million kilograms of grain in subsidies from other provinces per year. We just need to add to the quota after farmers convert their farmland."

"But it is more expensive to buy grain from other provinces than to grow it. Will farmers be happy about increased costs?" the emperor asked.

"We have to take into account the fact that growing mulberry and producing raw silk is more profitable than standard crops," Yan Song replied.

The emperor ceased his queries but, before ending the conversation, added a firm, personal mandate. "Farmers should pay the same amount of tax after they convert their farmland into mulberry fields," he decreed. "No extra tax levy is allowed."

"No living soul possesses such keen intelligence as Your Majesty," Yan Shifan exclaimed obsequiously. "With your approval, farmers in Zhejiang will jump at the opportunity to grow mulberry trees," he raved. "With an abundant source of raw silk, we shouldn't have problems adding a few thousand weaving machines in Nanjing and Zhejiang Provinces."

"Excellent," Emperor Jiajing clapped his hands lightly and descended from his throne. "It doesn't hurt to argue and fight over things," he murmured while pacing around. "Unrestrained arguments produce sound ideas. Let's assign this conversion plan to the Interior Department and the Ministry of Public Works to implement. Of course, we should involve the Ministry of Treasury too. All the proceeds should be collected at the Ministry of Revenue. I urge the council to formulate a detailed implementation plan and send it directly over to Hu Zongxian, governor of Zhejiang Province. Ultimately, we have to rely on him for full implementation."

"Yes, Your Majesty," Yan Song and Lu Fang promised in unison.

On the spur of the moment, the emperor strolled towards the front gate and was about to unlatch it himself. Two junior eunuchs quickly scurried over and opened it for him. A blast of snow-laden wind flew into the hall, sending the emperor's long sleeves flying.

"Aiya... Your Majesty, be careful – you could catch a cold," Lu dashed over to close the door.

"I'm not as fragile as you are," the emperor waved his hand dismissively to stop Lu.

The snow continued to blanket the region. The red lanterns were glowing in the white snow, forming a promising scene. As the emperor was inhaling the fresh air, he noticed several eunuchs kneeling quietly on the steps outside, like a cluster of snowmen. The one at the front held a tray above his head. Despite the heavy snow, the emperor could see a big jade tablet on the tray.

"Could it be that the Prince of Yu's wife has given birth?" Emperor Jiajing's eyes lit up.

"Congratulations, Your Majesty," the eunuch who held the tray announced loudly. "The heavenly god has blessed you and our Ming empire with a boy."

Lu, who stood behind the emperor, quickly hurried over and received the tray. Then, he dashed back and knelt before the emperor, raising the tray above his head. "Your Majesty, congratulations!"

His four deputies at the Interior Ministry quickly dropped to their knees. Yan Song and the other Privy Council members followed suit.

"Congratulations, Your Majesty."

Regardless of whether the Privy Council members were truly happy or merely feigning, it was the emperor's first grandson, a blissful event for the Ming dynasty. Under normal circumstances, it was considered a taboo to look the son of heaven in the eye, but on that occasion all eyes were directed towards the emperor – such exception was called "welcoming happiness". Jubilation flamed up on Emperor Jiajing's face and eyes – he did not seem at all surprised. Instead, a hint of gleeful smugness appeared on his face, as if he had planned all along to have the news arrive along with the snow.

"Please raise the tray higher," he instructed Lu.

"Yes, Your Majesty," Lu said, duly hoisting up the tray. Reaching his right hand into his long left sleeve, he pulled out a winter jujube, as big as a baby's fist, and placed it on the tray. Then, before the surprised crowd, the emperor mischievously reached into his right sleeve with his left hand and brought out a similar-sized chestnut.

"What do these two items symbolise?" he quizzed his ministers, who were still in shock.

With the tray over his head, Lu could not see what the emperor was showing. Lu's deputy, Chen Hong, responded instead. "Your Majesty, together, these two signify that an heir will soon be crowned," he stated.

Impressed by the "magic trick", many wondered how the emperor would have known that it would be a day of bliss for the country.

All the Privy Council members knew that it was an opportune time to sing praises for the emperor, and at the same time they also realised that no words were enough to express their praises. Even though he was in his 80s and had decades of experience serving in the Imperial Court, Yan Song simply stood there, stunned and delighted like everyone else.

"One cannot afford to be ignorant of family matters," Emperor Jiajing said with conceit. "He has to be on top of both national and family affairs."

His ministers and eunuchs prostrated themselves on the floor. "His Majesty's wisdom and talent are boundless."

Having got a thrill out of his magic trick, the emperor's jubilant face turned serious, and he said to Lu, who was still kneeling in front of him, "The winter jujube and chestnut were heaven's gifts to me, and I will pass them on to my grandson. What is the traditional custom? What kinds of gifts should we endow on the new parents and the baby?"

"Your Majesty, given that this is your first royal grandson, we would assign twenty eunuchs and twenty maids, in addition to the usual congratulatory gifts," replied Lu.

"OK, go and take care of it quickly," the emperor demanded.

"Yes, Your Majesty," Lu promised loudly.

Next, the emperor turned to Xu, Gao and Zhang. "For years, you have served as mentors and advisers for my son," he said, his voice exuding tenderness. "I assume you're eager to go and congratulate the Prince of Yu. I won't keep you here tonight to eat yuanxiao[2] and celebrate the lantern festival with me. Please go."

The three council members kowtowed before dashing away.

Yan Song and his son were still kneeling in the hall. The emperor watched pensively as his other council members disappeared in the snow. "I don't always know what is going on in the nation and my family," he murmured, as if to himself. "Grand Secretary Yan, now that we are alone, could you tell me if any of our council members are secret supporters of Zhou Yunyi?"

Yan Shifan raised his head and was about to speak when his father stopped him with a stern glance. Emperor Jiajing slowly turned his head and signalled for the father and son to rise. "It's the lantern festival – why don't you two stay and keep me company? Let's have yuanxiao together."

"Please accept my humble thanks," Yan Shifan replied. While his voice was filled with gratitude, it also conveyed a slight sense of grievance.

明

Lu Fang and his deputies stopped by the Interior Ministry's office complex before heading over to the Prince of Yu's mansion. When they approached the duty room, two junior eunuchs dropped to their knees to greet them. Near the stairs, Lu suddenly stopped because he caught sight of a kneeling "snowman".

"Who is this?" Lu asked.

"Daddy, it is Feng Gonggong."

Seeing that his protégé, Feng Bao, lay literally frozen in the snow, Lu looked conflicted. His four deputies exchanged quick knowing glances. "Why don't you go and eat some yuanxiao to celebrate the Lantern Festival," Lu told the group. Chen Hong, his senior deputy, felt a bit resentful knowing that Lu attempted to send them away so he could take care of Feng. Even though he wouldn't dare challenge Lu, Chen wasn't willing to let Feng Bao off the hook so easily.

"If we all go, who'll be on duty then?" Chen asked.

"I'll do it," Lu insisted.

"But we can't let you…" the other deputies, who had seen through Lu's true intention, joined Chen in begging to stay.

Lu waved them away. "Just go and have a good time." As the

deputies reluctantly stepped away towards the Moon Gate, Lu dispersed the rest of the eunuchs in the courtyard. "I only need two people to help me here. The rest can leave and celebrate the Lantern Festival with friends," he said in a moment of calculated generosity.

Once the small crowd exited the courtyard, Lu yelled at Feng Bao, "You can stand up."

Feng did not respond.

"Stand up," Lu repeated.

Realising that something had gone wrong, Lu instructed the two helpers to step over and check up on his protégé.

"Feng Gonggong, Daddy asks you to rise," they bent over and whispered to Feng.

When Feng did not move, they tried to lift him, but couldn't.

"Feng Gonggong is frozen stiff," one helper screamed.

"Carry him inside," Lu said, his face and voice betraying no emotion.

The two helpers strained to lift up Feng's iced-over body and lug him into the night duty room. After sitting him on a chair, they removed his wet clothes. Soon, the big charcoal brazier, which heated up the room comfortably, brought Feng to life. Even though his eyes remained closed, his teeth began chattering. The guards bolted out and came back with two buckets of ice. Scooping out some with their hands, they rubbed the ice gently on Feng's arms and legs. Lu sat on a chaise lounge next to a window, his eyes half-closed. Eventually, Feng began groaning.

Lu Fang slowly opened his eyes and glanced at Feng.

"Carry him to the bed, and feed him some ginger tea," Lu told the two helpers.

The two junior eunuchs lifted Feng from the floor, placed him on a bed in the duty room and spoon-fed him ginger tea. After a few coughs, Feng regained consciousness. Even though he was still weak, he managed to get up, drop on his knees and kowtow to Lu.

"Daddy, it was my fault..." he sobbed.

Lu waved his hands, ordering the junior eunuchs to leave the room. Then, he ambled over and sat on the edge of the bed where Feng Bao sat. "After all these years working for me, you haven't learned a thing," he scolded. "Even a cow knows how to play a rope trick after I teach it three times. Look how arrogant you were, so desperate to climb the ladder. On the twenty-ninth of December, you had Zhou Yunyi killed without consulting with me. Today, you tried to show off and report the good news without notifying anyone else. I don't hold grudges against you, but what about the others? Zhou Yunyi had many cohorts here. And the Prince of Yu is also one of them. If you wish to die, what you have done will certainly make your wish come true."

"I'm sorry. It will never happen again," Feng kept murmuring. "Your humble son will remember your words and start all over."

Lu stopped talking and gazed at Feng tenderly, which made his protégé more nervous. Feng could sense that Lu had something else in mind.

"I promise I'll turn over a new leaf," Feng pleaded.

Lu paused for a few minutes. "From tomorrow on, you'll be reassigned to the Prince of Yu's mansion," he said.

It took a while for the words to sink in. Shocked and stunned, Feng struggled to get up and stumbled off the bed. Kneeling in front of his mentor, he grabbed Lu's leg. "Please don't do it, Daddy," he begged. "It's probably better if you just have me killed on the spot. I'd rather die than work at the Prince of Yu's mansion."

"Get up," Lu ordered with an icy tone that sent shivers down Feng's spine.

"But Daddy," Feng said, shuddering uncontrollably while leaning his body on the edge of the bed.

"Let me gift you a few words," Lu said to Feng, who seemed to be in a stupor. "There is a popular saying among government officials: one needs to always ponder three things – think about danger, think about retreat and think about change. These three things are connected. If you sense danger, you need to plan your retreat right away and withdraw to a place where your enemies won't spot you. Once you retreat to a safe corner, you bide your time, slowly reflect on your mistakes and plan your comeback. This is called 'the contemplation of change'."

"I'll follow your teaching," Feng replied with a trembling voice.

"But sending me to the Prince of Yu's mansion is like putting me on the road to ruin."

"Listen carefully to what I'm about to tell you," Lu interrupted Feng with a fierce look. "There is another popular saying among officers who serve in the Imperial Army. It's called 'allowing a person to confront the danger of death and he will fight to live'. In your particular case, many officials, including the Prince of Yu, know that you are responsible for Zhou Yunyi's death. They despise you. How could you convince them that you didn't actually kill Zhou Yunyi? You won't have the opportunity to defend yourself if I keep you here. As you know, the Prince of Yu will take over and ascend the throne sooner or later. When the day comes, you'll be doomed if you don't redeem yourself right now. Listen to me. I'm going to send you over as part of His Majesty's gifts. Your job is to babysit and look after the royal grandson. Once you're there, you need to work hard and keep your head down, gaining confidence and trust from the prince and others around him. In this way, they'll change their perception of you and treat you better. Someday, when the prince is crowned, I'll have to rely on you for protection."

Lu became emotional, his eyes glistening with tears. Feng lay prostrated on the floor and began wailing. Lu was not sure if his protégé had truly grasped his meticulous intent.

For the Prince of Yu, time seemed to have stalled since dawn. Gao Gong and Zhang Juzheng had briefed him on their possible confrontation with Yan Shifan at the Privy Council meeting the night before. Their plan made him nervous. But his wife, Princess Li, went into labour at three o'clock in the morning; it was a difficult birth, and the prince could hear her painful howling for two hours as he waited nervously in a chamber outside his living quarters.

With his chief of staff keeping him company, the prince paced up and down the room. As the hours went by, he became increasingly worried about both his child's pending birth and, at the same time, the possible consequences of his mentors' actions at the Privy Council meeting. Personal and political tensions pressed down on him.

Thank heavens, the birth went smoothly, and he was now the father of a baby boy. Gao Gong and Zhang Juzheng braved the snow and arrived to offer their congratulations. It was obvious that they had been sent by his father, the emperor. As the period of suspense and tension subsided, the prince found his body weakening. When his two mentors dropped to their knees and kowtowed, he couldn't even summon enough strength to stand up and return the courtesy. He just moved slightly and waved his hand. "My teachers, please rise. I'm glad you're back safe and sound."

Several chairs in the room formed a circle around a big bronze brazier. The prince sat in the middle, Xu Jie and Gao Gong picked their seats on the right, while Zhang Juzheng and chief of staff Tan Lun were on the left. As the crown prince and his advisers clustered around the fire, they looked at each other quietly and became so emotional that they didn't know where to begin.

"The three of you probably had no idea how His Royal Highness survived the past several harrowing hours," Tan Lun started, his eyes moistened. "Princess Li had been in labour since dawn, and for two hours the midwives couldn't deliver the baby," he said. "Fortunately, someone remembered that Li Shizhen[3] had left a few herbal pills that would help induce labour. Thank heavens, the pill worked, and both the mother and baby boy are well."

Xu, Gao and Zhang glanced at the prince's pale face sympathetically.

"Meanwhile, the prince was worried about you three," Tan continued. "He went outside and stood in the snow several times to check if all of you were coming back. He feared that you could be taken away."

"Confucius once advocated benevolence, and Mencius emphasised justice," Gao interrupted Tan. "I'm not afraid of following Zhou Yunyi's example and sacrificing my life for our Ming empire. Now that Your Royal Highness has a son and our empire has a successor, there is hope. If I die, I'm sure others will step in. As a

Ming official, I have to do my job and fight for justice. Otherwise, I'd rather die."

"There aren't too many righteous officials left, and you all are pillars of our Ming empire," the prince remarked.

He seemed to have recovered from the mental exhaustion, but his voice still sounded weak. Stoking the fire in the brazier, the prince remarked, "The Imperial Government cannot afford to lose any of you. Otherwise, I don't know who will be able to help His Majesty to remedy the ills that beset our empire."

"His Majesty is wise and capable," Xu interjected. "With his leadership, I don't think we are likely to end up like that."

But Gao disagreed. "What happened at the council meeting today wasn't too encouraging," he complained. "Your Royal Highness, do you know that the council approved all of last year's bad debts and wasteful spending?"

"At least, we have had a promising start to this year," Xu argued. "Because of our efforts to control spending, we're not going to increase taxes. I hope that the land-conversion plan in Zhejiang goes smoothly."

"I doubt the conversion will work," Zhang said bluntly. His words drew the attention of both the prince and his chief of staff.

"Why?" asked the crown prince.

"Grand Secretary Yan Song proposed at the meeting today that farmers convert half of their prime farmland into mulberry fields," Zhang explained. "He claimed that the conversion would lead to an increase of 200,000 bolts of silk a year. Profits made from the silk would be able to bridge the deficit. Good as it sounds, it's quite pernicious. This gives the Yan clan just another excuse to rob local farmers of their land. If wealthy merchants control half of the farmland in Zhejiang, farmers there would be forced into dire straits and rise up against local officials. Besides, Zhejiang is rife with pirates. It wouldn't be long before we see chaos and uprisings there."

"Why didn't you state this at the council meeting?" the prince said impatiently.

"His Majesty approved the plan before Yan Song even finished it," Zhang said. "He simply instructed Yan not to levy more taxes on farmers who agree to the land conversion. But did it ever occur to His Majesty that farmers wouldn't be able to benefit from the land conversion and the no-tax provision? Yan's wealthy cronies in Zhejiang would collude with big merchants to purchase land directly from peasants and grow mulberry trees."

"I completely see your point," Tan Lun, the prince's chief of staff, nodded. "Theoretically, if the Imperial Court does not levy extra taxes on converted land, a farmer can earn up to fifty per cent more from growing mulberry trees and producing raw silk than he would from planting rice and other crops. But it doesn't work that way. Local officials would collude with merchants and use all different administrative means to force farmers to sell their land. In this way, the merchants can monopolise the silk production. They can grow mulberry trees, raise silkworms and then manufacture silk. The profits could be unimaginable."

"You're right on target," Zhang concurred. "When Grand Secretary Yan Song proposed the idea, his true intent might have been to make up for the rising deficit. But the fact that his son, Yan Shifan, has suddenly thrown his support behind it shows that they must have plotted beforehand."

Gao stood up. "We have to stop this. Even though we were not able to shoot down the project at the council meeting, we have to strategise, figure out a way to salvage the situation, and prevent this bad policy from being implemented in Zhejiang."

"How can we do it?" the prince asked Xu, who was unusually quiet during the discussion. "The Yan clan is quite influential, both at the Imperial Court and inside the Zhejiang government."

Xu didn't reply to the Prince of Yu. Shifting in his seat, he turned to Zhang. "Do you have a specific plan?"

Zhang considered it for a few minutes. "The Yan faction is not what many see as a monolithic whole," he said. "I'm sure there are some honest and upright officials in Zhejiang. We need to look for cracks. There is one person who I think we can win over."

"Who?" Gao asked sceptically.

"This person holds a powerful position there," Zhang said.

"Are you talking about Hu Zongxian?" Gao probed.

"Yes," Zhang affirmed. "He's not only the governor of Zhejiang

Province but also the imperial inspector, who has gained the trust of both Grand Secretary Yan Song and His Majesty. If only we could get someone to convince him of the policy's deleterious effect, he could make a case to His Majesty and kill it before it is implemented."

"I beg to differ," Gao said. "Yan Song plucked the governor of Zhejiang from obscurity and then nurtured, promoted and planted him there. I don't mean to say that we are not able to move any trees in Yan Song's garden, but Hu Zongxian is deeply rooted, and I doubt we can move him over to our side."

The prince fixed his gaze on Tan Lun, his chief of staff, seeking his opinions.

"We can certainly explore this idea," Tan said. "As his Royal Highness is aware, Governor Hu and I used to be close friends. He's smart and independent when it comes to state affairs. Ever since he's taken over the Zhejiang governor's post, he has stood his ground on many key issues, despite the fact that he seemed to obey Yan Song and his son in public."

"Even so, whom should we rely on to win him over?" Gao questioned. "As the saying goes, a mere acquaintance has no power over close friends. What makes you think he'll listen to us?"

"We won't talk to him directly, of course," Zhang said. "But we can send over a friend of his who can explain our position to him."

"Who should that person be?" asked the prince.

Zhang turned to Tan Lun, and the prince suddenly understood. So he shifted his head towards his chief of staff.

"Of course, I can go without question," Tan said. "But I need to have a legitimate reason, such as securing an appointment as an official in Zhejiang, where I could work alongside him and use the opportunity to convert him."

The prince and his confidants exchanged glances knowingly – everyone liked the idea.

"I think this is a good game plan, and we can certainly try it," said Xu cautiously. "With Tan Lun planted next to Governor Hu Zongxian, I'm sure we can achieve something. It's better than nothing."

"If that's the case, I'll give my permission," said the prince.

Standing up, he rested his hands on the arms of his rosewood chair. "As long as we can awaken his conscience, the situation won't get out of hand."

Zhang became flustered and said to Tan, "It's not enough to salvage a bad situation. Are you planning to come back after this assignment?"

Startled by this unexpected rhetorical question, Tan asked. "What do you mean?"

"If you want to come back in triumph, you should first start a fire in Zhejiang and then bring some sparks back to the Imperial Court, letting the flames destroy Yan Song and Yan Shifan. If you can't achieve that, you probably shouldn't even bother coming back to see his Royal Highness. There is also a possibility that you could lose your life there. You need to think it through before making a decision."

Gao slapped his knee in excitement and stood up to voice his support for Zhang. "That's an excellent point. If you really want to go, you should be prepared to do it in a grand fashion. It's not worth it if you simply want to do a little bit, with the attitude that it's better than nothing."

The fiery exchange of words made the Prince of Yu nervous. He turned to Xu, who didn't seem to mind that his younger colleagues challenged his attitude because he knew that as the prince's mentor and pillar of the Clear Stream faction, he needed to balance both short and long-term considerations. "Please remember, silk production falls under the jurisdiction of the South China Textile Bureau, which is directly under the control of the Interior Department," Xu pointed out.

"Sir, your concern is…" the prince asked politely, and then he suddenly understood. With his blank stare into the distance, he looked lost. "If the South China Textile Bureau is implicated in implementing the policy, many in the Imperial Court, including His Majesty, would be affected… Should I send Tan Lun or not?" he asked bluntly.

The prince's remarks saddened Tan Lun. When Zhang and Gao, two younger officials known for their blunt heroism, triggered him to take action, he did not appear to be offended. He considered himself a warrior who was not afraid of devoting his life to a bigger cause, even though it might mean brutal death as his end. However, Tan Lu looked disappointed at the prince's cowardly reaction to Xu's concern. Obviously, the prince, fearful of the Interior Department and Emperor Jiajing, cared more about his own interest than that of Tan's life.

This sense of bitter disappointment further strengthened his resolve. "Your Royal Highness, do not worry," Tan pledged. "I will not do anything that jeopardises your position or that of my colleagues here. All I need is a letter from the Ministry of Personnel, appointing me as the military adviser in the Zhejiang governor's yamen. I can leave tomorrow."

The room fell into an awkward silence. There was no doubt that the prince – a sensitive person – and his other cohorts understood Tan's sentiments.

"Your Royal Highness, it's the Lantern Festival today." Tan broke the silence and suggested that they enjoy a bowl of yuanxiao together. The way he said it echoed an ancient scene where the assassin Jing Ke bade farewell to Prince Yan before leaving on his mission to assassinate the tyrannical emperor of the Kingdom of Qin. Everyone, including the prince, became emotional. At that loaded moment, a palace maid walked in.

"Your Royal Highness, the princess just asked if we should invite everyone to eat yuanxiao since it's already past noon."

The prince suddenly came to his senses. "Yes, bring up the yuanxiao," he ordered, with a slightly hoarse voice. "Don't forget the liquor."

"Let's propose a toast to Tan Lun," Gao said loudly, totally forgetting about the emperor's grandson, whose birth they came to celebrate.

2

DESPITE A DRY WINTER SEASON, SPRING FLOODING REPLENISHED THE Xin'an River in the southeastern province of Zhejiang. By April on the lunar calendar, incessant rainstorms had pushed the water level of the Xin'an to its peak. Clear and serene, it generously irrigated the vast expanse of green rice seedlings on both sides of the bank as it confidently meandered forward. Local peasants praised the Xin'an's life-giving force, often citing a famous adage of Lao Tse, the founder of Taoism: *The top virtue is like water, benefiting all, contending with none.*

For the first time in ages, Master Lao Tse's adage could no longer be applied to the Xin'an River. All the irrigation canals along the river stood blocked. Like an arrogant government who ignored the needs of its people, the vigorous river now ran roughshod without stopping, and the abundant water went wasted.

Zhang and his cohort of reformers had accurately foreseen the dreadful outcome. From the very beginning, the Yan-led initiative to convert rice paddies into mulberry fields set off a domino-toppling chain of disaster for the locals, government, and beyond. Still, the plan continued apace.

On that day, fully armed soldiers and government officials lined up along the embankment. Ma Ningyuan, the mayor of Hangzhou, along with two magistrates, Chang Boxi and Zhang Zhiliang, had travelled there to forcibly implement the new land-conversion policy. Thousands of local farmers had shown up as well, and they now dropped to their knees in despair.

Alongside the rice paddies near the embankment, two rows of armoured soldiers on horseback waited ominously for orders.

"Crush the seedlings," bellowed Mayor Ma. Eager horses charged forward, sweeping across the rice paddies like waves of violent floodwater, transforming the rice paddies into a fierce battleground. Without guns or even enemy troops, the officials fought a brilliant battle. Muscular horses trampled on dry cracked farmland, killing the countless inch-tall seedlings. The deafening hoof beats failed to drown out the loud wailing by farmers who knelt along the embankment. Total destruction followed in the wake of the horses, who moved on like the unceasing deluge that lay ahead.

"Put up the markers," two officials standing next to the mayor barked at the soldiers who carried wooden billboards that prominently bore the characters *Mulberry Field*. The soldiers rushed over to the trampled farmland and hammered the billboards deep into the ground. The wailing became louder as the horses moved on to other plots.

"Dad!" a young woman's shrieks rose above the howling and crying.

Before the shocked onlookers, an old farmer ran as fast as he could and plunged into a rice paddy, thrusting himself to the ground. As he pressed his ancient face close to the soil, he stretched out his thin arms to encircle a patch of withering seedlings as if protecting his own children. As the horses approached, the old man remained flung across his trusted land.

"Let's fight it," a strong young man shouted to his fellow farmers. "They're going to kill us anyway." He leapt into the rice paddy and rushed through the swirling water towards the elderly man. Several other farmers joined them, and together they locked arms, forming a human wall in front of the prostrating old man. A local crowd nodded and murmured from where they knelt by the riverbanks.

Unprepared for the resistance, the soldiers on horseback

became nervous and baffled. Such combativeness was rare in the countryside. Finally, they looked to their officer for direction.

The officer who led the raid instinctively pulled on his reins. As other soldiers moved to imitate him, their horses refused to obey and galloped towards the human wall. Sweat broke out on the officer's face. Fortunately, the confused soldiers were able to halt their horses about twelve feet away from the protestors. Puffing and snorting, the agitated animals kicked and dug their hooves into the dirt.

"These unruly bastards!" cursed Zhang, the magistrate of Jiande. He stamped his feet.

"They're plotting an uprising," added Chang Boxi, the magistrate of Chun'an. "I just heard a young traitor calling for an uprising."

"Which one? Point him out!" directed Ma, the mayor of Hangzhou.

"It's that one there." Chang pointed at the young man who started the resistance.

"Lock him up," Mayor Ma howled.

A dozen yamen guards rushed over to the crowd with chains and wooden poles. Soon they shackled a dozen young farmers, including the so-called leader, and dragged them over. The arrests incensed the crowd so much that they rose from their supplicating postures. The formidable group began walking towards the soldiers and yamen guards; a riot appeared ready to start. In an attempt to stop the strapping farmers from advancing, the soldiers swiftly produced their weapons.

Meanwhile, the mayor and the two magistrates walked up to the shackled farmers.

"Who is the agitator?" asked the steely faced mayor. "Who gave the command, 'Let's fight it?'"

"I did," the young man said, stepping calmly forward.

Startled by his peaceful demeanour, the two magistrates exchanged quizzical glances at each other.

Mayor Ma sized up the young man and said sarcastically, "Wonderful. I always appreciate it when insurrectionists are so earnest and straightforward. What's your name?"

"Chee Dazhu," the young man replied.

"What do you do for a living?"

"I'm a mulberry farmer. My family has farmed mulberries for generations."

The mayor took a closer look at the young man and asked, "A mulberry farmer? Then why on earth are you making trouble here when we're merely converting all the other rice paddies over?"

After pausing for a few seconds, the young man said, "Because I don't think it is right to treat rice farmers like this. Without feelings of respect, what is there to distinguish men from beasts?"

"Confucius," muttered the mayor under his breath. "You are a real man!" Then, the mayor changed his tone abruptly. "What position are you holding under Wang Zhi?"

"Wang Zhi? Who's that?" the young man asked in complete confusion.

"As if you don't know – he's the leader of the pirates!"

Startled, the young man protested loudly, "I swear I don't even know him!"

"Oh yeah? When the time comes, you will divulge your relationship with Wang Zhi!" Mayor Ma uttered in a low voice before turning to the large crowd gathered outside the rice paddies. "Converting rice fields into mulberry farms will benefit both our country and individual farmers. It's a win-win policy for all of us and will lead to an even more prosperous future. Unbelievably, we are running into all sorts of stumbling blocks. Today, some people even gathered here to boycott the land-conversion policy. Now we understand why – the pirates are instigating a riot!"

The screaming and wailing suddenly stopped. Colluding with pirates constituted a capital offence, and the mayor's threat worked. The crowd fell into a stunned silence.

"Let the horses run to kill the crops," Mayor Ma ordered. "Anyone who dares to obstruct them this time will be arrested and sent to the prison in Hangzhou with this group!"

The two magistrates standing next to the mayor shouted simultaneously to the soldiers on horses. "Go!" The soldiers unleashed the horses, which ran rampant in the field, leaving thick trails of annihilated seedlings.

In the distance, a pack of five horses was dashing towards the embankment. At the sight of the advancing squad, the officer who directed the operation in the rice field immediately reined in his horse.

The squad came into clear view, led by a rider wearing a helmet adorned with a big red tassel. His black cloak flew in the air, making him look like a ferocious bat. "It's the general," the officer blurted out in surprise. He dismounted quickly.

General Qi Jiguang was the regional military commissioner. As he dismounted, the soldiers who had been tasked with maintaining order rapidly lined up in two neat rows to await their commander's arrival.

Perching on the edge of a rice field, General Qi scanned the damages and glared at his horsemen, who had abandoned their destructive mission and were galloping over towards the embankment. Once they climbed out of the rice field, the horsemen dismounted and stood at attention, facing each other in two rows. Slowly, General Qi rode around his troops. First, he glanced at the swarms of dejected farmers on the embankment, and then he fixed his gaze on the trampled crops. Qi's frosty expression sent chills down the spines of his soldiers, who stood there silently. Even their horses remained motionless.

The commotion on the edge of the rice field caught the attention of Mayor Ma and the magistrates.

"What's he here for?" asked Chang, the magistrate from Jiande.

"Is he coming to pull out his troops?" Zhang, the magistrate from Chun'an, speculated.

"No, he can't," Mayor Ma explained. "The troops were assigned to me by the Ministry of War."

The three officials strode towards General Qi.

"You were out when I went to summon your troops," Mayor Ma raised his voice and shouted to the general. "I left a letter from the War Ministry on your desk."

General Qi ignored him and glared down at the officer in charge.

"Did you command the soldiers to destroy the crops?" General Qi questioned.

"Yes... sir!"

Whop-eesh! General Qi cracked his bullwhip to lash the officer's face like a bolt of lightning. Despite the long bloody welt, the officer straightened his body without flinching.

"Who else has damaged the crops?" General Qi yelled. "Step out."

The cavalry moved a step forward simultaneously, without disrupting their formation. General Qi moved slowly between the two rows, waving his bullwhip. Each crack produced a welt on the face of his horsemen, who remained miraculously poised, at attention. The crowd watched in awe as the viperish bullwhip danced in the air.

The two magistrates, Chang and Zhang, stood there in a daze. The yamen looked baffled. Mayor Ma's face turned uglier by the minute.

"You have cut off the water and trampled the crops," General Qi stopped the whipping and reprimanded. "Do you know who supplies you with food every day?"

"Of course they do," Mayor Ma spoke up and answered on behalf of the soldiers. "The Imperial Government. It's quite obvious, isn't it?"

General Qi was forced to face Mayor Ma. "Then where does the Imperial Government get its food?" he asked the mayor.

"Under the heaven, every inch is His Majesty's land. And to the borders of the land, every individual is his subject," the mayor responded confidently in a raised voice. "Therefore, His Majesty provides food for us."

"Well deduced," General Qi complimented him sarcastically, his eyes boring into the mayor's. "If that's the case then, why are you cutting off water to His Majesty's rice field? The crops you have destroyed are His Majesty's crops."

Speechless, Mayor Ma had no answer as his face grew blue. General Qi straightened his back and turned to his soldiers again. "Do you know what offences you have committed by cutting off His Majesty's water and trampling on His Majesty's crops?"

"Yes, sir – death," the soldiers answered unanimously, smart enough to know at whom the questions were directed.

"I'm glad you understand it," General Qi said before ordering his troops to regroup and return to their barracks.

As the soldiers gathered to leave, the farmers began pleading. "General, don't leave yet," they shouted on their knees. "They have arrested our honest folks. Please release them."

Soon, more shouts broke out in the crowd. "Release! Release!"

General Qi did not respond to the crowd's plea. Instead, he turned to his soldiers as they prepared to depart.

"This is pure sabotage," fumed Chang, the magistrate of Jiande County. "Are you trying to boycott an imperial order?"

"Your Highness, we can't allow Qi Jiguang to withdraw the troops," pleaded Zhang, the magistrate of Chun'an, as he approached Mayor Ma.

The mayor raced over to General Qi. "The Ministry of War has assigned the troops to me," he yelled. "You have no right to take them away."

"The troops have to go to fight the pirates now," General Qi replied in a cold yet resolute tone.

"What? Do you have written orders from above?" the mayor questioned.

"Yes, of course!" said General Qi.

"From whom?" asked the incredulous mayor.

"I don't have to show them to you," General Qi replied haughtily. "If you really want to find out, go and ask those at the Imperial Palace in Beijing."

"I know who's behind this," the mayor said in an accusatory tone. "Did you receive the order from Tan Lun?"

General Qi paused for a minute then continued about his business without answering. Mayor Ma marched a few steps forward and stopped in front of General Qi's horse.

"Qi, you are a friend of governor Hu, and so am I," he reminded him. "If you want to undermine my work, you'll come to no good in the end."

General Qi tilted his body towards the mayor. "Given that we're the governor's friends, let me offer you a piece of advice," he whispered. "Release those farmers before my troops leave. Otherwise, the farmers may tear you to pieces and toss your remains in the river."

Before the mayor had time to respond, General Qi spurred his horse into a gallop and shouted to the soldiers, "Let's go!" The army and their horses followed their general and marched past the mayor, who was left alone by the side of the road.

Farmers gathering on the embankment began to gather force again, storming towards the mayor's entourage and wrestling with the yamen guards who held the shackled instigators. Someone thundered, "Release them," and hundreds responded. Panicked, the two magistrates nudged closer to the mayor. "Your Honour, why don't we release them first and figure out what to do when we get back to Hangzhou?" they begged.

"You coward! If you want to run, leave your official's hats here and go," reprimanded Mayor Ma with a fierce and disgusted look on his face.

As the two magistrates stood there, startled, the mayor turned to his apprehensive yamen guards who watched over the shackled farmers. "Without my order, nobody can release them," he pointed out.

The crowd was moving towards the mayor. Undaunted, he marched calmly towards them.

Surprisingly, they stopped.

"I'm standing here alone as your mayor," he taunted them with a stern voice. "If you want to start an uprising, come on over and get me. Throw me into the river – I dare you."

Unexpectedly, his ferociousness effectively deterred the crowd. For a few minutes, the embankment stood silent. "Converting rice into mulberry is His Majesty's new national policy," he continued. "You either convert the farmland yourself or sell your land and let others do it. Nothing can change it, regardless of how many people have to die for this – be it one thousand or ten thousand. Even if the whole population of our province perishes, the conversion will still continue. General Qi might have left with his soldiers, but the Imperial Court will send reinforcements – thousands of them – to keep order. If you want to use violence to boycott the imperial policy, do it. I'm here for you to slaughter."

The crowd stared in disbelief. "Take those pirates back to Hangzhou," the mayor barked. By then, the two magistrates had quickly composed themselves. "Tie them up and go," ordered Chang, the magistrate of Jiande.

The mayor turned around and marched at the front.

Submitting to the mayor's threats, the farmers, who were timid and kind by nature, did not rise up and riot. But Mayor Ma's threats failed to disperse the crowd. They simply followed the mayor as he was getting ready to return to Hangzhou.

Chang, the magistrate of Jiande walked up to the mayor and whispered, "If these people follow us all the way to Hangzhou, things could get out of control." Sweat ran down his cheeks.

"It's already getting out of control," the mayor said, striding forward. "Let's return to Hangzhou first and see what the governor has to say."

The crowd wriggled forward quietly behind the mayor's entourage, like the flowing water in the Xin'an River.

明

The governor in Zhejiang was Hu Zongxian, who simultaneously held the position of imperial inspector. On that afternoon, Governor Hu was entertaining a group of western merchants at the South China Textile Bureau's product exhibit hall. Yang Jinshui, a eunuch who headed both the South China Textile Bureau and the Zhejiang Provincial Maritime Affairs Department, had organised a show to illustrate the marvels of Chinese silk. Despite his reluctance, Governor Hu felt that he should be there to offer support.

Boom, boom, boom! The pulsating sound of the drums not only assaulted one's eardrums but also tugged at one's heartstrings. Drumbeats had only recently become a form of entertainment under Emperor Jiajing, rather than the traditional call for action in the bloody battlefield. As the drums faded out, the sound of flutes filled the cavernous hall – another recent addition to the established music repertoire. Even though the tender and melancholy melody came from the flautist sitting on the stage nearby, one felt as if it had flown down straight from the remote heaven.

Shimmering silk draped the handrails of a long spiral staircase that stood in the middle of the exhibit hall and led to the second floor. From the handrails, the gorgeous fabric extended upward and ended on the shoulder of a tall and beautiful young woman. She, in turn, had elegantly wrapped the tip around her neck.

Appearing both translucent and colourful at the same time, the silk looked magical. Similarly, from a distance it appeared to have rich patterns but grew smooth and blank when one moved closer. The flowing silk melded seamlessly with the soft, siren-like melody of the flute, another once-forbidden aesthetic pleasure recently allowed again as official entertainment. When the stirring tune ended, the silk-bedecked lady moved, turned her back and smiled at the guests who were sitting on a row of chairs across the hallway. When she walked, catlike, towards the end of the second-floor corridor, her elegant figure pulled the bustling silk like a bridal train. Captivated both by the model and material, the guests stood up and applauded vigorously.

Governor Hu sat in the middle of the row. On his left was Yang, who had orchestrated the performance. A few local officials and five opulently decked-out merchants flanked him on either side. The merchants stood out because of their foreign looks – they had unusual aquiline noses, deep-set eyes and dark skin. The entertainment obviously bedazzled them.

"Light the candles," Yang ordered with his high-pitched voice as he clapped his hands. Dozens of his assistants, each carrying a lit candle, emerged from the hall's dual entrances. They approached the audience and handed each member a gleaming candle. When Hu declined his, Yang looked puzzled. "You and other officials should go ahead and show them the product," said Hu, with an exhausted look.

"I understand that you've been really swamped lately," Yang said. "But I'm afraid that we can't let you go yet. We're going to start negotiating with our clients. Once we figure out how much silk they will order and how many gunboats we require to escort the commercial ships, we need your approval to seal the deals. Why don't you sit here and take a rest first?"

Holding a candle, Yang stepped away with his guests. As he

paused before the staircase, he shouted once again, "Lights off." The red silk lanterns that decorated the second-floor corridor went off, and the exhibit hall darkened. The candles flickered, forming an aura of light in the middle of the hall.

By the candlelight, Yang's pale, beardless and pudgy face, typical among eunuchs, became clearer. He led the group forward, and slowly they approached the spiralling stair to examine the silk that draped around the handrail. Seated nearby, Governor Hu closed his eyes. Then, a guard appeared at the entrance, carrying a thick wool cloak on his arm. He tiptoed over to Governor Hu and quietly placed it over his body before retreating into a corner.

When Yang and his guests were halfway up the stairs, they paused as two of Yang's assistants gently lifted the silk and held it aloft. "Please proceed to examine the fabric," Yang said, moving his candle closer to the silk. Butterflies and bees on the fabric came alive. They flew around clusters of flower buds; their wings appeared so transparent that one could see both sides. Each butterfly and each bee carried a different colour and pattern, and when they flapped their wings they took on different angles. The foreign merchants smiled but remained unimpressed.

"Let's go up," Yang said.

When they reached the landing on the second floor, Yang's two assistants took a few steps back and carefully held up the second stretch of the silk for the guests to examine. Several candles converged to shed light on the fabric – similar patterns of butterflies, bees and flower buds.

The guests merely smiled politely without showing much interest. Seeing their diffidence, Yang pointed his soft and slender finger at a flower bud on the fabric and declared in his feminine voice, "Look at this flower, watch it very carefully."

The guests bent over. Yang tapped one of his fingers on a flower bud. At Yang's touch, that flower bud began to move – it was slowly blooming.

"Kai Le," one of the merchants blurted out in Chinese, which meant "It's blooming". His fluent Chinese, with an awkward Zhejiang accent, suggested that he had taken many business trips to the region.

"You have a sharp eye," Yang complimented the Chinese-speaking merchant. "Based on the western time device, this part of the fabric can be made into a dress that is suitable to wear at seven o'clock in the morning. Since the flowers are still budding, the butterflies and bees simply fly around them."

The Chinese-speaking merchant translated Yang's words for his colleagues, who nodded vigorously.

"This other section of the fabric can be tailored into a dress for a woman to wear at ten o'clock in the morning when the flowers are blooming, and bees and butterflies are beginning to collect nectar and pollen," explained Yang.

After hearing his words translated, the guests abandoned their former restraint and uttered sounds of admiration. Their positive reaction pleased Yang and the other officials, who looked at each other proudly.

"Please allow me to continue," Yang said with a cautious grin. The group held their candles and climbed another flight of stairs. Their shoes stepped soundlessly into the thick carpet. The hallway was so quiet that one could hear Governor Hu's light snoring.

Outside the exhibit hall, the sounds of clicking hooves caught the guards' attention. The South China Textile Bureau was located inside the imperial provincial government office complex. Under normal circumstances, it was closely guarded, but on that day all the senior officials in the province who were invited to the show had brought their own guards. So a heavy presence of uniformed security personnel made the exhibit hall look more intimidating than usual. Therefore, it came as a shock to the guards that horses were even allowed to burst into the complex. Looking alarmed, the guards rushed out to the Textile Bureau's main entrance, and in came an angry-faced individual they recognised as Mayor Ma. While they were deciding whether to stop Mayor Ma's horse, he had already barged in and stopped right in front of them. The governor's personal aide knew the mayor well, and he went up to greet him.

"Is the governor here?" The mayor dismounted before tossing his bullwhip to a startled guard behind him.

"Yes, Your Highness," replied the aide. "What's the rush? An emergency?"

"There's an uprising," said the mayor, who strode towards the main entrance to the exhibit hall. "Some pirates have instigated it, and about a thousand unruly scoundrels are gathered outside as we speak."

Shocked at the news, the aide led Mayor Ma into the Textile Bureau's courtyard, a labyrinth of chambers and halls. After passing through multiple heavily guarded gates, Mayor Ma finally saw the exhibit hall, which, to his surprise, had no armed soldiers at the entrance. Only two eunuchs stood outside. The determined mayor made a beeline for the entrance, leaving the governor's aide scrambling behind. "Your Highness, we can't allow you to go in at this moment," two eunuchs said in a firm tone as they stopped him. "It's not the right time."

The mayor, who had acted arrogantly in front of the farmers, finally met his match here. Faking a smile, he whispered in a humble tone, "I have something urgent to report to the governor. Please, I really need to see the governor and the others now."

One of the eunuchs pointed a finger at the hall and whispered, "All urgent matters have to wait. As you can see, they're in the middle of…"

The mayor peeked in and saw shadows flickering on the walls. Yang and a few provincial officials were watching a silk product display in a room partially illuminated by candlelight.

Confused and out of his element, the mayor took a gulp of air and said in a hushed voice, "There's an uprising that I have to report."

"An uprising?" the eunuchs uttered, looking shocked and nervous. "Where? How many troops are involved?"

"At this stage, we haven't mobilised the troops yet," the mayor explained. "Only a thousand or so farmers are gathered outside the complex."

The two eunuchs, who had their hearts in their mouth, uttered a sigh of relief. "For a moment, I thought the pirates had attacked us," said one of them. "Why don't you just wait for a few minutes? It won't be long."

Just then, the governor's aide caught up with them. "Since Governor Hu is resting, would it be possible for me to take him inside and talk with him?"

"That's right," the mayor nodded ingratiatingly. "I promise I won't interrupt the show. All I need is to talk with the governor quietly and report the incident."

The two eunuchs looked at each other hesitantly. Obviously, it was not wise to stop the governor's aide from seeking out his boss.

"Well, if anything happens, I'm afraid you have to take the blame," a eunuch said to the aide.

"I swear that we won't cause any problems," the aide promised.

"All right then, please go in quietly," one of the eunuchs acquiesced reluctantly. "You know how upset Yang Gonggong can get when interruptions occur."

"Of course," the mayor added.

"Please go this way," one of the eunuchs said while stepping aside to let them in.

The mayor followed the governor's aide and tiptoed inside. Before they approached the governor, the aide signalled the mayor to halt. In the faint candlelight, they saw Governor Hu sitting there with his cloak covering his back. Even though the governor kept his upper body upright, the mayor could hear his light snoring.

The governor's thinning face betrayed stress and exhaustion. Realising his state, the aide became reluctant to wake him. He shot a glance at the mayor, who shook his head sympathetically, indicating for the aide to wait. They simply stood there, unmoving, so they wouldn't disturb their governor's nap.

The unusual activities on the second floor caught their attention. Mayor Ma and the governor's aide turned their gazes towards the stairs, where Yang, the eunuch who directed the South China Textile Bureau, was attempting to impress his guests with the elaborately designed silk samples. Yang and his guests moved closer towards the top of the stairs, where the young model was holding the tip of the beguiling silk sample. Two of Yang's assistants went ahead of everyone to straighten out the surface, which seemed to have retained the same pattern – butterflies and bees. But a closer look by the candlelight revealed a different picture: the butterflies and bees were actually falling flower buds.

"This part of the silk can be tailored into a dress that ladies wear in the evening," said Yang. "Based on your western custom, the material is good for a nightgown."

All the guests nodded with admiration and appreciation. One muttered something in his native tongue, and the Chinese-speaking merchant immediately turned to Yang and explained, "My friend is curious to find out why you want to embed these subtle changes in this pattern?"

Yang gave out a mysterious smile. "As you probably know, a true aristocrat seldom shows off," he said. "They're reluctant to bring attention to themselves. So they wouldn't want people to see right away that they have changed outfits. One has to be observant to notice that they have actually changed four times during the day. That's what we call a true aristocrat."

Yang's explanation triggered a round of lively discussions among the guests. When they finally dwindled, the Chinese-speaking merchant spoke up on their behalf. "They think this type of silk will sell well among the wealthy in their countries," he briefed Yang. "Of course, when I say 'they', it includes me as well. We'll each order a hundred thousand bolts. Do you have enough in stock? That's what we want to know."

Yang paused for a second. "Of... Of course, we do," he answered. "We'll have enough to meet everyone's need."

Once the orders were confirmed, Yang declared in a high-pitched triumphant voice, "Open the windows!" The curtains on the second-floor windows were lifted and daylight filtered in, carrying different colours – the windows were draped with a variety of colours and patterns of silk.

Music rose. Governor Hu opened his eyes and saw Yang descending the stairs, beaming with self-congratulatory delight. As Governor Hu stood up to greet Yang, his aide approached to remove the cloak from his back. From the corner of his eye, he was surprised to see Mayor Ma, who was too preoccupied to follow the usual etiquette of bowing. But he and the governor were close enough, and an occasional omission wouldn't do him much harm.

The mayor cupped his hands, whispering in the governor's ear what had happened along the Xin'an River bank. Hu showed no emotions. Having secured this high ranking within the government, Hu might have cultivated and attained his state of serenity at a time of crisis. Or perhaps he had long anticipated that such riots would happen sooner or later.

As Yang and his guests came up to him, he greeted them with a calm yet weary smile.

"Our guests have ordered half a million bolts of silk," Yang reported to the governor, grinning from ear to ear. "That will translate into seven and a half million taels of silver. Your Highness, it is now up to you to make it happen."

Governor Hu did not respond and wore only a contrived smile on his tired face.

Noting his response, the other officials refrained from expressing too much enthusiasm about the deal.

Meanwhile, the foreign merchants began chit-chatting in their native tongues. The Chinese speaker stopped his own chatter and translated their conversation to Yang. "Mr Sahari and his friends really like the model who was holding the silk there. Can you find some other young women like her and sell them to my friends?"

Yang sniggered. "That does not fall under my jurisdiction. Go and ask them," he said, pointing at Governor Hu.

Hu's smile vanished. "Our Ming empire sells silk, tea and china, but not humans," he said, sternly.

Even without the translator's assistance, the foreign guests understood what Hu had said from his facial expression. They stopped their jokes, their faces turning sullen.

"Please send our guests to the hotel for food and rest," Hu told Yang, who, by then, had noticed the anxious-looking Mayor Ma. His unannounced presence could only indicate one thing – there was an emergency that needed the governor's urgent attention. A flicker of annoyance flashed across Yang's face. He turned around and faced his guests with a chortle. "You have probably heard the Chinese phrase *Paradise in heaven, the cities of Suzhou and Hangzhou on earth*," he said. "We specifically invited these musicians from Suzhou to perform for you today. This evening, we have arranged a boat tour for you on the legendary West Lake in Hangzhou. Let's talk business tomorrow."

After hearing the translation of their host's words, the guests looked pleased and eager. Yang clapped his hands, and several young eunuchs appeared. They led the guests out of the exhibit hall.

"Let's go and have a meeting at my office," Governor Hu told Mayor Ma before marching to the door in big strides. Mayor Ma and the other officials followed.

明

The public space outside the governor's office complex covered four mu of land, symbolising that the earth was a flat square and the Imperial Palace commands all four corners of the earth.

In the middle of the square stood a thirty-three-metre-tall flagpole, which remotely faced the office entrance. The flagpole lay flanked on both sides by two gigantic stone lions. At other times, the empty square exuded authority through its spaciousness, but today the atmosphere was different. Farmers from Chun'an, a rural county outside the city of Hangzhou, swarmed the space. Even the stone pathway to the entrance, specifically reserved for officials visiting the governor's office, was packed with petitioners, all of whom fell to their knees soundlessly. The fluttering sounds of flags billowing in the wind accentuated the silence.

Armed with sabres, the governor's security guards lined up on both sides of the front entrance, with the stone lions towering over them. Tan Lun, former aide to the Prince of Yu, donned his military uniform and waited quietly on the steps. As the crowd knelt silently, the armed guards watched them nervously and vigilantly.

Soon, Governor Hu's entourage appeared in the distance. But given that the pathway was fully occupied by petitioners, the governor's sedan and the guards' horses could not pass through. Flummoxed, they stopped on the outer edge of the square. When Governor Hu and other provincial officials stepped out of their sedans, the petitioners cast their gloomy glances at the governor and then at the yamen entrance where Tan Lun waited, his eyes fixed on one person: Governor Hu.

Their eyes met. People noticed that the governor looked despondent, but Tan's eyes showed flickers of hope and expectation. Avoiding Tan's searching stare, Governor Hu quickly turned his face to the sky, towards the graceful and overhanging roof of the yamen building.

"Your Highness, take a good look at that person there." Mayor Ma stepped forward and pointed at Tan Lun. "He's the one who has colluded with General Qi and created this mess."

"Let's settle things with those two later," suggested Ho Maocai, who headed the Provincial Justice Department. "I think we should make arrests first. Once we capture the ingrates, we can interrogate and investigate them one by one. Those who are guilty will be punished accordingly. If necessary, we should report this to Beijing."

The crowd turned to Governor Hu, waiting to see where he stood on the protest.

"There are so many over here – how can you arrest them all?" Governor Hu spoke up.

"But this is the governor's yamen and they can't..." Ho stammered.

"Don't worry," Governor Hu interrupted him. "They won't dismantle this place. Even if they do, I'll take the blame. When the Imperial Palace removes me from my position, I'll just go back to my native village. Why don't we use the back door to get in?"

Instead of returning to his sedan, Governor Hu took a detour and walked towards a side street, where the back entrance stood. The other officials also abandoned their sedans and followed him. Yang Jinshui, the eunuch in charge of the South China Textile Bureau, began throwing a tantrum. With a sullen face, he scurried towards his sedan. A junior eunuch lifted the sedan curtain, and Yang clambered in.

Soon, Mayor Ma stood there as if in reverie, and it took a while for him to realise that he was the only official left in the square. Before hurrying away, he threw a few hateful glances at Tan Lun, who waited at the entrance with the stony expression of a statue.

Through the back entrance, Governor Hu's entourage entered the expansive Zhejiang provincial governor's yamen and gathered inside a conference hall. After they took their seats, an aide went out to summon Tan Lun, who was then serving as a military adviser to Governor Hu.

A few minutes later, Tan Lun appeared. Without greeting anyone, he walked over to an empty seat next to a long table on the right side of the hall. Barely had he sat down when Mayor Ma removed his official hat and tossed it on the desk in front of him. "We are risking our lives on the front line, but some people here are sabotaging us," he fulminated. "Converting land and growing mulberry is a national policy. What I want to ask is, shouldn't we go all out to implement it? But if we don't have everyone's support, I seriously doubt that I can do it."

All eyes turned to Governor Hu, who stared into the courtyard with a pensive look before drifting to Zheng Bichang, the chief administrator, who was the second most powerful person in the province of Zhejiang.

Zheng felt obligated to speak up. "I have to agree with Mayor Ma. It's been four months since the Imperial Court issued the policy. So far, we've only met ten per cent of the quotas. We've been receiving letters from the Privy Council every few days. Beijing is requesting progress reports. That's the reason I sent Mayor Ma over to check up on those who were implementing the land-conversion programme. Many of you who are sitting here attended the trade negotiation at the South China Textile Bureau early today. We all saw that the foreign merchants have ordered half a million bolts of silk and that the orders have to be fulfilled by the end of the year. Without the land-conversion initiative, we wouldn't be able to produce that much raw silk here in Zhejiang. If we allow this chaos to continue, the Privy Council will definitively call us to account. If Yang Gonggong and the South China Textile Bureau fail to generate enough silk for export, Lu Gonggong will be censured by His Majesty. Who's going to take the blame? By then, I doubt anyone can get away with it by simply quitting."

When Yang Jinshui's name was mentioned, he sat there with his eyes closed, as if he had been a mere outsider. Zheng was accustomed to Yang's shrewd calculated reticence – each time a sensitive topic came up, Yang would only put on his listening ear but seldom opine. On the contrary, Ho Maocai, director of the Provincial Justice Department, exerted no self-control at public meetings.

"I think some people are conspiring against the Imperial Palace," accused Ho, who banged a fist on the desk to strike home his point. "The provincial government has sent troops to assist with Mayor Ma's work and control those dangerous mobs. But now, those scoundrels are bold enough to stage a riot in front of the governor's office. Do we know who in the world ordered General Qi to withdraw his troops? Please stand up and explain it to Governor Hu and Yang Gonggong?"

It was obvious that Ho's remarks were intended for Tan Lun, especially after he and a few others glowered suspiciously in Tan's direction.

To the surprise of those in attendance, Governor Hu spoke up and claimed to be the alleged culprit. "I was the one who instructed General Qi to pull the soldiers," he said in his usual deep calm voice, which struck Ho and the other officials like claps of thunder. Even Yang was jolted awake before drifting into his feigned nap again.

Tan Lun had not expected that Hu would readily accept responsibility on his behalf. Feeling grateful, he was tempted to thank Governor Hu in front of everyone but resisted the urge. Instead, he remained still, with arms folded and eyes downcast.

"The government has planned to borrow sixty thousand tonnes of rice from private suppliers to make up for the loss of rice output during the land conversion. Any progress on that?" Governor Hu asked Zheng, his deputy.

"We haven't had much luck yet," Zheng answered, looking surprised that Governor Hu would suddenly change the subject. "We've approached several large rice suppliers, and they all claim they don't have much to spare."

"What about securing some loans from other provinces?" Governor Hu continued.

"We sent a representative to the neighbouring province of Jiangsu last week, and officials there sounded reluctant," Zheng replied.

"Your answers have helped explain my current position on the land-conversion programme," said Governor Hu, who peered at Ho Maocai, signalled for him to sit down.

"As the governor and imperial inspector of Zhejiang Province, I'm willing to take the criticism and punishment from the Privy Council. If folks in the field curse us, they can swear at me. I understand that growing mulberry is a national policy and we have no choice but to implement it. But aren't they aware of the fact that if we propagate those mulberry seedlings now, we won't start seeing new leaves until the autumn? This means that farmers can only harvest two rounds of silkworms this year – one in early autumn and the other in late autumn. Within such a short window, we wouldn't be able to generate enough raw silk. In other words, if our government simply urges rice farmers to give up their grain production and grow mulberry trees, they wouldn't be able to earn enough to support themselves. Without any government loans to tide them over, people will be starving in the winter. Hunger breeds rebels. I understand that we are required to produce an additional three hundred thousand bolts of silk every year. But if these three hundred thousand bolts of silk could lead to insurrections and produce three hundred thousand rebels, I don't think I'll be the only one who will end up having his head cut off."

When Governor Hu stopped, the conference hall fell into total silence.

Hu turned to Mayor Ma and ordered, "I want you to go out there and release those folks immediately. Open up the irrigation channels along the Xin'an River and allow farmers to water their crops."

Mayor Ma stood up, trying to defend his actions, but Governor Hu shot him down. "I don't need to hear your explanation," he said with a look of impatience. "Please go and take care of it now."

"Yes, Your Highness," the mayor responded in a husky voice. Picking up his official hat, he dashed out.

"Your Highness, I know I have no right to stick my nose in your affairs here in Zhejiang," said Yang Jinshui, who had strategically kept his eyes closed most of this time. "But I have been assigned to run the South China Textile Bureau on behalf of the Imperial Palace. His Majesty should be cognisant of the transactions we completed today. So it's really important that we fulfil those orders. As you probably know, the textile bureau has only about one hundred thousand bolts of silk in stock. The silk mills in Hangzhou and the nearby cities of Nanjing and Suzhou have to produce an extra four hundred thousand bolts. But, at present, we just don't have enough raw silk. Based on our assessment, the current amount of raw silk provided by mulberry farmers in the area is only good for two hundred thousand bolts. So we'll be at least two hundred thousand bolts short. If we can't meet the quotas, we could be in big trouble. The Privy Council might let you off the hook, but I can't get away with it because I'm a staff member of the Imperial Palace. I have to fulfil my promise for Lu Gonggong and His Majesty."

"I'll write up a report about today's events to His Majesty," Governor Hu countered. "If the Privy Council wants to implement the land-conversion programme, it has to urge our neighbours to loan more rice to us. The Ministry of Treasury needs to reach out to them directly. At the same time, we also have to persuade private rice suppliers to lend us rice or pressure them if necessary. I know many suppliers are concerned that the government might renege on its promises to pay back the loans. To boost their trust, I'll put the governor and the imperial inspector's stamps on all of the IOUs. Every day, I can see suppliers' junks loaded with grain travelling on the Grand Canal. Why can't they lend us some? Anyone who blatantly lies about their inventory and refuses to help out will be charged with hoarding. Extorting the rice suppliers is a better option than driving ordinary folks to rebellion, don't you think?"

Yang didn't answer. Instead, he closed his eyes again. Nobody around him openly objected to Governor Hu's proposal.

明

Governor Hu's report reached the capital city in seven days via the Imperial Express service. Instead of following the usual route and delivering it to the postal department, the courier ferried it directly to the Privy Council's reception room inside the Western Palace. Xu Jie, the deputy grand secretary, happened to be on duty. From a mere glance at the envelope, he could tell that the letter was no ordinary report and could cause huge ripples. Holding his cards close to his chest, he ordered an assistant to personally deliver the letter directly to Yan Song's home without opening it.

Local rumours long held that the nation's major decisions were made inside the Yan family mansion, rather than the Forbidden City. The sly supposition had some truth to it. Yan Song had turned seventy-five in 1556, and except for his daily thirty-minute private meeting with Emperor Jiajing in the Yuxi Palace early in the morning, he seldom showed up at the Privy Council's office. All the important government reports and documents were sent directly to his home. For urgent matters relating to national defence, Yan Song would summon council members to his mansion for discussions. Once he and his council members formed a consensus, he would draft an official response and submit it to the emperor through Lu Fang, who headed the Interior Ministry.

Under normal circumstances, Yan Shifan sifted and reviewed all major documents pertaining to the Privy Council before sharing them with his father. Governor Hu's report on that day was no exception. Yan Shifan tore off the envelope, and after skimming through the document's contents he exploded with anger and quickly sent a messenger to summon Luo Wenlong, his father's confidant as well as his most trusted friend.

Luo headed the postal department that handled key reports and letters submitted by officials from around the country. When Luo arrived, Yan Shifan brought him along to consult with Yan Song in his study.

Even though Yan Song did not show much emotion upon reading the letter, Yan Shifan knew that his father was equally upset. "Governor Hu claims that we'll lose the support from farmers if we grab their land, and landless farmers could pose a threat to the security of our country," Yan Shifan said contemptuously as he held up Governor Hu's report. "What does that mean? He's such an alarmist. These statements are so pompous. I think he is boycotting our plan because he's concerned about his own political future."

"I cannot agree with you more," said the scholarly-looking Luo. "I alerted and cautioned everyone here when the Prince of Yu decided to transfer his chief of staff, Tan Lun, to the Zhejiang governor's office last month. As you're probably aware, Tan Lun and Governor Hu have been friends for years. Governor Hu knows very well that Tan Lun is a confidant of the crown prince. Given that Your Highness is considering retirement and the crown prince might take over the country someday, it's natural that Hu would look for a fallback plan to hedge his bets. The fact that Governor Hu bypassed the postal department and had his report delivered directly to the Privy Council shows that he intends to curry favour with Xu Jie and other friends of the crown prince."

Yan Song, who had remained inert on his couch until then, interrupted. "But Xu Jie didn't open the letter. I think Governor Hu simply wanted to bypass you two so he can get his message to His Majesty and me directly. I can't vouch for anyone else, but I know for sure that Governor Hu is a loyal student of mine. I doubt he intends to betray me and undermine my authority. He simply has a different perspective on the land-conversion programme than yours, that's all. When judging others, one should put oneself in their shoes. What would you do if you were Governor Hu?"

Yan Song's reprimand disappointed Yan Shifan and Luo, both of whom had intended to drive a wedge between Yan Song and his protégé, Governor Hu. Little did they know that their seasoned elder would have dismissed their attempts so quickly. They looked at each other, speechless. Through their eyes, they seemed to be saying to each other: this man was eighty-one years old, but old age has not addled his brain.

"If you were in his position, you would have done the same thing," Yan Song continued slowly, ignoring Yan Shifan and Luo Wenlong's apparent disapproval. "It might not be a bad thing to have Tan Lung at his side. Tan has the backing of the crown prince, and the prince has the backing of His Majesty. It simply means that Governor Hu can't be too reckless with his decisions."

The old man certainly knew when to appear dull-witted, thought Luo.

"But the plan to convert rice fields to mulberry farms was also His Majesty's idea," Yan Shifan raged, angry at his father's prejudice in favour of outsiders, rather than his own kin.

"Governor Hu is not saying that he won't implement the policy," Yan Song insisted. "Tan Lun's presence is making him more prudent. The situation is pretty dire over there. If Governor Hu follows your plan without consulting with the Privy Council, he could give others an excuse to depose him."

"Dad!" Yan Shifan walked up to his father and tossed Governor Hu's report on a tea table next to the couch. "It's so obvious that Governor Hu has written this report to curry favour with the crown prince," he accused. "Anybody can see that, except you. Why are you always defending him? How could you claim that he's merely trying to bypass me because he doesn't like me? Who am I? I'm your son. You're eighty-one years old. Have you ever thought that someday, when you retire or die, all of your political enemies would take me out? I won't have any fallback."

"Oh, stop it," Yan Song interrupted his son. "Let me ask you, who is the crown prince's father?"

Once again, Yan Shifan felt blindsided by his father's question.

"Do you know who His Majesty is visiting this afternoon?" asked Yan Song, who gazed at the courtyard outside.

Yan Shifan and Luo Wenlong shook their heads.

Yan Song sat up in his couch and enlightened them. "He's going to the crown prince's mansion to meet his new grandson."

Yan Shifan and Luo now understood what the old man was trying to imply – the Prince of Yu's stock had just risen with the birth of his son.

"You're always so impatient." Yan Song shot his son a reproachable look before lying down on his recliner. "Why don't you two sit down? You make me dizzy."

"Now that Tan Lun has been transferred to Zhejiang Province, the Prince of Yu has been keeping a close watch on what is happening there," Yan Song said. "In other words, even if the postal department intercepted Governor Hu's letter, the Privy Council, the Interior Ministry and His Majesty would find out sooner or later. So stop fussing over protocols, and let's focus on the content of the letter. How will His Majesty react after he reads Governor Hu's report? To me, his arguments and suggestions are quite mature and wise. The conversion policy involves the conversion of many acres of farmland, and it directly affects the lives of thousands of farmers. Zhejiang has been rife with pirate attacks. If our policy triggers large-scale insurrection, it wouldn't be good for our country. What if His Majesty shares similar concerns but still insists that we increase the production of silk by four hundred thousand bolts at all costs? How should we respond to this? I would suggest you peruse Governor Hu's report. I understand that you support the idea of allowing large silk mill owners to acquire land from farmers and convert it into mulberry plots. But is there an alternative option that can accommodate both needs – boosting silk production while benefiting farmers?"

"I'm not aware of any other option that is better," said Luo.

"Like you just mentioned, our land-conversion policy aims to boost the supply of raw silk for export production," Yan Shifan responded in a testy tone. "Increases in silk exports can earn us more silver taels. But, if the quality of the silk is inferior, foreign merchants wouldn't buy it. So the silk has to be made at large facilities. If we allow farmers to grow mulberry and raise raw silkworms, they would inevitably sell the raw silk to smaller mills. Their cheap low-quality products will never meet the export standards. That's why we encourage farmers to sell their land to big mill owners. Dad, that's what our land-conversion plan is all about. Our ultimate goal is to reduce the national budget deficit. But, if we don't grit our teeth and stick with it, our national treasury will be depleted. Pretty soon, we won't need others to topple us. We'll collapse on our own."

Yan Song remained unconvinced. To win the old man over, Luo realised that they had to follow his logic by temporarily leaving Governor Hu out of the conversation and making Yan Song aware that they were on his side all along. "We don't have to speculate about Governor Hu's motive," Luo interrupted. "But your son is well-intentioned, and his analysis is right on target. As the saying goes, a desperate illness needs a desperate cure. The land-conversion policy was initially made to alleviate a perilous situation. We have to rely on large silk mill owners, who have the capacity to rake in several million taels of silver each year and help ease our deficit. If we're lucky, we can probably cover some of this year's expenses as well. As for those targeted farmlands, farmers have to sell them whether they like it or not. Otherwise, the export orders secured by the South China Textile Bureau will fall through. If we fail," he added, looking Yan Song directly in the eye, "the Privy Council and Your Highness would be held responsible. I doubt that Lu Gonggong and the Interior Ministry would want to have anything to do with it."

Luo's words touched a sore spot. Yan Song sank into silence and stared blankly at the garden outside while Luo and his son, Yan Shifan, were waiting for him to speak. A few minutes later, Yan Song picked up Governor Hu's letter from the tea table. "I guess we cannot always shoulder everyone else's problems," he sighed, waving it in his hand. "Take this letter to the Interior Ministry and try to talk with Lu Gonggong before His Majesty visits the Prince of Yu today. Tell Lu Gonggong to present the letter to His Majesty upon his arrival at the prince's mansion. If possible, request that His Majesty offer his feedback right in front of the prince."

Yan Shifan looked befuddled – he hadn't fully grasped the old man's true intentions.

"That is a very wise idea," Luo complimented Yan Song while trying to explain it to the grand secretary's son. "If His Majesty reads Governor Hu's report, he's likely to support the land-conversion policy, insisting that we meet the export quotas. Whatever suggestions or comments he makes in front of the prince would be known to everyone and exempt us from future liabilities. That's your father's first intention. Secondly, if the Prince of Yu opposes the policy, he wouldn't dare challenge His Majesty in front of everyone. On the other hand, if the prince fails to speak up, it would be political suicide for him. In the future, we can easily claim that he conspires with his allies inside the Privy Council to sabotage His Majesty's authority. Your Highness, have I interpreted this all correctly?"

Yan Song nodded appreciatively. "Thou hast certainly read my mind," he praised. "Nobody is as perceptive and insightful as you are!"

Yan Shifan did not seem to mind that his father favoured Luo over him – at least not in this instance. "Ah, I see," he blurted out loudly. "I'll take the document to the Interior Ministry immediately."

明

As Yan Song had correctly predicted, the news about Governor Hu's urgent report had reached the Prince of Yu. Since Tan Lun's secret letter to him arrived in Beijing simultaneously, the prince and his advisers were briefed on what Governor Hu had written.

Zhang Juzheng, the head of the Ministry of Defence, clapped his hands after reading Tan's letter. "Tan Lun is a true hero," he remarked excitedly. "It is quite a feat to persuade Governor Hu, a key member of the Yan faction, to submit this report. There is hope."

"I beg to differ," said Gao Gong. The deputy minister of the treasury, who was known for being easily excitable, was uncharacteristically calm. "Governor Hu must have proposed quite a few items in his report, but, except for Yan Song and his son, nobody knows exactly what has been included. There is a possibility that Yan Song could omit some items and present those less important ones to His Majesty. Then, Yan can write to Governor Hu, asking him in private not to mention those omitted items. I doubt Governor Hu would speak up to embarrass Yan, his mentor."

Gao's words dampened the enthusiasm in the room like a bucket of icy water. An uncomfortable silence ensued. The Prince of Yu shot a sidelong glance at Xu Jie, the deputy grand secretary.

"Governor Hu's report was first delivered to the Privy Council's duty room, and you happened to be there to receive it," Gao groused. "I wish you had gone over to Yan Song's house to hand-deliver the report. In this way, Yan Song would have felt obligated to share the report with you. That would have prevented them from rigging it. Please don't take offence – I know prudence is a virtue – but often, too much prudence can ruin things."

Xu's face flushed red with anger. The Prince of Yu and Zhang, who were too flustered to respond, sat there quietly. An infant's loud screaming from the inner chamber broke the awkward silence.

"What happened?" the prince shouted to the people inside. "We have so many adults in there, and nobody knows how to take care of a baby!"

"His Majesty is visiting this afternoon, and we're trying a new hat on him," a maid dashed out and explained, with her head lowered. "The boy doesn't want it."

"If he still cries, don't put it on him," complained the prince. "His Majesty will be here in an hour. Go and tell the princess that our son needs to wear the ceremonial robe. It's frustrating that nobody here is helping."

"Yes, Your Highness," the maid said before retreating hurriedly.

The guests, all of whom were mentors of the prince, knew what he was insinuating. Deputy Grand Secretary Xu wondered if the prince was venting because of Gao's previous remarks about him being overly prudent. So he stood up and dutifully offered his self-criticism. "Gao might be right in blaming me," he offered. "If you also agree with what Gao has just said, I can make up for it by going to Yan Song's residence right now and finding out exactly what Hu has submitted."

Realising that he had probably overreacted, the prince quickly corrected himself. "I didn't mean to blame or reprimand anyone," he explained. "I was just in a bad mood. It's kind of pathetic. Even though I'm His Majesty's son, you people are treated better than I am. The last time I saw His Majesty was two years ago. If it hadn't been for his grandson, he wouldn't have come this afternoon. It's a hopeless situation. I don't even have the opportunity to shoulder some of my father's responsibilities. What gives me the right to blame you? Oh well, His Majesty will be here shortly. Why don't you all go home. Let's discuss the affairs in Zhejiang some other day."

Seeing that the prince had stood up, the guests reluctantly rose as well. They had hoped to meet and strategise with the prince about speaking with His Majesty during his visit. But now, the group parted on bad terms – Gao's blunt criticism had soured the prince and left Xu in a dark mood.

"I'm sorry to be such a wet blanket," Gao apologised to the prince before turning to Xu. "Please don't take offence. I was just worried that Yan Song and his son could distort the messages in Governor Hu's report. Oh well, we might get a better idea during His Majesty's visit."

As the Prince of Yu walked his three guests to the gate to bid them goodbye, the royal grandson's loud wailing sounded again. He turned around and saw Princess Li stepping out of the inner chamber with their crying child in her arms. A maid followed, cupping with her hands a small crown embedded with tiny pearls. The delicate task had made her sweat profusely. An additional childcare cadre followed with the child's nanny and three other maids. Perspiration shone on their faces, as well.

The prince glanced at his infant and then shook his head. "His Majesty could be here any minute, and you people can't even get him to put on his royal hat," he scolded, looking crestfallen. "Don't you know how to take care of a child?"

The women visibly quaked, while the princess rocked the child gently and slowly in her arms. His crying diminished but started again as a maid hastily put the baby's hat on with her trembling hands. Distressed, the maid quickly pulled her hand back.

"Feng Bao is the only person who can stop this," Princess Li said to her husband. "I think we should get him here."

The mere mention of Feng's name disgusted the prince. He paused for a second then waved his hands in defeat. "Go and get him. His presence is required at the ceremony anyway."

A few moments later, the maid rushed in with Feng, who, in a matter of months, had transformed into a different person. Donning a grey coarse linen robe with a wide blue belt, Feng had the new look of a low-level servant, complete with a modest smile on his dusty face. Before stepping inside, Feng dropped to his knees outside the entrance, his forehead touching the ground. "Your humble servant, Feng Bao, is kowtowing to the prince and princess."

The prince, who was perusing a book at his desk, ignored Feng's obsequious greeting, but Princess Li quickly invited him in. "Go and play with his Royal Highness, and see if you can get him to wear his crown," she said, handing over her child to the nanny.

"Yes, Your Highness," Feng kowtowed again before sidling in.

The nanny walked over to Feng with the boy. Feng lowered his head and murmured to Princess Li. "Your... your humble servant had no time to change before he came in... I'm afraid that my grubby outfit might..."

"There's no time to worry about that," Princess Li said impatiently. "Take His Royal Highness now."

The nanny placed the little prince in Feng's arms. Feng tilted the boy's face towards his. "Your Royal Highness, can you recognise me?" he whispered mischievously. "Your humble servant and playmate is here with you."

Astonishingly, the boy immediately stopped crying when he saw Feng's grinning face. He stared at him, with his eyes wide open. The nanny and maids uttered a long sigh of relief, and hard-earned smiles appeared on their tired faces. Princess Li, looking visibly relieved, turned to her husband, whose head was still buried in the book. "Now, figure out a way to get him to wear the crown," Princess Li told Feng.

"Yes, Your Highness," Feng answered. When one of the maids handed the delicate valuable crown to Feng, the boy became scared and burst out crying again. The prince closed his book and rose from his desk with an irritated look. Before he had the chance to reprimand the servants, a eunuch appeared at the entrance and kowtowed. "A message for the prince and princess," the eunuch announced. "His Majesty has left the palace. His guards of honour are approaching the main gate."

The boy was still crying, and people in the room began to panic. The prince waved his long sleeves in agitation and strode out.

"Act fast!" Princess Li ordered anxiously. "We have to find a way to get the boy to wear his crown."

"If only you allow me to break the rules a bit," Feng asked. With the princess's permission, Feng slowly squatted down with the little prince in his arms, until his knees touched the ground. "Meow, meow," he began imitating the sound of a cat while moving about on his knees.

The boy began to giggle.

"Little Sister, could you bring the crown over and put it on my head first?" Feng asked the maid, who hesitated and looked to the princess for permission.

"Please go ahead," Princess Li said, her voice trembling with helplessness.

The maid walked over, leaned down a bit and carefully placed the crown on the top of Feng's head. It was too small to fit, but fortunately the maid was able to use a long attached string to tie the crown firmly around Feng's chin. As the benighted eunuch bobbed his head, meowing like a cat and barking like a dog, the accessories started to clank, which aroused the little prince's curiosity. He stopped giggling and kept his eyes fixed on the glittery and clinking accessories on Feng's head.

"I think you can put it on him now," Feng said in a low tone to the nanny. She bent over, removed the crown from Feng's head and cautiously moved to place it on the little prince. To distract the child, Feng rocked him back and forth, serenading him with long drawn-out sounds of cats and dogs while the nanny tied the string around his chubby, baby chin. The procedure worked as seamlessly as an experienced doctor feeding a bowl of bitter herbal water to a difficult child.

"Whew," Princess Li exhaled long and slow before slumping into a chair behind her. "Let's get ready to greet His Majesty."

The prince's mansion consisted of six layered courtyards, and from the front entrance to the reception hall there were twelve gates, all of which were kept wide open prior to the emperor's arrival. The compound was packed with guards of honour, who lined up on both sides of the gates.

Emperor Jiajing was his normal self. In contrast to the finery worn by the prince and his family, a casual loose-fitting robe covered the Ming ruler, along with a yellow Taoist headband. Now, as he perched comfortably on a chair in the middle of the prince's reception hall, a rare benevolent smile spread across his face. Lu Fang, standing behind the emperor on the left, also appeared gleeful.

The prince dutifully kowtowed to his royal father nine times then retreated to the left side, while Princess Li moved to a similar position on the right. Both the prince and princess kept their heads down, as dictated by custom. Feng knelt in the middle of the room, holding the wriggly little prince in his arms, with him facing the grandfather.

As the saying went, when a person is favoured by fortune, even his mind becomes keener. The royal infant was only a few months old, but he was not the least intimidated by the stranger in front of him. Instead of staging another tantrum, however, the infant gazed upon the old man's face, grinning and giggling. Charmed by his grandson's smile, the emperor clapped his hands before opening his arms. The prince quickly grabbed his son from Feng and offered him to his grandfather. Feng rose from the floor and bowed his way out.

Emperor Jiajing beamed with pleasure as he examined his grandson's face. The child beamed back. Jiajing's paternal instincts were rekindled after years of strict Taoist meditation and isolation.

As the two generations delighted in each other, Princess Li observed the protocol by keeping her head down. Without knowing how her son was reacting to the emperor's grand gesture, however, she became anxious. Sweat gathered in beads on her smooth forehead.

"You have rendered a great service for our empire," Emperor Jiajing said, placing the child on his lap and addressing Princess Li. "I will reward you handsomely."

Princess Li had no idea that the emperor was addressing her. Her husband quickly reminded her, "Princess, the Royal Father is speaking to you."

Princess Li quickly dropped to her knees. "The birth of the royal prince testifies to the virtues of our ancestors," she intoned. "His Majesty's veneration for heaven and his love of his subjects have produced karmic reward. As the humble wife of your son, I dare not claim and do not deserve any credit."

Emperor Jiajing's face brightened even more. "I must give credit where credit is due," said the emperor. "Since you come from a humble family, I will bestow a knighthood upon your father."

Dumbfounded by the news, Princess Li froze like a statue. The prince quickly knelt next to her. "On behalf of my wife, I want to thank my royal father for this heavenly gift," he said, followed by three kowtows.

Princess Li recovered from her shock and prostrated herself on the floor. As the prince helped her up, Emperor Jiajing noticed that her face was streaked with tears. "It's a happy occasion, and there is no need to cry," the emperor consoled.

"Please forgive me for the breach of etiquette," Princess Li apologised, holding back her tears.

In a moment of generosity, Emperor Jiajing tilted his head to his most senior eunuch, Lu Fang, and said, "If Jiangsu and Zhejiang Provinces produce an abundance of silk this year, please gift one hundred thousand bolts to Princess Li's family."

"Yes, Your Majesty," Lu Fang responded. "I will pass on the message to the South China Textile Bureau."

Princess Li was about to kowtow again to express her gratitude when Emperor Jiajing interrupted her. "There is no need to thank me," he said while picking up the boy from his lap. "Take good care of my grandson."

The prince hurried over, retrieved the boy from the emperor and handed him to Princess Li.

"On this auspicious occasion, your humble servant wants to report another small piece of good news," Lu Fang whispered to Emperor Jiajing. "The South China Textile Bureau has just secured orders of five hundred thousand bolts of silk from foreign merchants."

"How much will the transaction bring us?" Emperor Jiajing asked, looking visibly energised at the news.

"The domestic price for silk is about six silver taels per bolt, but, if we ship it overseas, each bolt can sell for up to fifteen silver taels. So five hundred thousand bolts can translate into four and a half million silver taels."

"This is excellent news," remarked the emperor. "Do you think there is enough raw silk in Zhejiang for us to fulfil those big orders?"

"Hmm…" Lu Fang paused deliberately.

"What is it?"

"We have received a report from Hu Zongxian, the governor of

Zhejiang," Lu Fang said. "The report is related to the land-conversion programme. Yan Song delivered it to me before we left the palace. I was planning to show it to you."

Emperor Jiajing, a shrewd and perceptive ruler, detected the overtone in Lu's words. "Has he run into problems?" he asked. "Is he trying to complain to me about the policy?"

"Nothing escapes your sharp eyes," Lu said ingratiatingly.

"I don't want to read about complaints," the emperor said dismissively. "Tell him to take his complaints to the Privy Council and talk to Yan Song."

"Yes, Your Majesty," Lu answered loudly while shooting a sidelong glance at the Prince of Yu, who stood with his head down. Lu thought he had detected a slight twitch on the prince's face.

"Tell the palace not to prepare supper for me," Emperor Jiajing stood up and announced. "I'm going to eat here."

The prince bowed to his father. "Thank you for the honour, Father," he said.

Emperor Jiajing foiled Yan Song's plan by sending back Governor Hu's report without even offering any comments. But Yan Song took comfort in the fact that the emperor had at least become aware of Governor Hu's report. Since His Majesty specifically delegated the task to the Privy Council, Yan Song felt obligated to obey and entrusted it to his son, urging him to handle it with caution.

The emperor's lack of interest emboldened Yan Shifan, who ignored his father's advice to proceed cautiously. Even though it was late at night, he summoned Luo Wenlong to the Yan family mansion. When Luo arrived, Yan Shifan paced up and down in the room, too absorbed to speak. Curious to find out about the emperor's reaction to Governor Hu's report, Luo picked a seat near a desk and looked at Yan expectantly.

"Draft a letter to our folks in Zhejiang," Yan Shifan dictated. "Tell them to ignore Governor Hu's interference and go all out with our original plan. The rainy season in May is a critical time, and we have to seize the opportunity. Destroy the sluice gates along the

Xin'an River, and flood the nine counties in the region. Once the rice paddies are submerged in water, we will send out leading silk producers in the region to seize the land by bartering for it with grain. Once the land is secured, we'll plant mulberry right away. I want to see silk this year!"

"Understood," said Luo. "What did His Majesty say?"

"His Majesty didn't even bother to read it," Yan Shifan replied. "Governor Hu's report is coming back unopened – untouched. This provides us with a perfect opportunity. I'll personally draft a rebuttal on behalf of the Privy Council. Damn it. I'm going to let Hu understand that the Yan family owns the halo over his head."

With that, Yan Shifan stopped pacing. After a few strenuous coughs, he spat out a ball of thick phlegm.

3

Governor Hu's face looked gaunt and tired, more so than two weeks ago. Sitting at a gigantic desk specifically reserved for reviewing and signing confidential documents, he stared at his report that had been returned after the Privy Council's rejection. Next to the report sat Yan Shifan's accompanying rebuttal letter.

"I've heard your report was rejected," Tan Lun stepped in, speaking with his usual strident voice.

"Take a seat," Governor Hu said, raising his grim eyes.

Tan Lun paused for a second. Instead of sitting down, he stepped around the desk and right up to Governor Hu. "I've received a letter from the Imperial Palace," he whispered. "I know what's happening. The whole thing sounds so turbulent! Listen – my source wants me to share some details with you. Are you interested?"

"No, I'm not," Governor Hu replied, closing his eyes.

Tan Lun stood there awkwardly. Governor Hu opened his eyes but did not turn his gaze to the young schemer. "I don't think it is a good idea for you to stay here," Hu said in his deep voice. "Go and pack, and get ready to leave."

"Are you worried about incriminating me, or are you just concerned that my being here could harm your career?" Tan Lun questioned, looking Governor Hu in the eye.

Governor Hu fixed his gaze on his desk and did not answer. His grave expression revealed displeasure at Tan Lun's words.

Realising that he had been too blunt, Tan Lun apologised.

"I didn't mean to be rude," he explained. "What I want to say is that, if the Imperial Palace puts the blame on you someday, my presence here might help absolve you."

"You have not learned a thing since I last saw you ten years ago," Hu said with a sigh. "I have no idea what the Prince of Yu sees in you."

In a fit of pique, Tan Lun retorted, "Are you saying that I have not grasped the so-called 'Three ponderings for government leaders'?"

Governor Hu looked Tan in the eye. "I don't know what you are talking about," he said slowly. "Are you referring to the saying about an official's ability to always 'ponder risk, ponder retreat and ponder change'?"

Tan Lun didn't respond.

"If that's what you were referring to, I want to tell you now that I'm not pondering any form of exit, and you shouldn't expect to change me either," Governor Hu continued.

"So I shouldn't have come over here," Tan lamented.

"No, you shouldn't have," Governor Hu said, pronouncing each word separately and clearly.

"Apparently, the people around me know you better than I do," said Tan Lun, who looked somewhat lost.

"You're talking about those who are mentoring and advising the Prince of Yu, aren't you?" Governor Hu asked. "Let me be honest with you. They are a bunch of big talkers – way too pedantic for my taste."

The comment irritated Tan Lun, and before he had the chance to defend his posse, Hu Zongxian cut him off.

"Let me finish," Governor Hu said. "I act the same way no matter who is around. Isn't that the definition of an ethical leader? If you hadn't come, I would have acted the same way I am now. Tomorrow, when you leave, I will continue walking the same path. Therefore, there's really no point in advising me what to do or volunteering to be my scapegoat."

Tan Lun, stunned by the old governor's candour, gave him a quizzical look. But Hu was having none of it. "The whole Imperial Court probably knows that I'm Grand Secretary Yan's protégé," Hu kept on, as if talking to himself. "In one thousand years, I'll still be written up in the history books as someone who was affiliated with Grand Secretary Yan's faction. Even so, why do people like you and members of the so-called "Clear Stream" faction still find some value in me?" He waved a thin hand. "I think it is because I've never allowed harm to come to our country and people. In my home town, villagers have built three memorial arches for me. Three! I'm over fifty now – if I can live up to seventy, I have about a dozen or more years to live. I will use everything I've got to keep my integrity so my fellow villagers won't dismantle those memorial arches."

Tan Lun sat there, listening intently.

"You and your scheming friends are under the illusion that you understand people and are well versed in what is happening locally," Governor Hu said, with more than a hint of sarcasm. "But how many of you truly know me and understand the situation here? Take the land-conversion policy as an example. This unwise new national policy will bring about a sea change in local politics. Many big silk mill owners want to take advantage of the policy and monopolise the land. As you know, seventy per cent of my province here is covered by mountains, twenty per cent by water and only ten per cent is farmland. If we allow the big landowners to acquire more land, nearly half of the farmers would immediately end up without any property! With such a large number of landless people hovering around, our province would be a breeding ground for turmoil and insurrection. If those farmers don't rise up this year, they will do it next year or the year after. History and human nature dictate that it will happen sooner or later. And when that happens, we'll be facing both external threats from the pirates and internal chaos caused by discontented farmers. There's no doubt that His Majesty would make me the number-one culprit, and my failure in Zhejiang would be printed in the history books. I have no interest in doing my people wrong like this and going down thus. So, for these reasons only, I won't allow this policy to destroy

Zhejiang, regardless of whether you had come or not. You might have arrived to assist me, or to proselytise to me. No matter what your motives are, the consequence is the same – you would mess things up for me."

"What do you mean?" Tan Lun said, looking a bit befuddled.

"Before you came over here, I had easy access to Grand Secretary Yan, and sometimes sought advice on things that I didn't agree with," Hu said. "Occasionally, I would even submit a report to His Majesty and explain why I chose to do things in a certain way. Truly wise governing requires diplomacy and dialogue. So when it came to implementing the land-conversion policy, such access to Beijing would have allowed me to buy some time and change things slowly in the direction that I wanted. For example, the original plan was to convert half the farmland into mulberry fields, but I could have submitted a request to try and do it over three years. Using such a method would have given me more room to alleviate the situation and probably even reverse the outcome."

Waving the rejected report in front of Tan Lun, Governor Hu continued, "After your arrival here, however, this is what I received from Grand Secretary Yan and His Majesty. Do you know why? Now they all see me as a raging partisan. If everyone perceives me as a partisan, I won't be able to accomplish the things that you and others want me to, will I? The Privy Council discussed this policy early in the year. If your friends truly had the ability to stop it, they shouldn't have allowed it to end up here in Zhejiang Province."

Tan Lun cast his eyes down on the floor.

"Now that you're here, the Privy Council no longer wants to hear what I have to say," said Governor Hu. "I bet they're conspiring to relieve me of my duties here in Zhejiang. Since you're such an avant-garde genius of strategy, why don't you sit down and read this letter yourself, then tell me how *you* interpret it?"

Picking up Yan's rebuttal letter, Governor Hu handed it over to Tan Lun. He meekly took it, picked a seat near a window and started reading. Meanwhile, Governor Hu rose and walked over to his filing cabinets that stood against the wall, where he pulled out a stack of documents and letters. Seeing that Tan Lun had already finished reading the short missive, he handed over the documents.

"These are letters from Grand Secretary Yan and his son, and these are official documents that detail the land-conversion plan," said Governor Hu. "Don't you want to read them?"

"No, I don't need to," Tan Lun said, shaking his head. His face showed a mixture of contrition and understanding.

"Why not?" Governor Hu asked.

"The more I know, the more difficult your job will be," Tan Lun replied.

Governor Hu turned around, with his back facing Tan Lun. "In the book *Commentaries of Zuo*, there is a saying – 'That which creates can also destroy,'" he said, growing misty-eyed. "Grand Secretary Yan promoted me, and any day now he'll be the one who demotes me as well. But now I have this – When the big tree falls someday, I can take comfort in the fact that a person named Tan Lun will speak in my favour and judge me fairly."

Tan Lun rose from his chair and became emotional as well.

"I've said everything that needs to be said," Governor Hu continued. "I don't think you should return to Beijing. At this critical moment, your presence here might make them more scrupulous. Since the Prince of Yu sent you here as a military adviser, I think it's better if you report to General Qi Jiguang and join his army. There's already chaos here inside the government. We have to make sure that the military is in good order."

"I'll take my leave now," Tan Lun said. Wiping the tears from his face with the back of his hand, he strode out without speaking another word.

Meanwhile, in what was probably the largest silk mill in the whole country, the owner was giving a tour to three special guests. Twenty rows of three-metre-wide silk-weaving looms stood in front of them, with six lining up on each row. A passageway, wide enough for two people to walk side by side, ran through the middle of the workshop. Each machine was weaving a different type and colour of silk fabric. The cacophony of weaving machines rose and fell rhythmically. The hectic pace at the workshop put Yang Jinshui, who directed the South China Textile Bureau, in a cheerful mood. He invited Zheng Bichang, the deputy governor and chief administrator, and Ho Maocai, the director of the Provincial Justice Department, to join in the inspection. The bigwigs beamed with delight. The owner, a scholarly-looking young man who wore a long blue cloth robe and black cloth shoes, showed the three officials around the bustling workshop.

"Mr Shen, how many bolts of silk can the workers here weave every day?" Yang asked. Due to the loud noises, he was literally screaming, making his otherwise high-pitched voice more piercing.

"We're now running two twelve-hour shifts every day," shouted Shen Yishi, Zhejiang's wealthiest businessman and a designated contractor for the South China Textile Bureau. "Even so, each weaver loom can only produce about eight inches of silk fabric per day."

"So you're saying that each workshop can produce a maximum eight thousand bolts of silk every year," Yang continued in his shrill voice.

"Yes," Shen replied. "I have twenty-five silk mills, which can probably produce two hundred bolts of silk per year. Why don't we discuss business in our visitors' room?"

When the three officials followed Shen into a spacious room, Shen clapped his hands, and numerous servants emerged from the side doors. They went about quietly, setting tables for tea. The visitors' salon was more like a huge hall; Yang had never seen such a classy place in the Hangzhou and Suzhou region. Against the north wall stood a large rosewood tea table with a marble top, flanked on each side by rosewood round-backed armchairs. Similar rosewood armchairs with matching tea tables lined the east wall and the west wall. The mono-coloured marble floor, each piece embedded with marbled starbursts, struck Yang as the most precious and impressive.

"Please take the top seat next to Yang Gonggong," Shen bowed slightly to Zheng, the chief administrator.

"You go ahead and take that one because it makes it easier for you two to talk," Zheng politely declined before taking a seat on the far left.

Ho took a seat on the right. Yang, who was seated in the middle, invited Shen to sit near him. Four young men, brisk and business-like, appeared, each bearing a shiny bronze teapot. They tiptoed to the tea table and, with impressive dexterity, removed the lids of the teacups with one hand and slightly tilted the teapots in the other. Clouds of steam rose as water flew out of the teapots into the cups. Green sprouts expanded, floating on the water surface in the cup. Yang held his cup under his nostrils and inhaled deeply. "Nice tea," he complimented, putting the cup down and waiting for the fragrant liquid to cool off.

"This is Lions' Peak Dragon Well tea, from the first harvest of the year," Shen explained. "Farmers collected the tea leaves at night, when the tea plants start to bud."

Both Zheng and Ho sipped their tea, smacked their lips and nodded approvingly.

"This is the best of the best," Zheng commented.

"We haven't harvested a lot this year," Shen said, somewhat apologetically. "I have prepared two pounds each for Lu Gonggong and Grand Secretary Yan. Sorry that I won't be able to do the same for everyone, but each one of you will get one pound."

As Yang reached for his teacup, he noticed that Shen himself was drinking plain boiled water. "Why don't you drink tea yourself?" he asked, curiously.

"This is an old habit," Shen said. "I like to retain my simple ways – it keeps me earnest and unadulterated."

"Look at you," Yang teased. "You're too hard on yourself. You have twenty-five silk mills, three thousand weaving looms and more than one hundred thousand mu of mulberry land, plus several hundred silk, tea and china stores. But you drink plain water, eat plain food and wear plain cotton clothes. Are you trying to make some sort of a statement?"

"Well, as the saying goes, a pomade vendor uses water for her own hair," Shen replied. "I'm setting up these silk-weaving shops for the South China Textile Bureau. I live frugally because, someday, when you can no longer bear the sight of me and kick me out of the door, I'll still be able to survive."

"Oh stop it," Yang said, raising his voice. "I wouldn't dare! If I kicked you out, Grand Secretary Yan and Lu Gonggong would have me killed."

"Sorry, I meant it as a joke," Shen said with a solemn look.

"I know," Yang replied cheerfully before his tone also turned serious. "Let's get down to business. We need to increase production by three hundred thousand bolts. Based on instructions from the Imperial Palace, the mills in Yingtian will handle one hundred thousand, and, of course, you'll handle the rest of the two hundred thousand bolts here in Zhejiang. Based on our calculation, you need to add three thousand weaver looms and build new mills. All these take time. Have you worked out a plan yet?"

"The order comes directly from the Imperial Palace, and I wouldn't dare procrastinate, no matter how arduous it can be," replied Shen. "But the challenge is to secure land to grow mulberry. No matter how many machines we add, we still can't silk merchandise without raw silk."

Yang glanced at Zheng and Ho, signalling for them to address Shen's concerns.

"We can get you the land to grow mulberry in a month or so," Zheng cleared his throat and promised. "The important thing is to gather enough grain to barter the land. Do you have the grain ready?"

"How many mu of land can you get me?" Shen asked.

"Based on our projected production quotas, how many mu do you need?"

"If the land has already been converted and mulberry trees mature, we only need two hundred thousand mu. But, if it's farmland and we have to convert it ourselves, we'll need at least five hundred thousand mu. This is because the mulberry trees we plant in the spring are still seedlings in the autumn and there wouldn't be enough to breed silk moths. Plus, the silkworms do not produce as much raw silk in mid or late autumn as they do in the spring."

"You're greedy, aren't you?" Ho couldn't help remarking. "You are now requesting an extra three hundred thousand mu of land. If you plant mulberry trees this year, they'll mature in two years. They can breed much more raw silk than we need for this order."

"As I said, the land I have purchased, the machines I have

acquired and the mills I have built are for the South China Textile Bureau and the Imperial Government," Shen said, laughing off at Ho's bluntness. "I don't have the guts or appetite to swallow it all and keep the profits for myself."

Zheng and Ho uttered an awkward chortle, while Yang gazed at the entrance distractedly.

"Where is Mayor Ma?" Yang asked. "When is he arriving?"

"I had an invitation delivered to him two days ago," Ho said. "He's supposed to come and join us from Chun'an County today. He should be here any minute. I've already told the guards outside to bring him here directly after he arrives."

"What's the rush?" a loud boisterous voice sounded outside. Speaking of the devil, here he came. Mayor Ma strode in. Before he had the chance to greet everyone, Ho jumped from his seat and pulled him aside to the corner of the room. They whispered something to each other before returning to join the conversation. By then, the mayor's face fell. He stood there, looking distracted and sceptical. Ho eyed Zheng and Yang, urging them to continue pressuring the mayor.

"So what do you think of the plan?" Yang asked the mayor.

"I haven't thought it through yet," the mayor growled. "This is a big decision. Why are we hiding it from the governor?"

"We're not trying to hide it from Governor Hu," Ho explained. "The grand secretary and his son specifically told us not to loop him in."

Taken aback by Ho's remark, the mayor barked, "So now the grand secretary and his son no longer trust the governor?"

"I don't think it's a matter of trust," Zheng added. "With Tan Lun by his side, we just want to be cautious so the news doesn't get out and reach those folks in Beijing."

"So, in other words, it shows that Grand Secretary Yan has lost confidence in the governor," Mayor Ma repeated.

"Why are you so stubborn?" Ho said with a tint of impatience. "What does it take for us to turn you around and point you in the right direction?"

Yang glared at Ho, signalling him to stop the badgering.

"I understand that you report to the governor and you want to remain loyal to him," Yang said to Mayor Ma gently. "But who is Governor Hu's mentor? Have you thought about that?"

"The grand secretary," the mayor said hesitantly.

"So the answer to your previous question is quite obvious, isn't it?" Yang said. "You're dedicated and loyal to Governor Hu. That's your strength. But you can't just blindly follow orders. I understand you only take orders from Governor Hu. But your boss reports directly to the grand secretary. You won't risk a mistake if you follow what the grand secretary tells you. Besides, by not telling Governor Hu, the grand secretary might intend to shield him from harm. Otherwise, if Tan Lun gets wind of it, he might rat on him and tell the Prince of Yu. If that happens, the first one they attack would be your friend, Governor Hu."

The mayor stood there, obviously struggling to make a decision as the others looked on.

"OK, I'll do it," he finally said, looking resolute as if he was ready to risk everything. "I just want to make sure that nobody will starve after the counties are flooded. Otherwise, the governor will be stuck with a huge problem."

Despite Mayor Ma's mention of such a dire outcome, Yang looked pleased. So did Zheng and Ho.

"The grain we currently have in the state granary won't be enough, of course," Zheng replied to Mayor Ma. "Mr Shen will prepare enough grain for the land purchase."

"There is no need to worry," Shen pledged. "When the purchase starts, I won't be short of even a single grain of rice."

Yang stood up and reminded everyone, "We're about two weeks away from the May rainy season. Troops need to be dispatched to guard all the weirs along the Xin'an River. Before we flood the area, nobody should be allowed to approach them. For security's sake, let's keep this plan a secret. If it leaks out, nobody will be spared."

The air thickened with tension. Zheng and Ho turned to Mayor Ma, seeking his pledge to keep things confidential. Instead of responding to their unspoken requests, however, Mayor Ma suddenly asked Shen, "Do you have any old ginseng roots?"

The request confounded the group.

"I only have two left," Shen replied.

"Do you mind gifting them to me?" the mayor asked solemnly, like a warrior who was making his last request before departing for the battlefield.

"What happened?" Zheng asked sympathetically. "Is your mother sick?"

"No, I just want to give them to the governor," Mayor Ma answered as he gazed at the courtyard.

"Could you promise not to be stupid enough and leak our plan to the governor?" Ho asked, with trepidation in his voice.

The remarks incensed Mayor Ma. "If you don't trust me, why don't you ask someone else to do it?" he retorted.

Ho appeared speechless.

"Even though we are hiding this plan from him, he'll still have to shoulder the blame if anything goes wrong," Mayor Ma continued. "He looks quite exhausted lately. What's wrong with gifting him two ginseng roots? It shouldn't warrant your suspicion, should it?"

"All right then," Yang interrupted, trying to smooth things over. "I admire Mayor Ma's loyalty and his strong sense of justice. You're bound for big things, Ma. Let's wait for Mr Shen to get the ginseng roots."

Shen nodded ingratiatingly before disappearing into a side room.

明

Carrying a red box smelling of ginseng, Mayor Ma showed up at Governor Hu's office. The governor sat reviewing files and reports.

"Have you sent people to open up the irrigation channel so farmers can water their land?" he asked without taking his eyes off a document.

The mayor was mute, and after a few minutes Governor Hu looked up. Mayor Ma seemed to be in a daze, with his hands behind his back.

"Did you hear what I just said?" Governor Hu asked again.

"Oh…" the mayor recovered from his reverie and stammered. "Yes, yes, I've taken care of it."

"What are you holding in your hands?" Governor Hu probed.

The mayor presented the red box haltingly. "Your Highness, these two ginseng roots..." he said, choking up. "I know you forbade us from giving you gifts. It's not a bribe... I just think you probably need it because you look quite exhausted lately... I..."

Governor Hu stared at him for a moment before resuming his reading. "Your stellar efforts at work will be better than any gifts," he said.

Still holding the red box, the mayor stood there without moving.

"OK, leave the box there and go to check the weirs," he ordered.

"Yes, Your Highness," the mayor said. Before stepping out, he took one last look at the governor.

The annual rainy season arrived in early May. In 1561, forty years into Emperor Jiajing's reign, a natural catastrophe triggered by a human conspiracy was about to strike unsuspecting farmers living along Xin'an River in Zhejiang Province...

Darkness descended but the rain continued. Soldiers packed the public square in front of the governor's office complex, each pulling a horse. Flickering lanterns hanging under the eaves swayed in the wind. In the dim light, the soldiers who were waiting for orders moved about like apparitions.

The heavy wooden gate suddenly flung open, and the soldiers saw Governor Hu striding out without a raincoat. Before he reached his sedan chair, bolts of lightning struck directly at the wooden gate – Governor Hu's elongated shadow from the dim lights was slashed into two equal parts, from his head to his feet. A rapid succession of lightning bolts, followed by deafening claps of thunder, illuminated the ghostly faces of soldiers and their horses gathering in the public square. Hu's top aide approached him from behind and held an umbrella over his head.

"Where is the river surveillance director?" Hu shouted to the top aide.

"He's gone to brief different agencies on the disaster situation," the aide replied in an equally loud voice, to be heard above the downpour.

"What did he say about the flooding?"

"Leaks have been spotted in all the weirs in the nine counties along the river," the aide reported. "All the sandbags we have placed down there to stop the leaks have been swept away. It's impossible to stem the flood."

"Benevolent heaven, why are you so heartless?" Hu uttered, but his words were drowned out by more thunder and lightning. His body shivered with emotion, and his face grew paler in the jagged flashes.

"Your Highness, what did you say?" his aide asked.

"Let's go to Chun'an County now," Governor Hu decided.

The aide turned to the soldiers waiting in the rain and shouted, "Bring the sedan over!"

"No, get my horse," Governor Hu interrupted before dashing down the stone stairs. As he stepped into the rain, the aide followed closely, holding his umbrellas and trying to keep pace with the governor.

"The horse!" his aide shouted. "Bring the horse over!"

A big black horse, powerfully muscled with thick mane and tail, stopped in front of the governor. Before he mounted, his aide opened up a raincoat. Governor Hu stretched both arms downward to allow the assistant to slip on the raincoat from behind him. As the aide was securing the hood and tying the strings in the front, another round of lightning struck. The rain poured down even more forcefully than before. But the black horse remained unfazed, planting its hooves firmly on the ground. A guard tossed his umbrellas to the side and held one of Hu's hands to help him mount the horse.

"Why don't you get two of our men and go to meet with General Qi and his military adviser Tan Lun?" Governor Hu ordered his aide. "Tell them to send one thousand troops to different weirs and help with flood rescue efforts. Then, ask the two of them to come and see me at Chun'an County."

"Yes, sir," shouted the aide. He and two soldiers leapt onto their horses and disappeared into the dark rain. Governor Hu kicked his black horse into motion and led the rest of the soldiers towards Chun'an County.

刎

"Daddy, Daddy," a feminine voice pierced the darkness, awakening Yang with a start. He climbed out of bed, put on a dark maroon silk jacket over his white silk pyjamas which featured subtle patterns of cicada wings. Sitting on the edge of his bed, he was poised to receive the unexpected guest.

A man burst into his room inside the South China Textile Bureau compound and stumbled his way to the bed. Plopping down on the floor near his feet, the man whimpered, his voice filled with panic. "Daddy, the weirs... have cracked... nine counties... are flooded."

Yang looked at him dismissively. The man was his protégé, Li Xuan, who managed the Xin'an River Flood Control Commission.

Li caught his breath. "Someone... someone is trying to sabotage the weirs... and harm my career... and ruin yours..." he continued in a somewhat more coherent but nervous tone.

"What are you talking about?" Yang Jinshui asked. "Who is trying to harm us?"

Yang's unusually calm response surprised Li. "All the weirs were repaired and fortified last year under my supervision," Li said. "They should be standing solid as iron. Leaks were impossible... just impossible... but now every single weir is damaged..."

"No weir can be as solid as iron, and there's no such thing as an impregnable dam," rebuked Yang.

Stunned by Yang's dismissive response, Li stood there, staring at his master silently.

Yang turned around and said to a woman in his bed, his harsh tone softening, "Madam Yun, could you get up and find an outfit for him to change into?"

A tall slender woman reluctantly rose from the bed behind Yang. She was the model at the textile bureau's silk exhibition. Wearing thin transparent silk pyjamas with pretty patterns of cicada wings, Madam Yun flew out of bed and made a beeline for one of the dressers. She opened a drawer, picked an outfit and tossed it on a chair. Without saying a word, she slowly climbed back into bed.

Kneeling before Yang, Li straightened his back and focused his gaze at the floor.

"Get up," Yang demanded. "Remove that wet outfit and change."

"Daddy, nine counties… if they are all flooded, they'll have me beheaded…" Li Xuan sobbed, without moving.

"Oh come on, you'll live," Yang said impatiently. "Get up! After you change, stay inside the Textile Bureau compound. Don't go anywhere."

Li stood up, looking sceptical. Then, an epiphany seemed to hit him. "Daddy, did you already know about this?"

"What do I know?" Yang asked. His eyes hardened.

"I… I don't know what you know…" Li shuddered with fear.

"Ignorance is bliss," he advised. "Let me tell you – some things can be simple if you choose to resolve them behind the scenes, but once you bring them out into the open they become complicated and can turn into huge scandals. We are part of the palace staff and our job is to handle tasks given to us by Lu Gonggong. Whatever happens locally is none of our business, regardless of how threatening it is. Let the local folks fight among themselves. In the next few days, there is no need for you to show up at work. It doesn't matter if the land is flooded or people are killed. Just stay right here."

Li Xuan seemed to have only half-understood. "Would it be possible for Daddy to switch jobs for me?" Li begged.

"I've already reported this to Lu Gonggong," Yang replied. "Let's wait patiently for him to make the arrangement."

"Understood!" Li said with restored confidence. He managed to get to his feet and walked over to the chair. Cradling Yang's clothes in his arms, Li swallowed his spit, inhaled deeply and began untying his clothes.

"Is this your place to change?" Yang's cold harsh voice stopped him.

Li quickly picked up the clothes. At the door, he turned around and glanced at Yang and the woman behind him. "Thank you, Daddy and Mommy," he said.

"You can leave now," Yang ordered. Li stepped out and closed the door behind him.

中

There's a popular saying among farmers: "Fierce wind never lasts a whole morning, and a rainstorm always ends in a day." Even though rainstorms are quick and short, they often trigger flooding. This is what happened in parts of Zhejiang Province during the rainy season in 1561.

A rainstorm that ravaged the region for a whole day finally stopped around midnight. In the ensuing days, torrential floodwater from the mountains poured into Xin'an River, rapidly raising the water levels. Even though the rain had stopped, the water rose by the minute. In Chun'an County, thousands of torches flickered on the big dam on Xin'an River, but in the vast darkness and against the roaring sounds of the river, those flickering lights seemed so tiny and feeble.

Countless soldiers and farmers raced towards the gigantic sluice gate, where two widening cracks appeared, one on each side. The roaring water in the river was bursting through a crack, forming two ferocious waterways ready to swallow the farmland along the Xin'an River. People carried sandbags with both hands, and some on their shoulders. Soon, the sandbags piled up on the weir like a wall. Several soldiers and young farmers stood in a row, next to the sandbags, waiting for orders from General Qi and his adviser, Tan Lun, both of whom stood perched on the edge of the cracks. With the help of the torchlight, they attempted to survey the situation below.

"Get ready to push the sandbags down," General Qi shouted out his order.

Soldiers and farmers stuck long wooden poles or the butts of their long firearms underneath the pile of sandbags and then pushed them hard with their shoulders.

"One, two, three. Go!" General Qi ordered. With minutes, a

huge wall of sandbags was toppled into the cavity in the weir, in the hope of blocking the water. Hundreds of eyes gazed down. Unfortunately, like pinches of salt tossed into a large boiling pot, none of the sandbags stayed. They were swept away without a trace.

The crowd froze. Frustration and disappointment set in. But General Qi refused to give up. "More sandbags," he ordered, with steely determination in his eyes. Soldiers and farmers began moving again, rushing to secure more sandbags.

On the far end of the weir, Governor Hu was standing alone on the edge of the river, his eyes gazing into the roaring waves. Guards holding burning torches stood a few feet from him. Tan Lun passed through the guards and quietly approached Governor Hu. He could feel Tan Lun's presence behind his back.

"Any success?" Governor Hu asked in his deep voice, without turning his gaze from the river.

"I'm afraid not," Tan Lun replied, his tone getting agitated. "This outcome shouldn't surprise us because we simply had no time to prepare. This is now happening in nine counties. If we can't block the leak here, the other eight weirs will meet a similar fate and burst. That's exactly what those people are expecting to see."

"When Mayor Ma came in to give me some ginseng roots last week, I should have thought of it and questioned him," Governor Hu mused. "This could endanger the lives of several million people... a crime for all eternity!"

"Such a ruthless act... Unprecedented in history... It's beyond anyone's imagination," Tan Lun ranted. "It looks like we have no other choice but to find a way to divert the floodwater."

Governor Hu did not respond.

"Rather than exposing all nine countries to such disaster, we can divert the water," Tan Lun proposed. "It's a much better option to have one or two counties flooded and save the rest. Besides, it will be easier to organise rescue efforts, and we'll have enough grain to cover the victims if we concentrate the distribution in one or two counties."

"Is this General Qi's idea as well?" Hu asked.

"Yes. But you have to make the final call."

Governor Hu sank into silence for a few minutes before he

sighed, "How am I going to tell the people in Chun'an and Jiande Counties if we divert the floodwater there?"

"Before making the decision, we're going to give one more try to block the leak," Tan Lun added. "As a last resort, General Qi is prepared to allow soldiers to plunge into the water and form a human wall near the crack. If it works, we'll do the same in other places. If we still fail after having made this sacrifice, people will understand it better."

Governor Hu turned around slowly. The torches lit up his gaunt face. "We need to help people evacuate their villages quickly," he demanded.

"We have already sent people to the villages," Tan Lun replied. "Fortunately, the region is surrounded by mountains and evacuation can be done quickly."

Governor Hu looked in the direction of the weir. Even from where he was, he could hear General Qi's desperate shouting. "I need volunteers... We need a human wall down there first before we push the sandbags down."

Governor Hu shuddered at the idea of sending hapless soldiers into the treacherous water. He strode over to the general, followed by Tan Lun and his guards. Volunteers lined up, arm in arm, on top of a large pile of sandbags, waiting for orders.

General Qi did not issue his order of action. Instead, he waited for the governor, who was walking up to him. His set eyes were filled with grief and determination.

"Do we have names for our brothers here?" Governor Hu asked.

The general nodded solemnly.

"If anything happens to them, we will make sure to compensate and take care of their families," Governor Hu pledged.

With a heavy heart, the general nodded again.

Governor Hu turned to the volunteer soldiers, offering his fist and palm salute.

"Thank YOU," he shouted.

"Yes, sir," the soldiers shouted back unanimously before turning around to face the fast-flowing river.

General Qi raised his right arm and shouted, "Go!" In unison, the soldiers howled at the top of their lungs before plunging into the turbulent water down below. Burning torches moved closer to the edge. While some people widened their eyes, trying to monitor the situation, many others closed theirs. Knowing the grim prospect of this mission, Governor Hu also closed his eyes.

General Qi kept his eyes fixed on his soldiers struggling in the ferocious water. They were supposed to steady themselves in the water, waiting for the sandbags to drop so they could manually fill the crack. General Qi's heart sank when he saw that his soldiers became immediately submerged in the water. Then, his eyes brightened when they reappeared, still arm in arm. Their heads bobbed in and out of the water. "Drop the sandbags!" the soldiers in the water seemed to be shouting, but their voices were drowned out by the roaring waves. Fearing that the fierce waves could swallow his soldiers at any moment, General Qi resisted calls from his troops on the weir behind him to drop the sandbags. Instead, he began to regret his decision. Balling both of his fists, he yelled at the soldiers on the bank, "Drop down the ropes and save our brothers first!"

A dozen rescuers quickly untangled a pile of thick ropes and threw them down into the water. But by then, those soldiers had all disappeared. On the dam, an eerie silence fell.

The waves in the river rumbled.

All of a sudden, some farmers fell to their knees, and many others on the weir followed. In the torchlight, General Qi shut his eyes as tears oozed from their corners.

"We can go down," a young farmer stood up and shouted. General Qi opened his eyes and recognised Chee Dazhu, the farmer who had been arrested by Mayor Ma earlier for allegedly "sabotaging" the land-conversion efforts. Chee Dazhu turned to his fellow villagers. "It is our turn to serve now," he howled. "If you're a real man, follow me."

Several strong young men got to their feet and followed Chee Dazhu as he walked towards a pile of sandbags. Governor Hu looked at General Qi and shook his head in disapproval. The general immediately caught up with Chee Dazhu and stopped the farmers from advancing.

Chee Dazhu got on one knee, and his followers did the same.

"General Qi, let me pledge in front of my parents, my wife and children who are over there," he said. "We will do as you tell us. If anyone should jump down there, it should be us. The other day, you came and stopped the troops from destroying the rice seedlings. We're greatly indebted to you. We are willing to serve you. Please accept our service."

"Were you the one who was accused of leading a riot?" General Qi asked.

"Yes, sir," Chee Dazhu replied.

"Do you know who ordered your release that day?"

"Yes. It was the governor."

"That's right," General Qi said. "Then we should all listen to him today. Please rise. Tell all of your folks to stand up. The governor wants to talk to you."

Meanwhile, Governor Hu, surrounded by torchlight, moved towards the pile of sandbags. Grabbing a hand that General Qi offered him, he steadied himself and climbed on top of the sandbags. Peering down at the sweaty mud-smeared faces and the flickering torches, he opened his mouth, but nothing came out of it. It was as if something was stuck in his throat…

四

In his spartan living room, Shen Yishi, the silk contractor, was entertaining guests. Even though the servants had laid out food and liquor on the big round table in the middle of the room, none of the guests took their seats. Instead, they sat on chairs against the wall, waiting.

An aide rushed into the room and whispered something to Zheng, the deputy governor and chief administrator. Zheng's eyes flashed with displeasure, then he stood up and declared, "Yang Gonggong is not coming. Let's toast Mayor Ma and his colleagues without him."

"He is supposed to be the mastermind of this plan, but when it comes to decisions he's conveniently absent," grumbled Ho, who headed the Justice Department. "How could he do this to us?"

His remarks rattled Mayor Ma and two of his magistrates. They stood there, looking gloomy. Even Shen, who was hosting the dinner, appeared a bit uneasy about Yang's absence. But he quickly regained composure. "What do you want to do?" he asked Zheng.

Realising that he had to take control of the situation quickly, Zheng motioned for Ho to shift everyone to the table. "Let's start the meal and discussion without him," he suggested. "Once we come up with a plan, we'll send it to Yang for approval."

Ho invited Mayor Ma to the place of honour at the table. "You're our hero today and deserve to be in the centre," he said.

"Hero? I feel more like the world's number-one criminal," Mayor Ma grumbled in a hoarse voice. "Someday, when I receive the capital punishment and my family gets raided, I just hope all of you here can show some mercy and take care of my surviving family members."

The mayor's wry remarks made the two magistrates uneasy. Seeing that Mayor Ma had declined the place of honour and picked a seat on the side, they decided to sit next to him on the far end of the table, leaving Zheng and Ho with no choice but to take the chief's seats. Zheng raised his cup to present the first toast of the evening. "We all work for the Imperial Court," he said. "It is not the job of ordinary folks like us to judge the merits and faults of our deeds. If we do a good job implementing the conversion policy, we'll bring honour to the country and long-term benefits to the people. It's not a major problem if the farmland is flooded. The important thing is to make sure that farmers are properly fed. Therefore, I urge Mr Shen to get the grain ready quickly. We'll be committing a cardinal crime if a deadly famine occurs."

"There is no need to worry," vowed Shen as he raised a glass and then emptied it. "It'll be a fair swap, and I'll compensate the farmers handsomely. If starvation occurs because of me, I'm willing to pay with my own life."

"I hope Mr Shen's words help put your mind at ease." Zheng raised his glass again to console Mayor Ma.

"This is not a matter of whether my mind is at ease," the mayor stood up and drained his liquor glass with one gulp. "I have no control over what will happen to me in the future. But I've been told that Governor Hu has gone to the weir to investigate the situation there. It would be heartless and unconscionable for us to drink here while he is there working. I need to go."

Before the host and guests had a chance to respond, the mayor put the glass down on the table and marched out. A few minutes later, a messenger crept in with news about the governor's decision to divert floodwater away into Chun'an and Jiande Counties to protect the other regions. The report unnerved Zheng, Ho and Shen, leaving them speechless. They quickly left the dinner and showed up at Yang's office.

"Are you aware of the flood-diversion plan?" Ho cried out nervously when he saw Yang emerging from a side door in his office. "I heard that only two counties will be affected by the flood."

Yang paused for a moment, pondering something before resuming his steps slowly. Then, under the glare of his three guests, he plopped into a chair.

"The diversion will make it hard for Mr Shen to buy up the five hundred thousand mu of farmland that we have promised," Ho said.

"Well, I can still purchase the land in the non-flooded counties, but I'm afraid there won't be enough grain to barter," Shen said. "It costs me five hundred kilograms of rice to buy a mu of flooded farmland. But for the non-flooded farmland, where the rice seedlings are already knee deep, the price for each mu could jump five to six times."

Yang listened silently. At one point, he shot a sidelong glance at Zheng and muttered, "It's a mess now."

"I heard that when the governor announced his diversion plan, Tan Lun was present," said Zheng; a worried frown crossed his face.

Yang's face twitched involuntarily.

Zheng continued, "We did this without the governor's knowledge because the grand secretary's son had instructed us to do so. Governor Hu should understand this. I can't figure out why he's decided to divert the flood. I truly have no idea what he is trying to do."

"When is the governor returning to the city of Hangzhou?" Yang finally spoke up.

"I think he's already back in his office," said Zheng.

"What?" Yang sprung to his feet. "If he's back, why hasn't he sent anyone to contact you?"

"We're just wondering about the same thing because my department should be handling the disaster relief efforts…"

Yang's mind was racing, his eyes rolling.

"What's to be afraid of?" Ho broke the silence. "The rice-to-mulberry conversion policy was issued by the Imperial Palace. If we fail, we could be all dead. Instead of supporting us, the governor is trying to defect to the other faction. Fortunately, our grand secretary is still alive, and the Interior Ministry is still in the hands of Lu Gonggong."

"You certainly have more guts than I do," Zheng grumbled. "I haven't been able to find Mayor Ma. He's nowhere in sight at the moment. If he leaks our plan and people know that we damaged the weirs deliberately, I don't think any of us can be spared capital punishment."

"You can't find the mayor?" Yang asked in earnest.

"Correct," Zheng replied. "I have sent several guards to search for him. He's not at the city yamen. People at the Flood Control Commission have no idea where he is."

"Then he must have been summoned by the governor," Yang pointed out.

"I should think so," Zheng agreed.

"If Governor Hu doesn't want to talk with you, you should go and see him," Yang suggested.

"What should we say to him?" Ho asked.

"It's not a matter of what you'll say to him," Yang corrected him. "It's what he's going to tell or ask you."

"Let's go then," Zheng urged.

Just as Yang had guessed, Mayor Ma was at the governor's office. Donning a blue cloth robe, he sat quietly on a chair in front of the governor's big rosewood desk. His face, covered with several nights' unshaven stubble, had slimmed down significantly. His deep-set eyes appear bigger. He had just placed a big bundle wrapped up in cloth on the governor's desk.

Governor Hu sat behind the desk with his eyes closed. Neither of them spoke. The silence accentuated the size of the bulging bundle on the desk.

"I want to apologise to Your Highness," Mayor Ma muttered in his hoarse voice. "But my loyalty and devotion to you never wavered."

Governor Hu did not respond; his face was expressionless, and his eyes remained closed.

"I was a certified scholar in my village, trying for years without success to enter the Imperial College," Ma stated. "If you hadn't discovered and promoted me, I would probably have been, at most, an assistant county magistrate. Neither I nor my family had dreamed that I would become the mayor of Hangzhou. The day when you plucked me from obscurity, I made up my mind that I would devote my whole life to you and that after I die I will continue to serve you as a ghost. I'm glad that I finally have the opportunity to pay you back."

Mayor Ma rose to his feet and reached over to the desk to untie the big bundle. From inside the bundle, he pulled out his mayor's official hat and robe. "Your Highness has changed my life by granting me this position, and I'm now returning it to you," he said, holding it reverentially with both hands. "Whatever punishment the Imperial Court deals out, I'm willing to take it on your behalf. I just hope that the grand secretary, his son and the people who are friends with the Prince of Yu will give you a pardon."

Governor Hu opened his eyes and slowly rose from his seat. Stepping out from behind his desk, he strolled over to the centre of the room, silently gazing at the courtyard through a large window. Mayor Ma slowly turned around. Holding the bundle that contained his official hat and robe, he stepped up and presented it to Governor Hu.

"Wham!" Governor Hu smacked him in the face. The mayor straightened his body, his hands clutching tightly at the bundle.

"You idiot!" Governor Hu scolded in his deep voice that was filled with anger and pain. "You think you know it all, huh? You think you're helping me get a pardon from the grand secretary and the Prince of Yu... Do you know how deep the water is down there? The land-conversion policy and flood control are such big complicated undertakings, but you schemed with those people and kept me in the dark. Do you consider that an act of loyalty?"

"I didn't mean to hide it from Your Highness," the mayor explained. "I would never collude with anyone and harm you... Like Confucius advises us, there are many things in this world to which one is committed even though he knows they cannot possibly succeed."

Governor Hu glared at Mayor Ma and shook his head in frustration. Slowly, disappointment turned into twangs of pain. Governor Hu had put so much trust in the young man facing him, but now the mayor felt like a stranger to him.

"I advised you time and again to read more history books, but you never took my advice seriously. When I urged you to read books by Wang Yangming,[1] a fellow countryman of yours, you snubbed him, claiming some nonsense like reading 'half of what Confucius wrote' would be enough to help you handle your job. Let me ask you, what did Confucius really mean when he said, 'There are many things in this world to which one is committed even though he knows they cannot possibly succeed'?"

The mayor did not answer.

"The true essence of Confucius is reflected in this quote – 'Before committing oneself to a task, one first asks if he should, rather than if he can.' Sabotaging the dam with the sole intent of flooding farmland is a heinous criminal act. You harmed the interests of our country and the people. How could you justify this criminal act with a Confucius saying?"

"I thought I was merely trying to help out by sharing your burden," Mayor Ma defended.

Governor Hu responded by stamping his feet in fury. "You were trying to ruin several million lives in nine counties. Such brutality is unheard of in history. How could you say you were merely helping me share my burden? For this crime, I wouldn't even consider it an excessive punishment to have you executed and eliminate nine generations of your family."

The mayor stood there in a daze. Governor Hu raised his head towards the ceiling. "Everyone says that I have hired the best people to work in the Imperial Government," he sighed. "How did I make this terrible mistake of appointing you as the mayor of Hangzhou and the regional commissioner of river flood control?"

The mayor dropped to his knees and uttered in total despair, "I shouldn't have entered government services in the first place. I have an elderly mother, a wife and a young son in the village. Your Highness is aware that they're honest country folks. Please spare their lives."

When Governor Hu didn't answer, he choked up and plopped down to the floor.

"Let me ask you one more time, who else is behind this scheme?"

Mayor Ma raised his head and pled, "Please do not question me on this. If you probe deeper, you could bring chaos to the Ming empire. I don't think this is something that Your Highness can stomach. Even the grand secretary could be implicated. Why don't you stick with the official line that nobody attempted to destroy the dam? Blame the Flood Control Commission, which obviously did a shoddy repair job that has triggered this catastrophe. But on the other hand, the massive flood would make it easier for the Imperial Court to implement the land-conversion policy. I just wanted to get you out of this so you wouldn't be stuck in the middle. That was why I did it. Even if I had to pay with my own life, it would have been worth it."

The mayor's words had touched upon a sore point – an issue that worried Governor Hu the most. His face darkened. "You are among us, and we're among you. You help me, and I help you," he sighed. "This is the source of all evil... They're gambling away your life and career for money. They're destroying the livelihood of so many farmers in exchange for money... Even so, you're still protecting them, all in the name of protecting the Imperial Court and a national policy. What kind of national policy is it? When the mulberry trees are taking over crops and start to yield profits, how much of the money goes to the Imperial Treasury? You're not the only one they are trying to take advantage of. I'm not the only one they are trying to deceive. They're going to hurt more people, including the grand secretary, who is surrounded by these evil and greedy people. He's 81 years old. I hate to see him fall into disgrace."

The mayor, stunned and regretful, stared at Governor Hu.

"Your Highness..." an aide came in and interrupted the conversation.

"Are Mr Zheng and Mr Ho here? Bring them in," said Governor Hu. Before he got ready, he turned to Mayor Ma. "I doubt you can be spared capital punishment this time," he warned. "After you die, I'll see to it that your family is well taken care of. Go and wait inside the room there. I want you to listen carefully and learn the true nature of the so-called friends you're trying to protect. At least, you can die with the comfort that you got to know the truth."

Mayor Ma kowtowed hard on the floor, collected the bundle in his hands and tottered into a side room.

By the time Zheng and Ho were ushered in, Governor Hu had slouched back in his seat with his eyes closed. The two guests paused, looking at each other hesitantly.

"Your Highness," Zheng tiptoed to the governor's desk.

"Please have a seat," Governor Hu invited him without opening his eyes.

Zheng and Ho sat down as told, waiting for the governor to begin. But, for nearly five minutes, Governor Hu seemed to ignore their presence. An awkward silence ensued. Zheng motioned with his head to Ho, who cleared his throat loudly. "It's hard to believe that such a catastrophe could have occurred," he said.

Governor Hu still did not move. Nor did he respond.

"After I heard the news, I visited some grain warehouses and did a quick calculation," Zheng added. "We have about one hundred and fifty thousand kilograms of rice in storage. At the moment, more than four hundred thousand families are affected by the flood. Even if we distribute everything we have saved, we wouldn't have enough. The food will only last them ten days or so. So the priority now is to buy rice from private suppliers. Unfortunately, we are short of funds. So we need to file a disaster report to the

Imperial Court immediately and request substantial disaster relief funds."

"What type of disaster are we going to report?" Governor Hu's mouth awakened below his still-dormant eyes. "What type of relief funds are we requesting?"

"Of course, we're going to report it as a natural disaster," Ho mumbled.

"Is it really a natural disaster?" Governor Hu opened his eyes and confronted Zheng and Ho, both of whom were startled by the governor's unexpected reaction.

"This is the flood season, and a terrible rainstorm battered the region for two consecutive days," said Zheng. "The water level has risen rapidly. Things happened so fast that we didn't have…"

Seeing how unabashedly Zheng was covering up the scheme, Governor Hu could no longer hide his contempt.

"If that's how you want to describe it, you should be the one to draft the report," he said.

"I can certainly draft it on your behalf, but Your Highness has to lead the effort, sign the report and submit it," Zheng proposed quickly.

"Since you're drafting the report, you will have to sign it and submit it yourself," Governor Hu retorted. "But in case you have forgotten, I just want to remind you that our climate condition is similar to that in the neighbouring province of Jiangsu. The rain hit them hard as well. They have two rivers flowing through their province, Baimao and Wusong. Just like us, they repaired and enhanced the weirs on the two rivers last year. In fact, we budgeted more funds for repairs and maintenance than they did, despite the fact that we only have one river in our province. Guess what, the weirs in Jiangsu Province remain solid and intact, and people are safe, whereas we're encountering an unprecedented disaster. How do you manage to explain away this so-called natural disaster and cover up your lie?"

Colour drained from Zheng's face. He eyed Ho, and they both realised that it was time to show their cards.

"Now that Your Highness already knows about it, we feel obligated to tell you what truly happened from our vantage point," Ho said. "As you know, the grand secretary's son wrote us a letter. You must have received a similar letter from him. So if the Privy Council's investigation implicates us, shall we show the letter to the investigators? Should we hold the grand secretary junior accountable? Is it necessary for us to urge His Majesty to rescind the land-conversion policy? Please advise."

Governor Hu suddenly turned around and asked, "Are you saying that the whole flooding scheme was hatched by the grand secretary's son?"

The question flew like a sharp dagger at Ho's face. "I, I... That's not what I meant..." Ho winced and stammered.

"Then what did you mean when you said that the grand secretary's son had written to you and that we should hold him accountable?"

"What I... I was trying to say is that... I was just talking about the land-conversion policy..." he mumbled nervously.

"What does the land-conversion policy have to do with the damaged weirs along the Xin'an River?" Governor Hu interrogated. "What does this have to do with the widespread flooding? If there is a connection, you should state it clearly in the report."

Ho was too stunned to speak, and Zheng pitched in. "The land-conversion policy has nothing to do with the flooding here..." he reassured Governor Hu. "But, at the same time, we can't really blame the extremely heavy rains for causing this widespread flooding... The culprit seems to be the River Flood Control Commission. Last year, they received a huge amount of funds to fix and fortify all of the dams along the Xin'an River, but apparently, they performed a shoddy job. In the past, several commissioners were indicted for embezzling public funds, neglecting repair work and causing severe flooding during rainy seasons. You probably remember a recent indictment that occurred in the thirty-first year under Emperor Jiajing's rule..."

"That makes a lot of sense," Ho jumped in.

Instead of confronting Zheng about his deception, Governor Hu kept his silence and glanced cynically at Ho, waiting to hear his response.

Zheng signalled to Ho with his eyes, encouraging him to continue.

"We should draft our report as Mr Zheng has suggested and attribute the flooding to the leaking dams, rather than to the unusually heavy rains, like we previously proposed. As for whether officials serving on the River Flood Control Commission have embezzled public funds or not, we'll launch a separate investigation at a future date. Causing the dams to leak in itself is a capital offence. Since Your Highness is authorised to impose the death penalty without obtaining permission from His Majesty, we should carry out summary executions of those who are connected with the case. Such tough measures will enable us to explain it and straighten things out with the Imperial Palace."

"Those who are connected with the case?" Governor Hu questioned. "Who are you referring to?"

"Some of the officials who are serving on the River Flood Control commission, of course," Ho replied.

"Which ones?"

Ho turned to Zheng for an answer.

"Naturally, the mayor of Hangzhou, who is the chief commissioner, should be held accountable," Zheng alleged. "The two magistrates who are commission members shouldn't be spared either."

"So you are saying Mayor Ma, along with Chang and Zhang, the magistrates of Chun'an and Jiande Counties?" Governor Hu asked.

"Yes," Zheng sheepishly lowered his voice.

"Who else?" Governor Hu demanded.

"It's probably not a good idea to implicate too many people," Zheng mumbled.

"What about the River Flood Control Supervisor appointed by Lu Gonggong at the Imperial Palace?" Governor Hu challenged. "Li Xuan is supposed to inspect every spending item and check the repair and maintenance on every weir. Do you really think we can absolve him of any blame?"

Zheng and Ho found themselves in a dilemma. "Your Highness, Li is a palace appointee," Zheng maintained. "If we want to take any measures against him, we should first consult with Yang Gonggong, who has to report it to the Interior Ministry under Lu Gonggong."

"If that's the case, our credibility would be challenged if we submit the report to the palace," Governor Hu pointed out.

Nobody answered – Zheng and Ho looked lost.

With a derisive smile, Governor Hu gestured to his aide who was standing at the door.

"Bring out Mayor Ma," he ordered. "Arrest him and take him into custody."

"Yes, sir!" the aide bowed before disappearing in the side room. Before Zheng and Ho had the chance to figure out what was happening, the mayor appeared, escorted by two of the governor's guards. By then, the two Mandarins realised that they had foolishly fallen into Governor Hu's trap.

Mayor Ma, with his bloodshot eyes, marched through the room. He paused in front of Zheng and Ho, who quickly cast their eyes down to avoid the mayor's scornful stare.

"Take him away," Governor Hu muttered. Under his command, the guards paraded the mayor to the door. Zheng and Ho kept their heads down until the sound of the mayor's heavy footsteps faded. They looked up and saw that Governor Hu was back at his seat, with his eyes closed again.

Zheng clenched his teeth and mumbled to Ho, "Let's go and talk with Yang Gonggong and see what he has to say."

"I guess so," Ho acquiesced. "His Highness might be correct. If we decide to attribute the flooding to the shoddy repair and maintenance, it wouldn't be fair to simply punish our people and let a palace appointee get away with it."

Governor Hu opened his eyes and got up from his chair. "If you agree with me, go and take your case to Yang Gonggong. Let's move fast on the rescue efforts and distribute food to flood victims in Chun'an and Jiande Counties. Also, please state clearly in our report that such catastrophic flooding has made it hard to implement the rice-to-mulberry conversion policy. We need more time. After you finish the report, make sure to get Yang Gonggong to sign it. You two should also put your names on the report. Then, I'll take over and submit it."

After Governor Hu stepped out, Zheng and Ho stood there motionless. They had no inkling of how they would persuade Yang – notorious for being maliciously difficult – to give up and hand over his protégé. The situation could turn ugly. If they did not tread cautiously, they could upset the whole coterie of powerful eunuchs in Beijing. Of course, before leaving the governor's office, Zheng and Ho had no time to ponder these echoing questions.

4

"Daddy," Li Xuan called when he entered Yang Jinshui's residential quarters inside the South China Textile Bureau's compound. The new décor in the room dazzled him. The whole place was blushing red – red lanterns, red candles, a red silk mosquito net, red bed sheets and quilts, and red cushions on the chairs. Surrounded by the ocean of unrelenting red, Li felt a bit light-headed.

But Li was most shocked to see a table covered with food and liquor in the middle of the room. Yang sat at the table, waiting for him. So did Madam Yun, who sported a red bridal cloak. Baffled by the beguiling festive scene, Li froze.

"Come over and have a seat here," Yang said to him, his face radiant with hospitality.

Li took a few halting steps forward and picked a seat on the far side of the table. "Go and sit over there," Yang said, pointing at a vacant seat next to Madam Yun. "You're the guest of honour tonight."

Li was more confused than ever. "Daddy, are you playing a practical joke on me?" he said, forcing out a smile. "You know I'm a shy and timid person. Please don't scare me."

"You think way too much," Yang said calmly. "Do as I say and sit down."

"It's very kind and generous of you, but I wouldn't dare break the rules," said Li, who insisted on taking a side seat. He could hear his own heart thumping. Yang gave in but urged Madam Yun to move over and sit next to Li. Holding her wine glass, the slender young woman snuggled against the junior eunuch. Springing to his feet like a startled monkey, Li asked in panic, "Daddy, please tell me what is going on. What do you really want me to do?"

"You are truly a smart boy," Yang conceded. "All the training and favours I have bestowed on you are not completely wasted."

The remarks sent Li reeling with fear. He fixed his gaze on Yang's well-groomed face.

"Bring that cup of globefish soup for my boy," Yang said to Madam Yun, who picked up a blue porcelain soup bowl from the table and placed it in front of Li. After she lifted the lid, Li involuntarily stared into the soup with a look of horror, as if the liquid had been laced with poison.

"What's the matter?" Yang reassured him gently. "I'm not going to poison you."

But Li simply sat there, refusing to touch the spoon. Shaking his head, Yang removed the lid from his own soup bowl and scooped up a spoonful of broth into his mouth.

"Of all the boys I have mentored, you're the most thoughtful and loyal," Yang complimented. "You brought me this globefish last year. I raised it in my pond, hoping that someday we could enjoy it together. I finally have the chance today. Earlier on, I asked a chef from Yangzhou to cook it for us. But you don't seem to like it."

"I'm sorry for being such an idiot," Li said, literally slapping himself in the face. "I'm going to eat it."

He removed the lid, cupped the bowl with both hands and took a big gulp directly from the bowl.

"It's hot," Yang yelled. "Pace yourself."

The soup had burned his tongue. Li put the bowl down, opened his mouth wide and grimaced with pain. Madam Yun picked up a pot of liquor, filled up a large mug and offered it to Li.

"This, this mug is too big…" Li stuttered nervously.

"You're truly perceptive," Yang repeated. "Daddy does want to tell you something today. Actually, my message boils down to three sentences. I'll broach a sentence each time you empty your cup. Now, drink up this one."

Li finished it at a single gulp and waited for Yang to utter his first sentence.

"Well, you mentioned several times behind my back that you would die a happy man if you could sleep with Madam Yun," Yang said nonchalantly. "Didn't you say that?"

Li leapt from his seat, pushed away his chair and dropped to his knees. Yang stood up and held out a hand, trying to pull him up from the floor. Li refused to get up.

"Look at you," Yang teased. "I've only uttered one sentence. If you keep acting like this, I won't be able to broach the other two with you."

Too scared to speak, Li kept kowtowing. Madam Yun, taking her cue from Yang, tried to help him, but Li sidestepped her as though she were a ghost.

"Get up," Yang finally hardened his tone. Li quickly obeyed. When he rose to his feet, his legs quivered uncontrollably. Madam Yun held his arm and sat him down. Then, she filled up a second glass.

"Drink it up," Yang demanded. Li could hardly hold the cup with his trembling hands. It took him a while to gulp it all down.

"My second sentence – how has Daddy treated you so far?"

Li was about to rise again, but Madam Yun pressed him down.

"Daddy treated me like his own son, and I'm forever indebted to you…" he mumbled.

"You are a good man," Yang nodded. "Give him more liquor."

Madam Yun filled up the cup again. Before Yang spoke, Li raised the cup and held it to his lips. Yang stopped him.

"Wait until after I finish my last sentence," he said. "Then, drink as much as you want."

Emboldened by the alcohol, Li responded loudly, "Daddy, you own my life, and you make every decision for me. Please finish what you need to say."

"Fine," Yang said. "My last sentence is – I want you to spend the night here and sleep with Madam Yun."

Yang's words dumbfounded Li. He stood there, stiff as a wooden board.

Yang rose and said, "I'm done with my three sentences. Now that you have heard what I have to say, I'll leave it to you to decide whether you want to empty the cup or not."

Then, Yang walked out and closed the door behind him.

By then, Li had finally seen through the charade. Turning around abruptly, he howled at Madam Yun, "Come over here and serve your man another drink."

At the crack of dawn, the public square outside the governor's yamen suddenly teemed with fully armed soldiers. Holding burning torches, they encircled the square, which appeared from the sky like nails spreading around evenly. The front gate stood wide open. Guards carrying swords and torches stood on both sides. The entrance pathway that led guests into the governor's inner courtyard was also flanked by soldiers with torches, which lit up the compound like daylight.

A suffocating silence spread across the square. There was no wind, not even a gentle breeze. Flags hung limply on tall poles. Two men stood tied to thick wooden stakes nearby, their heads slumping lowly over their chests. Chang Boxi and Zhang Zhiliang, two former county chiefs, would be executed on charges of "negligence of duty". Opposite them stood two more vacant stakes.

"Who is it?" a loud voice pierced the silence – a few lanterns coming towards the square. Several soldiers stirred, dashing over to intercept and question the newcomers.

"We're with the South China Textile Bureau," a person in the group replied. They explained that they had escorted Li over for execution. Two eunuchs took Li by the arm, and four soldiers carrying lanterns followed them. Li was too drunk to walk steadily.

"Is that Li Xuan, the River Flood Control Commission supervisor?" an aide to Governor Hu asked.

"Ye-yes... it is me, your Daddy," Li garbled. "I'm... I'm ready..."

The governor's aide pointed at a wooden stake and ordered, "Take him over there." By then, Li had noticed the two magistrates who once served on the River Flood Control Commission with him. "Ah, I didn't realise that you two were here before me," he greeted them.

One of them shunned him by closing his eyes, but the other one, the former head of Jiande County, pleaded with him, like a drowning person grabbing a rope. "This is so wrong," he cried. "Please, go and petition Yang Jinshui to save us."

"Pe-petitioning... what?" Li reproached him. "You... you're a damn coward. Come on, tie me up there."

Out of despair, the Jiande County chief burst into sobs, but Li giggled. "At the crack of dawn, the tears of the departed have turned the maple leaves red..." he began humming an opera tune.

The two eunuchs tried to stop him, but he resisted them. "I regret that we hadn't met each other earlier, and it is a pity that you're leaving too soon," he crooned, waving his hands like a soprano. "The willow leaves are long, but cannot restrain your white horses from galloping away..."

As he was trying to strike a pose, Li fell headlong to the ground. The two eunuchs quickly helped Li to his feet. Mortified by Li's drunken outbursts, the guards looked at each other in frustration, not knowing how to handle him.

"Hurry... up... put me up... there," Li shouted.

"No, no, we have received instructions that Mr Li is a member of the Interior Ministry," shouted the governor's aide. "We can't apply an instrument of torture to him. Take him to the guard's room first."

Li Xuan, assisted by two eunuchs and four guards, marched into the governor's yamen.

Inside the governor's office, the dour-looking Yang Jinshui, Zheng Bichang and Ho Maocai sat quietly, waiting anxiously for Governor Hu to review the report they had just drafted. Since there was no breeze, the room felt stuffy. The loud sounds of insects outside increased their irritation.

"I mentioned to you earlier that we need to request more time in implementing the land-conversion policy," groused Governor Hu, who placed the report down on his desk. "I don't see it here. Why is that?"

Zheng turned towards Yang, but the latter sat there with his eyes closed.

"We've had many discussions with Yang Gonggong over this," Zheng explained. "We just don't feel that we are in any position to request a delay because the rice-to-mulberry conversion initiative is part of a national policy. It is up to the Imperial Palace to decide whether we should postpone it or not. If His Majesty is concerned about the large-scale flooding we are experiencing now, he can certainly issue a new decree, putting a moratorium on the implementation this year. Then, we'll follow his decree accordingly."

"What if the Imperial Palace refuses to issue a moratorium?" Governor Hu asked.

"Then, we just have to bite the bullet and try to overcome whatever difficulties and barriers stand in the way," Zheng insisted.

Governor Hu jumped to his feet.

"Overcoming barriers that stand in your way? What kinds of barriers?" he vociferated. "Several hundred thousand people have lost their crops to flooding. They've been left with nothing to eat. These people will have nothing to harvest in the autumn, and no grain supplier is willing to loan them rice to help tide them over. Even so, you still want them to grow mulberry trees. They can't eat mulberry leaves, can they?"

"Even if we don't convert their land, they still won't have rice or money," Ho argued. "Their land has been flooded, and they have already lost their crops."

"We can urge the Imperial Palace to loan us money or to allocate grain from elsewhere to help us," Governor Hu suggested. "Besides, if farmers can replant some seedlings after the floods recede, they'll still be able to harvest something in the autumn. They might not be able to pay back the loans this year, but they should be able to in three years. Therefore, it is imperative that we postpone the implementation for three years. Please put this in the report."

When Governor Hu tossed the draft on the desk, Zheng and Ho sat there without stirring.

"If you want to include that request in the report, I'm not going to sign it," Yang protested, without bothering to open his eyes.

"So what are you suggesting?" Governor Hu asked, refusing to back down.

"I'm in charge of the Textile Bureau, and my job is to produce silk and generate revenue for the Imperial Palace," said Yang. "What else can I suggest?"

"I understand the importance of silk production. What if starvation occurs and people rise up against the Imperial Palace? Would you feel responsible?"

"That's your business, not mine." Yang opened his eyes in defiance.

An awkward silence followed. The loud churning of insects in the courtyard filled the room. Governor Hu stared at Yang, and his eyes sparkled with intensity. "Do you think it should be my business to cover up the scheme of breaking the dams to flood the farmland?" Governor Hu yelled suddenly, thumping the rosewood desk with his fist.

Yang looked startled but quickly regained composure. Banging on a tea table next to his chair, he rose to his feet. "What scheme?" he countered. "What are you implying? When you learned about the leaking dams, you were bent on looking for scapegoats. So I offered Li Xuan as a sacrifice. What else do you want? For regional officials like you, the grass is always greener on the other side of the fence. You can always jump over the fence when needed. I'm not as fortunate. I only have one lucky star, and he resides in the palace in Beijing. You don't have to follow the grand secretary's order. But I have to obey Lu Gonggong because I'm a member of the Imperial Palace staff. If there's any fallout, my boss, Lu Gonggong, can report it directly to His Majesty."

Even though he was burning with fury, Governor Hu decided to control his temper. "I don't need Lu Gonggong to tell His Majesty," he said. "As the Governor of Zhejiang, I can travel to Beijing and see His Majesty myself. But, first, let me show you something."

To everyone's surprise, Governor Hu summoned Mayor Ma into the room. The mere mention of Ma's name startled Zheng and Ho. Yang's arrogance and hostility seemed to have dissipated. They all looked towards the entrance.

Dressed in a blue cloth robe, the mayor stepped in, looking serene. He made a beeline for Hu, without taking notice of three of his former peers. Reaching into his breast pocket, he pulled out a stack of papers and handed them over to the governor. "Here is my confession," he said. "It has all the information you need, including the names of my collaborators and details of how we sabotaged the weirs. I have asked both of my county chiefs to sign their names in here as well."

"Please put it on the desk," Governor Hu said softly as he looked Ma in the eye.

Ma cupped his confession with both hands and carefully placed it on the desk. Then, taking a step back, he dropped on his knees.

"At daylight, I'll be gone..." he said. "You've treated me well, and I'll pay back your kindness in my next life."

After he finished, he kowtowed to Governor Hu three times before getting on his feet and marching out. The three mandarins stood there in a daze.

"Do you want to review the confession?" Hu asked his guests.

Nobody responded.

"If you don't want to read it now, that's fine," Governor Hu continued. "I hope I don't ever have to show this confession to another person. But, if the floods and the land-conversion policy turn local farmers into rebels, allowing the pirates to take advantage of the chaos and launch an attack on us, I'm afraid that I would not only lose my life over this but also earn myself eternal infamy. Therefore, I won't permit anyone to create chaos in Zhejiang in the name of implementing His Majesty's land-conversion programme. I won't tolerate any attempts by others, whether intentional or inadvertent, to cause instability in our nation. There's no backing out for me. There's no way out for you either. Let me ask you one more time, are you willing to rewrite and modify the report?"

The three guests sat still in their chairs, gazing downward.

Yang broke the silence. "Now that Your Highness has said it, I guess we'll just have to do it. After all, it's for the betterment of our empire. What else can we say?"

Zheng complied as well. "All right then," he said. Before leaving, Zheng moved over to the desk and picked up the draft report.

明

The flood report, along with a letter jointly signed by Zheng Bichang and Ho Maocai, reached Yan Shifan a few days later. After giving it a quick read, he forwarded the report to his father, Grand Secretary Yan Song.

"That's great, that's great," Yan Song said sarcastically, his lips quivering with anger. Soon, his head and his thick white beard started trembling as well. In fact, he looked like someone who had just suffered a stroke. Panicked over the grand secretary's strong reaction, Luo Wenlong, his confidant and director of the Imperial Post Office, and Mao Qing, the deputy minister of justice, rushed to his side. They held his arms and massaged his back.

"Your Highness, please don't take it too hard," Luo consoled.

The flurry of activities at the other end of the room jolted Yan Shifan, who had been lost in thought while pacing the room like a cornered lion. When he saw Luo and Mao fussing over his father, he quickly walked over. Slowly, Yan Song's trembling had stopped, but he was still too upset to speak. Holding the report in his hand, he simply stared at it blankly.

"Human hearts are as unfathomable as deep water," Mao observed while rubbing Yan Song's shoulder. "How could one have guessed that Governor Hu would do this to the grand secretary."

Yan Shifan clenched his teeth and said with a determined look, "Well, we raised him high, but we can also bring him down and crush him to death. Let's draft a report and initiate the impeachment process right away."

"Stop it," Yan Song said. The old man had recovered from his initial shock. Banging on the arm of his chair with his old bony hand, he asked, "Tell me, who came up with the plan of damaging the weirs to flood the farmland? What was that about?"

None of them responded. Yan Shifan was glaring at the floor.

"Tell me!' the grand secretary demanded.

"All right then," Yan Shifan replied. "To cut a long story short, we encountered tremendous challenges when pushing the land-conversion policy because Governor Hu couldn't make up his mind and resisted it from the very beginning. The rice-to-mulberry conversion wouldn't be possible without the help of big silk mill owners. We have to offer them land at cheaper prices. So we decided that flooding was necessary. That's the whole story."

Yan Song wanted to say something but failed to summon enough strength to utter the words. He paused and closed his eyes. Luo eyed Yan Shifan reproachfully, signalling him to calm down. Taking his cue, Yan Shifan plopped down on a chair.

"We apologise for not consulting with you about this," Luo whispered to Yan Song. "We just didn't want you to be worried. We had planned to give you a detailed report afterwards. The farmland in Zhejiang's nine counties is critical to the success of our land-conversion policy. It is imperative that rice seedlings are out this year and mulberry trees are in. We have to make it happen regardless of whether the land is flooded or not. Confucius admonishes us – the people may be made to follow a path of action, but they may not be made to understand it. Ordinary folks will never understand the difficulties we are facing. We have no other alternatives. Governor Hu could have easily cooperated with his colleagues there and submitted a report, claiming that the flooding was a natural disaster. Nobody here would have questioned the conclusion. But who would have known that Governor Hu could be so inscrutable? Fortunately, he has scrupulously blamed the flooding on shoddy repair and maintenance work on the weirs. I personally think that he's merely attempting to stop us from implementing the conversion policy. The whole thing is still manageable."

"The conversion policy is irrevocable," Yan Shifan interrupted impatiently. "Hu's now forcing others to sign on this report and has requested that His Majesty put aside this policy for three years.

With the current dire fiscal situation, can we afford to wait for three years?"

"He can request three years, but it doesn't mean that we are granting it," Mao added.

"Well, it's not up to him to decide, but, if the Prince of Yu gets wind of our plan, he and his friends can use this to attack us," Luo warned. "That would make things more difficult. What I'm also worried about is that Governor Hu might use Mayor Ma's confession as leverage. If Lu Gonggong knows that Governor Hu has solid evidence against us, he might withdraw his support and stop pushing for our agenda in front of His Majesty. An urgent task is to go and talk with Lu Gonggong and persuade him to see His Majesty together. As long as His Majesty remains resolute in his support, the rest should be easy."

Yan Shifan, whose anxiety and anger had receded, gave his stamp of approval to Luo's suggestion.

"I'm already eighty-one years old," Yan Song sighed. "It's about time you killed me."

Seeing that Luo and Mao had dropped to their knees to apologise, Yan Shifan, visibly annoyed at his father's reprimand, felt obligated to do the same. Putting one hand on the edge of his desk, Yan Song slowly got up.

Yan Song held the report in his hand and said helplessly, "I'll follow your order and go to see His Majesty."

明

Inside the Yuxi Palace, Lu Fang, the interior minister and chief eunuch, was reading aloud Governor Hu's report to Emperor Jiajing, who listened quietly and intently. Grand Secretary Yan Song sat on a small stool. When the emperor stepped down from his cushioned throne and started pacing around anxiously, Yan Song laboriously got up from his chair as a gesture of respect.

"In Chapter 58 of *Tao Te Ching*, there is a passage that reads, *When the country is ruled with a light hand, the people are simple. When the country is ruled with severity, the people are cunning*," Emperor Jiajing chanted. "People have been feeling lost for a long time.

Tolerance can be a fault. So is repression. No wonder the people are feeling lost. I'm also lost. Aren't you lost?"

Yan Song pressed his hand on the drum-shaped stool and dropped to his knees. So did Lu Fang.

"Be it tolerance or repression, it's all my fault," Yan Song stated. "Governor Hu knows the situation better than anyone else. I recommend that you summon him to Beijing. We can have a discussion and try to figure out if it is possible to accommodate both needs – disaster relief and land conversion. I'm sure we can work out a solution."

Emperor Jiajing sauntered towards his bookcase and paused in front of a section labelled "Zhejiang Province". Then, he mused aloud, "God descended from heaven to enquire about the happenings on earth. Let's invite the earth lord over."

"Yes, Your Majesty," Yan Song replied.

"We should also invite two more people," Emperor Jiajing added. "The first person's surname is Yang, and his given name is Jinshui. He's Lu Gonggong's protégé. The second one is Tan Lun, a trusted ally of the Prince of Yu. Of course, Governor Hu is the grand secretary's student. Bring these local lords and deities over. In this way, all factions will be represented."

Emperor's Jiajing's suggestion and sardonic comments shocked Yan Song. He shot a sidelong glance at Lu, hoping that he could help him push back on the emperor's suggestion. But Lu simply knelt there quietly, ignoring Yan Song's silent signal.

"Yes, Your Majesty," Yan Song reluctantly consented.

明

In May on the lunar calendar, the late afternoon sun still hung high in the sky. The slanting rays of the sun shone on the lofty and magnificent Qianmen Tower, and its glitter dazzled the eye. Even though the nine city gates were heavily guarded during the day, residents still could enter or exit freely. On days when the emperor held a special ceremony or summoned a senior official to the palace, all the city gates would be closed to the public until the royal guards of honour or the horse-drawn sedans of senior officials galloped through.

On the early afternoon of the twenty-first of May 1561 the Imperial Guards shut the Qianmen Gate and began clearing the area. Soon, a transportation official in the palace showed up and waited eagerly with four carriers who stood next to a green curtained sedan. From the colour and shape of the sedan, those who were familiar with the palace rituals knew immediately that a provincial governor would be visiting. Apparently, the governor was not the only guest. A senior eunuch was also standing in the vicinity with four carriers. The colour of the second sedan was blue.

Very soon, a string of horses sprinted towards the Qianmen City Gate, leaving behind them a trail of dust. Governor Hu's top aide led the entourage, and four bodyguards followed the governor. Shrewd observers spotted Tan Lun with the group. Yang Jinshui also arrived, escorted by four junior eunuchs.

At the Qianmen Gate, the coterie stopped and briskly dismounted from their horses. Governor Hu and Tan Lun tossed their whips to the aides and walked towards the official greeters. After exchanging pleasantries, the greeter lifted and held the curtain on the side of the sedan. Governor Xu bent his head and climbed in. The carriers lifted the sedan and sped right through the city gate. Tan Lun and the governor's aides marched in with their horses. Meanwhile, Yang remained on the horse, trying to catch his breath. It took two eunuchs to help him alight. His legs appeared so sore that he could hardly walk. In the end, he wobbled forward, with the eunuchs holding his arms.

When a greeter led Yang to his sedan and lifted the green curtain, he didn't hop in. Instead, Yang grabbed the greeter's wrist, pulling him closer. "Do you know why His Majesty has summoned me to the capital?" he asked in earnest. "Has Lu Gonggong mentioned anything?"

The greeter shook his head and said, "You know how Lu Gonggong is. His mouth is as tight as that of a Buddha statue. Nobody, not even his deputies at the Interior Ministry, can get him to leak anything."

Yang stood there with an abstract expression. "Lu Gonggong is waiting for you at the Interior Ministry," the greeter nudged him, snapping him out of his reverie. Yang dutifully grabbed the greeter's arm and clambered in slowly.

Close to a quarter of an hour later, Yang's sedan stopped in front of the duty room at the Interior Ministry. "Daddy!" Yang addressed Lu endearingly. The pain that had stunted his movement a few minutes before seemed to have vaporised. He jumped out of his sedan and made a beeline for Lu Fang, who sat inside the Interior Ministry's duty room. Falling to his knees, Yang kowtowed three times.

"Please rise," Lu said calmly.

Yang sprang to his feet. With both hands, Yang carefully picked up Lu's teacup from a small table nearby and ingratiatingly offered it to his Daddy. Like an accused criminal who was waiting for his verdict at his trial, Yang looked nervous but expectant. Seeing that Lu sat on his chair quietly, Yang began to feel the tremors inside his body.

"Why don't YOU drink it?" Lu finally spoke.

The patriarch's words, imbued with symbols and meanings, were treated like an emperor's edict. This was a routine that every regional appointee of the Interior Ministry would have to follow upon his return to the capital city. Before his meeting with his patriarch, the eunuch appointee would need to pick up Lu's cup and offer him tea. If Lu ignored the person or refused to take the tea, it meant that the Imperial Palace or Lu himself was not happy with the person's job performance. The appointee could face demotion, imprisonment or even death. But, if Lu drank up the tea, the appointee could utter a sigh of relief because it indicated "smooth sailing". On the rare occasion when Lu invited the person to drink the tea from his cup, as he did with Yang, it showed that he was treated like family.

As expected, Yang's eyes sparkled with gratitude. He removed the lid with his trembling hands and swallowed the leftover tea with one gulp. Then, he squatted down near Lu, and began patting and massaging Lu's legs.

"Daddy, it's been four years since I left here," he said nostalgically, with his face raising towards the patriarch. "You have aged."

Seeing that Yang was choking up, Lu sighed. "I live from day to day," he said. "But let's not dwell on me. Go and wash your face and change. I'm going to take you to see His Majesty."

"You mean now?" Yang said – he couldn't believe his ears.

"Since you have nothing to hide from me and told me the whole truth, I do the same for His Majesty," Lu pointed out. "He's aware of the flooding scheme. You just need to go and tell His Majesty in more detail."

"But what if he asks about my role? Am I going to be blamed?" Yang said distractedly.

"You did it for the sake of the Imperial Palace. Fortunately, you didn't lie about it. His Majesty appreciates your loyalty. Right now, only two counties are affected. His Majesty can stomach that. He has the whole country to rule."

"But Daddy, I…" Yang remained unconvinced.

"There's no need to say more," Yang interrupted him with a stern tone. "Go and get yourself ready."

For junior eunuchs like Yang, the honour of meeting with the emperor existed in name only. There was seldom any face-to-face meeting. Now that such an opportunity arose, Yang was required to wait on his knees at a spot near the gigantic silk curtains that separated the big hall from the emperor's meditation room.

Having washed and changed, Yang felt refreshed. More importantly, Lu's reassurance prior to the meeting calmed his nerves slightly, enabling him to keep a solemn and confident posture.

"Did you actually see the letter drafted by Yan Shifan?" the emperor's voice reached him from the meditation room.

"Yes, Your Majesty. Your humble servant saw it with his own eyes," Yang replied with his head down. "Yan Shifan's letter was delivered to Zheng Bichang and Ho Maocai, urging them to flood the farmland. In this way, it would be easier to implement the land-conversion plan."

"Have you seen Mayor Ma Ningyuan's confession?" the emperor asked.

"Your Majesty, I didn't. Governor Hu did invite Zheng Bichang,

Ho Maocai and your humble servant to read it, but none of us actually saw it."

"Why would Governor Hu do that? What could be his motive?" Emperor Jiajing raised his voice.

Yang hesitated. He looked to Lu, who was standing next to him, for advice.

"Answer it honestly," Lu advised.

"Your Majesty, your humble servant personally thinks that Governor Hu has three considerations," Yang raised his voice slightly.

"Three considerations? What are they?"

"First, as the governor of Zhejiang, Hu Zongxian is facing a lot of pressure. The pirates run rampant, posing a serious security threat to the coastal region. Plus, if peasants lose their farmland and their livelihood, they could rise up against the government. When external threats mix with domestic chaos, the government could lose control. This is probably what Governor Hu is concerned about. Secondly, Tan Lun, who worked for the Prince of Yu for years, might have some influence over him. Thirdly, Governor Hu feels indebted to the grand secretary, but he doesn't always see eye-to-eye with the grand secretary's son."

After Yang finished, Emperor Jiajing summoned Lu into the meditation room. Yang pricked his ears. "You've done a good job training and promoting Yang," Emperor Jiajing was heard saying. "He's quite capable. Award him something, but do it quietly."

Yang Jinshui knelt on the floor, with his head down. His heart was thumping with excitement.

"Tell Grand Secretary Yan Song to bring Hu Zongxian here tomorrow," Emperor Jiajing's voice lingered in the big hallway. "Invite the Prince of Yu to the meeting as well."

※

Governor Hu arrived at the Imperial Guest House, where he washed briefly and changed into civilian clothes. Then, he left again without supper. His sedan chair stopped at about three hundred metres away from Yan Song's mansion. It was seven o'clock in the evening, and darkness had just descended. Stepping off from his sedan, he paused. From a distance, he gazed at the sprawling courtyard house that he had visited countless times before. The façade hadn't changed much. Under the eave hung the same four big red lanterns, with the characters *The Yan Mansion* printed on them.

How time had flown past! Twenty years before, when he had scored the highest in the annual Imperial Examination, Grand Secretary Yan Song summoned him there for a meeting. Governor Hu could remember it as if it had only happened the day before. But things were different today. He had never felt so remote from the grand secretary, even though he was only about three hundred metres away from the Yan Mansion. To give himself enough time to mentally prepare for the possible insults and rebukes that the grand secretary could hurl at him, or some unexpected conspiracies plotted against him, he decided to walk the last three hundred metres.

"I'll go by myself, and you can all wait for me here," he said to his aide, who handed him a square package wrapped in cloth.

"Oh, it's you, Governor Hu," a guard at the entrance greeted him warmly – it was obvious that he knew Governor Hu very well. However, beneath the familiar tone, Governor Hu could tell that the guard sounded a little uneasy and guarded.

"How is the grand secretary?" Governor Hu enquired with smiles.

"Fairly well," the guard answered, quietly sizing him up.

"Could I bother you to take me to see the grand secretary?"

"I hate to broach this to you, but I received instructions from the grand secretary this afternoon that he does not think it appropriate to see you because you have been summoned back by His Majesty," the guard said haltingly.

Governor Hu was taken aback by the guard's message. On his way there, he had prepared himself for all sorts of awkward scenarios, but he hadn't anticipated that Yan Song would refuse to see him. A pang of disappointment and sadness overcame him. He stood there for a few minutes, contemplating what to do next.

"Could you go and tell the grand secretary that I need to see him first for both personal and work-related reasons?" he requested again.

"All right, Your Highness," the guard said reluctantly. "Why don't you wait here while I go and relay your message."

Since he had been away from Beijing over the past two years, Governor Hu had not been advised of the changes in the Yan family. The grand secretary had long ago lost the energy that kept him on top of every decision. His son, Yan Shifan, had taken over the Privy Council. It was more so at home. Everyone had to follow Yan Shifan's order. Everything, big or small, had to go through him. Earlier that day, Yan Shifan specifically instructed the guards to stop Governor Hu at the door.

"Grand Secretary Junior," the guard came to the study to notify Yan Shifan of Governor Hu's visit. It so happened that at that moment, Yan Shifan was dictating a letter to Mao Qing, the deputy minister of justice, who was arduously taking notes at a desk. Yan Shifan was so engrossed in the rebuttal letter that he ignored the guard.

> During my tenure, I neither shared His Majesty's concerns for the country nor alleviated hardships for the people," Yan Shifan read. "My failure was such that it could no longer be explained away by simply calling it 'ignorance or incapability'. Given the harm I had done to my country and the people, how could I continue to hold the governorship which you bestowed upon me? With your permission, I resign from my positions as the governor of Zhejiang and the imperial inspector of Zhejiang. With gratitude, Hu Zongxian.

He peered at the guard and asked, "Governor Hu is out there, isn't he?"

"Yes, Your Highness."

"Didn't you parrot what I told you to him?"

"Yes, Your Highness," the guard replied. "But Governor Hu insisted that I pass on this message to the grand secretary. He said he should see the grand secretary for both personal and work-related reasons."

By then, Mao Qing had finished copying Yan Shifan's dictation – it was a resignation letter that Yan Shifan had drafted on behalf of Governor Hu. Mao handed over the letter and, while reviewing it, Yan Shifan shouted to the guard, "Tell Governor Hu, this is the grand secretary's private residence. If he wants to talk about business, he can bring it up in the palace tomorrow, or we can send someone to the royal guest house to discuss with him. If he's here for a personal visit, tell him that the grand secretary has no personal relations with him."

The guard didn't leave. "If I tell him this, don't you think it'll hurt his feelings?" he mumbled.

"Hurt your mother's fucking arse!" Yan Shifan roared. He picked up an inkstone from the desk and hurled it at the guard, who quickly ducked his head.

"Your humble servant will follow your instruction..." the guard pledged before running out of the house.

Having witnessed such irate outbursts before, Mao Qing sat at the desk calmly. "I guess I have to find a new inkstone," he muttered.

"Why don't you ask?" Yan Shifan chided. "Can't you send someone to get it for you?"

Even though the guard dodged the inkstone, he was shivering with fear. Upon returning to the gate, he passed on Yan Shifan's message verbatim to Governor Hu, who mistakenly thought that the message had been dictated by the grand secretary. Standing alone, Governor Hu felt overwhelmed with sadness.

"I assume Your Highness will have the chance to see the grand secretary before going to meet with His Majesty tomorrow morning," reminded the guard, who couldn't bear to see Governor Hu suffer like that. "You can bare your heart to him tomorrow then."

"Thanks for your kindness," Governor Hu said slowly. "If possible, could you tell the grand secretary that I have something urgent? If we wait until tomorrow, it could be too late."

"I will definitely report what you said to the grand secretary," the guard promised.

Governor Hu turned around and strode away.

Inside the Yan Mansion, the grand secretary, known for his placid temperament, seemed unusually agitated and distracted tonight. Lying on a recliner in his study, he was wide awake while listening to books, which, under normal circumstances, tended to make him drowsy. Fixing his eyes on the horizontal beams on the ceiling, he was lost in thought. Luo Wenlong sat next to a floor lamp, reading aloud the verses in Chapter 58 of *Tao Te Ching*.

> *When the country is ruled with a light hand*
> *The people are simple.*
> *When the country is ruled with severity,*
> *The people are cunning.*
>
> *Happiness is rooted in misery.*
> *Misery lurks beneath happiness.*
> *Who knows what the future holds?*
> *There is no honesty.*
> *Honesty becomes dishonest.*
> *Goodness becomes witchcraft.*
> *Man's bewitchment lasts for a long time.*

Yan Song raised his hand to stop Luo. "When His Majesty chanted Chapter 58 this morning, do you think he had got wind of the secret plan to destroy weirs and flood the farmland in Zhejiang?" he asked, with his eyes staring at the ceiling.

"I doubt it," Luo replied. "We have full control of the Zhejiang government, and the South China Textile Bureau is staffed with Lu Fang's henchmen. Since several of the eunuchs were also involved in the scheme, I'm highly sceptical that Lu Gonggong would foolishly reveal it to His Majesty. Apart from them, nobody knows what happened, and no one has any evidence against us. Who would dare speculate and spread rumours?"

"Then, why did the emperor quote Chapter 58 in the middle of our meeting today?" Yan Song asked.

Yan Shifan barged in and shouted, "If you truly believe that His

Majesty knows something about it, Governor Hu has to be the leaker. Governor Hu personally travelled to Chun'an County with Tan Lun to direct the disaster relief work. After the two returned to Hangzhou, Governor Hu had Mayor Ma arrested. I think Tan Lun must have read Mayor Ma's confession and passed on the information to the Prince of Yu. If His Majesty is in the know, I'm sure he got it from the crown prince."

"I don't think so," Yan Song shook his head. "Governor Hu is prudent in nature. I know that part of him well. When he interrogated Mayor Ma, there was not another person on site. I doubt he has shown it to Tan Lun."

"Father, you are way too trusting!" Yan Shifan accused.

"I've mentored him for years, and I know him better than anyone else," Yan Song insisted. "If His Majesty learned about this scheme from the Prince of Yu, other Privy Council members, such as Gao Gong, Zhang Juzheng and Xu Jie, would have been briefed as well because they're the crown prince's advisers and confidants. If that's the case, I would have heard something."

Yan Song struggled to sit up, and Luo rushed over to help.

"Let's ask Governor Hu when he's here," Yan Song said expectantly as he peered at the courtyard. "He should be here any minute. Why don't you go and ask the guard? Bring him to me immediately upon his arrival."

"Don't count on it," Yan Shifan said dismissively. "I just asked the guard. He's not going to be here tonight. His betrayal is obvious to everyone, except you. Please don't be too trusting."

"I'm sure he will show up," Yan Song reassured his son.

明

Inside the Prince of Yu's mansion, Gao Gong, deputy minister of the treasury, and Zhang Juzheng, who headed the Ministry of Defence, were chatting with the Prince of Yu. The deputy grand secretary, Xu Jie, was absent. The prince paced about the room nervously.

"All we can do at the moment is to watch closely and wait," Gao suggested. "The fact that His Majesty explicitly summoned Tan Lun to the capital shows that he is laying the blame on us. It's probably not a good idea to see Tan Lun before he meets with His Majesty."

"If we don't see Tan Lun before the meeting, it'll give people a reason to suspect that the prince has something to hide," Zhang objected. "Tan Lun used to be your chief of staff. It would sound strange if he doesn't see you upon arrival. Besides, you're the crown prince. It is only natural you take a strong interest in national affairs. This land-conversion scheme could turn into a big political scandal."

"I understand what you are saying," Gao Gong argued. "But you don't have to be overly exuberant tonight. If His Highness, the Prince of Yu, sees Tan Lun tonight, what would he say if His Majesty asks about it tomorrow?"

"His Highness can just answer truthfully," Princess Li's voice came from inside the chamber. Her interjection took the two guests by surprise. They both stood up as a gesture of respect for the princess, but the Prince of Yu signalled for them to sit down.

"I personally think that Zhang Juzheng is right," said Princess Li, who argued from inside the chamber. "Your Highness should see Tan Lun tonight. It's better if you ask Feng Bao to bring Tan Lun over. Father and son should act as one. There is nothing to hide from each other."

The men's eyes brightened.

"I'm embarrassed to say that Princess Li is more insightful than us," Zhang quipped, and Gao Gong nodded in agreement.

As planned, Feng Bao brought Tan Lun to the prince's mansion. Just as Feng was about to exit, the prince stopped him.

"I want you to take tonight off and return to the palace," said the prince.

"Master, what do you need me to do?" Feng asked, his head bowed down.

"Tell Lu Gonggong that I have summoned Tan Lun to my house tonight."

"Master... Master... your humble servant wouldn't dare do something like this," Feng dropped to his knees and mumbled.

"There's nothing wrong with that," the prince reassured him. "There is no such thing as a private affair here. I'm the emperor's son. My private affairs are also part of our national affairs. Go as you're told."

Feng knelt there without moving.

The prince stamped his feet and asked, "Are you listening?"

"Yes, Master," Feng said. He rose to his feet and exited with a look of confusion on his face.

※

By the time Governor Hu returned to the Imperial Guest House, it was quite late. Despite the exhaustion from his week-long trip, he couldn't sleep. So he got up and decided to organise his thoughts before his meeting in the palace. Regardless of how things would develop, honesty was his best strategy to cope with the emperor and to tackle any unpredictable turn of events during his meeting.

As he was lost in contemplation, his door suddenly burst open. Yan Shifan walked in, surprising him only partially. In a way, he had somewhat expected Yan Shifan's visit.

Before Governor Hu had the chance to formulate a proper greeting, the grand secretary's son had already swaggered in and sat down on the only chair in the room.

"I'm told that you have in your possession a signed confession," Yan Shifan said bluntly. "That confession has something to do with damaging the weirs to flood the farmland."

"Grand Secretary Junior, I'm not aware of such a written confession," Governor Hu replied calmly but tenaciously.

Yan Shifan stared at Governor Hu; his eyes widened like two lanterns. After a long pause, he said, "All right, it's good to know that you don't have it. Even if you have it, it's not a big deal. The worst of it would be that His Majesty deposes my father and me, and puts us in prison. But I want to warn you – throughout history, those who served two masters always ended up in a bad way. Even if you drive us out, I don't think they'll grant you a seat on the Privy Council."

Governor Hu listened carefully and responded to Yan Shifan's accusation with silence.

Exasperated by Governor Hu's reticence, Yan Shifan yelled, "Are you trying to present the mayor's confession to the crown prince as a coronation gift?"

"Brother Shifan, you can always use this to gauge the motives of people around you, but it doesn't apply to me," Governor Hu retorted. "The grand secretary is already eighty-one years old. As his son, you should at least think first for your own ageing father, if not for the well-being of common people in our country."

Yan Shifan stood up and roared, "What gives you the right to lecture me? I've been given the responsibilities of managing two capital cities and thirteen provinces. Speaking of caring about the well-being of common people, you have to wait your turn. Answer me – are you willing to implement the land-conversion policy in Zhejiang, or are you not?"

"I've stated it clearly in my report," Governor Hu replied.

"Does that mean you're not planning to change your position?"

Once again, Governor Hu ignored his question. His silence further infuriated Yan Shifan, whose body trembled in frustration. Lifting his right hand, Yan Shifan suddenly began slapping himself across the right side of his face. "I smack this side on behalf of my father," he ranted. "He deserves it for mentoring and promoting you." Baffled at the show of self-punishment, Governor Hu was tempted to rise and stop him. But Yan Shifan lifted his left hand and slapped himself on his left cheek. "This smack is a reward I give to myself for trusting you. I have no idea how my father and I could be so blind and stupid as to appoint you as the governor of this important province."

Governor Hu rose from his chair and walked over to the door. "I have long lost interest in the governorship," he said. "Feel free to file a report with His Majesty and have me removed from my current position."

"I didn't force you to say it," Yan Shifan pointed out. "You said it yourself. I hope you mean it."

"Feel free to tell me what I need to do. There is no need to beat around the bush," Governor Hu said calmly.

"Fine. I've already drafted a resignation letter for you," said Yan Shifan, who brought out a letter from his pocket and tossed it on the tea table. "All you need to do is hand copy it."

Before Governor Hu had the chance to read it, Yan Shifan headed for the door.

※

Wealthy families in the capital city usually hired watchmen to mark the time by beating the clappers hourly. As Yan Song was lying on his recliner, he could hear the watchman's clapper coming from the front yard. He opened his eyes and asked, "How late is it?"

"It's close to bedtime," Mao Qing replied. "I don't think Governor Hu will show up tonight."

A rare expression of sadness flashed in Yan Song's eyes. "I guess I'm wrong about Governor Hu," he sighed. "What did you say about human hearts earlier on?"

"Human hearts are fickle like flowing water," Mao Qing repeated.

Yan Song shook his head in disagreement. "Water always flows downward, but a human heart always aims higher and higher," he added, implying that Governor Hu was dropping him for the Prince of Yu.

Mao eyed Luo, who stepped up and advised Yan Song to go to bed. "You need to get up early for the meeting tomorrow morning," he reminded.

"I'm just going to stay here for the rest of the night," Yan Song insisted.

※

At the crack of dawn, Governor Hu left the Imperial Guest House alone, with the resignation letter tucked inside his breast pocket. By the time the gigantic bronze bell on top of the Gate of Heavenly Peace boomed forth to signal the start of a working day, he was already standing outside the Yuxi Palace, waiting for the arrival of Yan Song and the Prince of Yu. When he saw a royal palanquin and an official sedan chair approaching, Governor Hu was seized with pain and dismay. He had no idea how to face Yan Song, his mentor with whom he desperately wanted to consult before the emperor's meeting. Following the previous night's snub, he knew that the greeting was bound to be awkward. Besides, how was he going to handle the Prince of Yu?

Based on royal etiquette, Governor Hu was required to greet the crown prince first. So he dropped to his knees when he caught a glimpse of the prince's golden robe and his boots, which were embroidered with a dragon. By the time the prince emerged from inside the palanquin, Governor Hu had kowtowed three times.

"Thanks for your hard work," the prince consoled Governor Hu, trying at the same time to tame his enthusiasm so he wouldn't offend Yan Song.

Two aides helped Yan Song alight from his sedan chair. Governor Hu, who was still on his knees, tilted his body towards the grand secretary. "Your humble subordinate is pleased to see the grand secretary," he greeted.

"All right then," Yan Song threw him a quick glance and replied coldly. "Let's go and meet His Majesty now."

The indifference pained Governor Hu. After pausing for a few seconds, he said, "Yes, Your Highness."

By the time Governor Hu got to his feet, the Prince of Yu and Yan Song had already entered the courtyard. He composed himself and caught up.

At seven o'clock, a eunuch on duty ushered them into the Yuxi Palace. The Prince of Yu took a seat reserved for the crown prince on the east side of the throne. Given his advanced age, Yan Song was granted a designated stool on the west. As usual, Lu Fang, the emperor's top eunuch, stood behind the throne. In the cavernous hall, Governor Hu was the only one kneeling.

Emperor Jiajing appeared in his usual baggy robe. Though the season was still in the middle of winter, he wore only a thin silk robe. What seemed odd was that the emperor would change into a thick cotton outfit with nine printed dragons in the summer. Based on his explanation, such unusual sartorial preference showed the power of his decade-long Taoist meditation and alchemic practice. But many around him knew that the immortality pills supplied by Taoist monks made his body hot in the winter and chilled it in the summer.

But nobody dared question this odd condition. Instead, they flattered him profusely on his diligent Taoist practices that had given him "magic" powers.

Emperor Jiajing started the meeting by directly addressing Governor Hu.

"You ordered the execution of four senior regional officials – a mayor, a palace-appointed river flood control supervisor, and two magistrates who had excelled in the Imperial Exams," the emperor charged. "How brazen!"

The opening remarks, abrupt and straightforward, startled Governor Hu. "Your Majesty, your humble servant closely followed the Ming Dynasty Law," he explained. "The negligence by officials in charge of dam repairs and maintenance caused severe flooding that led to the deaths of thousands. Their crime was no different from that committed by military officers who desert their cities at times of war. As the governor and regional military commander, I'm entrusted with the authority to order summary execution on behalf of Your Majesty."

"You could have obtained prior approval from the Privy Council before you applied the law, couldn't you?"

"Your Majesty, yes, of course."

"Then why didn't you?" Emperor Jiajing questioned. "If memory serves me correctly, you're prudent by nature. But this time, you acted quite recklessly and impetuously. The officials you beheaded included people favoured by the grand secretary junior or Lu Gonggong. Weren't you afraid of retaliation?"

"Your Majesty, this land is your land, and all of us who serve the Imperial Palace are solely at your disposal. There's no division among us," Yan Song interjected.

"The Imperial Palace is nothing more than a bureaucracy that owns a few palaces and government ministries," Emperor Jiajing retorted, in half jest. "We don't eat from the same pot, do we?"

Before Yan Song had the chance to respond, Emperor Jiajing turned to the Prince of Yu, enquiring about Tan Lun. "Early this year, you recommended that your chief of staff be sent to Zhejiang to undertake more training," he asked. "Has he accomplished anything?"

The prince looked visibly nervous. He thought for a few seconds before speaking up. "Father, Tan Lun served as a military adviser to Governor Hu at the beginning," he said. "Now, he's been assigned to the military there to assist General Qi Jiguang. Since he only started a few months ago, it's still too early to talk about accomplishment."

"Well, accomplishment doesn't mean that one has to conquer the enemy on the battlefield and take over a whole enemy city," rebutted Emperor Jiajing. "Don't you consider it an achievement for someone who has the audacity to step up and do things that others wouldn't dare to do?"

The Prince of Yu eyed the calligraphy on the wall behind Emperor Jiajing's throne. It bore the famous Taoist Teaching: *I have three treasures which I cherish. The first is called compassion. The second frugality. The third humility or not daring to step to the front.* To the Prince of Yu, the third one about "not daring to step to the front" seemed specifically glaring. He quickly dropped to his knees, and the others held their breath.

Governor Hu raised his head and broke the silence. "Your Majesty, I was a man of mediocre talent, but you championed on my behalf and appointed me to be the Governor of Zhejiang," he asserted. "After I took over the position, I followed the orders of Your Majesty and the Imperial Palace. I have not bowed to the will of others, and nobody can sway my decisions. But, unfortunately, I have not been able to implement the rice-to-mulberry conversion policy. On top of this failure, an unprecedented flooding occurred during my tenure there. If one gets to the roots of the problems, the blame is on me, not anyone else. I take full responsibility."

Then, Governor Hu paused. Pulling his resignation from inside his long sleeve, he presented it to Emperor Jiajing. "Your Majesty, this is my request for resignation. Please accept it," he said.

The sudden resignation took everyone by surprise. Emperor Jiajing did not ask Lu, his chief eunuch, to accept the resignation letter on his behalf. Instead, he gazed at Governor Hu for a few minutes before turning to the crown prince. "Did you listen to what he just said," Emperor Jiajing said. "He's trying to exculpate Tan Lun."

The prince sat there, with his head down. Emperor Jiajing eyed Governor Hu and fired a string of questions at him, his tone growing harsher.

"As you mentioned just now, the shoddy repairs of river dams caused severe harm to people and property," the emperor upbraided. "The offence was no different from that of deserting land or a city at time of war. On top of that, the flooding disrupted the implementation of the rice-to-mulberry conversion policy. If I were to punish you for such offences, do you think you can get away with it by simply resigning?"

"Be it thunders or morning dew, they are all heaven's blessings," said Governor Hu. "I will throw myself at the mercy of Your Majesty."

"I'm not done with my questions," Emperor Jiajing continued. "The Imperial Palace allocated two and a half million taels of silver to repair the weirs along Xin'an River last year. All the weirs leaked or collapsed in one big rainstorm. Didn't you have an inkling of what happened there before?"

The question caused jitters among Yan Song, the Prince of Yu and even Lu Fang. They all looked at Governor Hu.

"I inspected the weirs before, but failed to discover any potential trouble," Governor Hu replied. "It was an oversight on my part."

"Was it mere oversight?" Emperor Jiajing asked.

The other attendants were waiting nervously for Governor Hu's reply.

"Your Majesty, I have a written confession given by Mayor Ma and two of his magistrates who served on the Xin'an River Flood Control Commission." Governor Hu pulled out a folded document from inside his breast pocket. "It states whether it was oversight or not. Please review."

The air was thick with tension and awkwardness. Emperor Jiajing turned around and signalled Lu. The head eunuch reluctantly walked over, took the written confession from Governor Hu and handed it over to Emperor Jiajing.

As the steely-eyed Emperor Jiajing was reading the confession, Yan Song closed his eyes, but one could tell that his face was twitching slightly. The Prince of Yu cast down his eyes, trying to control his breathing and his emotions.

As he was perusing the confession, Emperor Jiajing bore an expression that changed from surprise to contemplation and calm.

"Grand Secretary Yan," Emperor Jiajing called.

Yan Song, who was deep in thought with his eyes closed, didn't hear his name being called. Emperor Jiajing's face registered a subtle expression of sympathy and perhaps a bit of disapproval. Instead of waiting for Yan Song's response, he asked Lu, who was standing behind him, "Did you know what is written in this confession?"

"Your Majesty, I did not know," Lu bowed his head.

"This confession provides some interesting details about how the weirs fell into disrepair."

Lu Fang was taken aback at first – he had thought the confession would shed light or expose the scheme of sabotaging the weirs to flood the farmland. Then, with a visible sigh of relief, he looked at the emperor. The two smirked, giving each other a knowing glance.

"Please hand over the confession to the grand secretary."

As Lu Fang was walking over towards Yan Song, Emperor Jiajing peered at the Prince of Yu, who sat there quietly and calmly, as if nothing important had been discussed.

"Grand Secretary," Lu spoke softly in his ear.

Yan Song opened his eyes and gazed at Lu. His eyes were filled with uncertainty.

"His Majesty has reviewed the confession," Lu raised his voice slightly. "It's about how the weirs fell into disrepair."

Yan Song's eyes brightened momentarily.

"His Majesty wants you to review it as well," added Lu, who handed over the confession.

With his trembling hands, Yan Song unfolded the confession, took a quick glance at the first page and then raised his head. "Your Majesty, the characters are tiny. My poor vision has rendered it impossible for me to read," he confessed.

"Take it home and share it with members of the Privy Council," Emperor Jiajing suggested.

"Yes, Your Majesty."

"We have one more thing on the agenda," Emperor Jiajing continued. "Let's discuss Governor Hu's resignation. He has requested that the Privy Council and I fire him. Do you think we should grant his request?"

After pausing for a few moments, Yan Song said slowly, "Promotion, transfer or dismissal of imperial officials are the sole decisions of His Majesty, and it is not something with which my peers and I dare interfere."

A shade of displeasure crossed Emperor Jiajing's face. "You know you're not speaking sincerely," he accused.

Yan Song sprang to his feet.

"You were the one who recommended Hu Zongxian for the position of minister of defence and subsequently the governor and imperial inspector of Zhejiang," Emperor Jiajing pointed out. "When was the last time I promoted or dismissed someone without consulting with my advisers?"

Stunned by the emperor's rebuke, Yan Song stood there speechless.

Governor Hu raised his head. "At that time, Your Majesty put me in an important position upon the recommendation of the grand secretary," he said. "Both of you had hoped that I would live up to your expectations and bring peace and economic benefits to people in Zhejiang. But I have faltered in my responsibilities. Obviously, I'm not the best fit for the position. Therefore, I sincerely request that you remove me from my current position."

Emperor Jiajing gazed into Hu's eyes. "Are you trying to throw up your job and dodge responsibility?"

"I wouldn't dare," Governor Hu lowered his head and replied timidly.

"Regardless of whether you have requested it, I won't let you get away with it," Emperor Jiajing insisted. "There are two things that I know about you. First, you have the ability to always see the big picture and put the interest of our country above all. Second, you are a hard worker. Zhejiang provides a large portion of income for the Imperial Palace, but it is under constant attacks from the pirates. Nobody can handle the situation there better than you do."

Before Governor Hu had the chance to respond, Emperor Jiajing turned to Yan Song. "What do you think?"

"The comments manifest Your Majesty's wisdom," Yan Song replied. "At the moment, Governor Hu's leadership is crucial to the well-being of Zhejiang Province. But I personally think that he's been shouldering too big a burden. Now that Your Majesty asks my opinion, I would recommend that he resign from the post of imperial inspector and retain his current governorship. In this way, he can oversee the major tasks there and focus on fighting and defeating the pirates. We have to clear the shipping routes for our merchants and fulfil the Textile Bureau's order of five hundred thousand bolts of silk. I urge Governor Hu to try his utmost to accomplish these tasks."

"These are the words of a truly experienced strategist," Emperor Jiajing complimented. "You should call a meeting for Governor Hu so he can discuss with other Privy Council members how to help out the rescue efforts in Zhejiang and implement the rice-to-mulberry conversion plan. It would be ideal if we can work out something that can accommodate both ends."

"Yes, Your Majesty," Yan Song bowed.

"Hu Zongxian, do you agree with what I just said?" the emperor asked.

"I will obey, Your Majesty," he answered, his face awash with tears.

"I understand your predicament," Emperor Jiajing sighed. "It's also a tough situation for me. We'll just have to do the best we can."

The Prince of Yu and Yan Song dropped to their knees. "It is our responsibility to serve you with all our heart," they chanted.

"Oh, I forgot about that Tan Lung," Emperor Jiajing said to the prince. "Keep him in Zhejiang and, as you wish, let him continue with his training there."

With that, Emperor Jiajing waved his long sleeves in the air and headed for his meditation room. "Beat your drums and hawk your sweets, we each return to our own trade and profession," he chanted.

"Long live His Majesty," all the attendants chanted after him.

Once everyone had left the palace, Emperor Jiajing sat cross-legged on his meditation cushion to prepare for his daily practice. Lu put on a pair of thick cotton gloves and pulled out a small tea kettle from the enormous bronze incense burner. Before putting the lid on the burner, Lu tossed a few pieces of sandalwood in there. Then, he carried the tea kettle to the table, poured some warm water into a brown clay cup and presented the water, along with a medicine box, to Emperor Jiajing.

"Master, it's time to take your immortality pills," he spoke softly.

Emperor Jiajing slowly opened his eyes, and, with three of his slender fingers, he pinched a bright red pill from the medicine box and swallowed it down with water. Then, instead of resuming his meditation right away, he asked, "Tell me which faction do you think Hu Zongxian belongs to? He's certainly tricked all of us."

"I don't think anyone dares to trick Your Majesty," Lu replied matter-of-factly. "I think he's stuck in the middle."

"Oh well, he's in a tough place," Emperor Jiajing observed.

"More tough days are awaiting him," Lu answered, while wiping the water marks on the table with a piece of cloth. "I don't think the grand secretary will trust him again. Based on his personal character, I doubt he'll join the other faction led by Gao Gong and Zhang Juzheng. While maintaining stability and keeping the farmers from rebelling, he also needs to implement the land-conversion policy. It will be tough because neither Yan Song's nor the Prince of Yu's side will trust him. Even if he doesn't work himself to death, he'll worry himself to death."

"The Imperial Palace cannot sustain itself without the stability of the southeastern region, and the stability of that region cannot be maintained without Governor Hu," Emperor Jiajing commented. "We need to defeat the pirates and appease the farmers. Let's make sure that he's not burned out fast. At the moment, we're relying on Yan Shifan to bring in more money and replenish the treasury. I don't mind if he takes a twenty per cent cut on the money he brings in. I can even turn a blind eye to it if he takes a thirty per cent cut. But if he becomes greedier, and if he cannot even tolerate a competent and honest official like Governor Hu, he'll have to face the consequences. If farmers in Zhejiang feel squeezed amid the land merger and start rebelling against the Imperial Government, I'm going to hold Yan Shifan responsible. It is good that the Prince of Yu has sent Tan Lun over to keep an eye on Yan Shifan's appointees. We need to protect Hu Zongxian. At the same time, we should recruit more people like Tan Lun. Please relay a message to the Prince of Yu, telling him in private that he has my permission to dispatch more of his people to Zhejiang."

"Yes, Your Majesty," Lu Fang replied.

"Please tell your boy, Yang Jinshui, not to create trouble for Governor Hu."

"Understood, Your Majesty."

5

Having recently advanced from his position as a mere editor at the Hanlin Academy to become the mayor of Hangzhou, Gao Hanwen felt more anxious than elated, especially after he received notice that Yan Shifan, known as the grand secretary junior, had summoned him for a meeting at the Yan Mansion.

At his office, Yan Shifan looked visibly pleased with himself for securing what he believed was an ideal candidate to fill the Hangzhou mayor's position vacated by the disgraced Ma Ningyuan, who had been executed by Governor Hu for his role in the dam-breaking scandal. In his self-congratulatory mood, Yan Shifan even assumed the air of an eager mentor who thirsted for and respected young talents. His unusually amicable attitude put Gao Hanwen somewhat at ease, mollifying some of his earlier fears. He felt less rigid, and his smile seemed less contrived.

Taking a box from an expansive mahogany cabinet with both hands, Yan Shifan stepped up to Gao, who quickly rose to his feet.

"Oh, please sit," Yan Shifan motioned to Gao while opening the box, which revealed four smaller similar boxes inside. Luo Wenlong and Mao Qing, both of whom were present, grinned at one another knowingly. Among the four smaller boxes, Yan Shifan slowly removed the lid from a thin rectangular one and plucked out a calligraphy brush which, from a mere glance, looked exquisite. The handle, as thick as that of an ordinary inkbrush, looked like it was made from mottle bamboo, with bluish black spots covering its body. The brush was securely sheathed in a jade cap – a piece of pointed Hotian jade with a hollow interior. "This pen handle was made from a rhinoceros horn that explorer and diplomat Zheng He had brought back from his overseas expedition one hundred and forty years ago," Yan Shifan boasted. "Since then, we haven't seen such a perfect-sized rhinoceros horn. The jade cap is quite ordinary, a piece of carved jade for good luck."

Pulling off the cap, Yan Shifan showed off a shiny red inkbrush. "It's made from a type of rare animal hair," he said. "About thirty years ago, a tribal leader in the province of Yunnan captured a rare weasel and shipped it to us as a gift. This brush came from the hair of the weasel's tail. I've shown the weasel to many experts. They all said it was a very precious specimen, one that is only seen in a thousand years. I'm not asking you to use it. Since you come from a family of scholars, you should keep it as an antique that can be passed on to future generations."

Gao's eyes sparkled. Yan Shifan placed the pen in the rectangular box and handed it over to Gao, who was overwhelmed with gratitude. "There are four identical calligraphy brushes in this box. They are all yours," Yan Shifan said before opening another box. "Here is a piece of ink stick from the Song dynasty, with Mi Nangong's[1] signature carved on it, an inkstone with Huang Tingjian's[2] signature engraved on it, and a stack of papers autographed by Li Qingzhao.[3] These are yours. Go and admire them in the comfort of your home."

Gao held the gift box and stood there in a daze. "My dear teacher, I can't accept these precious gifts," he said while declining to take the antique ink stick, the inkstone and the papers.

"I insist," Yan Shifan said while putting the gifts back in the boxes.

"It's like awarding a precious dagger to a warrior," Mao Qing observed. "In our Hanlin Academy today, there aren't too many scholars who deserve this gift. It shows that the grand secretary junior has full confidence in you. Please accept the gifts."

With trembling hands, Gao accepted the gifts, which prompted

Luo to joke in a melodramatic tone. "Oh well, well, these have long been my coveted items, and I've begged the grand secretary junior multiple times to gift them to me, but he never did. I guess he's found new talents, and it's time for us to retire."

Flushed with embarrassment, Gao quickly presented the gift box to Luo. "If that's the situation, I think you should take them," he pleaded.

"Oh, no, no, you'd better keep them," Luo declined. "You have a big job ahead of you. Implementing the rice-to-mulberry land-conversion programme in Zhejiang is a key initiative that is beyond my ability. When you succeed at the end of the year, we'll be waiting to hear your good news and read your report written with the brush and the ink stick."

Gao fell on his knees. "Thank you for your generosity, Teacher Yan, and two of my respected superiors. You can rest assured that I will get it done for the Imperial Court. If I can't accomplish the task in one year, I'll use the inkbrush and paper to write my own obituary," he pledged.

Yan Shifan helped him up. "I'm sure you'll do a good job and return with flying colours," he encouraged. "You will be rewarded in due time."

Gao nodded with tears shimmering in his eyes.

明

Zhang Juzheng, the deputy minister of defence, went to see the Prince of Yu right after the Privy Council meeting.

Tan Lun, who was also at the mansion, rose from his chair and asked in earnest, "What is the verdict?"

Even though the Prince of Yu did not appear too eager, his searching eyes glimmered with curiosity.

"The outcome had already been predetermined, and it didn't really make any difference whether we discussed it or not," Zhang complained.

Silence fell upon the room.

"Shouldn't the council at least grant Governor Hu's request to allocate more food subsidies for flood victims in Zhejiang Province," the prince spoke up.

Zhang shook his head.

The prince rose to his feet, appearing indignant. "Did the council say why?"

"It's quite obvious, isn't it?" Zhang said. "By refusing to grant food subsidies, they can drive down the land prices, allowing the large silk producers in Zhejiang to barter prime farmland with a tiny amount of grain. It's a blatant land-merger scheme in the name of helping flood victims with the land-conversion programme and killing two birds with one stone."

"Didn't you all speak up at the meeting?" the prince questioned.

Zhang did not answer.

"Where are Xu Jie and Gao Gong now?" the prince said, noticing the absence of his two advisers.

"Governor Hu refused to give up and dragged Xu Jie and Gao Gong to the Ministry of Revenue," Zhang explained. "He's hoping that the ministry could allocate some disaster relief fund for Zhejiang Province."

"Can the ministry do something about it?" asked the prince.

Gazing into the prince's eyes, Zhang fell into silence again.

Having realised that he had posed a redundant question, the Prince of Yu waved his hand dismissively and mumbled to himself, "I should know better about the Ministry of Revenue. They are not allowed to provide the funds Governor Hu needs."

"Your Highness, you might not want to hear this, but we wouldn't allocate the money to Zhejiang even if we could."

"What do you mean?" the prince asked, looking baffled.

"Why don't we simply allow Zhejiang to fall into chaos?" Zhang responded emphatically.

The prince widened his eyes in disbelief.

"We have reached the point where I need to share with you what my peers are thinking," said Zhang. "The Yan family has monopolised political power for twenty years. They are rotten to the core. They are able to get away with it because they flatter and curry favour with His Majesty. As a consequence, the palace staff's unrestrained and extravagant spending and rampant corruption at every level of the government have caused us such a huge budget deficit. Your Highness knows as well as we do that the rice-to-mulberry conversion policy is a desperate attempt on their part to fill the gap. But this is such a major undertaking, and even Governor Hu doesn't think they can fully implement the programme in one year. But those folks in the Yan Mansion can't wait that long. Their cronies also want to exploit the policy for their own personal gains. That's how they came up with the wicked flooding scheme.

"Even though they're snatching the food out of the mouths of ordinary people, they are eating away at the foundation of our empire. These are obvious facts, but the Imperial Court is turning a blind eye to such blatant robbery. Fortunately, we have Governor Hu who dares to speak out against it – he is also doing this for the good of the Yan family, but they now see him as an arch foe. The fact that they won't tolerate Governor Hu shows that they're at their wits' end. Your Highness, it's better to suffer the short-term pain than the long-term torture. Why don't we just allow Zhejiang to fall into chaos, just like the way we let a piece of our flesh become gangrenous. That'll get people's attention, making it easier for us to cut out the piece of rotten flesh and drain the abscess."

Zhang's rousing remarks prompted excitement as well as consternation. "Do Xu Jie and Gao Gong share your view?" the prince asked.

"Yes, absolutely," Zhang replied.

The prince turned to Tan Lun. "What do you think?"

Tan Lun rose from his chair and replied, "It is a wise strategy, but ordinary folks in Zhejiang will have to suffer on their account."

Suddenly, Tan stopped, turning his gaze into the prince's inner chamber – someone shuffled out of there. He quickly lowered his head. So did Zhang.

It was Princess Li who sauntered in with their son in her arms. "What are you doing here with our son?" the prince said in a tone that denoted displeasure. "We're in the middle of a meeting."

"Nothing in particular – I just want you to hold our baby," said Princess Li with a serious look as she handed him their son

"Oh for heaven's sake, what are you trying to prove here?" asked the Prince of Yu, who grew impatient but had no choice but take the baby.

"I just want to ask Your Highness a simple question," said Princess Li calmly. "How many sons do you have?"

"Don't beat around the bush. Tell me what you are trying to get at."

"Your humble wife wants Your Highness to answer this question," Princess Li insisted.

"Isn't it obvious that we only have one son?"

"It might be presumptuous for me to say, but your answer is both right and wrong," the princess claimed.

Zhang Juzheng and Tan Lun, who always held her in high esteem for her intelligence and insightful comments, raised their heads with the knowledge that she had something up her sleeve and was about to reveal it.

The princess faced the three men. "I happened to overhear what you discussed. I understand that some problems cannot be resolved in the short-term, but one should never forget the fact that every inch of this land and every person living on this land are part of our Ming empire. Your Highness is the crown prince, and the boy you are holding in your arms will be inheriting the empire from you. Based on this assumption alone, you should think afar to ensure that you and your son inherit an empire where the ruler has the wholehearted support of his subjects."

These words caught the prince's attention.

"This is what I meant when I just said that Your Highness was both right and wrong," Princess Li continued. "As the crown prince and future emperor, you will govern these people, who will also be the loyal subjects of your son. Therefore, how can a future emperor stand idle when his own people are suffering? Governor Hu knows how to take care of the people under his jurisdiction. What about Your Highness? And all of you here? Do you think you can do better than Governor Hu?"

The three men in the room looked at one another, flickers of guilt and embarrassment, typical with men in front of their female matches, passed through their faces. Oblivious to their reaction, the princess continued, "The Ming empire does not belong to the Yan family. Neither to those corrupted officials and wicked merchants. They can ruthlessly exploit and oppress the common people, but Your Highness, and your righteous officials, cannot simply watch passively without doing anything."

"This is the true spirit of righteousness," Zhang praised enthusiastically. "The princess's remarkable words put my peers and me to shame. She is right. Even though the dire situation in Zhejiang Province is irrevocable, we need to fight, piece by piece, for those flood victims. We cannot let the flood erode our support from those ordinary folks, who constitute the very foundation of our empire."

The Prince of Yu handed the baby back to Princess Li with a look of approval and affection before speaking to Tan Lun. "You've been in Zhejiang Province for quite some time," the prince said. "Can you figure out a way that we can help Governor Hu and alleviate, if possible, the suffering of the flood victims?"

"I think there is only one thing – I can help to make sure that local officials and big silk merchants don't take advantage of the disaster and acquire farmers' land on the cheap," Tan Lun said contemplatively. "To do this, we need to secure enough grain for the victims and tide them over until next year. I discussed this with Governor Hu before our trip. If the palace cannot provide timely help for the victims, he and I will go to the city of Nanjing and borrow some grain from Governor Zhao Zhenji."

The Prince of Yu nodded. "That might work. Zhao is also the imperial inspector in Nanjing. If I remember correctly, he's been friends with Governor Hu for years. I doubt it's going to be a problem if Governor Hu merely asks for a loan."

"Even if we get the loan, we still won't be able to stop the massive land acquisition," Tan Lun pointed out. "Now that Governor Hu is no longer the imperial inspector, some of the disaster relief supplies will be handled by Hu's deputy Zheng Bichang and the magistrates. Governor Hu ordered the execution of the Hangzhou mayor and two magistrates. If the Yan family appoints two of their people to take over these posts, the disaster relief supplies will no doubt be hijacked before they get into the hands of the victims."

"Have they appointed anyone to be the mayor of Hangzhou?" the prince asked.

"Yes, they picked one of Yan Shifan's protégés," replied Zhang. "His name is Gao Hanwen, an editor at the Hanlin Academy."

"Didn't he score the third in last year's Imperial Examination? Doesn't he consider himself a true follower of neo-Confucianism?" asked the Prince of Yu.

"Yes, that's him," Zhang said. "The Yan faction carried out an extensive search before they found him. This person has written several influential articles on neo-Confucianism. In comparison with other corrupt officials, he has a relatively clean record. At the meeting, Yan Shifan praised him to the sky. He's the one who came up with the idea to use the land-conversion policy to both accommodate the challenges of disaster relief and ease the budget deficit."

"If this person takes over the city of Hangzhou, and Zheng Bichang becomes the new imperial inspector of Zhejiang, the whole province is bound to be in chaos," the prince brooded.

"What about the other two counties, Chun'an and Jiande?" Princess Li interjected again.

"These two positions are still vacant," Zhang replied. "The Privy Council has entrusted Zheng Bichang and Gao Hanwen to pick candidates of their own choosing."

"Can we find two capable and honest men to fill the positions?" Princess Li asked.

"What's the point?" the prince argued. "These two magistrates will be reporting to the provincial imperial inspector and the mayor of Hangzhou, both of whom are Yan's surrogates. It would probably be a waste of effort."

"No, it's not," Tan Lun disagreed. "The princess's suggestion makes a lot of sense because county chiefs are critical. They deal with the grassroots. At the moment, Chun'an County has been completely flooded, and half of Jiande is under water. The greedy merchants are eyeing the prime farmland in these two counties, waiting to snatch it away from farmers. If the magistrates, especially the one leading Chun'an, really want to help ordinary folks, simply being nice is not enough. They have to be prepared to fight their superiors. Whoever is appointed has to be willing to sacrifice his life, if necessary."

"In our country today, it's hard to find someone like this..." Zhang sighed.

Silence fell.

"I have someone here who might fit the profile," Tan Lun said after a long pause.

"Who? Where? Bring him over now," the Prince of Yu said eagerly.

"I'm afraid that it wouldn't be possible to summon him here immediately," Tan Lun explained. "We might not be able to meet this person, but I can read you an article he has written on the harmful impact of land monopolies by the wealthy. Are you interested in hearing what he has to say?"

"Where is the article?" Zhang asked.

"Who would carry the physical article with him?" Tan Lun said. "Since this one was well-written, I have memorised it. If you like, I can recite a few paragraphs."

Seeing that the Prince of Yu was nodding, Tan Lun collected himself and began. "When a couple begets a son, they shoulder the responsibility of raising and nurturing the child. When heaven brings a person to the world, nature provides him with food and protection so he can survive. We call this nature's law of existence or even the basic principles of human existence. Is it not a violation of heaven's law and basic humanity to allow a few people to rob hundreds and thousands of people of their land, reducing them to hunger and abject poverty? Ignoring heaven's law and degrading humanity lead to chaos. When the people lose their land, the rulers will inevitably lose the support of their subjects. I don't know of an empire that can still prevent chaos and survive when it loses the support of its people."

"Wait," Zhang stopped Tan Lun. "The last few lines sound familiar."

"You are right," Tan Lun agreed. "Governor Hu modified them slightly and quoted them in his report. Hu's version reads, 'People without land will not support the ruling government. A government without the support of its people will be toppled.'"

"Excellent," Zhang patted his balled fist on his thigh and exclaimed. "Who is the author? Where is he now?"

The prince and his wife were also waiting for Tan Lun to answer.

"His name is Hai Rui, and he's currently a schoolmaster in Nanping County in Fujian Province."

"It shouldn't be a problem," Zhang championed with greater gusto. "Promoting a well-educated schoolmaster to the position of a mayor is a legitimate move. Your Highness, I personally think this person can be our precious dagger. He might not be able to rescue people from misery, but at least he could contain and combat the Yan faction with force. Could you recommend him to the Ministry of Personnel, urging them to send Hai Rui to Chun'an County immediately."

"Yes, I'll talk with the Ministry of Personnel," said the prince, nodding in agreement. "Sounds like he's a rare talent."

"Things might not be that simple," Tan Lun cautioned.

This threw a bit of cold water on the plan, taking everyone by surprise.

"What are the challenges?" Zhang enquired. "This is a legitimate promotion unless he himself declines it."

"It's easy to justify the promotion and persuade the Ministry of Personnel, but I am not sure if we can convince Hai Rui himself to accept the position," Tan Lun explained. "I know something about his personal character. If he's willing to take up a cause, nobody can stop him. However, if he's unwilling, nothing can change him. Political power never appeals to him. If we can spell out the significance of this appointment, making him realise that he can put into practice what he has written, I have no doubt that he would take it. But there's one hurdle that I don't know if he can cross."

"What is it?"

"His filial obligation," Tan Lun said.

Intrigued by the assumption, Princess Li asked, "Could you give us some more details?"

"Hai Rui was born in Hainan Province. At the age of four, the death of his father plunged his family into poverty," Tan stated. "His mother raised him by working for a clothing mill. He attended school and became a certified scholar in the county. When he was young, he harboured strong aspirations to right the wrongs in this world and wrote some remarkable essays. After his failed attempts to excel in the Imperial Examination, which could qualify him for senior government positions, he lost interest in politics and decided to devote his energies to taking care of his mother. You probably won't believe me if I tell you this – even though he's in his forties, he sleeps in his mother's room twenty-two nights out of a month."

"Isn't he married?" Princess Li asked curiously.

"This is a critical element for us to consider," Tan Lun added. "Yes, he is married because he's the only child in the Hai family clan. But, at the moment, he only has a daughter. If he takes the offer as the magistrate of Chun'an, the likelihood of him returning home is almost nil. It's like sending a warrior to the battlefield. If he goes, he won't be able to take care of his mother and produce a male heir for the Hai family."

Silence fell.

"Let's draft a letter and send it along with the appointment letter from the Ministry of Personnel," Zhang suggested. "We'll urge him to substitute his filial piety with loyalty to the country."

Tan Lun hesitated. "I can draft a letter, but I can't guarantee that it would convince him to serve," he said.

"Let's write it together," Zhang volunteered. "I can at least prepare the ink for you." He walked over to the prince's desk and poured a few drops of water on the inkstone before rubbing an ink stick on it. Tan Lun paced up and down, contemplating what to write in the letter. Once the ink thickened, Zhang retreated to the side while Tan Lun took over with his inkbrush and began writing. He finished it before everyone had time to finish a cup of tea. The Prince of Yu and Princess Li leaned over and nodded their heads approvingly. But when Tan handed it to Zhang, he expressed some reservations. "I like the first part," he said. "The second half needs a boost. Why don't I take a stab at it."

Zhang dictated his words, and Tan Lun jotted them down:

You used to harbour the aspiration to rid the world of injustices and bring the people out of misery. But at the age of forty, you have not been granted the opportunity. A pearl lay hidden in a corner, and it was piteous that none in this world discovered your talent. Heaven might have intended for you to step out and show your outstanding talent today. In the county of Chun'an, thousands of farmers live in abject misery, and they look forward to your leadership, like they do with clouds and rain during a famine, like an orphan craves the presence of their parents. With wild beasts running rampant, would you prefer to keep your dagger idle inside its sheath or would you rather use it to behead the ferocious monsters? Even if you die on the job in Zhejiang, your mother would be the mother of all people in our country and your daughter will be the daughter of all people. I'm aware of the fact that the Hai family has no heir, but your family name will be revered in temples; the incense and candles will never die off, and your life story will inspire generations to come.

"Wonderful," the Prince of Yu exclaimed while the princess grinned; a flicker of admiration, reserved by a young woman for a talented young man, flashed across her eyes.

By then, Tan Lun had finished transcribing it; his head was covered with dripping sweat. "Your literary talent is truly worthy of its stellar reputation," Tan Lun praised. "This passage goes hand-in-hand with Hai Rui's essay, like two shining stars hanging side by side. This letter has given me hope that he will take the job. But, on the other hand, I'm afraid that if for some reason this precious dagger breaks itself in Chun'an County, I will have another mother to take care of."

"If anything happens, we can bring his mother to the palace and take care of her here."

An old woman's unbound feet revealed themselves underneath the light blue cloth pantaloon skirt. They planted squarely on a stone slab next to a well. The grey-haired woman was pulling a hemp rope with both hands, trying to draw water from the well. Soon, a bucket was lifted in mid-air, filled to the brim with water. Holding the rope with one hand, she reached out the other to grab the bucket by the handle. Then, she poured the water into one of the two empty buckets on the floor next to her. The whole manoeuvre seemed a bit laborious, but she handled it skilfully.

As she was trying to put the bucket back and let it drop into the well, a man, who stood by her, grabbed the bucket from her hands, but she resisted. "I can do it," the woman insisted; her voice was soft but authoritative. At her persistence, the man let go of the bucket.

He was a mild-mannered man in his forties, and the elderly woman was his mother. Holding onto a shoulder pole with chain hooks on both ends, he looked on helplessly. When the old lady filled up her own buckets from the well, the son rushed over, trying to hook the buckets by their handles to his shoulder pole.

"Oh, I don't need shoulder poles," she waved her hand dismissively. "Put that away."

"Amah, I've told you many times that you can't do this alone," the middle-aged man persuaded, as he slowly unhooked the bucket. "Let your son carry the buckets."

Ignoring the man's plea, the elderly woman hoisted the two buckets, one in each hand, and walked over to her house in big strides.

Shaking his head helplessly, the man picked up his clanking shoulder pole and followed his mother.

Inside the house, a middle-aged woman removed the lid from a steamer on the stove. A plume of white steam rose, spreading through the room. Seeing that the steamer was packed with rice cakes wrapped in lotus leaves, a little girl, about five years old, jumped up and down, her eyes sparkling with excitement. "Mummy, Mummy, rice cakes, why so many?" Her mother wiped the sweat off her forehead with the back of her hand and picked up a cake from the steamer, flipping it in her hands as she tried to cool it off.

"These are for Daddy," she said, with a hint of sadness in her voice. "He's going on a long trip. Don't touch them today. Mummy can make some more tomorrow. Take this one to Grandma."

The girl, who was salivating over the cakes, nodded quietly.

Cupping the rice cake with both hands, she dashed out. In the courtyard, she saw her father, the middle-aged man, standing outside her grandmother's room with a shoulder pole in his hands. The girl slowed down and crept up to him. Suddenly, loud sounds of water splashing that came from inside the room startled her – her grandmother was scrubbing the floor again. Drops of dirty water splattered outside. The middle-aged man motioned to his daughter with his eyes, asking her to carry the rice cake inside.

The little girl stood at the door and shouted to her grandmother, "Granny, here is a piece of rice cake for you."

There was silence.

"What rice cake?" the elderly woman finally spoke up.

"Rice cake in lotus leaves," the little girl answered. "Mummy has steamed a big bunch. She says they are for daddy. He's going on a long trip."

"Who says your daddy is going on a long trip?" the elderly woman asked in a stern voice, which stunned the little girl.

"I heard it from Mummy," she mumbled.

The elderly woman stepped out. "Over my dead body."

The middle-aged man immediately fell to his knees. The little girl followed suit.

It was in the early evening and darkness was descending.

The official appointment letter, along with Tan Lun's note, had reached the government office in Nanping, Fujian, and an official there had delivered the mail to Hai Rui in person. When Hai Rui's mother learned about it, her face fell, and, for several days, she seldom talked to her son. As a way to vent her displeasure, she would fetch water from the well and then lock herself up inside, scrubbing the floor multiple times a day.

The starting date for Hai Rui's new job was approaching fast. The day before his scheduled departure, Hai decided to have a sensible conversation with his mother, but...

Now, the whole courtyard was enveloped in darkness. A crescent moon hovered over the south wall which was covered with sprawling vines. Crickets hidden inside the weeds started chirping.

Inside Hai's bedroom, a small stack of books and manuscripts, along with a few sets of neatly folded clothes, lay on top of a blue sheet on his bed. His wife sat distractedly by a lamp with a pea-sized oil flame. When Hai Rui stepped in, carrying his daughter in his arms, his wife rose and took the little girl from her father. The couple did not speak to each other. Hai walked over to a big armoire that stood against a wall and picked out a thin light blue quilt. As he stepped out, his wife asked from behind, "Are you still planning to leave tomorrow?"

Hai paused. Without answering, he kept on walking.

Outside his mother's room, Hai removed his shoes, placing them carefully near the doorstep. Then, he fumbled his way in and struck a match to light up an oil lamp on a small wooden table. The lamp gave out a faint glow. Putting down his quilt on a cot next to the table, Hai Rui glanced impishly at a bed across the room. His mother was curled up in bed quietly. A thick linen mosquito net was left wide open and her quilt was untouched. Hai tiptoed over and cautiously put the quilt over her body, leaving her big feet uncovered. His mother remained motionless. Hai grabbed a wooden stool and sat by the side of the bed.

A breeze rustled the leaves outside, and the sounds of bugs rose and fell. A few mosquitoes buzzed around the flickering lamp. Hai picked up a cattail-leaf fan, waving it vigorously to drive the mosquitoes out of the net before sealing it. "Leave the net open," his mother suddenly spoke up, with her back towards him.

Hai obeyed.

"Let me ask you a question," she asked without moving her body.

"All right," Hai replied, realising that his mother was wide awake.

"Tell me again what the letter says."

Hai pulled Tan Lun's note out of his pocket and planned to read it.

"I don't want you to repeat the high-sounding words," she stopped him. "I want you to tell me in your own words what this appointment is all about."

"All right, Amah," Hai complied. "Do you know how much grain you can get when you sell a mu of farmland?"

"During a bad harvest year, you can probably get three thousand kilograms of grain, so probably twenty-four thousand," she answered promptly. "Why are you asking this?"

"In Chun'an County in Zhejiang Province, where I'm going to work, farmers can only get five hundred kilograms of grain for a mu of land."

"They must have an abundance of land there," his mother said.

"Not really," Hai answered. "There's an old saying about Zhejiang Province – seventy per cent mountains, twenty per cent water and only ten per cent farmland. In other words, farmland is fairly precious there. On average, there's about one mu of land for each person."

"Then why is it that land is selling so cheap there?"

"Farmers are forced to do it."

"How?" Amah suddenly sat up to face her son.

Hai helped her move to the edge of the bed before answering her question. "Government officials and wealthy silk producers are bullying farmers there," he explained. "The Imperial Palace has run out of money. So the government is planning to convert the farmland in Zhejiang into mulberry fields so we can produce more silk, export it and make more money to replenish the treasury. Some officials at the South China Textile Bureau and large wealthy silk merchants there see this as a big opportunity to make a major killing. In order to force farmers to give away all of their farmland and sell it at cheap prices, local officials have colluded with big silk merchants. They deliberately damaged the dams during the rainy season, causing severe flooding in two counties. Many people have lost everything in the flood, but the local government won't loan them any grain to help tide them over. So farmers have no choice but to sell their farmland."

"How could the Imperial Palace allow such a scandalous thing to happen without intervening?" Hai's mother asked.

Hai Rui didn't answer.

"Answer me," his mother pressed him.

"I'm afraid it'll make you more concerned," the son said timidly.

"Tell me first," she insisted.

"The fact is, several people in the Imperial Palace know about this scheme," Hai said, dropping his eyes to the floor.

Shocked, Hai's mother asked, "Are you saying that the schemers have the approval of the Imperial Palace?"

"Well, yes," Hai confirmed. "I think several powerful people in Beijing, including the grand secretary and his cronies and a few people at the Interior Ministry are masterminding this."

Amah's eyes widened. She sat there, contemplating something. Then, out of the blue, she began rummaging through her quilt.

"Amah, what are you looking for?" Hai asked.

"The letter you showed me," she answered.

"I have it here," Hai said, bringing out the letter from his pocket and handing it to her.

She gazed at the letter with intensity. The faint glow from the small lamp on the table made it impossible to read, but it was apparent that she had not intended to read the words. It seemed that she wanted to penetrate the letter, trying to find something that she could feel but hadn't been able to articulate.

Hai understood her impulse. "The people who have written to me are loyal and honest officials," Hai said softly. "They're the ones who have made the arrangement for me to be the magistrate in Chun'an."

"They have designated you as their representative to fight those corrupt officials?" Hai Rui's mother said without taking her eyes off the letter.

Hai nodded.

"Why can't they pick someone in a senior position to take up the fight?" Amah shifted her gaze to her son. "Why do they send a mere magistrate to do the job?"

Like a sharpened cleaver, these simple words cut in half the befuddled mess that lingered in his mind, enabling him to discover many clues. However, as he pondered more, the clues themselves became entangled with others, forming two more piles of mess that he found impossible to sort out. Hai simply sat there, without knowing what to say.

"Why don't you answer me?"

"Amah, I'm sure the situation is more complex than we think, and I don't have a good grasp of it now," Hai admitted.

"Then why do you still promise them to go before you sort out everything?"

"Several hundred thousand people are affected, and nobody is willing to speak for them and seek justice for them. For this reason alone, I have decided to go."

"Why would they pick you?"

"Because they know that your son will go all out to fight for ordinary folks."

Silence fell. The crickets outside had stopped chirping. In the room next door, Hai's wife could be heard singing a lullaby to their daughter: *The sun is taking a rest, isn't it? Yes, it is. The moon is taking a rest, isn't it? Yes, it is... My little girl is taking a rest, isn't she, yes she is... Amah is taking a rest, isn't she, yes she is...*

Amah slowly stretched out her hands and tightly grabbed her son's.

The lullaby, melancholy and sad, continued in the other room: *When Amah is in bed, the sun dims and the moon also dims...*

"Why is it that the heavenly god always subjects all mothers in the world to such misery?" Amah mumbled, her eyes staring at the lamp distractedly.

Hai tightened his grip on his mother's hand.

"Why don't you go and bring Amah a bucket of water?" she said.

Hai hurried out. A few moments later, he returned to the courtyard, carrying two buckets of water on his shoulder pole. Removing his robe and shoes, and rolling up his trouser legs, he scooped out some water from the bucket and poured it onto the brick floor.

His mother got off her bed and said, "Why don't I pour the water and you scrub the floor?"

Reluctantly, Hai handed the ladle to his mother who scooped up the water and poured it onto the brick floor. Hai swept the water with a broom made of palm leaves. The water on the floor glistened with the lights from the oil lamp. The moon cast a faint glow on their bare feet.

"Do you know which part of you comes directly from me?" Amah asked.

"You have given me everything," Hai replied.

"No, I'm asking which part of your body resembles mine?"

Hai did not know. He wiped the water on the floor without answering.

"You have my feet," Amah reminded. "We both have big feet that are hot all year round, even in the winter. The doctor said that people with hot feet have too much internal heat and tend to be warm-hearted and hot-tempered. For this, you really take after Amah."

"I know that my ancestors were true followers of the Ming Jiao," Hai added. "Its core principle was to burn up yourself to warm others."

"I have been told that the founder of our Ming empire was also a believer of the Ming Jiao," Amah said. "That is why he named his empire Ming, isn't it?"

"Yes, Amah."

"Why is it that our current ruler doesn't act like the founder of Ming?" Amah asked.

Without knowing how to answer that question, Hai bent over and resumed scrubbing.

"Let's call it a night," Amah finally said, putting the ladle in the bucket.

"Why don't you go to bed first? After I clean up, I'll keep you company tonight."

"Bring your daughter over. You don't need to be here," Amah said with a sigh.

Hai stood there, with his head down.

"If the heavenly god has mercy, he will give us a boy tonight to carry the family name," prayed Amah.

At the crack of dawn, the stars scattered in the sky still twinkled brightly. In the Hai family courtyard, three people stood facing each other silently. With a bundle of clothes and an umbrella in his left hand and a small bamboo basket of rice cakes in his right hand, Hai bid goodbye to his mother and then his wife, who kept her eyes to the ground.

"Amah, I have to go now," he said, but his feet refused to move. Amah looked at her son, speechless.

"Please take care of Amah for me," said Hai as he turned to his wife. She nodded.

"You really should get going now," Amah urged. Hai Rui put his luggage on the ground and dropped to his knees. His wife followed suit. He kowtowed three times, and by the time he finished he noticed that his amah had already stepped away to avoid a sentimental farewell. Hai paused, his eyes glistening.

"Do you want to say goodbye to our daughter?" his wife asked, tears streaming down her cheeks. Hai shook his head. Grabbing his luggage from the ground, he rose and strode towards the door.

"Daddy!" His daughter's cry, which pierced through the early-morning quietude, tugged at his heart. He turned his head and saw the little girl standing at the living room door. He turned around to face her and his daughter scampered towards him. Once again, he put down his luggage and hugged his little girl.

"Is Daddy coming to fetch me later?" his daughter sobbed.

"Yes, Daddy will come back to fetch you soon," he promised. Reaching his hand into his basket, he brought out a rice cake and stuck it into her hand.

"Daddy, you should have it because you're going on a long trip," the little girl said.

"But Daddy wants you to take it," he insisted.

His wife came over and picked up the little girl from the ground. Hai reloaded his luggage into his arms, took one more look at his wife and daughter, and then marched through the narrow courtyard entrance.

明

In Beijing, Gao Hanwen, the new mayor of Hangzhou, left with an impressive entourage, creating quite a spectacle. His carriage was flanked on each side by a guard on horseback. At the front, four soldiers on horses led the way, and four more followed behind. Gao's entourage traversed several provinces, and, at each rest stop, special personnel had been instructed to greet the entourage and change horses for them, providing the best stallions they had. Such royal treatment, unprecedented for a mayor, was meticulously arranged by Yan Shifan, but outsiders saw it as the works of the

Privy Council. Before Gao even reached Hangzhou, his reputation preceded him. His arrival heralded the Imperial Palace's determination to make the rice-to-mulberry conversion a success.

Inside his carriage, Gao's mind remained as turbulent as his ride. It had been barely four years since he passed the Imperial Examination and joined the Hanlin Academy. Securing this appointment as the mayor of Hangzhou was a milestone for him, an avid follower of the political philosophy of Mencius, who urged rulers to provide material conditions for the livelihood of common citizens and moral and educational guidance for their edification. Throughout his life, Gao had been pursuing the dream of becoming a politician, like he was today, who travelled with an entourage of guards and horses, and made decisions that affected people the world over. Yan Shifan had made his dream come true, plucking him from obscurity, offering him a rare opportunity to put his abilities to good use. However, given that many Confucian scholars and members of the "Clean Stream" faction within the palace took a dim view of the Yan family, Gao was concerned that this appointment might have tainted his reputation.

He had been tasked with implementing the rice-to-mulberry conversion policy while appeasing several hundred thousand flood victims. Even Hu Zongxian, renowned for his political experience and ability, felt at the end of his wits. Would he be able to accomplish anything? If, by a stroke of luck, he succeeded in the land-conversion programme, he was unsure how farmers would react to it. How would the emperor and the rest of the Imperial Palace treat him if farmers rioted for the loss of their land? He did not even want to think about it.

Despite the trepidation, he decided to take the job because the monotonous and neglected life at the Hanlin Academy had become unbearable. After all, one nurtured one's talent and aspiration for the purpose of applying them someday. Even though the road to success was paved with perils, it was still worth it. Such thoughts motivated him. He ordered his entourage to travel night and day without a break. It was late May, and the scalding sun made it unbearably hot inside the carriage. He removed the top of the carriage and took down the curtains. At times, when the carriage was accelerating, he would stand with both hands holding the horizontal bar. The hot air assaulted his face, sending his baggy robe flying. He felt both inspired but also apprehensive, like a warrior going to his death.

The horses were galloping. For most of the trip, the thrash of his carriage seemed to have jolted the soul out of his body, and he allowed his mind to roam freely. Suddenly, the carriage slowed down, and the breeze that fanned his cheeks stopped. Waking up from his reverie, he found himself in front of a small inn. "Why don't we take a short break here?" he suggested.

His guards led their horses into the courtyard but paused at the entrance. The inn served as a relay station for the Imperial Palace. A dozen or so horses sauntered around the small courtyard, and a few uniformed guards were feeding and washing the animals. There was hardly any space left.

Gao's personal aide got out and asked, "What is happening inside?"

The guards did not answer. Instead, they urged him to go in and survey the situation himself.

Gao's aide stepped into the yard and yelled, "We're from the capital city. Do you know who's in charge here?"

People went about their business, feeding and washing their horses, and nobody answered him. The aide raised his voice. "Anybody in charge here?"

There was silence. By then, Gao Hanwen had stepped in. An innkeeper emerged from inside the stable and greeted Gao. "I've met Your Honour before," he said with a grimace.

"His honour has been appointed mayor of Hangzhou, and we're passing through here," said the aide. "Why is it that nobody comes out to take care of our horses?"

"As you can see, another official got here first, and we're taking care of them," replied the innkeeper. "We're out of feed now. We have to make do with our own food to keep the horses going."

Gao and his aides glanced at the troughs and noticed millet and beans, over which the horses were fighting.

"I don't care what the situation is – our horses can't leave here with empty stomachs," said the aide.

"Why don't you go and talk with them and see if they can share some of their feed with you," the innkeeper pointed at a group of uniformed guards who were escorting another official.

"Do you know who that official is?" Gao Hanwen asked.

"I didn't dare ask," the innkeeper replied, somewhat mischievously. "With so many guards around him, he must be at least a level-two."

"Could it be Governor Hu Zongxian?" the aide speculated.

"Probably," the innkeeper nodded.

"All right, let's go somewhere else," said Gao Hanwen.

As he was about to leave, he heard someone calling his name. "Is that the mayor of Hangzhou?" Gao turned around and saw a uniformed guard walking towards him.

"Yes, I am Gao Hanwen."

"Your Honour, Governor Hu Zongxian has been waiting for you here for a few hours," Hu's aide said. "Please follow me."

Initially, Gao Hanwen appeared reluctant, but it would have been highly inappropriate to decline an invitation from the governor of Zhejiang Province, where he would be serving. After pausing for a few minutes, he followed Hu's aide and went in.

At first glance, Gao Hanwen thought Hu had been taken ill. He was lying on a recliner with his eyes closed and a wet handkerchief on his forehead. His aide tiptoed over to him and removed the handkerchief before whispering in his ear, "Mr Gao is here."

Hu opened his eyes and motioned to Gao Hanwen, who was standing at the door. "Please come in and take a seat," Hu invited.

"If I may be bold enough to ask, are you Governor Hu Zongxian?"

"Yes, I am."

Gao took a deep bow and introduced himself. "I have long heard your great name."

"Do sit down." Hu Zongxian pointed at a chair. "Even though I'm still the governor, you're no longer under my jurisdiction. You report directly to the imperial inspector of Zhejiang, and we have no direct reporting relationship. But I want to see you today for the mere sake of Zhejiang Province and for the sake of our Imperial Palace."

"Your Honour, please go ahead," Gao said, with his head down.

Hu did not start the conversation right away. Instead, he asked his aide to go out and share their horse feed with Gao's guards.

"Mayor Gao, do you know how many people are being affected by the flood in Chun'an and Jiande Counties?" he asked. "Also, as of today, do you know how much rice we have in storage? If we distribute half a pound of rice to each farmer per day, how long can we last?"

"As far as I know, we have about two hundred and ninety thousand flood victims in Chun'an County and one hundred and forty thousand in Jiande," Gao responded readily. "Before the flood, Zhejiang Province had ten million kilograms of rice in storage. At the moment, each victim gets about four pounds of grain per day. That amounts to three hundred and fifty thousand kilograms. It's been like this for twenty days. There isn't much left. At most, we can probably last ten more days."

"I'm impressed by your familiarity with the situation," Hu said, nodding his head. "But what are you planning to do after we run out of supplies in ten days?"

"Your Honour, do you have any reservations about my proposal?" Gao raised his head and confronted Hu, who did not answer. "As you're probably aware, I'm the one who has put forward the proposal of using the land-conversion policy to rescue flood victims. Based on my idea, the wealthy silk merchants will be asked to barter for the farmers' land with grain after the government runs out of supplies ten days later. Once the situation is stabilised, the merchants who have purchased the land will be asked to grow mulberry, rather than rice. I think the proposal is reasonable and practical, and it is the only option we have now, don't you think?"

"But what price would you set for the land purchase?" Governor Hu asked.

Gao was taken aback. "As the saying goes, land changes hands from year to year in north and south," he said. "Land transactions are based on market prices, and I personally do not think it should be the government's responsibility to interfere."

"But when farmers run out of food supplies at the end of ten days, they will be desperate and have to sell their land way below the market price," Hu replied. "Don't you think the government should intervene?"

"We have stringent laws," said Gao. "If this happens, the Imperial Government would definitely intervene."

"Which government agency are you talking about? The mayor's yamen? The imperial inspector's yamen or the civil affairs yamen or the Justice Department?"

By then, Gao felt that he had grasped what Hu was trying to get at.

"Are you implying that the Imperial Government in Zhejiang might be encouraging the wealthy merchants to take advantage of the flood and buy farmers' land cheaply?" Gao asked.

Hu gazed into his eyes and asked, "If this is the case, what would you do then?"

Gao paused for a minute before answering, "I'll fight them every inch of the way."

"How would you fight them?"

Gao looked at Hu Zongxian and became speechless.

"If this happens, you cannot raid rich people's homes and force them to distribute the rice that they have hoarded," Hu continued. "Neither can you force farmers to sell the land on which their livelihoods depend at lower prices. In other words, you can't use force on either side. If peasants rise up against the government, our province could be plunged into chaos. When that scenario occurs, it is likely that the proposal you have put forward to the Imperial Palace will be blamed for causing the chaos. I doubt this is what you originally intended."

Shocked by the analysis, Gao quickly asked, "What should I do then? Please advise."

"Since you proposed the strategy of using conversion to rescue flood victims, you should have the right to interpret the way you intended," Hu counselled. "First, you should set a minimal land-transaction price, making it mandatory for silk merchants to buy up the land at no lower than one thousand five hundred kilograms of grain per mu. In this way, you would allow some farmers in Chun'an and Jiande Counties to keep their land. For example, a family may have three sons. The eldest can sell his share and will have enough grain to lend to his two brothers so they don't have to sell theirs. If by next year, two-thirds of the farmers still have land to grow food, there wouldn't be riots."

Gao nodded in agreement. "But, if we encourage farmers to keep their land, how are we going to reach the land-conversion target and produce three hundred thousand bolts of silk?" he asked. "There wouldn't be enough raw materials to go around. How do we resolve it then?"

"This land conversion itself is not a wise proposition," sighed Hu. "It's like cutting off flesh to cure a boil. At this point, we probably don't have any choice but to do it. That's actually my second point. We should also encourage the big silk merchants to buy land in counties outside the flooding zone, and they should pay the regular price of two thousand five hundred kilograms of rice per mu. If the land conversion is spread across the counties, the impact might not be as big, and we can probably prevent chaos."

"What if the silk merchants refuse to pay high prices and buy land in other counties?" Gao asked.

"Then, you submit a report to His Majesty, requesting the Privy Council to come up with ideas," Hu suggested. "Make sure you don't propose anything."

Gao looked befuddled.

"Do not worry," Hu reassured him. "I won't allow you to fight alone. You go to Zhejiang first. I'm going to Suzhou now to see if I can get a loan from Zhao Zhenji, who is the imperial inspector for Nanjing. I think I should be able to get us a loan in ten days. Once that's done, you can go and fight the land purchase price with the big silk merchants. Besides, the newly appointed magistrates for Chun'an and Jiande Counties, Hai Rui and Wan Yongji, would be able to help you. You need to trust them and share the responsibilities with them."

Following a long pause, a still-confused Gao ventured to ask, "Your Honour, I wonder if it's appropriate to ask you a question."

"Please go ahead."

"Why didn't you share what you just told me with His Majesty?"

"Sometimes, one doesn't grasp the full implications of life's difficulties until one experiences them," Hu said, with a wry smile. "You'll understand as time goes by."

Hu took a glance outside and rose from his recliner chair. "It's already past noon," he said. "You have another forty kilometres to go before you reach your next inn. You should get going."

Gao, who had by then let his guard down, fell on his knees and kowtowed before striding out of the room. "Your Honour, please take care of yourself," he said.

Hu followed Gao out with his eyes. Suddenly, a fainting spell struck him. As he was trying to grab the recliner chair, he lost balance and fell to the floor. His aide, who happened to be outside, heard the plop and rushed in.

Tan Lun appeared at a side door and ordered, "Don't touch him yet. Please go and get the doctor." After the aide left, Hu opened his eyes and struggled to get up. Tan Lun lent him a hand and put him back on the recliner chair.

"It takes another three to four days to reach Suzhou," Tan Lun said. "If you're not up to it, we can stay here for a couple of days. You need more rest."

"If we can't get the loan and transport the grain to Zhejiang in ten days, what was the point of talking with Gao Hanwen then?" Hu said.

"Do you really think that Gao would heed your advice?" Tan Lun asked.

"Do you truly think that the two magistrates that you people have recommended, Hai Rui and Wang Yongji, would follow your advice?" Hu retorted.

Tan Lun knew that Governor Hu was upset that he had kept him in the dark about his discussions with the Prince of Yu regarding the appointment of Hai Rui as the magistrate of Chun'an.

"Nowadays, there's no longer such a thing called friendship among officials," Governor Hu sighed.

"Zongxian," Tan Lun said, blushing with embarrassment. "I didn't intend to hide it from you…"

"There is no need to explain," Hu interrupted him. "As I said before, I would do what I have to do, regardless of whether you share the information with me or not. I'm just hoping that Gao would follow what I told him today. With Gao, and the two new magistrates that your people have appointed, we may have a chance to win the battle."

Hu leaned on the arms of the recliner chair and stood up. "Get the carriage ready, and let's go," he ordered.

At dusk, Hai Rui reached Hangzhou. Walking on the blue-stoned streets at dusk, one felt like stepping into a painting, with green hills mirrored in the clear waters of the lake. Hai felt a bit out of place here. He led a big mule which carried his luggage and his bamboo basket, and he was wearing a long blue cotton robe with mud stains and a pair of straw sandals that revealed his big toes. The mule trod on the blue stones with weary steps, but Hai felt invigorated. The Zhejiang imperial inspector's yamen was coming into view. Gradually, he saw a big flag pole and the gigantic wooden entrance.

The lanterns and torches in and outside the yamen illuminated the big characters *Zhejiang Imperial Inspector*, which were emblazoned in gold on a red plaque above the entrance. Within the bureaucracy, the imperial inspector used to hold the highest administrative position in a province. However, during Emperor Xuande's rule, the governor's position was elevated to the top. Even so, the imperial inspector still held more de facto power. Therefore, the layout for the inspector's yamen was designed similarly to that of the governor's – tall roofs, a grand entrance flanked on each side with a red wall, and a spacious public square with flagpoles. On this particular night, luxury sedans, specifically reserved for senior local officials, occupied the public square.

This was Zheng Bichang's first meeting since his appointment as the imperial inspector of Zhejiang Province. Upon hearing that Gao Hanwen, the new mayor of Hangzhou, would arrive from Beijing that evening, he quickly summoned officials from different departments to devise strategies overnight on how to implement the land-conversion-and-flood-relief policy. Despite the challenges ahead, they had to convert five hundred thousand mu of rice paddies to mulberry fields within a month.

That explained why the area around the imperial inspector's yamen had been blocked off since mid-afternoon. Stores on nearby streets had closed. When Hai and his mule plodded towards the yamen, it was eerily quiet, and the sound of the footsteps of Hai and his mule broke the silence as if the steps were distant thunder.

"Stop there," a guard shouted at Hai when he was a few feet away from the yamen. "Can't you see this is the imperial inspector's yamen?"

Hai stopped and took out from his pocket the appointment letter from the Ministry of Personnel. The guard was illiterate, but his attitude softened when he saw the big red imperial stamp on the letter. "Which yamen do you belong to?"

"I'm the magistrate of Chun'an."

The guard eyed him with suspicion. "Does anyone know if the magistrate of Chun'an has been invited to attend tonight's meeting?" he shouted to a scholarly-looking person by the entrance.

"Let him in," the man replied.

The guard returned the appointment letter to Hai. "You can go in, but not your mule," he said.

Hai paused for a second before tossing the rein to the guard and then marched into the yamen.

"Hey, why do you leave the mule to me?" the guard yelled.

By then, Hai had already disappeared behind the screen wall. It was 1561, the fortieth year under the reign of Emperor Jiajing. Hai was appointed the magistrate of Chun'an County in Zhejiang Province. The moment he walked into the capital city of Zhejiang Province and marched into the imperial inspector's yamen to report for work, he began a new chapter in life, declaring war against the corrupted forces within the Ming government. He was on a path of no return.

6

The imperial inspector's yamen was so enormous that it was equipped with two rooms for visitors, one on each side of the entrance with different services. Those who maintained a perch high up on the hierarchy were normally ushered into the one on the left, while the right-side one was reserved for lower-level officials.

Upon learning about Hai's official title, the greeter led the new magistrate into the room on the right, a Spartan space with two rows of benches against the wall. "Take a seat here first," said the greeter before he turned on his heel and walked away. "When your name is called, I'll come to get you."

Having waited outside in the well-lit public square, Hai found it hard for his eyes to adjust to the dim light in the visitors' room. After sitting a few minutes, he noticed another man was also seated inside, eyeing Hai with curiosity.

The man stood up and introduced himself. "It is an honour to meet you here. I'm Wang Yongji, the newly appointed Jiande magistrate."

Hai quickly rose and greeted Wang. "It is my honour as well. I'm Hai Rui, the new magistrate of Chun'an County."

"Your reputation precedes you," Wang said. "I've read your articles and heard a story about how you refused to kowtow to a corrupt local official."

"I'm truly flattered," Hai replied. "What is the proper way to address you?"

"Call me Yongji. Tan Lun is my former classmate and a good friend," Wang said.

The mention of their mutual friend, Tan Lun, brought them closer. "Did Tan Lun recommend you for this position?" Hai asked.

"Oh, not quite," Wang explained. "I served as the magistrate of Kunshan County for years, and it was quite a cushy job. But Tan Lun captured me and insists that I come and work here. You know how persuasive he can be. After a few correspondences, he just had me under his spell."

Fascinated by his story, Hai said, "Your transfer from Kunshan is truly a blessing for the people of Jiande County."

"Chun'an is beset with more challenges," Wang said reverentially. "With you taking the lead, I feel much better. I'll try my best to follow you."

As the conversation progressed, Wang noticed that Hai looked a bit worn out. "Did you just arrive in the city?" he asked.

"Yes. I was on the road for five days and got here before dusk."

"Have you had supper yet?"

Hai shook his head.

Wang got up and said, "Let me go and see if I can scrounge up some food for you."

Hai stopped him. "There is no need. This is not the proper place."

Untying his luggage, Hai Rui brought out a piece of dry rice cake. "I've got food here," he said while removing the lotus leaves. Watching Hai taking a big bite of the rice cake, Wang was filled with the sense that knowing a person by repute is not as good as seeing him in the flesh. He stood up and walked over to grab a warm teapot from a table, trying to serve his new friend, but the teapot was empty.

At this point, Gao Hanwen also arrived. Seeing the flaming torches and the sedans sitting in the public square, he ordered his entourage to stop. "I'll only need two guards to wait for me here, and the rest can report to the mayor's yamen," he said.

Alighting from his carriage, he walked towards the imperial inspector's yamen alone. A guard, who had questioned Hai before, had learned to be more tactful with people in civilian clothing. Instead of shooing away Gao, as he normally would, he accosted him by asking, "Which county do you represent?" Gao handed him an appointment letter. Taking a quick glance at the big red stamp, he said, "Please go ahead."

Strangely, nobody greeted him at the entrance. As he was waiting, he saw a receptionist yelling at Wang Yongji, who was holding the empty teapot.

"I've told you that it is not my job to get water for you," he said impatiently. "Why don't you wait until you're called to the meeting. They'll serve you tea inside."

"May I ask..." Gao stepped up and asked.

The receptionist glanced at him and interrupted, "Which county are you from?"

Repressing his disgust and anger at the receptionist's behaviour, Gao asked, "Are all of the county officials waiting here?"

"Yes," said the receptionist. "Sit down and wait."

"What about the two magistrates from Chun'an and Jiande? Are they here?" Gao asked.

"He's there," the receptionist pointed to Wang with his eyes and left.

Wang was about to bow and greet Gao when he saw the newcomer caught up with the receptionist. "Sorry to bother you, but could you get us a pot of tea?" Wang pleaded.

"What happened to you people..." the receptionist glared at Gao.

Removing a piece of decorative jade from his belt, Gao placed it in the receptionist's hand. The receptionist shifted his gaze from the jade to Gao, and his face softened. "All right, give me a few minutes," he said. Accepting the jade from Gao and snatching the teapot from Wang, he stepped out.

"I am Wang Yongji, the new magistrate of Jiande." Wang bowed as they retreated into the waiting room. "And you?"

"It doesn't matter who I am," Gao said, waving his hand in modesty. "The two of you have a big task ahead. The devastating flood struck most of Chun'an. Half of Jiande was also affected. I wonder what your views are relating to the Imperial Palace's strategy of using land conversion to help with disaster relief? How can we implement it?"

"It's not an easy task," Wang replied. Hai ignored Gao and continued munching on his dried rice cakes.

"Why is that?" Gao asked. "I want to hear more."

From his demeanour and the questions he raised, Wang figured that the newcomer was likely to be their new boss, Gao Hanwen. Seeing that Gao was reluctant to reveal his identity, Wang did not probe further. Instead, he turned to Hai Rui.

"Your Honour should probably get your answers from the new Hangzhou mayor," Hai said indifferently.

Gao was shocked at Hai's sarcasm. Wang also attempted to make eye contact with Hai Rui, signalling for him to show some courtesy, but Hai paid no heed. Putting a piece of unfinished rice cake on his chair, he stood up and continued, "I hear that the new mayor of Hangzhou has come up with the idea of disaster relief through rice-to-mulberry land conversion. Based on his reasoning, the conversion programme would be accomplished if farmers in Chun'an and Jiande Counties sell their land on the cheap. In this way, the wealthy silk merchants could make a big killing on this, and officials in Zhejiang can obtain their deserved promotions. But nobody cares to ask what would happen next year. When farmers run out of food and have no land to farm, starvation would occur. By then, it would be time for us two magistrates to be fired. So I wonder if the new mayor of Hangzhou intends to see this outcome from his new initiative."

Surprised by the vehement response to his policy initiative, Gao Hanwen fixed his eyes on Hai, wondering if the new magistrate had discovered his identity. Wang Yongji, helpless because he was unable to stop Hai, cast his eyes down on the floor.

"Do you really think that the disaster-relief-through-conversion initiative could lead to starvation in your two counties?" Gao asked.

"It won't happen this year, of course," Hai replied. "The silk merchants have stored enough grain, and they're willing to buy flooded farmland at four hundred or at most five hundred kilograms per mu. The grain that farmers get from the land sale can probably last them a year or so."

"How do you know that the Imperial Palace will allow those wealthy landowners to purchase land at such cheap prices?" asked Gao.

"I don't," Hai said. "That's why I'm going to consult with the new mayor. When land conversion becomes a priority, the government refuses to give out loans to flood victims. Instead, it encourages farmers to sell their land. Imagine if your family is affected by flood and you have nothing to eat, would you sell your land at four or five hundred kilograms per mu?"

The argument seemed to chime with Governor Hu's words. Gao Hanwen did not answer. Fearful that Gao could take offence at Hai's fiery rhetoric, Wang Yongji had attempted to bow to his new boss and interrupt the conversation, but he resisted the urge because he did not feel it appropriate. In the end, the three of them simply stood there, falling into an awkward silence.

Fortunately, the tea arrived. The receptionist even brought three clean cups. "Please forgive us," he said while pouring. "The yamen is getting bigger, and there are too many idlers around. Take today for example – a fair number of big shots are here, but the people who work in the kitchen and tea room are playing cards. Nobody bothers to tell me where they store the tea leaves. Fortunately, I have some fresh dragon-well tea leaves in my bag. It's fresh and tastes good. I know that it's a trying time for you. Enjoy the tea."

To his surprise, none of his visitors stepped up to take the tea.

"I'm not going to drink it because it's not clean," Hai protested before sitting down to finish the rest of his rice cake.

Assuming that the three visitors had been complaining about him all this time, the receptionist glared at Hai. "Are you here for your appointment, or to find fault with me?" he spouted. "Let me be clear – this is the imperial inspector's yamen."

Hai Rui looked the receptionist in the eye. "I know it's the imperial inspector's yamen. Do we have to bribe someone for a cup of tea here?"

"You... you're..." The receptionist choked on his own words.

"Our discussion here had nothing to do with you," Gao intervened. "You can go now."

At this moment, an official appeared at the door. "Do you know if Mayor Gao has arrived?" he asked the receptionist.

"Let me go and find out," he said. Before leaving, he glanced at Hai and mumbled, "Full of nonsense."

"There is no need to ask about," Gao said. "I am the new mayor."

The receptionist stopped, as if his feet had been nailed to the floor.

"Your Honour, we didn't realise that you're already here," the official said apologetically. "Please... everyone is waiting for you."

"Could you tell the imperial inspector that we'll be there shortly?" Gao said.

"Sure, but please hurry up," the official said before striding away.

Gao Hanwen turned to his two magistrates. Wang was about to conduct the fist and palm salute when Gao stopped him. "It doesn't matter whether you recognised me or not," he said. "I'm glad to hear Magistrate Hai's honest view on the land-conversion policy. As he said, it's very important that we don't plunge ordinary farmers into misery. I know that you care about your people, and I just hope that you can back me up during the meeting. Let's go."

After Gao stepped away, Wang and Hai exchanged guilty glances. At the same time, the receptionist suddenly came to his senses. He reached into his pocket and brought out the jade. "Please wait," the receptionist called out to Gao.

As Hai rose slowly from his chair, Wang advised, "We have a lot to do, but we need to pace ourselves."

"But if folks in Chun'an and Jiande are starving, do you think you and I can walk out of here alive?" Hai said before marching out.

Wang followed Hai out with a solemn expression.

The conference hall was packed with officials in red and purple robes, who sat behind two rows of desks on the left and right sides of the room as they waited for Gao's arrival. Bored and impatient, two officials sitting next to each other were toying with a fine porcelain tea set produced by pottery mills inside the Forbidden City. Another pair was poring over a new opera aria, hand-copied on a sheet of paper, and at times crooning while tapping out the rhythm with their fingertips. The imperial inspector, Zheng Bichang, hunched over a large desk in the middle, waited quietly, with his eyes closed.

"Hey, hey," Ho Maocai, the director of justice howled with a look of annoyance. "Could you people act a bit more professionally? This is not an opera house or an antique market."

Silence fell. The officials sat up straight and put on a serious look.

"By the way, I was told that some farmers in Chun'an and Jiande are instigating trouble by stopping others from selling their land," he continued. "Are you aware that some families are banding together to scrounge up silk and silkworms so they can buy rice? In this way, they don't have to sell their land."

"We're closely monitoring the situation," responded the official who was playing with his teacup. "We have spotted a dozen boats lingering along the river in these two counties, waiting to buy rice from merchants. I think they're negotiating the price now. After they conclude the transactions, we'll detain them."

Zheng Bichang opened his eyes and commented, "We need to control the rice market. We want to make sure that the transactions don't sabotage the rice-to-mulberry conversion. Those who secretly sell rice to flood victims should be arrested on charges of disrupting the implementation of a national policy."

"Understood," the official replied. "We will confiscate everything and arrest both the sellers and buyers."

"That's good," Ho Maocai said. At this point, an official rushed in and whispered in Ho's ears.

"The mayor from the Hanlin Academy has finally arrived," Ho announced with a hint of impatience.

Before he even finished, Gao marched in. Hai Rui and Wang

Yongji paused at the entrance. Seeing that Zheng Bichang had risen from his chair, the others stood up reluctantly.

"Your Honours, I apologise for keeping everyone waiting," Gao said. "The trip has been arduous."

"I totally understand," Zheng Bichang said with a smile. "It is not easy to compress a month-long trip into fifteen days. Please take a seat."

Gao was given a centre seat, next to Ho Maocai. For a mere mayor, the seat arrangement seemed to have violated the basic imperial etiquette. Zheng Bichang's intention was obvious: Gao was selected by Yan Shifan, the grand secretary junior, and the preferential seat arrangement for Gao reflected Zheng's respect for Yan. More importantly, Gao authored the disaster-relief-through-land-conversion strategy. If Zheng could secure Gao's full endorsement of the land-acquisition plan he and the South China Textile Bureau had formulated, it would make things much easier. Within a month or so, the programme could conclude swiftly and successfully.

As part of the protocol, Gao should have thanked the organiser and politely declined the seat with official jargon such as "I wouldn't dare take the seat" or "I don't deserve the seat". Then, others would stand to flatter him, insisting that he should take the seat. He, in turn, would then bow to Zheng in gratitude before sitting down. Finally, he would sign off on whatever plan his peers had devised and promise to implement it the next day.

On the contrary, Gao did not follow the protocol at all. Instead of politely declining the seat, Gao walked over and sat down, as if he deserved it. Worse, he did not even bow to Ho Maocai and the other senior officials, who looked displeased but resisted the urge to chastise him. After all, they needed Gao to implement their plan.

Once Gao was seated, he noticed that Hai Rui and Wang Yongji were still standing by the door, like two pens stuck in a holder. Gao rose and requested, "Your Honour, could you arrange two seats for two of my county chiefs?"

"We never invite county officials to provincial meetings," Ho Maocai said dismissively. "There is no such precedent. Their job is to implement whatever we have decided."

Then, he paused and motioned for Hai and Wang to leave. Wang was about to leave when he saw, through a quick glimpse, that Hai was planting his feet squarely on the ground, glaring at Ho Maocai. He decided to stick with Hai.

When Ho looked up and noticed Hai's cold stare, which lit up like two beams of dazzling light, he felt a cold shudder travelling down his spine. He wondered: What is going on today? The new mayor, who has kept everyone waiting for hours, turns out to be an insolent bookworm. Now, a menial magistrate is giving his superior such an icy menacing stare.

Ho Maocai was not the only one who felt the chill. Zheng Bichang experienced it too, and so did others. Given his senior position, not to mention the fact that he was in charge of all of the criminal investigations in the province, Ho felt that he had to put this rookie in his place. Adopting an air of authority, he asked in a harsh tone, "Did you hear what I just said?"

Gao decided to intervene. "The whole county of Chun'an has been flooded, and half of Jiande County is also affected by the disaster," he stated. "Our plan to convert rice paddies into mulberry fields concerns the lives of several hundred thousand farmers. If we want the magistrates to implement the plan, we need their input so we can do it in a proper way. That's why I have invited them to our meeting."

Gao's remarks infuriated Ho so much that he couldn't breathe. As he turned around to vent his fury, he caught sight of Zheng Bichang's stern look signalling him to stop.

"Set two chairs and bring two cups of tea for the county chiefs," Zheng Bichang announced.

Two of Zheng's aides carried two benches into the room, placing one on the left and another on the right. Hai chose the left bench while Wang sat on the right. Then, the receptionist came in with a tea tray. First, he went up to Gao and raised the tray – the cups were arranged in the shape of a triangle, with one cup facing Gao and the other two closer to the receptionist. Gao picked up the cup near him, and, as he was planning to put it down on the desk, he was puzzled that the receptionist still held the tray in front of him. Then, he noticed the jade that he had used to bribe the receptionist earlier was hidden underneath the cup. A smile flickered around the corner of his mouth. He used his other hand to pick up the jade from the tray and then held the teacup with both hands. Nobody took note of it. Grateful that Gao had handled it subtly without a hint of blame, the receptionist gave an awkward smile. He took the tray to Hai and Wang, placing their tea on the vacant end of their benches.

Clearing his throat, Zheng declared, "Let's start."

The conference hall quietened down.

"I assume that you have been briefed on the situation in Zhejiang," Zheng addressed Gao. "The Imperial Palace has sent us an express letter, outlining your proposal to use our land-conversion programme to assist with the disaster relief efforts. All of my colleagues here are impressed with your talent, and we're in full support of your idea. For the past several days, we have deliberated your proposal and finalised a specific plan. Please take a few minutes to review it. Once you sign off on it, we'll start implementing it tomorrow."

Zheng motioned his secretary to distribute copies of the plan to Gao Hanwen and the two new magistrates, all of whom began reading it earnestly. The so-called plan was nothing more than a one-pager, which listed in two hundred words a summary of six actionable decisions. Zheng and the other officials looked down at their desks, waiting. It was widely anticipated that the new mayor would applaud the items of action listed and give his written authorisation. Once the plan gained approval from attendees, the two new magistrates would pledge to accept the plan on the spot and start implementing it the next day.

Gao Hanwen and his two magistrates finished simultaneously. Hai stood up, and all eyes fixed on him. But, before he had the chance to speak, Gao rose and stopped him. "Magistrate Hai, please sit down first," he said.

From the glint in Gao's eyes, Hai knew that Gao's order was well-intentioned. He paused and then sat down. Meanwhile, Zheng, the imperial inspector, turned to Gao. "I assume that you have no objections to the plan," he said.

"I do!" Gao Hanwen replied; his voice, though soft, resonated in the room, taking everyone by surprise. "This plan contradicts the spirit of the Imperial Palace's strategy of using land conversion to support disaster relief."

Zheng's face fell. The others looked baffled by the unexpected turn of events. Hai's eyes sparked with expectation.

Zheng suppressed his anger and demanded an explanation in a harsh tone. "Please tell us which part you do not like."

"The current plan only reflects the first part of the Imperial Palace's strategy, but not the second half," Gao replied emphatically.

"Excuse me, this is not the Hanlin Academy," Ho blurted out in frustration. "Don't be too scholarly. Please clarify in simple terms what you are trying to convey."

"All right," Gao organised his thoughts and began. "A couple of days ago, someone confronted me with a question, which I found hard to answer – if farmers in Chun'an and Jiande Counties sell their land cheaply and survive the flood with the grain from their land sales, how are they going to support themselves next year or the year after?" Gao paused for a second and exchanged glances with Hai before continuing. "Initially, I took offence at the question. As the saying goes, land changes hands from year to year in north and south. There is no such thing as permanent land ownership. By allowing the wealthy silk merchants to first buy up land from flood victims and then grow mulberry on the land they have purchased, we hope to achieve financial gains for the palace and help flood victims at the same time. My original intent was to make this a win-win situation for both the country and for individual farmers. But a quick look at this plan makes me think twice about what I have proposed earlier. If we approve and implement this plan, farmers in Chun'an and Jiande Counties would have nothing to live on next year. A single focus of this plan is to help big silk merchants buy up the farmland and accelerate the pace of rice-to-mulberry conversion. There is not a single mention of how to prevent silk merchants from exploiting the flood situation and fixing the land prices. Your Honour, what if the silk merchants decide to lower the land prices to five hundred kilograms of rice per mu or even four hundred kilograms per mu? Should farmers sell their land or not? Should the government intervene? My initial proposal was to accommodate both our national priorities and the livelihood of ordinary farmers. If we don't intervene, we will bring misery to ordinary people, who could be forced to rebel against the government. If we don't resolve it, this plan could lead to chaos and costly trouble."

While Gao's tirade shocked the bureaucrats at the conference, it captivated Hai and Wang, who looked at Gao with admiration, agreement and support.

Regardless of the attendees' negative reaction, Gao continued to address his concerns. "Therefore, I believe that the imperial inspector and other senior officials in attendance today should reconsider the plan."

When Gao finished and sat down, there was total silence.

Zheng did not anticipate what he disdainfully characterised as high-sounding remarks from the new mayor, which almost amounted to an open challenge to him personally and to the government of Zhejiang. This was something that he could never tolerate. On the other hand, since Gao was the author of the proposal to offer disaster relief through land conversion and it had won the approval of the Imperial Palace, one had to take his interpretation seriously. However, if this person was recommended by the grand secretary's son, how could he be vehemently opposed to the plan? Why hadn't the grand secretary's son briefed him beforehand?

Baffled and lost, Zheng looked to Ho for clues, but Ho seemed as clueless as he was.

In fact, Yan Shifan, the grand secretary junior, had other considerations when he and his advisers handpicked Gao and sent him to Zhejiang at this critical juncture. Even though the government yamen in Zhejiang was staffed with people he trusted, Yan Shifan felt they had become complacent and corrupt after serving in the government for too long a time, to the point of being disloyal. In meetings and correspondence, officials there appeared compliant and even obsequious, but, when it came to action, they always put their own interests ahead of that of the Imperial Palace. In other words, they were mercenary, and Yan knew that very well. But he had no intention of beating them too hard. As the saying goes, when you drop a piece of soft tofu on a dusty floor, you can only pat it lightly to remove the dust. If you hit it too hard, the tofu could be crushed to pieces.

This dilemma had been plaguing Yan Shifan for several years. With the severe floods in Zhejiang and the pending implementation of the land-conversion policy, Yan became worried that those avaricious bureaucrats could mangle the situation if left to their own devices. After careful consideration, he settled on Gao Hanwen, a Confucian scholar with a clean record who also expressed firm support for the land-conversion policy. He hoped that Gao could restrain the powers of local officials, making sure they did not stray too far.

However, Yan Shifan had not anticipated that his protégé would "accidentally" run into Governor Hu on his way to Hangzhou. Their private conversation had profoundly changed Gao's views, leading to his fierce clash with his superiors in Zhejiang upon his immediate arrival in the city of Hangzhou.

The new mayor's vocal opposition to the land-conversion plan took Zheng by surprise. He felt he had to bite the bullet and put the newcomer in his place before more damage was done.

Zheng eyed Ho, who recollected himself and began his line of questioning. "Land transactions are conducted between sellers and buyers," Ho said to Gao. "Why does the government need to intervene?"

"If the transactions are conducted fairly – I mean if the land is sold at a fair price – the government has of course no reason to interfere," Gao replied.

"What do you mean by 'fair price'?"

"In a good year, a mu of land is bartered with three thousand kilograms of rice, and in a bad year it should be twenty-five hundred kilograms of rice. At the moment, even though Chun'an and Jiande Counties have been struck with terrible floods, the price for a mu of land should not be lower than fifteen hundred kilograms of rice."

Ho uttered an incredulous gasp. "If farmers sell their land at the price of fifteen hundred kilograms of rice, the local silk merchants wouldn't be able to buy up fifty thousand mu of land in Chun'an and Jiande counties to grow mulberry," he blurted out, revealing the unspoken motive that Zheng and others had tried to cover up. "There is no way we can fulfil the quotas of three hundred thousand bolts of silk for export."

Gao jumped at the slip. "I don't understand why we only target farmland in these two flooded counties for conversion? What about the farmland in other counties that have not been affected by the flood?"

"In those non-flooded counties, a mu of land can fetch at least three thousand kilograms of rice," Ho admitted. "Who would buy it?"

"If growing mulberry is more lucrative than planting rice, why wouldn't they buy it?" Gao asked.

Ho was speechless. His face turned pale and grim, frozen and immobile like that of a corpse. It finally dawned on him that Gao's arrival meant that they could lose an important source of revenue and profit. Regardless of Gao's connections with the grand secretary junior, Ho decided that he had to take the political risk and defeat Gao. There was no way he would allow a subordinate, a new transplant, to disrupt a well-established plan. "You can restrict the purchase in these two flooded counties, but the government's disaster relief grain can only last five days or so," he pointed out, his voice quavering. "If the land buyers don't make any purchases five days later, starvation could occur. If this happens, who is taking responsibility for it?"

"If it happens, the Imperial Palace would make a fair judgement on whose fault it would be," Gao persisted.

"How dare you utter such a presumptuous statement?" Ho yelled. Smacking his fist on the desk, Ho rose and turned to Zheng. "Your Honour, this mayor is acting impudently in front of his superiors," he accused. "This is not only a blatant breach of etiquette but also a violation of ethical standards. Our empire has laws and rules governing this type of behaviour. Aren't you going to report him to the Imperial Palace and have him censured?"

"There's no need to censure me," Gao said calmly. "I can submit my resignation if you think it appropriate."

Once again, Ho found himself at a loss for words. Zheng was also fumbling for an answer.

Hai Rui stood up abruptly to offer his resignation. "I'm also requesting to be dismissed from my position."

"Given the challenges of implementing this plan, I'm also asking to be removed from my position," said Wang Yongji.

The situation was threatening to get out of control. Three new officials appointed by the Ministry of Personnel had just offered to resign before they even began. Zheng felt that his hands were tied. Even if he was authorised by the Imperial Palace to fire those new political hires, he lacked the nerve to act on it.

Another deadly silence followed. All eyes turned to Zheng, who finally rose slowly from his chair. "Since we are convening today to review and discuss this plan, we certainly must allow free discussions and different viewpoints," he said, trying to pacify all sides. "Besides, since we rely on the mayor and the county chiefs to implement the plan, we have to make sure they are on board with us. However, the three of you are still new to the region and may not be aware of certain thorny and complicated issues, which are specific to the region. For example, how much land do we need in order to fulfil the export order of five hundred thousand bolts of silk? How much rice can we secure from the market and private suppliers to subsidise flood victims? At what price are big silk mill owners willing to pay for the farmland? These are tough issues. I want to put forward a suggestion. Why don't the three of you go around the counties tomorrow and get some first-hand insight? We'll reconvene here and resume our discussion the day after tomorrow."

Ho waved his hand and declared, "All right then, the meeting is adjourned." His face was contorted in disgust and anger, and he raced out the door before the other officials had the chance to ask questions.

明

Half an hour later, Zheng Bichang and Ho Maocai showed up in the spacious visitors' room next to Shen Yishi's silk mill. Upon hearing that Shen was not available, Ho burst into an angry rant. "Go and find him," he taunted Shen's servants. "Wherever he is, go and find him before I break your legs. Tell your master that he will have to pay two thousand kilograms of rice for a mu of land if he doesn't come to see us quickly."

Shen's personal aide stood there helplessly with his hands hanging at his sides. "Sir, I can try, but it's quite late, and my master hasn't told us where he has gone," he said. "What if I can't find him right away? I hate to keep you waiting…"

"Don't worry – we do not mind waiting," Zheng reassured him. "Go and find him."

The servant went reluctantly. Ho plopped down on a chair, fuming. "I still cannot figure out what the grand secretary's son is playing at? They have many options, so why send a troublemaker? What are they thinking? Besides, what's happening with Yang Gonggong? Does he know that his own backyard is on fire? When is he returning from Beijing? If he doesn't care, why should we? Why don't we just rescind the land-conversion policy? Let the South China Textile Bureau handle the export orders. They can find another source to produce an extra three hundred thousand bolts of silk."

Zheng had toyed with different solutions, but none satisfied him. He saw himself as the helmsman for Zhejiang Province, and, when a storm arose out of nowhere, he had a lot to reckon with; the situation put him in a bad mood. Therefore, when Ho let loose on him during his uncontrollable rant, he became incensed. "I hope you can stop it here," he castigated. "What did you mean by saying we should rescind the land-conversion policy or ask the Textile Bureau to handle the export order? If you're that gutsy, why don't you write to the grand secretary directly and put down what you just said in the report? Or, you can tell Yang Gonggong in person when he returns."

Ho Maocai's eyes widened, and his face flushed red with poorly suppressed anger.

"You and I have worked together in Zhejiang for years, and I have always treated you like a confidant," Zheng cajoled with a soft tone. "When something bad happens, you have to learn how to hold back and act calmly. I'm the imperial inspector, and you're in charge of the Justice Department. In this region, you and I are considered senior ranking officials. But if we mess up this deal and offend the Imperial Palace, our punishment wouldn't be any different from that of Ma Ningyuan."

Even though Ho was nursing a grievance, he held back. After all, Zheng was his superior and the captain of this ship. Ho simply sat there, sulking. But soon, his temper got the better of him again. He rose and dashed to the door. "Where the hell is your master?" he yelled at Shen's assistant. "Does he still want to buy land or not? Where are the servants? Are they all dead or what? Why can't they send more people to look for him?"

With a dour expression, Zheng shook his head helplessly.

明

Actually, Shen's personal aide knew his master's whereabouts – Shen was staying the night at a secret courtyard house next to his residence. Since Shen had specifically requested that nobody disturb him, the aide wouldn't dare burst into the house as he normally did when something urgent was happening. Quietly opening the door to Shen's secret sanctuary, the aide paused, trying to figure out an unobtrusive way to notify his master. The yard stood very quiet. He could hear faint music floating out of a room in the back.

The big room, inconceivably unique in the city of Hangzhou or in the whole country at that time, served as a music studio. Fifty-five feet deep and one hundred feet wide, it covered an area as big as the Palace of Heavenly Purity inside the Forbidden City. To hide it from government officials or curious onlookers walking past the courtyard, the room only stood twenty-two feet high. The inside walls were covered from top to bottom with pieces of one-by-two-inch sandalwood panels, a feature that was absent in the Palace of Heavenly Purity. Shen left the large space in the middle unfurnished. Rows of clothes racks made of ebony wood lined the walls on the south, north and west. On each rack hung a dozen women's silk dresses, in various colours, styles and fabrics. On the east side stood a large, eleven-foot-long by eleven-foot-wide wooden platform bed. A short mahogany music stand was placed in the middle of the bed. Shen, dressed in his usual blue cloth robe and with his long hair hanging loose over his shoulder, sat cross-legged behind the music stand on the bed, playing the guqin. Wisps of smoke from incense burners wafted around the bed past his gaunt face, which, in the dim light, seemed pale. His long slender fingers plucked at the strings, and, from a distance, they seemed to be dancing back and forth on the guqin. A beautiful melody seeped from those fingers.

In another part of the room, a flowing silk dress, thin and transparent as cicada wings, suddenly came alive, gliding away from the clothes rack and into the middle. Shen's eyes sparkled, and his fingers moved wildly. As the music began to crescendo, the dress swirled around, revealing, in a dreamlike sequence, the tall willowy body of a young woman, her long jet-black hair floating in the air. Suddenly, both the music and the dance came to an abrupt halt. One could see that the lovely face belonged to Madam Yun.

Shen picked up a flute next to the guqin and started playing. The soft gentle tune sounded like a woman's weeping. An air of melancholy filled the room, and Shen's eyes exuded sadness. Madam Yun stopped her dizzying dance, and her long sleeves fell onto the floor like feathers. "You and I fly side by side, like wild geese; and we traverse the sky like dragon and phoenix," crooned Madam Yun. "A wrecking storm broke us apart; each is yearning for the love of the other…"

Shen put down his flute with a long sigh. Madam Yun also paused, tears glistening in her eyes. Moving slowly towards Shen, she climbed onto the platform bed and snuggled next to him, gently touching his hair. But when Madam Yun gazed into his eyes, he looked away. "Before he died, Li Xuan claimed to the guards that you had made his death worthwhile," he said, grabbing her wrist and pushing it gently away. "What did you do to make his death so worthy?"

The colour drained from Madam Yun's face.

"I spent twenty thousand taels of silver getting you out of the whorehouse," Shen continued, without looking at her. "The fact that you can make a eunuch so madly in love with you shows I've certainly got my money's worth."

Tears welled up in Madam Yun's eyes; before they streamed down her powdered face, she wiped her eyes, rose and got off the bed. Then, she removed her long silk robe and changed into her everyday clothing. Shen sat there motionless.

As Madam Yun was walking towards the door, Shen spoke up. "Where are you going?"

"To be with the eunuchs at the Textile Bureau," she replied, coldly.

"Do you know that Yang Jinshui's appointment at the South China Textile Bureau will expire in a year?"

Madam Yun turned her head and said, "Of course, I know. You gifted me to him when I was seventeen. Since then, I've been counting with my fingers every day. As of today, I've been serving him on your behalf for one thousand five hundred days. When he returns to Beijing next year, you can send me to a convent, if you still allow me to live." She could see hate and murder in Shen's eyes.

"What about your mother and your siblings?" Shen said, his voice was sharp and cold like a dagger. "Do they have to go to the convent with you as well?"

Madam Yun stood there, her body shaking

"Do you see this string over here?" Shen pointed at his guqin; his voice had calmed down a bit and did not sound as murderous as before.

Madam Yun shifted her gaze to the instrument in Shen's long slender fingers. Shen pulled hard at the string. *Bam* it was broken. Madam Yun winced involuntarily.

"From now on, I won't touch that body of yours," Shen vowed, without looking at her. "But I do have a request. Show me what you did to Li Xuan that night. Do it again right here."

"You really want to see it?" Madam Yun asked; her voice turned equally icy, and her eyes glistened.

"I want you to re-enact it for me," Shen repeated, looking up at the ceiling. "It's up to me to decide whether to watch it or not."

"I can't do that," Madam Yun replied, her eyes cast downward.

"Is it because what you did was too cheap and disgusting?" asked Shen, his voice filled with contempt.

"Yes, I am cheap and disgusting."

"Then go ahead and show it to me," Shen demanded.

"I can't," Madam Yun said. "It involved two people. How can I do it alone? If you truly want to find out how cheap and disgusting I was, why don't you try, for once in your life, and play Li Xuan's part?"

Shen didn't expect that Madam Yun would mock him like that. Grabbing the guqin with his cigarette-thin fingers, he smashed it on the floor. The precious instrument bounced around, and the strings broke with a snap. Two remaining strings boomed with vibrations, followed by total silence.

Then, there was a soft tap on the door. "Master," called the personal aide in his timid voice.

"What is it?" Shen shouted without opening the door.

"Master, Mr Ho and Mr Zheng are waiting for you in the visitors' room..." the aide replied in his trembling voice. "They want to discuss with you the farmland purchase... There seem to be some changes..."

"Tell them if they want to make a fortune, they can buy the farmland themselves," Shen yelled. "Get out of my courtyard."

Silence resumed outside.

Having vented his frustration, Shen slumped into the bed, his face as white as the fine sheets. Then, he jumped off the bed and moved, with his socked feet, towards Madam Yun.

"Did you ask me to imitate Li Xuan, the eunuch?" he asked.

Madam Yun, who could feel his heavy breath on her face, was unusually calm. "You won't be able to," she replied softly. The tears in her eyes had dried up.

"What if I really want to?" Shen said, pursing his mouth in a creepy smirk. "Show me what he did to you."

Madam Yun shook her head slightly and said, "I've already told you that you're not capable of doing it. Li Xuan treated me like a fairy, and you see me as a disgusting whore. How can you imitate him?"

Her remarks shamed Shen into silence. Raising her head to face the ceiling, as if she were watching a replay of the scene with Li Xuan before his execution, Madam Yun recounted, in her calm voice, "I was sitting on the bed while he sat on the floor. He wept while drinking one cup of liquor after another. For hours, he wouldn't even dare look at me. Finally, he became so intoxicated that he fell asleep on the floor. I went down and took him in my arm. His head reclined on my bosom. Before dawn, the eunuchs at the Textile Bureau came to get him. Since he was still drunk, they poured cold water over his head to sober him up. Then, he was dragged to the execution ground. So, if you are willing to get yourself drunk, weep in front of me and lie down on the floor, I promise I will put your head in my bosom and keep you company until tomorrow morning."

Shen was dumbfounded. The coldness in his eyes gradually melted. Looking apologetic and sympathetic, he stretched a hand out to take Madam Yun's.

"Don't touch me," Madam Yun said, pulling her hand back. "Didn't you just say that you won't touch me again?"

Shen had never experienced such rejection from a woman. The fleeting apologetic and sympathetic feeling was taken over by embarrassment and his inborn arrogance. He felt as if he had been nailed onto the floor.

"Since you paid money to get me, my life is yours," Madam Yun said. "But you can't touch my body in the future. You have an inexhaustible supply of money, and, in this city, you have an endless supply of prostitutes who are willing to service you."

"Good," Shen was at a loss for words. "You're right."

Without putting on his shoes, he dashed over to the door in his socked feet. Before he opened the door, he mumbled without turning his head, "It is true that I have a lot of money and that I have an endless supply of prostitutes to give me pleasure. In fact, I'm going to spend my money on them now. Since I'm the owner of your life, I want you to stay here until Yang Gonggong comes back. Let me tell you something. The day when I paid money to purchase you, I no longer saw you as a fairy or even a virtuous woman. You're nothing but a hussy."

When Shen finished, he pulled the door open and walked out. A breeze blew in. Madam Yun stood there, stunned.

明

"I'm terribly sorry," Shen resumed his usual humble self and bowed to his two guests, who had waited a long time in the visitors' room. "I had to handle an urgent matter. Several dozens of boats loaded with rice from Jiangxi Province are being detained at the provincial border. Authorities in Jiangxi demanded fifty taels of silver per boat before allowing them to come to Zhejiang. The people who work under me wouldn't pay the money until I gave approval."

"Why don't you ask the boatmen to show the authorities in Jiangxi the disaster aid document issued by my office?" asked Zheng.

Shen shrugged his shoulders. "The paper you have issued doesn't work in another province. Money works the best."

"We should write a complaint letter to the imperial inspector in Jiangxi," Ho suggested. "It's so corrupt over there."

Shen waved his hands and sat down. "There is no need now. It's only a matter of ten thousand taels of silver. We don't want this to ruin relations between the two provinces."

"Let's get down to business," Zheng said to Shen. "The plan we have put forward was rejected by the new mayor this evening."

"Was it Gao Hanwen, the one chosen by the grand secretary junior?" Shen asked in surprise.

Zheng nodded.

"How come? What did he say?" Shen asked.

"He says we have to set a minimum price for farmland sales, at two thousand kilograms of rice per mu," Zheng said. "We did a quick calculation just now. Based on his idea, it would cost an extra five hundred thousand tonnes of rice to buy five hundred thousand mu of farmland. That amounts to seven million taels of silver."

"If that's the case, I wouldn't be able to come up with that much money," Shen replied, somewhat shocked by the figures.

"This is the best scenario," Zheng argued. "The truth is that in the flooded counties of Chun'an and Jiande, we probably won't be able to buy up five hundred thousand mu of land at this price. With the exorbitant rate of two thousand kilograms of rice per mu, farmers only need to sell some of their land to cope with the food shortages caused by the current flooding. In other words, we have to find alternatives in those non-flooded counties, where a mu of land is sold at three thousand kilograms of rice. If we take this into account, the price tag could go up to ten million taels of silver. This could jeopardise the whole land-conversion plan."

"Why would this person want to do something like that?" Shen said, looking baffled.

"He wants to have it both ways," said Ho Maocai furiously. "As the saying goes, he leads the life of a whore and expects a monument to his chastity. I think offering him a cheque of a hundred thousand taels of silver would shut him up, don't you think?"

"If this works, I can write him a cheque right away," promised Shen.

"Let's not get too far ahead of the game," Zheng interjected. "This person is a well-known Confucian scholar, but deep down he's harboured big political ambition. That's probably the reason the grand secretary junior picked him to appease the opposition. Knowing his character, I doubt he's going to openly accept bribe money."

"So, with your prestige and authority, the two of you still can't rein him in, can you?" Shen asked.

"Well, he's only a mayor, and we can easily keep him under control if we want," Zheng mused. "But he comes highly recommended by the grand secretary junior, and he has authored the disaster-relief-through-land-conversion strategy. If he rejects our plan and reports us to the Imperial Palace, we could face inquisition. Nobody would back us – not even the grand secretary junior."

"We have to find a way to rein him in or at least to shut him up," Shen replied with a crafty smile.

Zheng and Ho fixed their gaze on Shen.

"How much do you know about this person?" Shen asked.

"Two friends of the grand secretary junior corresponded with me last month, saying that this person writes good poetry and he's well versed in music," Zheng said.

"Really?" Shen's eyes sparkled. "Could you postpone the discussion about land conversion and disaster relief for a day or two?" he asked.

"Of course," Ho replied. "Mr Zheng has already done that. We have decided to discuss the plan again the day after tomorrow."

"I actually only need one day," said Shen.

"Do you have a plan in mind?" Ho asked in earnest.

Shen rose and said with a determined look, "As the saying goes, there's always a way to make money in the world, and there's always a way to kill your enemy if you put your mind to it. As long as you two give permission, I can make him change his mind at your meeting the day after tomorrow."

Ho patted his lap and said with gusto, "If you can make him change his mind, we'll do everything. What's your plan? Just tell us."

Shen turned to Zheng, who was obviously better at reading Shen's unexpressed thoughts than Ho.

"If you use beautiful women as a trap, I doubt it'll work on him," Zheng said with some hesitancy.

"Your Honour, I know sex traps don't always work, but what if we make a real match?" Shen said with a cunning smile.

Ho finally figured out what Shen was getting at. "This person is the pick of the grand secretary and his son," he questioned. "If we orchestrate this, it would probably be hard to explain away to the grand secretary."

"I know it is inappropriate to get you two involved," Shen assured them. "What about having someone at the Textile Bureau handle this? Like someone from His Majesty's staff?"

Zheng thought about it for a minute and answered, "That might work. We'll let you take care of it."

"But Your Honour needs to arrange a meeting for me," Shen added, trying to smile so he didn't betray his disgust at Zheng.

"Can you suggest a legitimate business excuse for your meeting with Gao Hanwen?"

"You can use the excuse that he needs to visit the South China Textile Bureau and meet with a silk merchant to understand the full impact of the land-conversion policy," Shen replied. "I'll take care of the rest."

"That sounds good," Zheng said contemplatively. "I think I can do it."

Ho banged his balled fist on the tea table and bragged, "Excellent. The two new magistrates are no angels. Once you have taken care of Gao Hanwen, let me handle the other two."

Since the Hangzhou municipal government yamen was located in the city centre, Gao Hanwen was able to move into his living quarters in the yamen's backyard after the meeting. Hai Rui and Wang Yongji stayed temporarily at a government guest house. Before dawn the next morning, the two new magistrates arrived at the municipal yamen, waiting for Gao Hanwen – they had been scheduled to visit the rice market at the Caoyun Wharf.

Hai had changed into a new grey cotton robe, and Wang, who grew up in a well-to-do family, wore a thin silk outfit.

"Brother Hai," Wang said somewhat hesitantly after they were seated in Gao's living room. "Why don't you buy a couple of silk robes? In this way, people won't think you're my aide-de-camp or something."

Hai, who sat there silently, lost in thought, raised his head and looked at Wang for a few seconds before answering. "I don't mind being your aide-de-camp," he joked.

"I'm not worthy of that," Wang immediately said, flustered. "You're at least ten years older, and you deserve my respect. If you don't mind, I can gift you a couple before we depart tomorrow."

"Thanks, but I only wear cotton robes."

"I apologise for being so presumptuous," Wang said, looking embarrassed.

"No, that's not what I mean," Hai quickly explained. "The region I come from is quite remote and poor. Only a few people can afford silk clothing. Besides, it's hot all year round, so we don't actually need silk clothing. Except for formal events, we seldom wear shirts. So I have got into the habit of wearing cotton robes. Speaking of being your aide-de-camp, I don't think age has anything to do with it. For example, Mayor Gao is very young, but I don't mind being his aide at all, as long as he's devoted to the Imperial Palace and the people."

Even though they had known each other for barely a day, Wang already saw Hai – a man of few words – as a friend or someone in whom he could confide. Hai's remarks about Gao further confirmed his judgement and warmed his heart. "I was about to tell you the same thing about Gao," he nodded.

"Then why did you bring up the subject of my clothing?" Hai teased.

"Well, no matter what one does, one has to eat and clothe oneself, right?"

"I still prefer my cotton robe," Hai replied with a rare grin.

As they were bantering, Gao emerged from his bedroom. He was also wearing a thin silk robe. "Sorry to have kept you waiting," he said. "Let's get going."

In the courtyard, two men came up to them with ingratiating smiles. The one at the front was the mayor's personal attendant. Dropping to one knee and bowing his head, he announced, "Your Honour, the imperial inspector has entrusted us to bring you his letter. He has invited you to visit a silk mill this morning and see how silk is produced."

"We've been here for a while to wait for Your Honour." The man standing behind the mayor's personal assistant stepped up and bowed.

Gao thought for a moment. "Could you tell the imperial inspector that I have made plans to visit the rice market with two magistrates," he said. "I can visit the silk mill another time. There's really no rush."

"Your Honour, I wouldn't be in a position to relay this message of yours," Zheng's attendant replied. "The imperial inspector has already notified the Textile Bureau to expect you this morning."

The mention of the Textile Bureau gave Gao pause. He turned to Hai and Wang and said, "Since the invite comes from the Textile Bureau, I guess I have to go. Why don't you two go ahead and check out the rice market without me?"

As the litter carried Gao off, Wang saw a glint of worry in Hai's eyes.

Gao Hanwen found himself in a large silk mill. He had never seen so many machines weaving different types of silk fabric. Despite his natural inhibitions, Gao had to admit that he was impressed. "Half of the silk that the Imperial Palaces use is made here." Shen talked loudly so he could be heard above the noise of the machines. "Before the sea route was blocked in 1553, half of the silk we exported to the west came from here."

Gao nodded. By then, he was already overwhelmed with the feeling that there was such a lot to know about this large industry and he knew so little of it.

"It's too noisy here," Shen suggested. "Why don't we go and see the silk samples first?"

Shen took the unprecedented step of taking Gao to his secret residence – a sanctuary that he had never shown to anyone before. Outside the cavernous house, Gao stopped suddenly, his face awash with surprise. "Someone is playing *The Guangling Melodies*," he murmured to himself. The music wafting out from inside a studio enthralled him.

Shen also stopped. Taking a side glance at Gao, he knew that his plan had started to work its magic. "Your Honour…" he jolted Gao out of his reverie.

"Where are we?" Gao asked. "Are you going to show me the silk samples here?"

"Oh yes. We used to bring western merchants here to see silk samples."

Gao eyed Shen curiously. "You've hired a guqin virtuoso to play *The Guangling Melodies* and entertain western merchants who are here to see the silk samples?" Gao asked.

"I'm impressed that Your Honour can tell that she's playing *The Guangling Melodies*," Shen remarked with feigned surprise.

Distracted, Gao did not respond.

"Both guqin music and fine silk are part of our cultural heritage," Shen bragged. "When we do business with the west, we don't just sell our silk. It is also our responsibility to spread our culture. I'm in awe of your deep knowledge about music. We'll have a lot to talk about. Please go in."

Gao felt that his legs no longer belonged to him as he followed Shen mechanically to the spacious music studio. Even during the day, Shen left the lanterns burning, which, along with rows of transparent silk dresses, had transformed the room into a dreamland. Gao, dazzled and distracted, scanned the chamber. It was apparent that the young official was not paying attention to the silk, but rather searching for the source of the music, which seemed to come from behind a flowing silk curtain.

"Your Honour, please look at this," Shen presented a piece of silk with embroidery on both sides. "This sells really well overseas, but its name sounds really plain. It's called 'Flowers in Four Seasons'. The foreigners really like it."

Gao felt obligated to show some interest in the product, or at least pretend to be enthused about it. But, after briefly studying the fabric, he became immediately captivated. On one silk dress alone, craftsmen had embroidered more than one hundred different species of flowers in various stages of blooming, and their colours and shades matched perfectly.

Shen put down the dress and led Gao towards a silk curtain, behind which the music arose. Gao's eyes were filled with anticipation and curiosity.

As they were ambling across the room, Gao suddenly stopped. Shaking his head in disapproval, he mumbled, "A pity, a pity."

"May I ask, what do you mean by that?" Shen asked, feigning ignorance.

"I'm talking about the music," Gao expounded. "Many musicians who play *The Guangling Melodies* tend to err at this spot. As you know, Ji Kang[1] was a non-conformist by nature, and yet for some reason he was offered a senior post within the government in the Kingdom of Wei. He despised his job and was critical of the ruling Confucian philosophy. Instead, he worshipped nature and spent his whole life studying the life-cultivating methods. For years, he was searching for a resting place where he could consecrate his heart, and he subsequently found his inspiration in Mount Mang, which he saw as the beginning of all creatures in China and the true destination of his soul after death.

"Therefore, before his execution, he was seized with mixed emotions – both grief and joy – and at his request, his executioners allowed him to play *The Guangling Melodies* on his guqin. While his fingers danced on the instrument, his spirit rose and flew towards Mount Mang. In this piece, one traditionally would use *jue* in the pentatonic scale to play the part about Mang Mountain, so a low pitch would be applied. However, nowadays, many musicians have turned to a high pitch, falsely presuming that Ji Kang was grief-stricken before his death. That's a wrong presumption."

Gleams of excitement flickered in Shen's eyes. While congratulating himself on ensnaring Gao in his trap, he also felt a strong attachment to the new mayor, someone whose talent he truly admired and who shared similar interests.

"I have a humble, or maybe unreasonable, request, and I wonder if Your Honour is willing to grant me the privilege," Shen requested.

Gao had guessed what Shen would say next – inviting him to guide and teach the musician. A sense of pride surged through him. "Please go ahead," he said to Shen.

"I would invite Your Honour to critique the work of this musician because your guidance will not only help promote our products and culture to the west but also ensure that the true spirit of *The Guangling Melodies* will not be misinterpreted by future generations."

"We'll learn from each other," Gao replied immediately, with an air of presumptuous confidence.

"I want to thank you in advance." Shen bowed before lifting the silk curtain. With a light pull, the whole piece fell down like a wisp of cloud. Gao's eyes were fixed on the platform bed; a red rug covering the platform surface transformed it into a stage. The virtuoso was actually a young woman dressed in a flowing white silk costume, with a tinge of lotus pink. She was beautiful and full of grace. Her attraction retained a perceptible aura of worldliness and the sophistication of a fille de joie.

As he quickly shifted his bashful gaze to the silk curtain, he caught a glimpse of her slightly parted lips under her arching eyebrows, reminding him more of *The Guangling Melodies*. Like Ji Kang, he was willing to pull his heart out and consecrate it, but to whom and where?

"You're a lucky girl," Shen said, his voice bringing Gao back to reality. "We have a true master here, and I hope you can learn from His Honour."

Shocked slightly at the coldness in Shen's voice, Gao could not fathom why the silk merchant would treat a woman of heavenly beauty with such indifference, which almost bordered on cruelty.

In her kneeling position, Madam Yun gently straightened her upper body. Crossing her two long sleeves in front of her chest, she bowed slightly and said, "Your Honour, I will play from the beginning, and I welcome your guidance."

As her slender fingers moved deftly on the strings, *The Guangling Melodies* rose, filling the whole room with music even though the room was insulated with sandalwood panels. Gao stood there, transfixed by the music and by Madam Yun, who gradually immersed herself in her performance.

Seeing that everything was going smoothly according to his meticulous plan, Shen sidled towards the door, pulled it open slightly and stepped out with his body tilted sideways. When he closed the door behind him, he left them alone in the room.

At the time this story took place, China's handicraft industry and commerce had reached a peak, especially in the southeast region around the Tai Lake. Music and arts also flourished in the region, making it the cultural centre of China and creating a large group of music- and art-loving officials and merchants. These practitioners of beaux arts hovered between their political careers and their artistic pursuits. Those who passed the Imperial Exams entered the bureaucracy, while those who failed indulged in women and music.

In those days, it was very common for officials and merchants to frequent brothels and befriend courtesans. The literati helped nurture many beautiful young courtesans who were well versed in the arts, music and literature, most of whom set up shop in the booming cities of Nanjing and Hangzhou. Theatres and brothels competed to host operas and music performances, and visiting those venues had become a fad and national pastime.

There was a popular saying among officials that illustrated the rich cultural traditions in the south and the lack thereof in the north: "One would rather be a county chief along the Yangzi River than a mayor along the Yellow River." Another saying among the ordinary folks stated, "One would rather be a dog in the cities of Hangzhou and Suzhou than a human being in the north and northwest."

In other words, Hangzhou, this paradise on earth, had become a coveted destination for China's cultural elite. Gao grew up in a family of distinguished scholars and was greatly influenced by the literati of his time. Not only was he a talented and accomplished writer, artist and musician but he also held a true passion for these artistic activities. However, one could not have it both ways. His political aspirations took precedence over his artistic bent as he began shifting his interest in arts and music to the study of neo-Confucianism.

An aficionado of literature and music, Shen shared Gao's literary temperament. His familiarity with the cultural elite and his knowledge about Gao's past gave him the confidence that he could succeed in luring the magistrate into his trap and eventually bring him to his knees. The literati might be incorruptible by money because of their self-righteousness, but they would never refuse an offering that displayed true elegance and good taste.

Shen was right. At this very moment, Gao sat with his eyes shut. His mind broke free from the enclosed music studio, travelling to Mount Mang, where Master Ji Kang was laid to rest. Meanwhile, Madam Yun was playing the finale, which Gao had critiqued earlier. She suddenly stopped. Too shy to look Gao in the face, she gazed at Gao's chest, with her beautiful eyes that shimmered like water. "Your Honour, I understand what you just said about using Jue in the pentatonic scale, but none of the music scores that I have read had such mention. Could you tell me why?"

Across the bank, a deer bleats, in the wilds where it eats.[2] Gao felt as if a deer were bleating, hopping up and down violently in his heart. For a while, he simply stared at the woman, rapt.

Curious at the silence from Gao, Madam Yun moved her gaze from Gao's chest to his face. Their eyes met. Gao's scalp was tingling. He quickly looked away and noticed that Shen was no longer in the room.

Having studied the Confucian moral teachings for more than a decade, Gao was well-aware of his boundary. A precious shining pearl was beckoning him, but he knew that darkness was lurking behind. Conscience whipped him in like a horseman's rein. Gao quickly became alert at Shen's absence. "Mr Shen, where are you?" Gao shouted. There was no answer. He quickly strode to the door. As he was about to pull it, the door opened. In came Shen, looking self-possessed. "Your Honour, are you looking for me?" he said.

Gao eyed him suspiciously.

"When Master Ji Kang played *The Guangling Melodies* before his execution, three thousand of his disciples crowded around him, listening to the music, but none fully comprehended its essence and impact," said Shen. "That explains why Ji Kang's version of *The Guangling Melodies* has been lost forever. It's truly lamentable. A few years ago, a fellow music-lover friend of mine said something that I didn't quite grasp at first. This person said *The Guangling Melodies* can only be played by one individual to another. Adding another member to the audience would create dissonance. I did not understand that, but later on, when I tried playing the piece a few times, I realised that he was absolutely right. We are very lucky to have a true expert today. After you mentor her today, I myself have many questions to consult with you about. I wonder if you would grant me the honour."

Impressed by Shen's sincere compliments, which clearly showed the silk merchant's own expertise, Gao let his guard down a little and began to warm to Shen.

"Can I ask you something," Gao said. "What is your position at the Textile Bureau?"

"I spend most of my time working with silk weavers on new fabric patterns and designs. My other job is to negotiate business deals with foreign merchants."

"What a pity," Gao said, casting a side glance at Madam Yun.

"Your Honour, I am sorry that I forgot to make the introduction," Shen said with an apologetic smile. "She's my niece, Yun. Her parents died when she was a little girl, and I brought her here to live with me and to teach her music and literature. As she is cultivating her trade, she's turned down many marriage proposals. Now she's turning twenty, it really worries me. While I'm anxious, I have to make sure she finds the right young man."

"What a rare beauty," Gao blurted out and quickly felt embarrassed by the slip. "Well, we have more important matters to take care of today. People are starving, and it's probably not the appropriate time for us to banter about music here. Why don't we continue with our conversation about the silk production quotas."

Bottling up his disappointment, Shen slowly followed the young official out. However, before Gao stepped across the threshold, Shen noticed that he involuntarily glanced back at Madam Yun and caught her adoring gaze. Embarrassed, Madam Yun quickly dropped her eyes. As much as Shen wanted Gao to fall into his trap, the subtle eye contacts between Gao and Madam Yun triggered an unknown feeling of jealousy in him.

"Try to digest Master Gao's words." Shen broke the awkwardness with his interjection. "Keep practising."

Madam Yun detected a touch of desolation in Shen's voice.

Junks and sampans, big and small, black-roofed or white-sailed, moved about in an orderly fashion. After more than a thousand years, the river port in Hangzhou, which marked the start of the Grand Canal, was functioning efficiently and smoothly. Hai Rui and Wang Yongji stood at the tip of the port, quietly watching the different types of moored vessels loading and unloading. Silk-robed merchants and bare-shouldered longshoremen with heavy sacks on their backs scurried back and forth.

"Is this your first time to be in the region?" Wang asked Hai.

"Yes!"

Wang blurted out one of Liu Yong's poems about Hangzhou. "'Blessed by nature / Seat of the Wu region / From the old has been thriving / Qiantang River/ With bridges beautiful, willows misty.'

After Liu Yong failed repeatedly to secure a career within the Imperial Government in the tenth century, he became a vagabond and traversed the region, leaving many beautiful poems behind. In a way, his misfortune turned out to be a blessing."

"I would rather live in the poor remote mountain village where I grew up," Hai replied curtly. "Wandering around in booming cities like Hangzhou is not my thing."

"There's nothing wrong with living in a prosperous city like Hangzhou," Wang retorted. "In this big country of ours, if we didn't have towns and cities, farmers wouldn't have a market to sell their silk, cotton and tung oil. You can't make a good living planting rice alone."

"You're absolutely right, but I'm just worried that the wealthy in the city will become wealthier and the poor in the villages will be poorer."

"It is impossible to eliminate inequality between the rich and the poor, but we try our best to bridge the gap a bit," Wang said.

"You must be one of those wealthy ones," Hai half joked. "No wonder you want to gift me some silk robes."

"Truth be told, my family owns about seven or eight hundred mu of farmland," Wang admitted. "My family is probably slightly better off than yours. But I just hope that the Imperial Palace doesn't appoint you as the magistrate of my home county. Your belief in 'robbing the rich to help the poor' won't bode well for my family."

"I'm targeting the super-rich whose fortunes are built by exploiting the poor," Hai teased. "Small landowners like you will be spared."

"If that's the case, I'll lobby Tan Lun, asking him to use his connections in the Personnel Ministry and transfer you to my county. At least, I can take some credit for securing a clean official with a strong sense of justice for my people."

Hai turned his eyes to the river and said, "I think you have overestimated my abilities as a government official. I don't even know if I can walk out of Chun'an alive."

Hai's remarks dampened Wang's cheerful mood.

"When is the rice market open?" Hai asked.

"About this time of the day. I think it's going to start at any moment."

"Why don't we go down there together," Hai suggested.

They were about to leave when they heard hurried footsteps behind. Turning around, they saw a group of uniformed soldiers running up with their matchlock harquebus and handguns.

"Hurry up," an officer with a dagger strapped to his waist ordered. "See those junks on the left sides? Get them all and don't let any run away."

The soldiers dashed down towards the port, running over several longshoremen who were too slow to move to the side. "Get out of our way," the soldiers yelled. "Seize those illegal rice boats."

Hai's face turned grim. "Let's go and find out what's happening," he said to Wang as they hurried down towards the port. The soldiers were relentless. As soon as the sampans pulled in, the soldiers used mooring ropes to tether the grain-carrying sampans to docks and then fired at the grain sacks on deck with handguns. As the magistrates watched, the masts collapsed, and the sails flew in the air before falling down. Sacks of rice were riddled with holes, like beehives. Rice flew out onto the deck and into the river. Farmers on the sampans scurried around out of desperation to block the holes with their bare hands but to little avail. Some even threw themselves onto the sacks, hoping to stem the flow…

"Don't move," the soldiers lining the port barked at the farmers on the boats as they reloaded their guns. "Raise your hands and kneel on the deck there."

The farmers couldn't bear to drop their hands plugging the holes on the grain sacks, but the soldiers jumped onto their sampans, beating them with gun stocks. Many farmers dropped to their knees helplessly.

On one sampan, the farmers were resisting, standing there in defiance. The officer immediately ordered his soldiers to aim their firearms at the boat. "Did you hear me?" the officer yelled. "Kneel down before I shoot you."

Under the threat, some farmers bent their legs and were about to comply when a young man urged his fellow farmers to remain standing. "We're not violating any laws," he said. "Let me go and talk with them."

The young man was Chee Dazhu, who had attempted to block the horsemen earlier when they attempted to destroy the rice seedlings. As he climbed onto the gangway, the officer ordered his soldiers to be ready to shoot at Chee. "This man is their leader," he shouted lividly. "Go and get him."

Chee paused in the middle of the gangway and decided to address the crowd gathering at the port. "My fellow countrymen, we are farmers in Chun'an County. A terrible flood has destroyed our crops. With each passing day, people are dying of hunger. We have collected some money to buy rice here so we can go home to feed our starving villagers."

Loud murmurs spread through the crowd. The soldiers, sympathetic to Chee's predicament, stood there, frozen.

"The government troops are here to arrest us and seize the lifeline to flood victims," Chee continued. "If we're killed, I want you to bear witness to such brutality."

The officer collected himself and changed his order. "Capture him," he howled. But a soldier who misunderstood his order pulled the trigger on his gun in a moment of sheer panic.

Bam!

Before the crowd figured out what was happening, Chee faltered, his hands grabbing the handrail on the gangway. The shot triggered an uproar in the crowd. Baffled by the commotion, the soldiers who had been ordered to capture Chee panicked. The individual who accidentally fired the shot dropped his gun to the floor in fear. His officer kicked him in the shins. "Why the hell are you dumping your weapon?" the officer howled. "Pick it up. Go and get him."

The soldier bent over to collect his gun before aiming at the boat. Meanwhile, two other soldiers dashed over to the gangway, where two young farmers came to Chee's rescue, trying to help him to his feet. Chee urged his fellow villagers to withdraw from the scene and step away from the soldiers.

The two soldiers approached Chee, pointing their long firearms at his head. "Stand up," they ordered. Chee rose slowly and straightened his body. Fresh blood oozed out of his right leg, prompting a few sympathetic soldiers to stand aside and let Chee take care of the bleeding. Tearing off his shirt, Chee wrapped it around his leg. When he got to his feet, he asked his captors, "Are you two from Zhejiang?"

The soldiers exchanged glances with each other and said nothing.

"We are farmers from Chun'an County and just suffered a terrible flood," Chee continued. "We're not stealing rice here. If you take our rice and our boats, many in my village could starve to death."

Seeing that the soldiers were standing still, listening to Chee's plea, the officer yelled, "Why don't you arrest him? Take him."

Once again, the soldiers pointed their guns to Chee's head. As they were about to seize Chee, a loud voice sounded in the crowd. "This is outrageous," bellowed Wang, who looked furious as he stepped forward in front of a large group of surprised onlookers. Hai, who was taken aback by Wang's action, followed him.

"Who has sent you here?" Wang questioned the officer.

"The Provincial Justice Department," the officer said, eyeing him suspiciously. "We're merely following orders. Please stay out of our way."

"Haven't these folks told you that they're flood victims and are trying to buy rice to save lives?" Wang chided. "When you arrest and hurt people like this, aren't you worried that someone might report you to the Imperial Palace?"

"Who are you? Where do you work?"

"I'm the new magistrate of Jiande County."

The office looked visibly relieved. "These people are from Chun'an, not Jiande. I have orders from the provincial yamen, and I think Your Honour should mind your own business."

The officer turned to his soldiers and demanded, "Arrest them and seize their boats."

"Wait," Hai stepped forward and stated calmly. "This should be under my jurisdiction then. You claim that these folks are thieves. What have they stolen?"'

Judging from Hai's appearance, the officer initially thought Hai was Wang's assistant, but the tone in Hai's voice indicated that he might be more powerful than the magistrate of Jiande. Baffled, the officer asked, "You are..."

"There is no need to tell you who I am. Answer my question first."

"The imperial inspector's yamen has put up a notice, banning the sale and purchase of rice this month," the officer recited. "Violators will be subject to arrest and confiscation of vessels."

"I was just there yesterday," Hai retorted. "How come I don't know about it?"

The officer shook his head vigorously. "Don't ask me. I'm merely carrying out an order issued by the Justice Department."

"All right, let me take care of it," Hai commanded. "Please order your soldiers to get off the boats."

"I don't think I can. For us to withdraw, I'll need another order from the Justice Department."

"Why don't you release these people first, and I'll go with you to the Justice Department," Hai promised.

Before the hesitant officer had a chance to respond, Hai strode towards Chee's sampan. The crowd stepped aside to let him pass. "Get out of there," Hai yelled at the soldiers guarding the gangway. Noticing that their officer had shown restraint in front of this unknown person, the soldiers complied and backed out.

Hai mounted the gangway and stopped in front of Chee. "Are you truly from Chun'an?" he probed gently. "Is your family affected by the flood?"

"Yes, sir. I'm a mulberry farmer, and my name is Chee Dazhu."

"Are you buying rice to help with flood victims?"

"Yes, sir. The price of land has gone down to five hundred kilograms of rice per mu. We don't want to sell so cheap. So we've collected some money to buy rice so we could survive the flood and keep our land."

Chee's description seemed to match what he had learned about the situation in Chun'an. Hai nodded and advised, "It is not a good idea to fight the yamen. Take the rice and go home with your fellow villagers. Let me take care of the stuff here."

At this urging, two farmers came over to carry Chee back to the boat, but Chee wouldn't move. "Your Honour, may I ask who you are?" Chee asked.

"I'm Hai Rui, the new magistrate of Chun'an County."

Chee's eyes glistened with tears. He fell on his knees. So did the other two farmers.

"This is not the place to give salute. Leave now. I'll be in Chun'an in the next couple of days."

After Chee embarked on his sampan, Hai remained on the gangway and turned to the soldiers on the other boats. "Get off their boats and come down over here," he shouted.

The soldiers looked to their officer for command.

Wang, who stood next to the officer, nudged him. "We have already promised to go with you to the Provincial Justice Department. Why don't you order your men to retreat from there? Do you want your job or not?"

The officer complied and gathered his men from the sampans. Before jumping off the gangway, he waved at the farmers on the boats. "Set sail and ship the rice home!"

Some farmers climbed up onto the mast to fix the broken sails while others hoisted their sails and moved slowly away.

"Let's go to the Justice Department," Hai told the officer.

7

When Ho Maocai learned about the events earlier in the day at the port, he flew into a rage. If he could have his way, he would definitely send his soldiers to arrest these two trouble-making magistrates and throw them in prison.

Unfortunately, Ho realised that he was not authorised to touch them. The Ming Law stipulated that only an imperial inspector had the power to impeach or detain current officials who were accused of criminal offences. All he could do was summon Hai Rui and Wang Yongji to the imperial inspector's yamen. Before he went in to see Zheng Bichang, Ho ordered the two magistrates to wait in the visitors' room.

"Before we even figure out how to rein in Gao Hanwen, we now have other troublemakers," Ho fulminated. "The two new magistrates colluded with bandits and resisted orders from the provincial yamen. If these people keep messing with us, we won't be able to get anything done. How are we expected to purchase the farmland? Once June is gone, we're going to miss the mulberry-planting season."

Zheng sat by a tea table, looking petulant. "How do you expect me to fire them?" he ranted.

"You're the imperial inspector," Ho suggested. "You can certainly submit a report to the Imperial Palace, requesting that they be censured and their positions terminated. While they're waiting for their verdicts, I'll notify the public and appoint the deputies in the two counties as acting chiefs."

"All right, let's work hard on getting rid of these two," said Zheng, who rose from his chair and slowly walked towards his desk. "If possible, why don't we remove Gao Hanwen from his position as well?"

"We probably need to be more cautious when it comes to Gao," Ho replied before realising that Zheng had been ridiculing him all along. Pausing for a few seconds, he suppressed his anger and switched gears. "You've heard back from our friend Old Shen, have you? Did Gao take the bait?"

"No, I haven't heard a word from Shen," Zheng uttered a long sigh. "But I have received a bunch of letters from Beijing, telling me to put a temporary brake on purchasing farmland and implementing the rice-to-mulberry conversion. I have no idea what is going on."

From Zheng's defeated look, Ho knew that something bad was about to happen. "Where are the letters?" he asked. "What else do the letters say?"

Zheng picked up a stack of unsealed missives, picking one on the top and tossing it to Ho. "They just arrived – one from the Privy Council and the other from the Interior Ministry," said Zheng. "The one I gave you is from the grand secretary. Read it carefully."

Ho skimmed the first few lines quickly and stopped. "These two new magistrates came at the recommendation of the Prince of Yu?" Ho remarked with an expression of disbelief.

Zheng ignored Ho's remarks. "Read this one." He handed another letter to Ho. "It's from Yang Gonggong."

Looking perturbed, Ho surveyed the pages quickly. "Yang Gonggong is going to stay in Beijing for a few more days?" Ho asked. "The land conversion is a major undertaking, but he chooses to be absent. What does it mean? What are we going to do?"

"The picture is getting clearer now," said Zheng, who sat down and stared distractedly at the garden outside. "The grand secretary junior has appointed a new mayor for us, but this new mayor took sides against us the minute he arrived. Then the Prince of Yu has chosen two new magistrates for us. Those two have started to boycott and tried to overturn the ban on rice sales before they even assume office. Yang Gonggong's absence is also intriguing. Why is he hiding in Beijing when we need him the most? There is only one explanation... Up there inside the palace, there's chaos. Two factions are engaging in a sword fight, and they are getting back at each other by hacking away at us in Zhejiang. Do you understand what I mean? Stop talking about dismissing these new appointees. If you have any ingenious ways to get rid of me, I'll be forever grateful and gladly let you take over."

While shocked by Zheng's diatribe, Ho did not fully share Zheng's pessimism. "Your Honour, do not forget the fact that the Imperial Palace is facing some huge budgetary problems and the treasury is almost empty," Ho pointed out. "They see the rice-to-mulberry conversion plan in Zhejiang as a lifesaver. If we fail, those in Beijing will not let us get away with it. We have to make it happen. That's our only option. Look at Governor Hu Zongxian. He lost his imperial inspector's job because of his opposition to the land-conversion policy. Regardless of who their backers are, the new mayor and two magistrates will follow Hu's footsteps and embark on a self-destructive path if they don't jump on the bandwagon fast."

"Do you still believe that Hu Zongxian got the short end of the stick?" Zheng asked.

Ho looked baffled.

"We naively thought that Hu had lost his bearings as he was climbing up his career ladder. We thought he had become muddleheaded and out of touch," Zheng said. "Looking back, it was actually one of his shrewdest political gambits. Now, we have no clue where he stands."

"I just don't get it," Ho shook his head.

"I didn't get it either," Zheng explained. "Come to think of it, though, Governor Hu recognised earlier on that the Imperial Palace's rice-to-mulberry policy would be a suicidal move. So he designed a ruse that could get him out of the mess at the cost of losing his mentor. By openly standing up to the grand secretary, he knew very well that it would incur the wrath of his mentor and get him fired. It was like a cicada sloughing off its skin – using camouflage to create an illusion to distract people so you can hide your real intention and protect yourself. Guess what – the grand secretary junior and his people totally fell for it. They removed him from the imperial inspector's position and made me his replacement. You also end up getting a promotion as the chief administrator. For a while, the two of us stupidly clutched these promotions as precious gifts. Now, we are stuck and can't even reverse if we want to."

Ho tilted his head, trying to detect the proper logic in Zheng's explanation. The more he thought about it, the more confused he became. "I still have problems following you," Ho rose from his chair and pleaded. "Could you be more specific?"

"How specific do you want me to be?" Zheng said, with a hint of impatience in his tone. "Now that the Imperial Palace is running out of money, His Majesty passed the bucket to the grand secretary and his son, who have been forced to find ways to lower the budget deficit. If they can bring in money, the father and son can stay around for a few more years. If not, His Majesty would undoubtedly kick them out. Therefore, the Prince of Yu and members of the Clear Stream faction are scheming to sabotage the land-conversion plan here. Their ultimate goal is to topple the grand secretary and his son. If they prevail, you and I will be the first to fall. There's no doubt about that."

"If that's the case, the grand secretary and his son would go all out to make it work. Why would they send an obstructionist over to contain us?" said Ho.

"I'm wondering about the same thing," Zheng reasoned. "If the land-conversion policy succeeds and we generate enough money for the financially strapped treasury, we could probably help the grand secretary and his son survive the ordeal they're facing. That would give us a pass as well. As the saying goes, one good deed will sometimes redeem several bad ones. But Gao Hanwen's fierce opposition yesterday aroused my suspicion, making me rethink this whole deal. If the grand secretary junior truly wants to get this done, he had many candidates to choose from, but why did he choose Gao? I finally figured it out today. The grand secretary junior must have been under a lot of pressure from people who are rallying around the Prince of Yu. Besides, Governor Hu's betrayal further complicated things, throwing the plan into disarray. That's why they picked a person who was acceptable to both sides. Everybody knows that the land-conversion policy is like 'cutting off a piece of flesh to patch up a boil' – a terrible stop-gap measure. But, now, they want us to carry out this challenging dirty job. At the same time, they don't trust us and send a self-righteous 'doctor' to oversee the operation. In other words, they not only need money to reduce the budget deficit but also want to look respectable. So we have to buy farmland to convert it into mulberry while keeping the farmers at bay. Once the money comes in, every single penny will have to be turned over to Beijing. It's going to bleed us dry. How can you expect a horse to run faster without feeding it?"

"As the saying goes, leading the life of a whore but expecting a monument to her chastity," Ho interjected. "Let them get the chastity monument, and I don't mind being the whore. If the worst comes to the worst, we just don't share the profit."

"If only they allow you to be the whore! I'm afraid it's not that easy," Zheng continued. "We might not take any commission from the land-conversion deal, but what about the eunuchs and members of the Privy Council? Besides, if we allow Gao Hanwen and his two new magistrates to have their way and fix the land prices at two thousand or twenty-five hundred kilograms of rice per mu, do you really think Shen Yishi would want to pay that much?

"If Shen refuses, our plan to increase silk production by three hundred thousand bolts of silk per year will go up in smoke, and there is no way we could fulfil the five-hundred-thousand export order. We're already approaching the end of May. If we keep messing around with these people and delaying the implementation of the land-conversion programme to late June and July, the whole deal will fall through. When that happens, the Imperial Palace would no doubt launch an inquisition, and it wouldn't be hard for them to find out about who deliberately broke the dams to cause the flooding. As you and I know, the grand secretary junior and the South China Textile Bureau would try to wash their hands of it and shift the blame to us. It's only a matter of time. They probably already have the meat wagon ready, waiting to take you and me to the capital city for our trial."

Ho felt as if his head were about to explode; his face flushed red, and his eyes flashed with anger. "If so, we'll drag them down with us," he muttered through his teeth. "We're not fish and meat on their chopping board, and we will not simply throw ourselves at their mercy. We can always muddy the water. If they dare touch us, we'll hurt them as well." Despite his short temper, Ho was full of ideas, especially when it came to sabotage.

"How would you muddy the water?" asked Zheng.

"Didn't you say that Gao Hanwen came on the recommendation of the grand secretary junior? Didn't you also mention that Hai Rui and Wang Yongji were sent by the Prince of Yu? We'll let them take on the task, forcing them to accept the land purchase price of sixty or eighty kilograms of rice per mu."

Zheng was incredulous. "You saw Gao's reaction to our plan yesterday," he said. "Even though Shen is trying to lure Gao into his trap, we still don't know if Gao will fall for it or not. Besides, Hai Rui and Wang Yongji are friends of the prince. There is no way they'll follow our ideas."

"If so, we will probably need to take a big gamble," Ho whispered before stepping out. Zheng overheard him telling the receptionist not to let anyone barge in. Then, he re-emerged, shut the door behind him and went over to Zheng.

"What kind of gamble? Tell me!" Zheng asked eagerly.

"Cooking up a 'collusion with the pirates' charge," Ho blurted out.

"Colluding with the pirates?" Zheng asked, his face turning pale. "Are you crazy? Colluding with the pirates is a cardinal crime, and it's punishable by the extermination of our whole families."

"We're not doing that," Ho explained. "We'll charge them with colluding with the pirates."

"How? Where is your evidence?"

Ho stepped over, sat on a chair next to Zheng and whispered, "Do you remember the farmer who was captured last month?"

"Do you mean the mulberry grower from Chun'an who

attempted to instigate a riot when we sent troops to destroy the farmland there?"

"Yes. The former mayor of Hangzhou arrested him on charges of colluding with the pirates, but Governor Hu set him free. I just heard from my men at the port that this same person has gathered a bunch of unruly folks in Chun'an, trying to buy up rice and dissuade farmers from selling their land. Our folks got him again, but Hai Rui has ordered his release. I assume he's going to scout around for more rice during the next few days. I'm going to figure out a way that can lure him and other farmers into buying rice from the pirates. If we can catch both the farmers and the pirates in action, they are doomed. Then I'm going to give that case to Hai Rui to handle."

Zheng was intrigued. "Please go on," he encouraged.

"Based on *The Great Ming Code*, those who are found colluding with the pirates would be executed on the spot. I'll hand this case to Hai Rui. He'll have to kill a farmer on the first day at his new job. The execution would help deter those who refuse to sell their land."

"What if Hai Rui refuses to carry out the executions?"

"He already intervened and had those unruly folks released today," Ho said. "If he continues to resist the execution order, it will give us the excuse to arrest him on suspicion of colluding with the pirates."

"That's not too far-fetched," Zheng nodded.

"If Hai Rui follows through and allows the execution to go ahead, nobody in Chun'an would dare to raise money to buy rice again," Ho recounted confidently. "Without food, farmers will have no alternative but to sell their land. By then, it will be futile for Hai Rui and Wang Yongji to block the plan because farmers won't even listen to them any more. Besides, refusal to sell farmland could inevitably lead to starvation and death, which could be the basis for us to do them in."

"How can we entice farmers to buy rice from the pirates?" Zheng enquired with scepticism.

"I'll take care of it," Ho promised. "You go and check with Shen Yishi. If Gao could turn around and accept our proposal at our meeting tomorrow, it would make things much easier. We'll use the collusion-with-pirates excuse to nab the two maverick magistrates as well as those leading rebels. It is critical that we trap Gao Hanwen tonight, at whatever cost."

Zheng sat in his chair, quiet and pensive. Then, he spoke up slowly. "If you want to press the collusion charge, make sure you do a clean job. Don't leave behind any damning evidence."

"No need to worry," Ho bragged. "I have done this for more than ten years."

Zheng rose from his chair and made his decision. "Since they've left us with no choice, let's do it. By the way, where are the two magistrates?"

"Waiting outside in the reception room."

"You've played the bad cop all day, and I probably need to say a few kind words to calm them down. Go ahead and take care of your business."

"All right." Ho nodded and left. Before he reached the door, he turned around and urged, "Please check with Shen to make sure the plan is going smoothly."

※

Led by a dozen prison guards holding blazing torches, Ho strode along a wide passageway in the dungeon. In the glaring light from the torches, he could see a row of thick metal bars, behind which were individual cells with exposed sturdy rock walls. In a cell at the far end of the row, a Japanese ronin was imprisoned; fully shackled by thick metal chains. Unlike other prisoners, he was clean-shaven and dressed in a clean silk kimono, with a bun on the top of his head – a typical Japanese pirate hairdo.

Ho sat on a chair outside the ronin's cell, flanked on both sides by guards and soldiers, who were carrying long firearms. "We always mean what we say," Ho said gently to the ronin. "For two years, we've kept you alive and haven't killed any of your friends and followers. Each day, we give you whatever you request. Why are you still so distrustful?"

"You didn't kill me and my men because you wouldn't dare," the Japanese replied in a fluent Hangzhou dialect. "Don't forget that we killed your predecessor and his family after he ordered the execution of my brothers."

The prisoner's insolence upset him. Knitting his brows, Ho hardened his tone. "Stop bragging," he mocked. "If you are truly that powerful, why don't you go and take revenge on Hu Zongxian and Qi Jiguang and exterminate their families?"

Ho's words touched a sore spot. Giving a snort of disgust, the Japanese prisoner smashed a low wooden table into pieces. "One of these days, we're going to kill Hu Zongxian and Qi Jiguang," he vowed.

In response to his violent reaction, the guards raised their guns and formed a human wall in front of Ho.

"Move away." Ho brushed his guards aside and continued his conversation. "Mr Inoue Toushirou, I've told you what I need you to do. I know you Japanese are known for being faithful to your words and to those who have helped you. If you agree to my request, I'll release a dozen or so of your friends who are being locked up here. If you do a good job, you'll be awarded with bolts of high-quality silk. Are you willing to do it or not? I'm waiting for your answer."

Sitting with his legs crossed and his eyes closed, Inoue Toushirou heaved a deep sigh. It was obvious that he was pondering Ho's offer. He and the guards held their breath, waiting quietly. Occasional sparks from the torches made loud cracking noises.

"Get me a fugu fish," Inoue Toushirou suddenly mumbled, with his eyes still closed.

"What?" Ho didn't catch what he was saying and turned to a guard. "What did he say?"

"Sir, he wanted us to get him a fugu fish," the guard replied.

"Go and get him one."

"But sir, where do we get it at this late hour?"

"Go to the yamen of the River Flood Control Commission now, and tell the eunuchs there to find him a Fugu fish, regardless of the cost!"

In the bookkeeper's office next to his silk mill, the grim-faced Shen Yishi piled up a stack of ledgers on top of a desk. Gao Hanwen sat on a chair nearby, watching. "Now that you and I are alone, let me be bold enough to show you these books, which I haven't shown anyone yet – not even the imperial inspector. "

"Then I shouldn't read them either," said Gao, who immediately rose.

"I'm not asking you to read them."

Gao looked baffled.

"I just want to confide something in you, both for your sake and mine," Shen said calmly. "It's purely for selfish reasons – I'll enlighten you later. It's totally up to you to decide whether to believe it or not."

Gao fixed an intense gaze at Shen.

"Here's what I'm going to do," Shen said, picking up a ledger. "You don't need to go through all of them. I'll just pick a few important items from the past two years and read them aloud to you. Let's just pretend that I'm mumbling to myself and you haven't heard a word of them."

Out of curiosity, Gao sat down again, his face turning serious. Shen opened one book on the top and started:

In May 1560, the thirty-ninth year under the reign of Emperor Jiajing, fresh raw silk became available on the market. In June, the South China Textile Bureau ordered one hundred thousand bolts of high-class silk and sent it to eunuchs at the inner palace. In July, the governor's yamen in Zhejiang and Yingtian purchased with taxpayer's money fifty thousand bolts of high-class silk, one hundred thousand bolts of medium-class silk and one hundred thousand bolts of printed cloth and shipped them to the Ministry of Public Works, which used them to gift the dukes and princes, as well as kings of the tributary states, on behalf of His Majesty.

In October, the Textile Bureau concluded a trade deal with Persian merchants, who purchased two hundred thousand bolts of silk, translating into two million and two hundred thousand taels of silver. The payment went directly to the Interior Ministry coffers. Note: No need to notify the Ministry of Revenue.

The transactions jolted Gao out of his seat, but Shen ignored his reaction. Picking up another book, he resumed reading and kept his tone calm.

> In February of 1561, the Interior Ministry issued an imperial edict, ordering all silk manufacturers in Yingtian and Zhejiang to support a trade deal with western merchants. The previous year, there were one hundred and twenty thousand bolts of silk in reserve. All the reserves should be kept and used for export this year. In March, the Interior Ministry issued an imperial edict, ordering the Textile Bureau to take one hundred thousand bolts of silk in reserve and ship them to the family of Princess Li in Beijing on behalf of His Majesty.

By then, Gao had become too stunned to breathe.

"Why don't I stop for now," Shen said, putting the ledger back on the pile. "As you probably know, there are three large silk manufacturers in the cities of Nanjing, Suzhou and Hangzhou. You'll find hundreds of other smaller ones in the provinces of Jiangsu and Zhejiang. We also produce lots of cotton fabrics. Theoretically, if we collect half of the profits from these textile sales and give them to the national treasury, the money would be sufficient to cover a third of the national spending."

Gao held his breath and stared at Shen.

"But, unfortunately, despite the large amount of silk and cloth we have produced, we still need more, and the national treasury is still in the red. Why? This year, the Imperial Palace even proposed that we produce three hundred thousand more bolts of silk. Where are we getting the silk? That's how the land-conversion programme came into being."

"Why are you sharing this with me?" Gao asked.

"As I said, I'm doing this for a selfish reason. What you're hearing today will help you get a better idea of the local situation. It also helps you get smarter at your job. By confiding in you, I hope that we can be friends, even though I might be unworthy to be connected with Your Honour."

Gao simply stared at Shen without talking.

"When the imperial inspector notified me last night, asking me to brief you on the silk industry here in Zhejiang, I was planning to tell you about these transactions," said Shen. "But, hearing you talk so eloquently about music and history, I've recognised that you are the musically talented son of the well-known Gao family in southern Jiangsu Province. I started to feel attached to you. You probably remember the story of poet Su Dongpao. He was accused of implicitly criticising Emperor Zhenzong in his literary works. After the emperor read about it, he had planned to have Su Dongpo executed. But the empress consort opposed the decision on the grounds that it was not auspicious to eliminate a talented poet. That simple advice saved Su Dongpo's life, who, during his subsequent exile, left us many literary masterpieces. I don't mean to compliment you, but I really think it a pity for such a talented scholar like you to fall into this big messy political vortex. What a waste. It's such a loss to the literary circles in southern China."

Shen's words, even though a bit grandiose and sycophantic, sounded sincere and personal. Gao was deeply touched by the silk merchant's gesture. "Mr Shen, what are you trying to say?" he asked.

"I shouldn't have shared these records with you because I have many friends in the government, such as Mr Zheng, Mr Ho and Yang Gonggong at the Textile Bureau," Shen admitted. "But my relationship with these people is purely business. One might know many people for life without any true connections, but, for a special few, one feels like old friends at their first meetings. If you see me as a good friend, I want to offer some heartfelt advice."

"Please! I'm all ears."

"You should urge the flood victims in Chun'an and Jiande to sell their land as soon as possible so we could start planting mulberry in June," admonished Shen. "Once this major task is complete, you should leave Zhejiang. I'll lobby Yang Gonggong, asking him to use his connections to transfer you back to Beijing or to another province."

Gao became alarmed. "If I understand you correctly, Mr Shen, you are suggesting that I should vote yes to the imperial inspector's proposal and allow flood victims to sell their land at six hundred kilograms of rice or less per mu."

"The arrow is fitted to the string, and we're at the point of no return," Shen replied resolutely. "If you don't support this proposal, there is no way we can implement the land- conversion policy this year. If we fail, you'll be the first scapegoat. They'll put all the blame on you."

"If the sole purpose of the Imperial Palace is to implement the land-conversion policy, I wouldn't have accepted the assignment and come over here," Gao said, his attitude changing from mere eagerness to righteous indignation. "When I proposed the policy of land conversion through disaster relief, my intention was to both help our country resolve a financial crisis and relieve flood victims of dire poverty. I want to thank you for taking the risk of sharing this inside information with me – it is eye-opening. But these shady transactions that you have shown me shouldn't prevent me from acting on behalf of the one hundred thousand farmers who could lose their livelihood next year. If I did otherwise, I would be selfishly putting my career above public interest."

"Please forgive me for saying this... If I put it mildly, I would say that Your Honour lacks familiarity with the local situation. If I'm being harsh – I would call your views too bookish and one-sided."

"May I ask what you mean by bookish?" Gao asked, looking disappointed.

"You argued against the proposal because you think farmers would lose their livelihood after selling their farmland. But you have overlooked some critical facts. After the silk merchants buy up their land, who do they hire to grow mulberry and weave the silk?"

Gao did not answer.

"Many farmers today don't own an inch of land. They simply lease the land from landowners and split the profits at harvest time. They make a pretty good living. Are you aware of any starvation among this population? At the same time, when we convert farmland and start to grow mulberry, we need to hire people to plant mulberry seedlings, pick mulberry leaves and rear silkworms. In the end, we also have to employ workers to weave them into silk. Think about it. Rice farmers who sell their own land this year could all become hired hands of big silk merchants next year. They can make a living growing mulberry or rearing silkworm. Nobody will be starving. Besides, our Imperial Government will not turn a blind eye to starvation if it occurs, will it?"

Gao thought about it for a few minutes before looking up at Shen. "Based on what you just told me, big silk merchants who have acquired farmland from flood victims will hire them next year. Is that correct?"

"Of course. Silk merchants don't do field work. Without hiring those farmers, who is going to grow mulberry for them?"

"Will the flood victims get the sixty-forty split on the profits, like they do with planting rice?"

Shen was stumped by the question.

"As we can predict, there would be a large number of landless farmers competing to lease land. If landowners increase their profit split to seventy-thirty or eighty-twenty or even ninety-ten, what would farmers do? Are you going to lease or not?"

"I apologise for being unable to answer your detailed queries, but, since time immortal, people have always remained unchanged while officials come and go like flowing water," Shen sighed. "If all the Ming officials are so concerned about ordinary folks like you are, we don't even need to have this conversation."

"Regardless, it is an honour to make your acquaintance." Gao rose from his chair. "When I have a moment of peace one of these days, I'll have to come and chat with you about music. Thanks for sharing with me the information regarding imperial spending. I promise I will keep it to myself and give your ideas some serious thought."

"You seem to imply that we won't be able to see each other again," Shen said with a charming smile. "It's still early. Would it be possible if I could take up another half an hour of your time?"

Gao knew exactly what Shen wanted, but he asked anyway. "What do you have in mind?"

"I wonder if you could spend a little time with my niece, enlightening her with your understanding of *The Guangling Melodies.*"

Gao looked hesitant; though excitement appeared on his face, deep down he had already said yes.

"Only half an hour," Shen pleaded. "Then, if she gets it, it's her good karma. If not, I can take comfort in the fact that I have tried."

Gao turned his gaze to the sky outside the window. It was still light outside. "Mr Shen, you've put me on the spot," he said. "Your niece plays elegantly."

Shen took those remarks as "yes" and bowed deeply to thank Gao.

When Gao re-entered the studio with Shen, he saw that Madam Yun was standing in the middle of the room, rather than sitting on the platform bed, practising her guqin. There was an embroidered silk cushion next to her feet.

"It is my honour and your luck to have His Honour as your mentor," Shen said to Madam Yun. "Please pay respect to your teacher now."

Madam Yun slowly dropped to her knees and bowed.

"Oh, please stand," Gao interjected, looking flustered.

Madam Yun bowed three times before rising. Then, she stood there with her head down. Silence fell.

"We only have half an hour," Shen finally spoke up. "Why don't you ask His Honour to play the piece and then tell you why you did it wrong. Try to learn it by heart. Once you have taken lessons from His Honour, I don't think I'll be able to coach you any more. In comparison, my knowledge and skills are too limited."

Gao might have taken Shen's remarks at face value, but Madam Yun understood their hidden meaning – Shen was not talking about music. Rather, it was a statement of how their heart-wrenching breakup felt. Conceited and ambitious, Shen set up a lethal trap for this talented young scholar, who could have swept any woman off her feet. How could outsiders see through such deceit and rancour?

"Understood," replied Madam Yun, who was slightly choked with emotion. When Shen shot a parting glance at Madam Yun, their eyes met. Gao seemed to have sensed something odd between the "uncle" and the "niece". As Gao was trying to figure out what it was, Shen quickly moved his stare away from Madam

Yun's face. "Please start," he said softly. "I'll wait outside and listen."

Shen left the studio and closed the door behind him. Music wafted out from inside. Shen returned to his office and sat by his desk. He kept his eyes wide open but had problems focusing. His mind wandered unfettered in the air like the sound of Madam Yun's guqin music, which he carefully monitored. Holding his breath, he attempted to capture every single note. Sometimes, the melody became so intricately gentle that it blended seamlessly with the sound of nature.

Suddenly, urgent footsteps sounded outside the door. Involuntarily, Shen knitted his brows and looked up impatiently. His personal aide tiptoed in, announcing the arrival of four eunuchs from the South China Textile Bureau. Shen looked away. Thinking that his master was deeply immersed in the music, the aide backed out. He put a finger to his lips and urged the eunuchs to keep quiet and wait until the music was over.

The eunuchs felt slighted and annoyed. "You are the one who called us over," one of them whined loudly. "But then you kept us waiting outside. What's going on?"

"Forgive me, my friends," the aide whispered. "Just bear with me for a few more moments."

Barely had the aide finished his sentence when the study door opened. Shen emerged.

"Mr Shen," the four eunuchs bowed in respect.

Shen motioned for them to be quiet before inviting them inside. The four eunuchs, of diverse body types and shapes – one tall, one short, one fat and one thin – were trained like military men. They sat down on four chairs in unison. Shen walked over and handed each eunuch a money certificate.

"Please have some tea," the aide offered.

The eunuchs ignored the tea. Without any pretence, they quickly looked down at the certificates – each carried one thousand taels of silver. The generous amount on the certificates brought satisfied smiles to their faces. Tucking his cheque into his breast pocket, the fat eunuch asked, "Do you want us to act now?"

"No rush," Shen said. Then, he sat down on his chair and

resumed listening to the music, with his eyes closed. The four eunuchs waited patiently. The music from the studio reached a crescendo.

Inside the music studio, Gao Hanwen sat next to Madam Yun on the stage, solid like Mount Jade. The fingers on his left hand, which pressed and slid across the strings, moved so swiftly that it gave the illusion that multiple hands were flickering. At the same time, his right hand deftly plucked at the strings, dancing across like blurry raindrops pelting against a window. His silk robe flew like clouds surrounding a mountain. Madam Yun sat on her knees on the far left side of the guqin, looking catatonic and oblivious to the violent rhythm of the music.

His two hands stopped abruptly in mid-air. The sudden change jolted Madam Yun from her stupor. She fixed her eyes on Gao's hands. He seemed to have forgotten about Madam Yun's presence. Slowly, his left hand struck the strings at an angle while his right hand plucked it gently. The guqin gave out a forceful dint, which sounded like a howl or the cry of a final farewell, followed by a sorrowful and yet enchanting melody that captured what Gao described as the essence of Ji Kang's spirit before walking towards the execution ground. As the poet Qu Yuan wrote: *Because straight is the gate, and narrow is the way that leads into life, and few there be that find it.* Seeing the glistening tears in Gao's eyes, Madam Yun started to weep silently, tears streaming down her cheeks.

Outside, Shen sat there, transfixed. Holding back his own tears, he moved both of his hands slightly in the air, as if he were playing the guqin himself. The four eunuchs observed him, looking baffled. Suddenly, the music came to another abrupt stop. It took a while for Shen to realise that the music had come to an end. He stood up. The four eunuchs also rose. "Can we go and snatch him now?" the fat one asked.

Shen paused for a moment before sitting down again. "Let's give it a few more moments," he said.

Inside, Gao collected himself and turned to Madam Yun, who was sitting on her knees, rapt. The sight of Madam Yun made him dizzy, and his heart was beating violently. This feeling must have been what poets call "a high mountain being joined by a flowing stream". Gao no longer avoided Madam Yun's gaze. "You come and play it for me," he urged.

Madam Yun did not move. "Your Honour, it's time you left," she suddenly said. "We've already exceeded the half-hour limit. You'll be late for your next appointment."

Gao was shocked and somewhat offended by the abruptness of her words. But, when he looked at her again, he saw the sincerity in her eyes.

"Overstaying a few more moments wouldn't make much of a difference," he said with a smile. "I already promised your uncle that I was going to offer some guidance on the last movement. Come and play it."

Gao slid his body away and vacated the seat in front of the guqin, but Madam Yun did not move. Then, her eyes sparkled with determination, as if she had made an important life decision at that instant. "Your Honour, we all have to die anyway," she said. "When death arrives, would you be willing to make Mount Mang the final destination of your spirit?"

Gao was taken aback, but seeing the solemn expression on Madam Yun's face, he turned serious as well. "Of course, I would follow Ji Kang's path," he pledged.

"I will too," Madam Yun said before sitting in front of the guqin. Pressing a finger firmly on the guqin at an angle, she gently plucked a string, producing a similar howling sound, followed by a melody that bore a close similarity to that produced by Gao. While Madam Yun's rendition began to echo that of Gao, capturing the pain and sorrows of Ji Kang's last moments before his execution, it was also imbued with a sense of fearlessness, which accurately reflected Ji Kang's upright character and his uncompromising disdain for the ruling class in the Kingdom of Wei. Gao's heart leapt with admiration.

Outside, Shen noticed the unexpected tone in the music. Livid, he muttered to the eunuchs, "Go and get him."

The four eunuchs, who had waited impatiently for this moment, jumped up and swarmed towards the door like bees dashing out of the hives.

"Wait," Shen stopped them. "All I want is a piece of written proof. Don't hurt him."

"Understood," the fat eunuch replied. "Let's go."

The four eunuchs kicked the door open and burst into the studio. Their sudden appearance startled Gao.

The fat eunuch shot Gao a disdainful glance. "Your Honour is certainly a talented and romantic person."

"You're not only romantic but also bold," the thin eunuch jumped in with sarcasm. "How dare you seduce Yang Gonggong's feeder?"

"What shall we do?" the tall eunuch asked, feigning helplessness. "We're supposed to keep an eye on her. If Yang Gonggong finds out, we're all going to be in big trouble."

"I have an idea," the short eunuch suggested. "Can we bother Your Honour with a request? Could you be kind enough to write a note, claiming that your affair has nothing to do with us. I'm sure you understand our situation. Please have mercy and spare us the trouble."

"What are you talking about? Who is Yang Gonggong? What is a feeder?" Gao shouted. By then, he had realised that someone had set up an elaborate trap and he had fallen right into it. But still, he was incredulous and turned to Madam Yun, who sat in front of the zither, calmly.

"Yang Gonggong is the director of the South China Textile Bureau, and I'm the girl who services him," Madam Yun replied. "In the palace, people like me are called feeders."

Gao's face turned pale, and his body trembled. "Who is Mr Shen, really?" he asked. "Is he your uncle?"

"No, he's the largest silk merchant who bought me while I was a little girl in Suzhou and gifted me to Yang Gonggong."

The revelation stumped Gao, who felt as if someone had struck him on the chest with a blunt instrument. Meanwhile, Madam Yun gazed at him unabashedly. Her eyes showed guilt and deep affection.

"Please tell your owner who orchestrated this that I'm NOT going to write anything," he told Madam Yun. "By the way, please do not play *The Guangling Melodies* again. Maestro Ji Kang will condemn you from above for your treacherousness."

As Madam Yun lowered her head to hide her tears, Gao strode towards the door. The four eunuchs quickly formed a human wall and blocked him.

"We can't let you go," the fat eunuch said. "If we allow you to escape, what are we going to say to our master?"

Gao confronted the eunuch with disdain. "Are you asking my advice on what to do?"

"Yes," the fat one replied.

"Let me give you an idea," Gao said.

The four eunuchs made eye contact with each other and said, "All right. Please advise."

"Go and get your daggers, and kill me right here."

The four eunuchs were stunned momentarily before collecting themselves. "Are you blackmailing us?" asked the short one. "We're so scared."

"He is a mayor – killing someone means nothing to him," the thin one muttered sarcastically.

"Stop it," the fat eunuch chastised his colleagues before turning to Gao. "We don't have the right to kill you, but Yang Gonggong can kill us. All four of us have been assigned to watch Madam Yun while our master is away. But now, this woman has snuck away to cheat on him. If Yang Gonggong is back, he's going to kill us. Since we're going to die regardless, why don't you kill us first before you run away?"

Tearing his shirt open, the fat eunuch bared his chest, revealing a pile of pale flesh. Then, he dropped to his knees in front of Gao. The other three followed suit and fell on their knees with bare chests.

Gao stood there, exasperated at the eunuchs' shameless exhortation, but he had no idea what to do.

※

Darkness was descending, and there was no sign of Gao Hanwen. Hai Rui and Wang Yongji anxiously rose and walked to the door. They had been waiting inside the visitors' room at the mayor's yamen for hours. An aide stepped in to light the candles. "Could you go again and find out when His Honour is returning?" Wang asked. "Does anyone know where he has gone?"

"He went to visit a silk factory in the morning and came out of there in the early afternoon," replied the aide. "Then, he sent all of his assistants back here and went elsewhere. Nobody knew where. All he said was that the South China Textile Bureau would arrange a sedan chair to take him home. May I recommend that you take a rest at your hotel? Once His Honour is back, I'll let him know right away."

Hesitant, Wang looked to Hai, who insisted that they should stay.

"All right," the aide said. "I'll prepare some food for you."

After the aide left, Wang became more concerned. "We're discussing the proposal tomorrow morning, but our mayor is nowhere to be seen," he said. "Do you think something might have gone wrong…"

"Let's just wait a bit longer," Hai suggested. "If he doesn't show up at seven o'clock, we'll look for him at the imperial inspector's yamen."

As they were talking, Gao Hanwen stepped in with the aide, who carried a lantern. Both Wang and Hai rose to greet him, but Gao looked too distracted to notice them.

"You can go now," Gao said to his aide; his voice sounded a bit hoarse.

After the aide exited the room, Gao realised that Hai and Wang were standing there, waiting to greet him. He quickly collected himself and said, "I'm sorry – I didn't realise that you two would be still waiting for me at this late hour."

"Since we're revisiting the proposal tomorrow, we hope to strategise and hear your views," said Hai.

Gao shifted his gaze away uneasily. "I have nothing to be ashamed of before the heavenly god and men," he said. "I hope the two of you can fight for the interests of people in Chun'an and Jiande."

Shocked and baffled, Wang looked at Hai, who fixed his eyes on Gao's face. They both suspected that something had happened, but neither knew what it was.

The meeting to discuss the land-conversion proposal resumed. What a difference a day made. The mood in the room had changed from sombre to confident. Zheng Bichang was sitting in his old chair behind the centre of the desk. Despite his grave expression, he remained alert. His eyes scanned the room, sizing up everyone in attendance.

Ho, surly and disagreeable at the previous discussion, looked unusually relaxed. He sat slumped on a chair on the left side of the desk, playfully tapping his fingers on the desk. What was officialdom, anyway? It was the domain of officials. Outside the domain, one hankered after the pomp and style. Once inside, Ho tried to build charisma, creating a positive aura around him.

The officials who attended the discussion today could feel a different vibe from Zheng and Ho, even though they had no clue as to what had happened after their previous meeting.

Could the proposal sail through? They couldn't help scrutinising Gao's face, trying to find some clues. Gao sat upright on the right side of Zheng, looking his usual self. But upon closer inspection, one could discover a subtle difference on his face, which looked haggard and showed traces of fatigue – probably from the long journey. He stared off into space. In addition, there was no aura of excitement in the meeting that typically surrounded a new appointee. In fact, he seemed to be a bit lost.

Hai and Wang sat on two benches that had been brought in at the last minute and placed at each end of the desk. With a heavy heart, Wang watched Hai at the opposite end while Hai was studying Gao's reaction.

"Let's start," Zheng spoke up, looking straight ahead at the garden outside. Attendees straightened their backs and became attentive.

"As the saying goes, one does not realise the difficulty of an undertaking until one has experienced it oneself," he said. "Mayor Gao visited the Textile Bureau yesterday. Our two new magistrates had the chance to walk around the rice market. By now, I assume that they should have a better idea of how to implement the disaster-relief-through-land-conversion policy. Let's take another stab at the proposal today."

Zheng's aide picked up a stack of newly copied proposals and began walking around the room, placing a copy in front of each attendee. Since Hai and Wang sat on benches without a desk, he handed them the proposal. Except for the faint sounds of the pages turning, the room was quiet. It didn't take long to peruse the two-page document, which merely contained six paragraphs of more than two hundred characters. Everything remained the same – not a single character had been changed or added.

People exchanged glances knowingly before turning to Zheng, who was still gazing straight ahead into the garden outside. Wang peeked at Hai, who had closed his eyes with the proposal sitting on his lap.

Meanwhile, Ho kept his eyes trained on Gao. When he noticed that the new mayor did not even touch the proposal in front of him, he couldn't help asking, "Mayor Gao, are you done with both pages?"

"Do I have to?" Gao raised his head and replied with an uncompromising tone. "Not a character has changed since I last read it."

"It's true that we haven't changed a word," said Ho, who leaned back in his chair, with an arrogant demeanour as if he could instantly crush any opponent into flying ashes. "Mr Gao, you started out as a scholar and should know that a good article often requires no addition or deletion, and it stands as a masterpiece regardless."

When Ho deliberately emphasised the word *masterpiece*, Gao flinched, as if someone had thumped at his chest, but he managed to stare right into Ho's eyes in defiance.

"If we do need to modify anything, I would change the slogan to *Resolving both challenges without a single word change*," said Ho with complacency.

Gao held on to the edge of the desk, attempting to rise, but suddenly looked like he was experiencing dizziness. Meanwhile, Zheng stood up. Scanning the room, he said, "Yesterday, we held a long discussion with Mayor Gao regarding how to implement the rice-to-mulberry land conversion in Zhejiang, especially in the counties of Chun'an and Jiande. At the moment, we only have three days' worth of rice for flood victims. At the same time, the mulberry season is upon us, and the seedlings will need to be planted by June. Also, the flooding problem is still pretty dire. If we keep postponing and can't make a decision soon, we will be condemned for failing to live up to His Majesty's expectations as well as for ruining the lives of ordinary people here. Therefore, after getting a better grip on the situation, Mayor Gao has agreed to our plan. Now that we don't have any opposition, let's sign off on it."

Calligraphy brushes and ink had been prepared for every official, most of whom quickly hunched over the proposal to sign their names on it. But Gao sat there without picking up his brush.

Zheng looked Gao in the eye and reminded him, "Mayor Gao, are you going to sign it?"

"Without any changes, I can't give my approval," Gao said, after summoning up whatever courage he had left.

Zheng eyed him critically. "Why don't you think about it more?" he asked Gao calmly.

As Gao struggled to stand up, Zheng shouted out to the servants, "Bring out the tea."

As if on cue, a male servant stepped in carrying a tray with eight cups of tea on top. Rather than following the order of each official's ranking, the servant reversed it, starting with Hai and Wang, two low-level magistrates who had been invited as guests. After placing the tea on their benches, the servant went around the room, serving those who were sitting behind the long desk. Soon, there was only one cup left on his tray. The servant stopped in front of Gao. With a faint smile, he raised the tray slightly.

Gao did not take the cup. "Please put it down on the desk," he mumbled.

The servant ignored him. Instead, he pushed the tray closer to Gao, who responded with a look of disgust. But then, Gao noticed that the servant tried to signal something on the tray with his eyes. When he glanced down, he saw a piece of letterhead paper with writing on it under the teacup. Gao's face went pale. He stood there, stunned, without picking up the teacup. The servant did not force him. Instead, he lifted the cup from the tray and placed it on the desk. Before walking away, the servant tilted the empty tray slightly towards Gao. The letterhead paper revealed two lines of characters – *I take sole responsibility for my meeting with Madam Yun*. Gao's own signature was printed at the bottom.

The servant exited quietly like a breeze. All attendees, except Hai, fixed their eyes on Gao, waiting for him to express his views. Hai's eyes remained closed. Gao slowly raised his right hand and reached out to grab the paintbrush from the holder. Even though he tried to control his emotions, his hands were still trembling.

Seeing that Gao was about to sign on the proposal, Zheng and Ho looked visibly relieved. They leaned back in their chairs.

Wang rose from his chair all of a sudden and shouted, "Your Honour, Mayor Gao,"

Holding the paintbrush in his right hand, Gao stopped and looked up. So did Zheng and Ho. Hai also opened his eyes.

"I have a few questions that need your attention," Wang pleaded.

"Please go ahead," Gao replied. Like a person who had been abruptly pulled back from the edge of an abyss, Gao looked jolted. He put the paintbrush back in the holder.

"The imperial inspector stated that he had conversed with you about the proposal yesterday," Wang said. "While it is true that the rice allocated for flood victims can only last three days and that mulberry seedlings need to be planted by June, these are the same facts that we discussed during our previous meeting. You opposed the plan the day before, citing that it wouldn't work. With the situation remaining unchanged, what makes you think it will work today? Could you help us understand the rationale?"

Boom, boom, boom! Ho banged on his desk, yelling at Wang, "Why is the document confusing to you? The plan is based on facts. It should have been approved the day before."

"Sir, please allow me to finish," Wang said, joining his hands in front of his chest respectfully. "Even though I have just been transferred from Kunshan County, I know Jiande very well because I served there before. Based on my knowledge, there are two hundred and seventy thousand registered households in Jiande, with four hundred and forty-four thousand mu of registered farmland. About one hundred and fifty thousand mu are covered with mulberry trees, and they are currently owned by large silk merchants. The rest, two hundred and ninety thousand mu, grow grain. For each season, farmers can expect a yield of one hundred and twenty-five kilograms of grain per mu. In a bad year, the yield is about one hundred kilograms. On average, each farmer can get one hundred and fifty kilograms of grain per year. Once the husks are removed, it's about one hundred and twenty-five kilograms of rice. In other words, each person has about three hundred and fifty grams of rice per day. That might be sufficient for young children and the elderly, but it's not enough for an adult. Fortunately, Jiande is rich in natural resources. Families can grow tea or Tung trees, or they can catch fish or shrimp in the river to sell them on the market for extra cash. With the money, they can pay their taxes and use the leftover to buy oil and salt. Most families live from hand-to-mouth. Life is hard."

"We can get those stats from the Civil Affairs Department," Ho interrupted impatiently.

Wang did not look at Ho. Instead, he continued with his argument. "The flood this year has destroyed half of the farmland, about one hundred and forty thousand mu. If farmers sell this land, they'll have no choice but to grow crops on leased land. If they plant rice, they could split the yield with landowners. This means that they could probably get seventy-five kilograms of grain each year. Once you remove the husks, each person can probably get one hundred and fifty grams of rice per day. But, if they grow mulberry trees, the landowner wouldn't split the silkworms at fifty-fifty. It would be less. If farmers barter the silkworms with rice, they will get less than one hundred and fifty grams per day. Your Honour, would you be able to subsist on one hundred and fifty grams of rice per day?"

Gao did not answer. His eyes were filled with pain as he stared at Wang. "It's certainly not enough," he finally replied.

Wang went on to cite Mencius. "Yu, the Great[1] thought that if anyone in the kingdom was drowned, it was as if he drowned himself. Sheji[2] thought that if anyone in the kingdom suffered hunger, it was as if he famished himself. Your Honour, whatever you're going to write with that paintbrush in your hand could affect the livelihood of tens of thousands who are drowning and starving. I strongly urge prudence."

The attendees, most of whom were locals, knew that Wang was telling the truth. But having worked inside the government bureaucracy for so long, they had become numb and inured to the harsh realities. To protect their own interests, they often chose to look the other way. Wang's remarks touched them deeply. Everyone looked grim. Silence fell.

Knowing that his peers expected him to issue the final word on the proposal, Zheng stood up. "Everything that Magistrate Wang has stated is true," he said. "I used to head Zhejiang's treasury department and took charge of grain distribution. I was very familiar with the situation in Jiande. In fact, I knew by heart what was happening in every county. Every county has its own difficulties, and every province faces its own challenges. But all these are trivial if one takes into consideration the grim fiscal situation of our country – our national treasury is empty. Along the north and northwestern border, we are facing constant invasion from the Mongols. Here, along the coasts in Zhejiang and Fujian, the pirates are rampant. We need to strengthen our military to protect our borders and build ships to fight the pirates and safeguard our sea routes. All these efforts require money, and we don't have it. That's our reality."

Then, Zheng suddenly raised his voice and reprimanded Wang. "You're a menial magistrate. All you care about is your county. How dare you hijack a national initiative with your ranting and try to stop senior officials from signing the proposal? Based on the rules here, lowly magistrates like you have no right to intervene in provincial decisions."

Before Wang had the opportunity to respond, Zheng called out to his aides waiting outside, urging them to remove Wang and Hai from the room.

The servant who had served tea to the attendees came in. He walked up to Wang, who was standing, and grabbed his bench from behind. Then, he stopped in front of Hai. "Sir, please rise as I need to take your seat away," he pleaded.

Hai stood up reluctantly. The servant snatched the bench. With the two benches secured under each of his arms, the servant dashed out. Hai and Wang stood there firmly, waiting for Gao to speak up.

Gao turned to Zheng and begged, "Your Honour…"

"Don't forget who is in charge here," Ho interrupted Gao. Pointing his fingers to Hai and Wang, he yelled, "Did you hear what the imperial inspector just said? Get out."

"Where do you want us to go?" Hai asked calmly.

"You can go wherever you want," Ho said with utter indignation.

"All right then. We'll want to go to Beijing and visit the Ministry of Personnel and Ministry of Justice," Hai said. "Then, we'll get ready for our execution at the Meridian Gate."

"What are you talking about?" Ho glared at Hai.

"We're going to ask whoever has appointed us – Why did you send us here?"

"Are you threatening the Ministry of Personnel or are you simply threatening the provincial yamen in Zhenjiang?"

"In a matter of hours, you have succeeded in cowering the newly appointed mayor of Hangzhou into silence," Hai replied in sarcasm. "I'm a mere magistrate – who do you think I can threaten? Nobody."

Hai's bold remarks infuriated Ho, but Hai disregarded him. Instead, he confronted Gao. "Mayor Gao, we made an arrangement to visit the rice market yesterday morning and a silk mill later, but you were called away by the imperial inspector at the last minute," Hai said. "Just now, the imperial inspector told everyone that the two of you had a deep conversation over the proposal. Where did the conversation take place? We went to look for you at the imperial inspector's yamen and the Textile Bureau, and nobody knew where you were. Would you mind sharing with us what you discussed? I'm asking this because it strikes me as odd. You were strongly opposed to the proposal the day before. But today, you suddenly agree to the very same proposal. What has made you change your mind?"

"That's offensive!" Ho banged on his desk. "Come in and get him out of here," he shouted to the guards outside.

Ho's aide and two uniformed guards stepped in.

"Don't you dare!" Hai howled, his voice vibrating in the hall.

The guards stood there, stunned. Hai glowered at Zheng and stated, "You don't have the right to detain me. Read the Ming administrative law. For an official appointed by the Ministry of Personnel, unless he has committed the crime of colluding with enemies, deserting the city of which I have custody during war or embezzling public funds, an imperial inspector can report him but has no right to detain him. Your Honour, please order your guards to withdraw."

Nobody had expected that such a daredevil would emerge among them. The attendees looked at each other in shocked silence. Zheng was trembling with anger, but he also knew that Ho's decision to detain Hai was highly risky and could lead to a political deadlock.

Taking a deep breath, Zheng conceded, motioning the guards to withdraw. "All right, all right, I won't put you in detention," he muttered under his breath with a fierce menacing look; his trademark calmness and civility had evaporated. "But I want to warn you… It is not because I don't have the right to detain you. Given your disruptive behaviour at the meeting and your attempts to derail the implementation of an important national policy, this office of mine can lock you up in a cage and ship you to the capital for punishment. But I have decided not to do that now. I want you to travel to Chun'an County and work on the disaster relief and land-conversion programme right away. The government food subsidies for disaster victims are running out in three days. If your county doesn't implement the land-conversion policy, if starvation occurs, if there are riots, I'm going to request an order to have you beheaded. I don't have to seek permission from His Majesty – do you know that? You're probably aware that the former mayor of Hangzhou, your predecessor, Chang Boxi, and the former magistrate in Jiande County, met their ignominious fate this way."

Hai remained undeterred. "The former mayor and my predecessor deserved capital punishment. In fact, that's the very topic that I intended to bring up myself," Hai said in defiance. "Last year, the neighbouring province of Yingtian spent three million taels of silver to repair and boost the dams along two rivers, which have remained intact during this year's flooding. Here, in Zhejiang, we allocated two-and-a-half million taels on one river. But the dams broke in nine counties. Sir, you were in charge of the treasury, and the money was spent under your supervision. How do you explain the sudden dam breaks along the Xin'an River? I know I will not be able to get an answer from you today, but one of these days someone may want an explanation. Chun'an and Jiande Counties became flooded due to the government's emergency flood-diversion plan. All government agencies should focus on finding ways to help the victims. But, unfortunately, none is doing it. Instead, you allow ordinary people to shoulder the burden by themselves and take advantage of their dire circumstances. If starvation and riots occur, the Imperial Palace will no doubt launch investigations and get to the bottom of the matter. You can certainly have me executed for saying this, but in the end it won't exonerate the true criminals from facing justice."

Zheng's face turned pale while Ho and the other officials looked flabbergasted. With his trembling hands, Zheng grabbed his gavel and banged on the desk. "Hai Rui, you're fabricating stories to frame your superiors," he shouted. "Do you know that there are specific clauses in our law to punish people like you?"

"I used to be a teacher in Nanping, a small county in Fujian Province," Hai replied calmly. "I've only been here for three days. It is probably not a good idea to assign blame on me for the breaking dams in nine counties along the Xin'an River, is it? Last year, Zhejiang Province allocated two and a half million taels of silver to river repairs. I didn't fabricate that figure, did I?"

Before Zheng had the chance to repudiate Hai's accusations, the Chun'an magistrate turned to Gao. "Your Honour, this motion contains six provisions with a little more than two hundred words. But, in the future, if you want to probe into the true stories behind this motion, you can probably fill up a whole archival room with files. No matter what happened to you yesterday, I think it's your personal matter, and, if any injustices have been done to you, I'm confident that they will be cleared. But if you have erred, you should confess and seek redress. Regardless, the current proposal involves a crucial national policy and concerns the lives of several hundred thousand. The water is deep and murky, and there's a lot that we don't understand. You've only been here for three days. If you sign off on it and the whole thing proves to be a trap, the consequences could be irreversible."

There was dead silence in the conference hall. Gao looked up, and his eyes, filled with confusion and pain, met Hai's, which were sparkling with anger. Gao seemed to be touched, and his body shifted slightly in his chair. Zheng, Ho and the other officials looked on with murderous hostility.

At this moment, a guard rushed in and got down on one knee in front of Ho. "Your Honour, we have received an emergency report from Chun'an County."

Ho sprung to his feet and grabbed the report. After skimming through it, Ho glowered at Hai and Wang. "That's just great," he said sarcastically. "Thanks to your delay and boycott, the scoundrels in Chun'an have teamed up with the pirates and started a riot. Magistrate Hai, did you know that you released a rebel leader called Chee Dazhu yesterday? He led a group of peasants in Chun'an and tried to instigate an uprising with the help of the pirates. Fortunately, we have captured him."

Wang appeared shocked, but Hai stood motionless. He still fixed his gaze on Ho's wrinkled face, waiting for him to finish.

Ho looked away and turned to Gao, who turned ghastly pale. "Mayor Gao, both Chun'an and Jiande fall into your jurisdiction," Ho said. "What do you think we should do?"

Summoning all his strength, Gao stood up. "We still need to find out if those peasants from Chun'an have colluded with the pirates," he said. "If the allegations prove to be true, they should be punished right away. But Magistrate Hai just arrived in Zhejiang two days ago. I don't think he should be held accountable…"

"He is the one who ordered the guards to release the rebel leader," Ho replied, banging his fist on the desk. "How can you claim that he has nothing to do with the case?"

Even though Gao was lucid enough to know exactly what his opponents were trying to do, he felt helpless. This sense of helplessness gradually moved up in his heart, making him dizzy. He closed his eyes, reminding himself not to fall. But then, a sharp pain in his lower abdomen struck him. He clenched his teeth and muttered to himself, "Don't fall... don't fall..."

Those were the last words that Gao remembered before collapsing on his back like a cheap wooden stake. His sudden fall took everyone by surprise. Zheng jumped to his feet, and the others rushed over. Hai and Wang looked utterly confounded. They stared at Gao's empty chair and desk.

"Can we get some help?" Zheng shouted. Footsteps sounded in the hallway, and soon several guards barged in. "Who has ordered you to come?" Zheng yelled. "Please leave." Before the guards retreated, Zheng left instructions for his aide. "Get someone to take Mayor Gao to the back and call a doctor right away."

The aide ran to the door and shouted, "I need two people here." Two office assistants, one of whom had brought in the tea, rushed in and went behind Gao's desk. The new mayor was lying flat on the floor, unconscious. "Please be careful," the aide instructed the two assistants. "Put your hands underneath his shoulder and back, and let's carry him with his face up."

Slowly, the three men lifted Gao in the air and, amid everyone's shocked gasps, carried Gao to an area segregated by a screen at the back of the hall.

"Let's forget about the proposal today," Zheng announced decisively before turning to Hai. "We're going to find out later if you have anything to do with the case involving peasants colluding with pirates. For now, I'm sending you to Chun'an with police officers from the Justice Department. First, I order you to supervise the execution of the pirates and their collaborators. Then you start implementing the land-conversion programme, as we have discussed."

Hai stood there without moving. Wang shot him a worried glance.

Seeing that Hai Rui looked reluctant, Ho barked at a police officer who had been called in. "Get your men ready, and escort Magistrate Hai to Chun'an immediately."

"Yes, sir," the officer saluted before going up to Hai. "Magistrate Hai, this way please."

Hai remained still. He looked at Zheng and asked, "May I pose a question? If these policemen go with me to Chun'an, should they listen to me or is it the other way around?"

Startled by Hai's unexpected question, Zheng replied, "They'll listen to you if you follow the instructions from my yamen."

"What if I handle the case truthfully? Will they follow my orders?"

"What do you mean by truthfully?" Zheng asked.

"The provincial police allege that several peasants in Chun'an have colluded with pirates," Hai answered. "How did they do that? Which pirates did they contact? I have to look into these allegations carefully. If they prove to be true, I'll apply the law accordingly. But, if these are false, do you intend for me to have them executed even if they are innocent?"

"Are you trying to instigate a boycott against our national policy?" Zheng accused.

"Your Honour, I'm merely asking if you want me to ignore truth, abuse power and kill the innocent?"

"I would never ask you to ignore the truth and kill the innocent," Zheng yelled as he slammed his fist on the desk.

"That's exactly what I want to hear," Hai said, putting his palms together in front of his chest to show his respect. "I will handle the case in accordance with the truth."

Before departure, Hai said to the police officer, "You just heard what His Honour has said. Get everyone ready and let's go to Chun'an."

Baffled by Zheng's words, the officer stood there, looking to Ho for guidance.

"Don't stare at me," Ho scolded him. "Do whatever you need to do. Go."

As the officer was dashing to the door, Wang's eyes anxiously searched for Hai, who had by then reached the outer entrance. "Magistrate Wang," Zheng called out. "You know what to do in Jiande, don't you? Leave now and start the land-conversion plan immediately."

Wang bowed to Zheng before marching out.

In the public square outside the imperial inspector's yamen, Hai mounted his horse. "Let's go," the officer ordered. Police officers, about thirty or so on horses, escorted Hai onto the street. As they galloped away, Wang waved at Hai. In the distance, Hai's body bobbed up and down among the horses, which looked like moving hills. In a few minutes, they disappeared in the setting sun, which painted the sky in bloody red.

Back in his hotel room, Wang sat down behind his desk and struck a match to light up a candle. "Go and pack your stuff," he told his aide. "I'm going to draft a letter for you to deliver to Mr Tan Lun in Suzhou."

"But who's going to accompany you to Jiande?" his aide asked.

"I can go by myself," Wang replied impatiently. "No need to worry about me. Go and pack."

After his aide left, he pulled up a chair next to his desk, set out a piece of paper on the desk and began writing with his paintbrush.

Then, there was a soft knock on the door.

"Who is it?" Wang asked, sounding alarmed.

"Someone from the imperial inspector's office wants to see you," his aide answered from outside.

Wang quickly hid the letter inside a book. "Do you know what the visit is for?" he enquired.

"The person said Your Honour left some documents at the meeting today, and he has brought them over," his aide answered.

Wang picked up the book from his desk and tucked it underneath his bedding. Then, he walked over to open the door. It was the imperial inspector's assistant who served tea at the conference. He walked in with a nervous smile on his face. Wang did not offer him a seat.

"Where are the documents?" he asked. The assistant handed him a stack of papers.

"Thank you for doing this," he said. "Anything else?"

The assistant simply stood there without saying anything. Knitting his brow in annoyance, Wang walked over to his bed and took out a few coins from his wallet. When he turned around, he saw that the assistant had closed the door. "Is there anything else you need?" Wang handed him the change. "If not, please leave."

The assistant shook his head and refused to take the change. "What the hell do you want?" Wang asked again.

The assistant tried to move closer, but Wang winced and involuntarily took a step back.

"Sir, I have something important to tell you," he said quietly. "You have to memorise it."

Wang looked at him with scepticism.

"The Provincial Justice Department released a pirate from prison and sent him to Chun'an to sell rice to peasants," the assistant whispered to Wang's ear. "So the whole thing is a trap."

Wang was shocked; his eyes bored into the assistant's.

"The imperial inspector set another trap for Mayor Gao," the assistant continued. "They sent him to visit Mr Shen, an important silk businessman here. Mr Shen arranged a seductive young woman for the mayor. I think he might have fallen for it and they caught him red-handed."

"Why are you telling me this?" Wang asked, shocked and alarmed.

"Your Honour, I've worked at the imperial inspector's yamen for more than four years."

Wang failed to comprehend what he meant by that.

The assistant stomped his feet on the floor and said impatiently, "Don't you remember the previous imperial inspector?"

Wang understood, but he didn't say anything.

Seeing that Wang would not respond to his hints, the assistant felt obliged to state it more explicitly. "I started my job when Hu Zongxian was the imperial inspector. I'm his man."

Convinced by his explanation, Wang began to warm to him and nodded in gratitude.

"Both Governor Hu and Tan Lun are in the city of Suzhou at the moment," he reminded. "You should probably send someone to deliver the news as soon as possible."

Then, he turned around and bolted out. Wang stood at the door, watching him disappear in the darkness. The news sent his mind into a tailspin. He shut the door, pulled out the letter that he had written from under his bedding and set it over the candle. The letter quickly went up in flames. Blowing the ashes onto the floor, he sat down at his desk, laid out a piece of paper and began writing a new letter.

8

The crimson cinnabar ink inside the violet gold alms bowl brought to mind the image of fresh blood. When Grand Secretary Yan Song dipped his paintbrush in the bowl, the ink rippled. He was sitting opposite his deputy, Xu Jie. The two old men, one in his eighties and the other in his sixties, were hunched over their desks, contemplating and composing what was known as the "blue essay", a laudatory paean to the heavenly god and the emperor on a special porcelain blue paper made from a special recipe of fibres and ground leaves. Every now and then, they stared at the crimson characters through their thick reading glasses, while pondering what words would come next.

The blue paper looked sumptuous, and the crimson calligraphy manifested strength and elegance.

The outside world might be in chaos, but nothing was important enough to distract the two senior ministers from their regular writing routine – composing grandiose prose inside the Western Palace for Emperor Jiajing, who, according to historians, was a big fan of blue essays. Given that this type of prose had its origin in Taoist ceremonies during the Tang dynasty, it came as no surprise to his ministers. Rumour had it that Emperor Jiajing frequently assigned essay topics to his two senior ministers. After reading their essays, he would burn them as tributes to heaven. Since Grand

Secretary Yan Song and his deputy Xu Jie knew how to write in the styles that the emperor liked, their compositions had won much praise. Historians sometimes referred to Yan and Xu as "blue-essay ministers". Those essays might sound flowery and superficial, but deep beneath the sometimes ludicrously sumptuous prose lay hidden the two men's philosophies and concerns about national affairs, as well as their complex relations with the capricious monarch.

"I'm too old for this," said Yan Song, as he put the finishing touches on his essay and then carefully placed his paintbrush inside a holder. Removing his reading glasses, he rested his hands on the edge of the desk and slowly got up.

"Are you finished already?" Xu looked across at Yan. He was still working on his ending but felt obligated to take off his glasses and rise.

"It took me more than a whole hour to write one hundred and sixty-nine characters," Yan sighed, patting his lower back. "Age creeps up on you, whether you like it or not."

"If that's the case, I'm the one who's truly old and dim-witted," Xu said. "For that one hundred and sixty-nine words, I'm a couple of lines behind you."

"I know you deliberately write it slowly to make me feel better," Yan said with tenderness in his tone. "Given your talent and energy, you could easily finish one thousand six hundred and ninety words within the time frame, not to mention one hundred and sixty-nine."

"Grand Secretary…"

Xu attempted to explain, but Yan interrupted him. "You're a good honest man," Yan said. "You and I have served His Majesty for more than twenty years. Now that I'm over eighty, I thought I could retire, but still can't. One might not feel a thing if one only does this job for a day or even ten days. But ten or twenty years are exhausting. It is not hard to remain alert and cautious for a year, but life-long prudence is a nearly impossible task. You've been my deputy for years, and I appreciate that you always humour me and let me have my way."

"To outsiders, you are occupying a powerful position, second only to His Majesty," said Xu. "But those of us who are close to you know that the grand secretary has the most difficult job of serving our wise emperor while guiding his loyal ministers."

Yan had no way of knowing if Xu's words were true, but of one thing he was certain – Xu was telling the truth as he saw it. Touched by Xu's compliment, Yan decided that it was time for him to share with Xu what he had pondered the previous night. With his fading eyesight, he could not discern Xu's facial expression, but he gazed at him regardless.

"Since we don't have to turn over the essay to the emperor until this afternoon, you can finish your sentences later," Yan suggested. "It would probably take you only a few minutes anyway. Why don't you move over? I want to discuss a few things with you."

"Of course," said Xu. Even though he was in his sixties, Xu was healthy and agile. He lifted his rosewood armchair effortlessly, strode over to Yan and placed the chair next to him.

Yan sat down and motioned for Xu to do the same. Xu bowed before taking the seat.

"I don't mean to be impudent, but could you promise me to be truthful when answering my questions?"

"I wouldn't dare lie to you," Xu replied. "Please feel free to ask anything."

With Xu sitting next to him, Yan could see Xu's face clearly now.

"That's good," Yan started, with his eyes fixed on Xu's face. "Tell me what type of relations is considered the closest and most intimate in the world?"

Surprised that the grand secretary would suddenly bring up such a clichéd and superficial question, Xu hesitated before answering. "I... I would assume it's between father and son."

"Not necessarily," Yan shook his head slightly.

The sullen expression on Yan's face prompted Xu to probe cautiously. "Please advise," he said.

"In the ancient *Book of Songs*, there's that famous phrase – *Alas! Alas! My parents, with what toil ye gave me birth!* So, theoretically speaking, one should never forget repaying the debt of gratitude to one's parents, and it should be the noblest thing in life. But how many of our children really think that? Nine out of ten probably take their parents' sacrifice for granted, thinking it natural for parents to pamper their children. You and I are both grandparents now, and I assume that you share my observations. The so-called care and endearment between father and son is seldom reciprocal. When do you ever hear that a son truly cares for his father?"

Yan's words sounded not only genuine but heartbreaking. Xu could completely identify with the sentiment. While feeling empathetic, Xu also saw the need to quickly restrain himself. After all, Yan was a shrewd manipulator who had accompanied the emperor for more than twenty years. The two of them never considered each other as a bosom friend. More often, they were adversaries. But why would Yan, all of a sudden, confide in him in this way? These words were obviously intended for Yan's own son. What was he trying to imply?

Yan paused, expecting his deputy to respond and keep the conversation going, but Xu simply sat there like an obedient child and listened intently.

Slightly disappointed, Yan switched gears. "There's no easy answer to this, is there?" he said warmly. "Why don't we talk about something else? For our writing assignment today, His Majesty asked us to focus on the theme of *zhen*? Do you know why?"

"As the saying goes, there are four important virtues in this world: *heng, li, zhen* and *yuan* – compassion, harmony, loyalty and purity," replied Xu. "So my interpretation is based on this context."

"Xu..." Yan uttered a sigh of disappointment. "This is intended as a heart-to-heart talk, and I really mean it. There's no need to be worried about what you say. Are you sure you don't know why His Majesty asks us to incorporate this word into our essays?"

An intelligent and sensitive man, Xu had no problem comprehending the emperor's implied message in today's assignment, but he put on his inscrutable face instead. As the saying goes, still water runs deep, and a man of wisdom often appears deceptively dim-witted. "The character *zhen* also means integrity," Xu attempted a guess. "Could it be that His Majesty advises you and me to retain our integrity in our old age?"

The warmth in Yan's face disappeared. Looking solemn, he looked into Xu's eyes and asked, "How do you manage to keep your integrity?"

"I respectfully yield to you for advice," Xu responded with an equally serious look.

Yan did not feel the need to beat around the bush. "My advice is to wisely use people you trust and keep the dire situations under control," he said.

"Could you be a bit more specific?"

"All right, allow me to be candid with you," Yan said. "I mentored Hu Zongxian, and his school name contains the character *zhen*. You have a student, Zhao Zhenjie, whose name also carries the character *zhen*. In my view, His Majesty is trying to tell us that we need to rely on these two to handle the current mess in Zhejiang Province. Don't you agree?"

Xu felt obligated to state his mind. "This is truly the underlying message of today's assignment, thanks to His Majesty's wisdom and the grand secretary's intelligence."

"That is the reason I posed the question to you, asking whom you consider to be the closest person in life," Yan postulated. "Sometimes, the closest person might not be your own son, but rather your student. Children often see what they have received from their parents as a given, but students accept your teaching and care with gratitude. When opportunities arise, they'll always repay your kindness. As you know, the land-conversion policy is important to His Majesty and crucial to the fiscal well-being of our empire. We have to implement it and do it well. But, at the moment, my son, Yan Shifan, is making a mess of it. Therefore, we both need to rely on our students to redress the situation before it gets out of control. Given the dire circumstances in Zhejiang, officials in the nearby provinces have to loan grain to Zhejiang to tide them over. Otherwise, starvation and riots could occur. Please tell your student, Governor Zhao Zhenji, to contact Governor Hu Zongxian as soon as possible and ship grain to Zhejiang."

"You can rest assured that I'll write to him today," Xu promised. "I'll order the military to deliver the letter to Zhao via express post, urging him to make the loan to Governor Hu."

Yan leaned on the edge of his desk and stood up. Before departing, he held Xu's hands. "I'm over eighty years old," he said. "When I retire, I won't allow my son to inherit this position. You're the only one who can do the job."

明

Governor Hu was lying on a recliner inside an official guest house in the city of Suzhou. A doctor with a long jet-black beard sat next to him, pinning his wrist down on the arm of the chair to take his pulse. Tan Lun rushed in, and Hu struggled to get up.

"Don't move," the doctor ordered sternly.

Hu laid down helplessly. Tan stopped at the door and watched silently as the doctor, who seemed to be in his forties, was examining Hu. Even though his eyes remained half-closed, they looked fiercely focused. The doctor was Li Shizhen, a legendary figure under the reign of Emperor Jiajing.

"Give me your other hand," Dr Li told Hu.

"Sir, do you mind if I stop for a moment to talk to him and see what he has brought me?" Hu begged, pointing to Tan Lun.

Li shifted his gaze from Hu to Tan Lun, who forced out an awkward smile and uttered a sigh of helplessness.

"Go ahead," Dr Li said. "But I have to warn you that there's no cure for your illness if you keep acting like this."

Hu motioned for Tan Lun to come in. "The conversation you had with Gao Hanwen has apparently worked," Tan said with giddy exuberance. "He vetoed their land-conversion proposal upon arrival."

"It doesn't surprise me," the governor waved his hand dismissively. "What about the grain loans? Has Zhao Zhenjie agreed to loan us any grain?"

"Not really." Tan Lun thought for a moment before continuing. "For the past two days, he's only cobbled together ten boatloads of grain, even though he promised that he would work hard on it."

Governor Hu sighed with a stern look on his face. "If government subsidies run out in a few days, I doubt Gao can hold out against his opponents," he warned. "Why don't you go and talk with Zhao Zhenji? Tell him that I don't need his loan any more. I just want him to come and see me right away."

"I will do that right now," said Tan before stepping out.

Leaning back in his chair with another sigh, Hu massaged his temple distractedly.

"You have taken all the trouble to get me here," Doctor Li said reproachfully. "Do you want me to treat you or not?"

Hu suddenly remembered that he was in the middle of a doctor's visit. Putting his wrist back on the cushioned arm of his chair, he apologised profusely. "Please continue with your examination," he said. "I didn't mean to be so rude."

Dr Li simply glanced at Governor Hu's arm without touching it. Governor Hu looked up with a bemused expression.

"It's the wrong arm," Dr Li said with his arms crossed.

Governor Hu burst into awkward giggles. As he was about to put his other arm out for Dr Li, Zhao Zhenji, the governor and imperial inspector of Nanjing, walked in, with Tan Lun at his heels. Hu quickly rose to greet the guest.

Zhao looked apologetic but tactfully guarded. "I would have come to see you, regardless of whether you sent Tan Lun to fetch me," he said. "Your health is more important. Why don't we discuss the loan after the doctor finishes here? If it hadn't been someone like you, Dr Li wouldn't have travelled this far to see a patient here. Let's wait until Dr Li makes a diagnosis and writes out his prescription for medicines. Is that all right?"

Hu closed his eyes, and Zhao turned to Dr Li, addressing him as "the Imperial Doctor".

"I have long left my post at the Imperial Hospital," Li corrected him, with a long face.

Zhao was taken aback by Li's reply. "Sorry about that," he said. "One can easily locate one thousand imperial doctors in our country, but there is only one Dr Li Shizhen."

Dr Li seemed to like the flattery. Even though he still sported a dour facial expression, his tone softened. "Are you sure you want me to write the prescriptions now?"

"Of course," Zhao replied. "Governor Hu is one of the pillars of our country. If you can cure him of this illness, you'll be doing our country a great service."

"If I put you in charge of filling the prescriptions, would you agree to do it?"

"I promise," Zhao said half-jokingly. "Whatever precious herbs you have chosen, be it a flying insect or a type of rare weed in deep water, I'll send people to gather them for him. But please don't prescribe things such as dragon's liver or kidney – I don't think I can get that."

"Don't worry, I don't use fancy stuff like that," Li said with a mischievous smile. "The herbs that I prescribe are fairly easy to get. In fact, you can find them everywhere in your province."

"All right then," Zhao said. "Do it now, and I'll gather it for you right away."

"Now that everyone has heard your promise, you'd better keep it," Li said. Sitting down by a desk, Dr Li dipped his paintbrush in a bowl of ink and wrote carefully on a piece of special rice paper.

Governor Hu was seized with another violent spasm of coughing. Zhao and Tan Lun rushed over to Hu's chair. Tan handed him a cup of hot tea, but Governor Hu shook his head.

"No, I don't need it now," he said feebly.

Li put down his pen and said, "Here's my list." Before handing out the prescription, he blew on the paper to make the ink dry. Zhao rose quickly to receive it.

"No rush," Dr Li said. "Why don't I show it to Mr Tan first?"

Tan accepted it with both hands.

"Why don't you read aloud the list for us?" Dr Li demanded.

Tan scanned the list quickly, and his eyes brightened.

"Go ahead and read it for us," Dr Li urged.

Zhao fixed his eyes on Tan. Governor Hu's coughing stopped. He lay on his chair quietly, waiting.

Tan cleared his throat and started. "Cause of the illness – a senior imperial official in charge of a major province finds his hands tied by forces both inside and outside, and he suffers from fear of slander and for his reputation."

A gleam of surprise flashed across Zhao's face, and even Hu opened his eyes.

Tan raised his voice and continued, "Treatment – ship one

hundred boatloads of rice to Zhejiang immediately. External use only."

Hu looked at Dr Li, his eyes beaming with gratitude.

Tan handed over the "prescription" to Zhao, who was standing there, stunned and stupefied. It took a few minutes for Zhao to regain his composure. Turning to Dr Li, he said with an awkward smile, "Dr Li, this is too big a joke for me to stomach."

"I've spent half of my time practising medicine, be it tending His Majesty at the Imperial Hospital or treating villagers in their shabby homes," Dr Li said matter-of-factly. "A doctor's goal is to cure people of their illnesses and save lives. There's no room for jokes. When we save one life, we feel accomplished. If we save ten, we consider it a significant contribution to humanity. Governor Zhao, a simple gesture of yours can now rescue several hundred thousand lives. To me, it's the greatest accomplishment. Why would I joke about it?"

"Help me up," Hu asked Tan Lun. Once he was on his feet, Hu dropped into a deep bow before Dr Li, who quickly rose and returned the courtesy.

"I have a big favour to ask you," Governor Hu said to Dr Li.

"What is it?"

"After the flood in Chun'an and Jiande Counties, starvation is not the only threat," said Hu. "We could face an epidemic. So it's important to teach people how to use herbs to prevent an outbreak. Would you like to go and take up the cause there?"

"When are you leaving?"

"I have to go today, regardless of whether we can get a loan or not."

"I can go with you today," Dr Li pledged.

"Please accept my thanks in advance," Governor Hu bowed again.

"That's enough," Dr Li stopped Governor Hu before turning to Zhao. "Governor Zhao, are you going to fill the prescription for me?"

With the list in his hand, Zhao grinned awkwardly. He looked at Hu, who turned his eyes away.

"Governor Hu, there's something I want to share with you,"

Zhao said. "Could you come out for a few minutes so we can chat about it?"

Governor Hu slowly raised his head and faced Zhao.

"I'll step out and leave you two alone," Dr Li volunteered.

"But, Imperial Doctor, I didn't mean…" Zhao tried to explain.

"I told you not to address me as an imperial doctor," Dr Li said before stepping out.

Governor Hu quickly motioned Tan Lun to go out and entertain Dr Li.

Now, the two governors were alone in the room. Hu lay down on his chair, and Zhao sat next to him, slowly massaging Hu's arm.

"I can't hide this from you, and even if I do lie you'll find out sooner or later," Zhao said. "To me, one hundred boats of rice are nothing. I could even lend you two hundred. It's not that I don't want to do that, but the current situation here doesn't allow me. You understand that, don't you? Besides, you finally got yourself out of this swamp while you were in Beijing. Why do you want to jump back in again?"

"Do you also think that I submitted my resignation to get myself out of the mess?" Hu straightened his back and argued. "I didn't resign on my own. I was forced out."

"It doesn't surprise me. What you did in Zhejiang caused jitters among many in the palace. Regardless of who the grand secretary is, he would do the same thing and fire you."

Hu saw that as a harsh but honest criticism.

"I don't mean to berate you," Zhao continued. "Inside the government, you rise one day and fall the next. Your situation is nothing unusual. But you and I have been friends for twenty years. I'm going to risk everything and tell you the truth. Someone inside the Imperial Palace specifically instructed me not to loan you the grain."

"Who is that?"

"I can't tell you."

"Is it the grand secretary's son or Deputy Grand Secretary Xu?"

Zhao paused before speaking. "Do you want to remain truly clueless or do you want to pull me into the slough with you?"

"I have no intention of pulling you into the slough with me. All I want is for you to stand on the bank and tell me the truth."

"The truth is that neither faction wants me to loan it to you."

It was Hu who became silent. A few minutes later, he muttered to himself, "That's what I figured. But thanks for sharing it with me. You're a true friend."

Touched by Hu's affectionate words, Zhao consoled his friend. "You should take things as they come," he said. "Everyone knows that you're here to borrow grain. The Imperial Palace and officials in Zhejiang have all been notified. Despite the fact that you have not obtained the loan, people understand it. It's the thought that counts. Now that you're ill, you should stay here and rest. I'll submit a report to the Imperial Palace, informing them of your illness and your decision to receive treatment in Suzhou."

"What about Zhejiang? Should we allow it to fall into chaos? We need to stay put and observe the situation carefully from afar. People have to die in order to call His Majesty's attention to this scandal. As the Taoist saying goes, *Heaven and earth are heartless – to them, the myriad creatures are but as straw dogs. The sage too is heartless – to him, also, the people are but as straw dogs.* Life goes on regardless of what happens. It doesn't matter if ten thousand people die or one hundred or one million people lose their lives. They're mere numbers, and there's nothing you and I can do."

Hu's eyes examined Zhao's face like two sharp knives, sending chills down his spine. Regretting that his words had offended Hu, Zhao said with resignation, "If you don't like what I just said, discard it as if you had never heard it. Yes, I take back everything I said."

"Don't worry, I'm not someone who betrays friends," Hu explained. "But I want to discuss the loan with you. I'm still the Governor of Zhejiang and your region, and I intend to borrow grain on behalf of Zhejiang. When I make the request as the governor, you have no choice but to comply."

"But Governor," Zhao said. "Even though my region falls into your jurisdiction, you cannot force me to do it. Without authorisation from the grand secretary's office, I can't ship grain to Zhejiang. It's not my responsibility."

"What about requesting grain on behalf of the military?"

"Are you going to stage a war?" Zhao asked.

"Well, the pirates have been planning attacks against the coast of Zhejiang for quite some time. General Qi Jiguang has received reports that the enemies have been converging, and we have to stay prepared. You and many others might automatically assume that I'm dodging my responsibilities. I might have removed myself from the land-conversion programme, but I still have to be involved in commanding the war against pirates."

"If it's for military operations, I can do that," Zhao said. "But they wouldn't need that much, would they?"

"Where is that fearless and idealistic young man who used to spend long nights arguing with me about neo-Confucianism?" Governor Hu reminisced. "What are you afraid of? You can certainly allocate more grain for me in the name of supporting military operations. Rescuing disaster victims can also help stabilise the region. If anything happens, nobody would blame you."

Zhao thought for a moment and said, "All right then. I'll try my best, but there is one thing that I want to advise you. If possible, stay away from the land-conversion programme. Allow yourself some leeway in the future."

"Thanks," Governor Hu said, his tone pessimistic. "As long as I'm the governor, there is no way out for me."

The sun had set, but the white sails on the sampans rose up against the darkening sky. Lanterns hanging from the boat's masts were lit up, each revealing three prominent characters: *The Textile Bureau*.

A fleet of junks, loaded with sacks of grain, docked along the river, and the lanterns illuminated the whole pier. On the stone steps leading to the water stood soldiers, fully armed and brandishing burning torches. Two big sedans were waiting a few metres away from the stairs, where Zheng Bichang and Ho Maocai paced back and forth impatiently.

"He's always like this," Ho whined. "He always disappears when we need him the most. The boats are ready to set sail, but where is Mr Shen?"

Shen's personal aide, who was standing nearby, quickly came up and said ingratiatingly, "Mr Shen should be here at any minute. I just sent someone to fetch him."

Ho shook his head in exasperation.

"Please send another person over, and find out what has happened," Zheng urged anxiously.

The manager ran away to search for Shen.

"I really can't stay here long," Zheng said to Ho. "I need to rush back to my office."

"You can't leave," Ho said. "We don't even know where Shen is. Why do you need to go back to your office now?"

"I need to check up on Mayor Gao," Zheng explained. "After all, he's sent by the grand secretary junior. Now that he's embroiled in a mess, we need to console him a bit. You also need to write to the grand secretary junior right away and tell him that we're coping with a well-coordinated pirate assault. We have no choice but to purchase the farmland immediately."

After a moment, Ho suggested, "I personally think the letter should come from you."

"Couldn't you at least draft the letter, and I can copy it when I come back?" Zheng said, looking irritated.

"All right then."

明

Shen Yishi's quiet courtyard was flooded with moonlight. When his personal aide walked into the door, he was shocked by what he saw: Shen had left his long hair hanging loose around his shoulders, and he was smashing his precious guqin on the ground. An oil bucket sat next to a pile of broken instruments and furniture. The familiar music stand was also among the rubble. In a few seconds, the guqin that he used to play fell to pieces. Shen picked up the bucket and poured the oil all over the small heap. Then, without appearing to know he had an observer, Shen threw the empty bucket to the corner and ignited a flint, tossing it onto what had become a pile of wood chips.

A blaze broke out, lighting up Shen's flushed face. The icy look in his eyes made his personal aide shudder with fear. Quietly, he moved a few steps back. But, as the flames shot higher and higher, the aide panicked and turned around to search for help. A huge bronze vat near the courtyard wall caught his eye. He walked over stealthily, but Shen saw him. "Come over," he ordered the aide, his eyes still fixed on the blaze.

Holding his breath, the aide toddled over.

"What is it that you want to tell me?"

"Sir, the boats are all loaded," reported the aide. "The imperial inspector and other officials are looking for you. They're waiting at the pier. Are you still planning to escort the boats to Chun'an and Jiande?"

"Leave me alone," Shen said dismissively, as if he had not heard the manager's words.

"But, sir, what am I going to tell the imperial inspector who is waiting at your office?"

"Tell him I'm dead," Shen said, staring into the blaze.

"I wouldn't dare..."

"Get out of here," Shen bellowed.

The aide quickly retreated, but, soon after he left the courtyard, he changed his mind. The fire in the middle of the courtyard worried him. He turned around and noticed the bronze vat.

At this moment, Shen picked up a drum and a drum stand that he had brought with him, and then he sauntered over into the music studio. The aide crept up to the bronze vat, scooped out a bucket of water and carried it to the studio entrance. With the bucket of water sitting beside him, he quietly watched the fire to make sure that it remained contained.

Loud booming noises burst out from inside the music studio. Mesmerised, the aide listened. He had no idea that drums could produce such lyrical and rhythmic sounds.

Shen alternated skilfully between two drumsticks, one beating the centre and the other on the edge. The drum in the centre emitted a series of thunderous booming sounds, like the roar of a male lion, while the side one pitter-pattered like raindrops or the high-pitched echoes of a lioness.

The aide was also surprised to see Madam Yun there. She sat motionless with her guqin on the big platform bed, which looked bare without the red rug. Her eyes, lacklustre and clouded, fixed on the entrance.

Shen began to beat the drum in the centre with both sticks, the rhythm accelerating.

Madam Yun remained unmoved, staring catatonically into the distance.

Blood seemed to have drained from Shen's flushing face. Strands of loose hair plastered on his forehead, and sweat quickly flooded his cheeks.

Gradually, the sticks moved from the centre of the drum to the edge. When the tempo slowed down, it seemed as if Shen was reminiscing about his romantic encounters under the midnight moon.

The sound of the drumbeat was slowly fading, and sadness and desolation occupied the air. Madam Yun's eyes shifted to the surface of the drum briefly before turning towards the door.

Shen held the drumsticks in mid-air, and his eyes tilted towards the ceiling. "You're allowed to go now," he muttered.

Madam Yun stirred and shifted her body slightly but did not rise.

"You've paid back all your debts," Shen reassured her. "You're free to go."

Slowly, Madam Yun straightened her body and alighted from the bed. Before walking towards the door, she lifted her skirt and knelt in front of Shen, who was standing there, with drumsticks in his hands. Kowtowing three times as silent gestures of gratitude, she rose and walked out.

Tears welled up in Shen's eyes.

A moderate-looking sedan, flanked on both sides with men carrying lanterns with *South China Textile Bureau* printed on them, glided in the darkness towards the river pier.

"He's here," Shen Yishi's personal aide shouted. "Mr Shen just arrived. Get the boats ready."

The soldiers who had been designated to guard the grain quickly stood in formation near the dock before scattering to their assigned boats.

The sedan pulled into a stop. The aide went up to lift the curtain, and Shen stepped out. Under the dim light of the lanterns, the aide was shocked to see his boss, known for wearing his cheap blue cotton outfits all year round, donning a glamorous long, silk gown embroidered with cicada wings. His hair was tied up with a golden flower silk ribbon. When a river breeze rustled his gown in a gentle sweep, Shen looked as if he were flying.

Even though the weather was by no means hot, Shen carried a gold-plated folding fan. After waving the fan leisurely in his face for a few minutes, he folded it and swaggered towards the stone stairs that led to his boat. Two men holding sizeable lanterns led the way, while two others walked side by side with him. They all noticed something unusual about their master, who had apparently applied oil to his hair and powder to his face, like a dandy rather than the unassuming silk producer they had known. Before he came to the stairs, his aide and guards caught up with him, lifting the bottom of his long gown to keep it from touching the mud-covered ground. Together, they walked towards an immense boat moored in the middle of the pier. "Watch your step," the aide kept reminding him.

In his unusually long stride, Shen marched onto the boat through a wide walkway. A boatman quickly removed the board and untied the anchor ropes.

Loitering at the bow, Shen suddenly turned to his aide, who was standing behind him. "Go and get me four girls from the Qiantang Brothel."

"You mean now?' his aide said, shocked at his master's request.

"Put them on a grasshopper boat," Shen instructed. "They should be able to catch up with the fleet in an hour."

"Yes, sir," the aide hurried away. Since the walkway had been removed, he climbed onto the edge of the boat and tried to leap across to the pier. But it was too wide a gap, and he fell into the water. Fortunately, the water was not deep. The lower part of his gown was fully soaked. Without time to fuss over it, he ran towards the stone stairs.

The river unfurled like an endless jade belt, and the mountain along the river sat like clusters of giant green spiral conch shells. The fleet went at full sail, progressing smoothly on the Xin'an River. The boats were moving, the water was moving and the mountain also seemed to be moving.

About an hour later, the grasshopper boat from the Qiantang Brothel caught up with the fleet, carrying the aide and four gaudily dressed and heavily powdered girls. After they boarded, the aide saw a shabby sampan sailing closer to Shen's boat.

The aide shouted at a fisherman on the sampan, "Toss us the anchor ropes!"

Once the sampan was tied around the boat, two fishermen climbed onboard, each with a bucket of live fish.

"Follow me to the bow," said the aide

The fishermen carefully placed the buckets on each side of the edge.

"I bought two buckets of koi for you to release to the river for good luck," the aide whispered to Shen, who cast a quick glance at the buckets. A few red koi were splashing around inside.

Shen bent over and reached into the bucket.

"Watch your sleeves," the aide cautioned.

Shen ignored his warning. By the time he pulled one out, both of his sleeves were dripping with water. He leaned over the edge of the boat, stretched both hands towards the water and dropped the fish.

The water glinted in the moonlight. The fish dived in and then leapt high in the air before swimming away.

A faint satisfied smile flashed across his gaunt face. His eyes swept across the dark mountains that flitted past.

"What do you want to do with the rest of the koi?" his aide asked hesitantly.

"Get those whores out and let them release the fish."

"Understood," the aide said before shouting to the prostitutes inside the cabin. "Girls, come out and help your master release the fish and get yourself some good luck."

The four prostitutes, in bright red and green outfits, stumbled out, giggling and laughing. They were well aware of the fact that Master Shen despised them, but their profession dictated that they put on smiles regardless. In jaunty small steps, they dashed over to the bow and gathered around the buckets.

"Sir," one girl purred.

"Master Shen," another called flirtatiously, "Come and watch – I'm releasing this fish."

"Have fun," said Shen, who was standing at the front of the bow. "Releasing the fish will enable you to collect enough merits and virtue in this life so you can be reincarnated into decent and respectful women in the next."

The prostitutes eyed each other awkwardly.

Shen's biting sarcasm did not stop one from ingratiating herself. "You're a man with virtues. I'd rather service you than leave you so I could become a respectful woman."

"Despicably cheap," Shen muttered between his teeth. "Lift the bucket and empty all the fish into the water."

The prostitutes were cowed into silence. Puckering their lips, they painstakingly dragged a bucket to the side of the boat. But, no matter how hard they tried, they couldn't lift it.

"Brother, please help us," one prostitute begged Shen's aide.

"Don't help them," Shen warned his aide. "These women have no intention of reforming themselves. It's probably better that they drown themselves in the river. I can afford to compensate the whorehouse if they die."

The women stood there, stunned and scared.

"Hurry up," the aide shouted.

"All right, all right."

Shen's insults and threats worked. The four women summoned enough strength and raised the bucket to the edge, tilted it and emptied the water and the fish into the river. The loud splash in the water startled them.

"Ask them to come over," he instructed the aide.

"The master needs you now." The aide motioned for the women to move over. They walked towards Shen timidly.

"I'm going to read a few lines from an ancient poem," Shen said, with his back to them. "If any of you can tell me the name of the poem and who wrote it, I'll buy you out today."

The four women glanced at each other. Surprised, and then excited at the proposal, they faced Shen's back, waiting.

Shen cleared his throat and intoned:

> *Passing the Xia's head, we then drifted westwards,*
> *I searched for the Dragon Gate but all in vain.*
>
> *Yearning racked my heart and grieved my mind;*
> *Going so far away, the path uncertain.*
> *Tossed by wind and waves, aimlessly drifting;*
> *Embarked on an endless journey without hope of return.*
>
> *Riding the rough waves, these thoughts filled my mind;*
> *When, oh when, will this drifting ever cease?*
> *My heart enmeshed could not be disentangled;*
> *My thoughts trapped in a maze with no escape.*

Shen's voice echoed and quickly dissipated in the evening wind. The waves lapped against the boat. The four women stared at each other, looking clueless.

"Who knows the answer?" the aide urged.

"I think I know," one prostitute shouted excitedly. "It's from Qu Yuan's poem."

"Which poem?" Shen turned around quickly and fixed his gaze at the woman who claimed to have the answer.

"The Sorrow of Separation," the woman replied hesitantly.

Shen's eyes darkened. Shaking his head in disappointment, he said to her, "I'm afraid that you just lost your chance, but given that you have guessed the poet's name correctly, I'm going to award one hundred taels of silver."

Shen turned his back on her and gazed at the moon over the mountain, his silk gown flying in the breeze.

It was approaching dawn. The moon on the backyard wall inside the South China Textile Bureau was fading away.

The four eunuchs who had blackmailed Gao Hanwen at Shen Yishi's music studio filed into Yang Jinshui's room. The fat one walked at the front, carrying a gold-plated face-wash basin filled with hot water. He was followed by the thin one with a silver-plated foot-wash basin in his hands. The other two eunuchs, one tall and one short, each held a piece of linen towel and a pair of fine cotton foot-dryer cloth. If one looked closer, one would notice that the hands holding the water basins were trembling so badly that water spilt out onto the floor. The four of them stopped at the door, looking nervous and scared.

Yang's personal aide greeted them. The quartet searched his face for clues as to how they would be treated inside. But, to their disappointment, the aide put on a poker face. He simply tilted his head slightly and held the door open for them. Without knowing if Yang would punish them for mistreating Gao or be pleased that they did it, the quartet simply stood there. The aide glowered at them impatiently, motioning with his eyes for them to go inside.

With trembling limbs, they stumbled in.

On a chair in the middle of the room sat Yang, who was still wearing his travelling clothes, which had been tainted with dirt from the journey. He stared at the ceiling with a surly expression.

The quartet stood in a horizontal line, trying to control their trembling legs.

Yang peered at his aide who was standing by the door and asked with an icy tone, "Who else knows that I'm back from Beijing?"

The quartet shook their heads vigorously.

"Daddy, these four came in from the back door," the aide explained. "Only two or three people within our circle are aware of your return."

"Go and tell the guards outside that if anyone leaks the news, I'm going to have them killed right away," he threatened.

"Yes, sir," said the aide before striding out.

Yang turned his gaze back to the ceiling. "Oh, I can't believe how hot it is here," he whined.

The soft bleat immediately sent the quartet scurrying, as if the bodhisattva Guanyin had just uttered a new mantra. They hovered around Yang, one removing his hat, the other untying his shoes. The thin eunuch soaked the face towel in the hot water, wrung the water out and handed it over to the fat eunuch, who unfolded the towel and slowly cleansed Yang's forehead.

"So dirty!" Yang muttered through his tightly clenched teeth.

The quartet froze. So did the thin eunuch who was about to dip Yang's feet into the silver basin. They stared at each other. It didn't take long before they figured out what Yang was trying to insinuate. The fat eunuch quickly put the towel back in the gold basin, reached into his breast pocket and brought out the cheque that he had received from Shen a few days before for threatening Gao. The other three followed suit. They all dropped to their knees, asking for forgiveness.

"Good dogs never take treats from outsiders," the fat eunuch said, slapping his face. "We accepted the cheques from Mr Shen so we could keep them as evidence. We have been waiting for Daddy to come back and to show them to you."

"Don't you know that treats from outsiders can be poisonous?" Yang glared at them before examining the cheques. "Four thousand taels of silver, that's very generous of him," he said sarcastically.

"He wanted to bribe us with this tainted and evil cheque," the fat one replied with a feigned look of disgust. "Who does he think we are?"

"He forgets the fact that Daddy is the one who has made him rich," the thin one pitched in.

"If he tries to hurt Daddy, I'm going to kick his arse…" the tall one quickly added.

Yang stopped the short eunuch before he even opened his mouth. "Eat them up," Yang barked at his four protégés.

Silence fell. The four eunuchs were at a loss about what to do.

"Daddy… Do you mean to say that we should swallow the cheques?" asked the short one, who was also the youngest.

"Yes," Yang ordered.

Without hesitation, the quartet each shoved the cheques into their mouths and began chewing them loudly, as if they had been eating sweets. During the Ming dynasty, the cheques, for the sake of durability, were made from hemp paper, which was hard to chew. As the quartet were trying to swallow them down, their faces turned red, and their eyes bulged.

"Is it fully digested?' Yang asked.

"Yeah... Yes..." the quartet replied, even though the tough pulp still appeared to stick in their throats.

Yang looked them in the eye and said, "Are you sure?"

Each member of the quartet made one last effort to get the wet pulp down his oesophagus, but Yang wasn't satisfied.

The fat eunuch was smart enough to decipher Yang's next move. "Daddy, do you mean to say that the cheques are not considered fully digested if they still remain inside our stomachs?"

"Are you saying that we have to wait until we pass them out..." the short one added.

"You boys are so smart," Yang said sarcastically. "You don't have to wait. I'll get some guys to spank your arses and help you pass quickly."

"Oh, please, spare us," the quartet howled.

"Stop the wailing," Yang shouted. "Nobody is dead yet."

The quartet stopped immediately.

"Tell me, did Mayor Gao sexually assault Madam Yun?"

"No, they were sitting apart, and I swear to heaven that he didn't touch her."

"Then who sent you over there?"

"Daddy, we received a note from Mr Shen," the fat eunuch admitted. "He must have schemed with the imperial inspector and the director of justice."

"You have all seen the boats loaded with grain?" Yang asked. "Who do you think came up with the idea of sending Mr Shen to buy up land in Chun'an and Jiande in the name of the Textile Bureau?"

The quartet lowered their heads without answering.

"Speak up," Yang scolded.

"We really don't know whose idea it was," the fat eunuch said.

"But we saw Mr Zheng and Mr Ho at the pier. They saw the Textile Bureau's lanterns."

"I also noticed that Mr Shen's escorts also carried the Textile Bureau's lanterns around," the thin one reported.

"Well, well," Yang mumbled angrily, his face turning purple. "Those people want to drag His Majesty's name through the mud… well, well…"

The quartet was too scared to move.

Yang's aide stepped in. "Daddy, I've told everyone in the compound to keep it confidential and not to share the news about your return home."

"Good. But first, take these four out and award them each with twenty floggings."

The quartet sat there in a trance

"That's awfully mild and forgiving, don't you think?" the aide reminded the quartet. "Did you thank Daddy?"

The quartet kowtowed and said in unison, "Thank you, Daddy."

"Daddy, the spanking could probably get us some unnecessary attention in the courtyard," the aide suggested to Yang. "Could you be kind enough to substitute the spanking with the low-key lover's smack?"

"That's way too easy on these four," Yang said. "But given the circumstances, I'll grant your request…"

The aide quickly winked at the quartet. "Thank Daddy for his kindness," he urged. "Get out of here and administer the spanking among yourselves."

"Thank you, Daddy, and thank you, Brother," hummed the quartet before they exited with relief.

Yang's aide scooped out the towel from the gold basin, wrung out the water and slowly wiped Yang's face. "I just heard that Zheng and Ho managed to bring Mayor Gao to his knees," the aide whispered. "Now, the two just sent Hai Rui, the new magistrate, to Chun'an to supervise the execution of some farmers who are charged with colluding with the pirates. At the same time, they sent Mr Shen to buy up the land in the name of the Textile Bureau."

Yang opened his eyes. "This is an urgent matter," he said to his aide. "Why don't you contact the Ministry of Defence, and tell them to send a letter of mine via military express post. I need to notify Lu Gonggong right away."

Two wide benches were laid out in the courtyard, one on the left and the other on the right. The fat eunuch lay face down on the left bench, while the tall one lay on the right. Their trousers were pulled down to their ankles, and their mouths gagged with small thin wooden sticks. The thin eunuch flogged the fat one's bare bottom with bamboo strips, and the short one beat up the tall one. *Bam, bam*; the spanking produced very loud sounds, but neither of the two eunuchs was moaning. Soon, it was time to rotate. The thin and short eunuchs took their turns on the benches to receive a flogging from the tall and fat ones, who struggled with the excruciating pain on their own bottoms.

During the Ming dynasty, the eunuchs were assigned to take up different imperial posts all over the country, and if anything went wrong they could be punished severely. Among the seventy-two different punishments, the most severe one involved a beating on the back with wooden staves. A few heavy strikes could damage a person's internal organs and kill him instantly. Flogging with a whip or stick was also a common practice, rendered by a professional flogger. After a few lashes, the victim's bottom would be badly bruised and swollen. The person could end up in bed, face down, for at least half a month.

In comparison, a patting, or "lover's smack", was nothing more than a light reprimand, like parents spanking their children. Since the punishment involved two people smacking each other with bamboo strips, these lashes were more lenient. Oftentimes, it became more of a performance with "loud thundering and small raindrops". Therefore, the palace eunuchs gave it the pet name "lover's smack". During the process, the person who smacked would usually pace each strike so the recipient on the bench could have a bit of time to recover. At the end of the ceremony, their bottoms might be swollen, but there wouldn't be any severe bruises.

As the bamboo strips swatted down on the bare bottoms,

Madam Yun sauntered into the courtyard. Shen Yishi had given her away as Yang's indentured mistress for four years, during which time she had become accustomed to Yang's many abuses. But it was the first time Yang had invited her to witness the beatings of eunuchs.

Madam Yun did not appear shocked; she likely connected the punishment to Yang's knowledge of Shen's plot against Mayor Gao. She lowered her head and walked calmly but directly to Yang's bedroom.

Yang was sitting on his chair with his feet soaking in the silver basin. He gave Madam Yun a cunning grin, but she looked unperturbed and smiled back. Surprised by Madam Yun's calmness, he stopped grinning and gazed at her.

Madam Yun bent over and started to wash his feet.

"Don't do it," he stopped her, putting both of his feet squarely on the edge of the basin. "Yours are the precious hands of a musician – don't ruin them."

Madam Yun rose and chose a seat next to Yang.

Yang eyed Madam Yun's face while his feet curled up to rub each other.

"You now have two men after you – Shen Yishi and Gao Hanwen," he said. "One has money, and the other has talents. They're both members of the educated elite. I'm proud of you..."

Madam Yun sat there in a daze, her eyes fixed on the floor.

"Look at my feet," he said. "When I put both of them on the edge of the basin, I manage to balance them very well. But, if you try to balance yourself on two boats, you could fall and drown yourself. Tell me the truth, which man do you like the best?"

Madam Yun looked up at Yang without responding.

"This stuff between you and me is fake, and I know it," Yang said with a look of rare kindness on his face. "Besides, I'm going to be in Hangzhou for no more than a year, and there's no way I can take you with me to Beijing. Given that you have serviced me for these years, I should grant you a dignified identity. Why don't you make me your godfather?"

Madam Yun's body trembled slightly.

"Come over to Daddy and wipe my feet dry."

Madam Yun picked up a foot towel from a rack and began wiping Yang's feet slowly.

"You haven't answered me yet," Yang asked. "Which one do you like the best? Shen or Gao?"

Madam Yun's hands stopped.

Yang looked down at her and noticed tears dropping down from her cheeks into the basin.

"You find it hard to part with either one, don't you?" Yang said, his face falling.

Madam Yun did not move.

"Why don't I make the choice for you," Yang said, putting both of his feet back in the water and standing up. "If you go with Shen, you'll have no future."

As Yang stomped on his feet inside the basin, water spilt out onto the floor.

9

PEOPLE OF CHUN'AN HAD NEVER SEEN SO MANY PROVINCIAL TROOPS stationed in their county before. Fully armed soldiers with helmets filled up the square in front of the county yamen. Their long guns glinted under the glaring lights of the flaming torches. A large flagpole lay half buried in a pile of firewood logs. Shaped like a pyramid, the firewood logs reached nearly four metres high. On top sat two men whose bodies were hogtied around the flagpole.

One of the men was Chee Dazhu, the farmer from Chun'an, and the other was

Inoue Toushirou, the notorious Japanese pirate. On one corner of the square stood a dozen young farmers locked up in wooden cages. Their bodies were chained up inside, and their heads popped out through a hole on the top. Troops guarding the prisoners stood at attention, waiting for orders.

The whole county seemed to have turned up for the public execution. Many tried to jostle their way to the front. Their eyes, filled with hostility, darted from the two men sitting on top of the firewood to the young farmers imprisoned inside the cages.

The tension was palpable. Soldiers circled the public square, aiming their guns at onlookers, who might disrupt the public execution.

Moments later, a loud commotion could be heard on a street

north of the square. People turned their heads in that direction, and the crowd began to stir. "Don't move," a squad leader shouted, firstly to people at the front and then to his soldiers. "Someone from the province is here. Stop and control the mob."

The soldiers quickly raised their firearms, pushing people to step back, but it was impossible because the whole area was packed solid.

A group of yamen employees came to their rescue. Carrying big paintbrushes and bowls of black ink, they dipped the brushes in the bowls and sprayed the ink into the back of the crowd. Many retreated to dodge the black liquid.

Meanwhile, soldiers drove away onlookers on the nearby streets to clear a path for new arrivals from the province.

Soon, Hai Rui emerged on the street. He was walking with his horse, flanked on both sides by policemen from Hangzhou.

When Hai entered the square, the crowd began to shift towards him. The ink spraying could no longer deter people from thronging forward. So the yamen employees brought out a dozen benches and placed them next to the soldiers. Climbing onto the benches, the employees began waving their whips, lashing at those who were trying to elbow their way to the front. One employee cracked his whip and yelled at the top of his lungs, "Step back!"

Hai walked past, oblivious to the chaos. But when he approached the pile of firewood logs, he suddenly stopped and looked up.

The prisoner who was hogtied to a flagpole on top of the firewood pile gazed at him. Their eyes met. Hai thought for a moment and remembered – that was Chee Dazhu, the farmer whom he had released at the pier in Hangzhou. With a mouth gag, Chee looked desperate. Hai could tell that Chee was eager to tell his side of the story. The timing wasn't right. Hai quickly shifted his glance away from Chee to the Japanese pirate, Inoue Toushirou, who glared at the sky in defiance.

Hai moved on. The young farmers locked inside the cages widened their eyes and watched him expectantly. Two faces looked familiar to Hai – they were mulberry farmers who were detained at the pier with Chee Dazhu. The farmers had also recognised Hai and begged for help with their eyes.

Hai walked past them without showing any emotions or sympathy. Before he reached the county yamen entrance, he heard screaming behind him. "Seize him, seize him."

He paused and turned around. An elderly farmer who had once stood up to block the horses from trampling on rice seedlings attempted to break the barricade, but soldiers quickly wrestled him down. "Your Honour, our righteous magistrate, please help us," the old man clamoured to get up from the ground. "Those people are innocent. Nobody here colluded with the pirates…"

From a distance, Hai gave him a quick sideways glance.

"They're innocent, innocent!" some in the crowd shouted. Soon, more people joined in the shouts.

Worried by the unruly crowd, the squad leader ordered his soldiers to point their guns at the sky and shoot. The fiery muzzle blasts effectively silenced the shouting.

Meanwhile, the squad leader marched up to the old man. "This man here is also a suspect," he ordered. "Put him in a cage."

Several soldiers dragged the old man into an empty cage and locked him in, but he kept shouting, "Righteous magistrate, please help us."

Hai merely looked on without a word. The squad leader came up to him and bowed. "Pleased to meet you," he greeted. "My name is Xu. I'm the group leader here."

Hai turned around and walked away towards the yamen without even acknowledging him. The squad leader's face turned red. Near the yamen entrance, a uniformed official rushed over from the makeshift podium that had been set up on top of the stairs for Hai to supervise the execution. Taking a deep bow, he introduced himself as Tian Youlu, the deputy magistrate. "Welcome," he said enthusiastically.

Hai simply stared at him silently.

"The execution is going to start soon," he reminded. "Please go and change to your official uniform. If things go smoothly, it will take place at three-quarters past noon."

Hai strolled past the podium without speaking to him and

stepped inside the yamen. Hai's insolence irritated Tian. He followed the new magistrate inside.

Meanwhile, Officer Xu, who was still sulking over Hai's deliberate slight, strode over to a provincial police officer who had come with Hai to vent his frustration. "This new magistrate is truly obnoxious," he cursed. "He's so arrogant and didn't even bother to talk to me when I greeted him."

The police officer's name was Jiang, and he witnessed what had happened. "Well, I was about to warn you," Jiang said to Xu. "Hai seems to be well connected. At a meeting yesterday, he was quite rude to the imperial inspector and Mr Ho. My goodness, he argued with them so fearlessly. Regardless, the execution has to take place at exactly three-quarters past noon. That's the order we have received from the province."

"Understood," the squad leader replied. "How can a mere magistrate be so bold and disobey the imperial inspector? We should find a way to beat him into submission and retaliate against what he did to our superiors."

"It's not the time to do it," Jiang advised. "Once the executions are done, he is tasked to buy up the farmlands and convert them into mulberry fields. We're merely here to carry out orders. Don't be upset and take it personally."

"I've also been told to make the arrests and supervise the executions," Xu said. "I'm not going to stay and get involved in the land-conversion implementation."

"That's right," Jiang said. "Once the executions are done at three-quarters past noon, you and I can leave. They have assigned the task to different squads."

"That's more like it," Xu replied.

At that moment, a commotion interrupted their conversation. Xu turned around with a ferocious look. "Who's making trouble this time?" he asked. "Beat him up! Use whips!"

The soldiers mounted the benches and began lashing at the crowd with whips.

The execution time – three-quarters past noon – was set by the Imperial Palace, and locals saw it as a divine order that could not be altered. At about noon, the sun dazzled in a crystal clear and spotless blue sky. Thousands of impatient onlookers sheltered their eyes with their hands to check the position of the glaring sun, which seemed to be moving unbelievably slowly.

The moment finally arrived. The executioners emerged and walked out in military formation from inside the yamen.

Four trumpeters and four guards lined up on both sides of the podium. The trumpeters set their instruments to their lips, and the guards lit up the fire torches.

Since the Justice Department ordered the executions by burning and gibbeting, a dozen executioners clothed in red uniforms did not carry any cleavers. Two of them, who held fire torches in one hand and buckets of oil in the other, stopped before the pile of firewood logs. The other ten executioners walked over to handle the farmers imprisoned in their cages.

Death by gibbeting involved a hanging cage with a movable bottom connected with a loop handle on the side. When the executioner pulled the handle, the bottom part would be pulled out. As a result, the unlucky person inside the cage would have his head stuck in the round hole on top of the cage and would suffocate.

The crowd started to stir. The guards, tense and nervous, yelled and cracked their whips while the soldiers aimed their loaded guns directly at people at the front.

Xu, the squad leader, raised his head to take a peek at the scalding sun and then shifted his gaze to the empty podium. Magistrate Hai was nowhere to be seen. He became impatient.

"Keep an eye on those people," he shouted to his soldiers who were attempting to rein in the crowd. "The execution will take place on time, at three-quarters past noon."

At that moment, Jiang, the police officer who came with Hai from Hangzhou, appeared at the yamen gate. Xu climbed over the podium to talk with him.

"It's almost noon, and we still haven't seen the new magistrate," Xu asked. "Do you know what is happening?"

"I have no clue," Jiang replied. "Let's go in and find out."

The two stormed into the yamen, but when they reached the hall they were stunned by what they saw.

In the middle of the hall, Hai sat resolutely in front of a desk in his magistrate's uniform. His eyes were fixed on the entrance, and his steely appearance instilled fear in the people around him. The silence in the big hall accentuated the new magistrate's authority.

Tian, the deputy magistrate who sat next to Hai, looked timid and withered. When he saw the two military officers coming in, Tian rose as a courtesy, but Hai ignored them completely. Sensing that Hai was in no rush to attend the execution, the two officers simply stood there, trying to figure out what to do next.

A loud commotion could be heard outside.

In ancient China, the imperial civil servant recruitment system, which had inherited many of the practices from previous dynasties, judged candidates not only based on their merits, but also on their looks. As the saying goes, an official who shepherds the masses should have the good looks of a leader; without them, one has no air of authority. Therefore, during the Imperial Examinations, a young candidate would have to meet an extra criterion – he had to have a well-shaped figure and standard facial features. Different standards were set for different types of faces. If a person happened to be born with a less desirable look, he would be rejected, no matter how remarkable his literary or other talents might be.

When he was young, Hai easily passed the provincial exam, but when sitting for his National Imperial Exam he was supposed to write an essay with a designated theme that he disliked. Instead, he picked his own topic and discussed a pressing political issue without restraint. His defiance enraged the officials in charge. As expected, they failed him in the first round, and he never got to the interview stage, where he would be judged on his looks. Therefore, nobody knew what he looked like or if he carried the air of a magistrate. The two squad leaders saw Hai twice in Hangzhou when he was dressed in his civilian clothing. Now that he had donned his magistrate hat and uniform, they were surprised by his new look – he was undeniably handsome with his intense almond eyes, thick eyebrows and a straight nose. Sitting there in his magistrate's chair, Hai conveyed confidence and an indisputable air of authority.

As the top of the hourglass on the desk was becoming half empty, people around Hai, the deputy and the two military officers, appeared nervous. Summoning enough courage, the deputy stood up and pointed to the hourglass. "Your Honour, it's a quarter after noon," he bowed and pleaded. "We should proceed to the podium."

The two military officers also bowed and stretched out their hands, urging Hai to step out and preside over the execution.

Hai sat there, motionless.

"Bring me the case files," he suddenly requested. That was the first time that the people around him heard him speak. His Hainanese accent was so thick that the deputy didn't quite catch it. Or to be precise, his deputy didn't expect that he would speak.

"I beg your pardon?" the deputy asked.

"I want to see the case files," Hai Rui repeated.

"I, I don't have them," the deputy stammered.

"How do you expect me to sign off on the execution orders without seeing the case files first?" Hai asked.

Startled with the unsolicited reprimand, the deputy looked to the two military officers for answers.

"Magistrate Hai," replied Jiang, one of the military officers. "The execution orders were issued by the Provincial Justice Department. Nobody told us to prepare the case files for you."

"I specifically pledged to the imperial inspector while I was in Hangzhou that I would handle the case in accordance with the Ming Law," Hai said. "If the collusion charges prove to be true, I will dutifully carry out the execution. But, without the case files, I can't prove anything, and I will not allow the killing of innocent people. Since you have submitted an execution list, one should expect case files. Where are they?"

"Your Honour, we captured the criminals yesterday," Hai's deputy explained. "Based on the Ming Law, those who are found to have colluded with the pirates shall be executed on the spot. So we had no time to prepare case files."

"Let me ask you a question then," Hai demanded with a stern look. "I want you to answer it truthfully."

"Please go ahead," the deputy said nervously.

"You mentioned just now that the suspects were captured yesterday. What time of the day?"

The deputy looked to Officer Xu.

"Before dawn yesterday," Xu answered. "Why do you ask this? Was there anything wrong?"

"Where did you arrest those people?" Hai asked.

"On the Haijiapu Pier about fifteen kilometres away from here," Xu said. "I think this line of questioning falls outside your jurisdiction."

Hai rose from his chair, raised his voice and said emphatically, "It is my responsibility. If you captured the suspects at dawn yesterday and your report was delivered to the imperial inspector's office that very morning. How did you manage to get your message there so fast? Chun'an is about one hundred kilometres away from Hangzhou. Did anyone fly over there like a bird?"

Stunned by the accusation, Xu realised that he had made a slip. At the same time, he realised that Hai was a tough nut to crack. Involuntarily, he shifted his gaze to Officer Jiang and Tian, the deputy, both of whom stood there, speechless.

Holding a thick book in his hand, Hai said, "Speaking of *The Great Ming Code*, I have a copy here. Tell me which article entitles you the right to execute suspects accused of colluding with the pirates without conducting interrogation and preparing case files? You submitted a report to the imperial inspector's office before you even arrested the suspects. You have neither interrogated nor filed any official charges. What were you trying to do?"

The three stood there, speechless.

"This case has many unexplained gaps. We cannot carry out the execution today," Hai decided. "Tell the soldiers and police officers to move the suspects over to the county prison and watch them closely. At the same time, Officer Jiang should return to Hangzhou immediately and report the case to the imperial inspector's yamen and the Provincial Justice Department. I'll send someone to Suzhou and notify Governor Hu. The case has to be reviewed and investigated jointly by the imperial inspector's office, the governor's yamen and the Justice Department."

"Before I left Hangzhou, I was told that my job was to help carry out the execution – nobody mentioned a trial," Officer Jiang challenged. "Your Honour, I'm part of the Justice Department. My job is to oversee the execution, and I'm in no position to ask questions."

"That's a good point," Hai said sarcastically. "If we execute the wrong people, who should be held accountable then? You or the Justice Department?"

Officer Jiang refused to back down. "I'm merely following orders," he said. "Mr Ho at the Justice Department and Mr Zheng, the imperial inspector, would be the ones to shoulder the responsibility. Even if they need a scapegoat, it wouldn't be me."

"Do you have an authorisation letter from Mr Ho and Mr Zheng? Show it to me." There was no way that Zheng and Ho would leave any written evidence, thought Hai.

Officer Jiang was at a loss for words.

"Let me explain it to you." Hai gave a stone-cold glare at the two military officers. "If the case proves to be a non-issue, you can carry out the execution right here in Chun'an without any complications. But it could also evolve into a major scandal that has the potential to implicate the Justice Department, the imperial inspector's office and the Imperial Palace. I understand that you are merely following orders, but you don't even have any authorisation papers. As the magistrate in Chun'an, I'm tasked with overseeing the execution. Based on the Ming Law, you have to follow my orders here. The execution cannot go on without my signing off on it. If you dare go ahead, nobody would speak on your behalf when the Imperial Palace investigates the case."

The two military officers accepted Hai's explanation but resisted the idea of reporting back to Ho and Zheng in Hangzhou.

"By the way, please make sure that none of the suspects is mistreated in prison before their trial," Hai warned. "If any of them dies of maltreatment, illness or starvation, I'm going to lock you up instead."

The two officers looked at each other in blank dismay.

"How much grain subsidies do you have left?" Hai turned to Tian, his deputy.

"I, I think we're going to run out of it tomorrow," the deputy, who was taken aback by the topic switch, stammered.

"Do we have a backup plan?"

"There... there isn't much that we can do..." the deputy replied.

Hai's predecessor Chang Boxi, who had been executed for sabotaging the dams, was a corrupt and avaricious man. The deputy who had served under him for years learned to curry favour and ingratiate his way into Chang's circles. As time went by, Chang and his deputy became literally partners in crime and shared whatever they had embezzled. Now, with the arrival of a new superior, the deputy faced uncertainty in his career.

"If you don't have any backup plan, I think you would be the next to be executed," Hai threatened.

"Your, your Honour, you're bluffing," the deputy argued. "The grain subsidies come directly from the provincial government. Why do you make me the scapegoat?"

"After this magistrate's position became vacant last year, you stepped in. You know very well that we're going to run out of grain subsidies tomorrow, but you have no backup plan. If starvation occurs and local people revolt, who do you think would be held accountable and executed?"

"I've been told that more grain subsidies will arrive no later than tomorrow..." the deputy quickly added.

"Who promised you that?" Hai asked.

"Officials in Hangzhou, of course."

"What will happen if the shipment doesn't arrive? Shall I kill you, or shall I punish those officials in the province? Besides, the current situation is evolving. We now have to review this case. Before we reach a verdict, we cannot force local farmers to sell their farmland. Regardless, if we run out of grain subsidies and people start a riot or something, I'm going to hold you responsible."

"This is a huge responsibility," the deputy ranted. "You can't dump it all on me."

"I'm the new magistrate and will take responsibility for whatever happens after today," Hai said. "You're responsible for things that happened before I assumed this office. If I were you, I would borrow grain from the wealthy landowners. We don't really need much. As long as you can make up enough subsidies for three more days, you should be fine."

"How am I supposed to do that?" the deputy asked.

"You can borrow in the name of the county yamen, and I'll make sure to pay them back later."

"I still cannot guarantee that they will loan it to us," the deputy admitted.

"If you can't secure the grain, you'd better pack and get your family out of here as soon as you can."

"How, how could you threaten me like this?" the deputy grumbled before bolting for the exit. Before reaching the entrance, he heard a loud commotion outside. He stopped, shuddering with fear – the execution time had lapsed. He quickly turned around and shouted, "It's over for us... What are we going to do? We have missed the deadline."

The military officers quickly checked the sandglass, which showed three-quarters past noon. By then, they realised that Hai had duped them.

"Now that the execution time has expired, let's move the suspects into the county prison and then submit a report to the province," Hai stated calmly.

The deputy shook his head helplessly. Dodging the crowd at the main entrance, he took a detour through a corridor and headed towards a side entrance.

明

Having procured a loan from Zhao Zhenji in Suzhou, Governor Hu felt more relaxed. The mild sunny weather propelled his boat back to Hangzhou smoothly. Moreover, Dr Li's herbs seemed to have produced visible results. Governor Hu looked much more spirited than he did a few days before in Suzhou.

"When you saw His Majesty in Beijing, how did his eyes look?" enquired Dr Li Shizhen, who was sitting next to Governor Hu on a cushion on the right side of the boat. When Hu shook his head, Dr Li persisted. "Think hard."

"If I remember correctly, I think his eyes looked sharp and steady," Governor Hu said. "There was no sign of insipidity."

"Did you detect redness in his sclera?"

"Yes, a little bit."

"Did he have dark bags under his eyes?"

"Somewhat bluish," Governor Hu said after contemplating it for a few seconds.

"These are the signs of mercury poisoning," said Li, who gazed into the water.

"Is it something serious?" Governor Hu asked with concern.

"If he keeps taking those pills concocted by the alchemists, he can last three to five years, regardless of how well he takes care of himself."

Governor Hu sat there stunned, his eyes moistened.

"When I served as the imperial doctor, I advised His Majesty not to believe in the art of alchemy," Dr Li said. "I tried to stop him from taking those pills, but he ignored my advice. That's the main reason I quit." Dr Li rose and began pacing about on the deck. "It was quite discouraging," he continued. "The Imperial Palace has attracted a large group of famous scholar-officials who are supposedly well versed in the studies of Confucius. But there is not a single person who dares to speak out or dissuade His Majesty to stay away from alchemy. Grand Secretary Yan Song and a few other prominent scholars are competing for attention by writing flattery essays to stroke his ego and encourage his bad behaviour. If we allow this to go on, this dynasty's days are numbered."

Governor Hu lowered his gaze in shame.

"If you don't mind, I would like to ask you a question," said Dr Li.

"No, I don't mind at all," Governor Hu said, lifting his head to face Dr Li.

"You're a very intelligent and upright person who puts the interest of the country and people above your own. Why would you attach yourself to Yan Song?"

The unexpected and straightforward questioning shocked Governor Hu, leaving him scrambling for words.

"Even though I have long left the Imperial Palace, I still hear all sorts of gossip from my patients who are senior officials. I've heard quite a lot about you. Would you want to know what people say about you?"

"Yes, please go ahead," Hu said eagerly.

"Let me touch on the positive ones first," Dr Li said. "The overall comments can be summarised in two sentences – You have the insight to identify talented people and bring out the best in them. You are practical and hard-working. People also commended you for cooperating with General Qi Jiguang in the fight against pirates. Your efforts have brought peace to the coastal region in the southeast. At the same time, you helped repair sea walls, reduce taxes for farmers and promote silk trade. These measures have really benefitted ordinary people. These accomplishments will certainly gain you a prominent place in history."

Embarrassed, Governor Hu lowered his head.

"As for the negative comments, I really don't need to bring them up, and you know exactly what they are," Dr Li continued pensively. "I admire your courage to buck authority and travel around to collect grain subsidies for the disaster victims, but I want to offer you a piece of advice because I might see things more clearly as an outsider. I think Yan Song and Yan Shifan could be toppled within a couple of years. When that happens, your connection with them will wipe out all the good work you have done."

Hu simply stared at Dr Li without any response.

"One could always forsake family relations for righteousness. Why can't you stand up and expose their villainous deceit?"

"But, doctor, I hate to disappoint you," Hu said resolutely. "People can go all out to topple the grand secretary, but I can't."

"Why?' Dr Li asked, looking dejected.

"It doesn't matter if I go down in history as a prominent official or not, but it does matter that I don't become a petty person."

Dr Li paused for a few minutes. Then, he nodded appreciatively. "Well, the fact that Yan Song recognised you shows that he is not all that evil," he said.

Tan Lun suddenly burst into the cabin with a grim look.

Knowing that something ominous had happened, Governor Hu rose and excused himself. "I'll be back in a few minutes," he said before stepping out with Tan.

The two of them moved to the bow, and the guards who occupied the area quickly vacated to the side.

"It's quite intriguing," Tan reported. "Three days after he arrived, Gao Hanwen suddenly changed his mind and signed on the farmland conversion action plan. Then, he passed out at the conference. At the same time, there was news that farmers in Chun'an county had been arrested on charges of collusion with the pirates. Hai Rui had been sent to supervise the execution."

"Did the execution take place?" Governor Hu asked, looking shocked.

"No, he postponed it and ordered the soldiers to lock up the suspects in a county prison," Tan said. "He sent you a letter, urging you and the imperial inspector to jointly investigate the case because he believes the charges don't stand up to scrutiny."

Governor Hu's mind was racing.

"We have also received a separate report, claiming that Shen Yishi has left for Chun'an and Jiande with boatloads of grain," Tan showed a letter to Governor Hu. "He's going to purchase farmland in the name of the South China Textile Bureau. I think he should have reached there today."

"The day is finally here," Hu said with a heavy sigh. "All factions – the grand secretary and his son, and the Prince of Yu and his advisers – are about to show their cards. But why are they dragging His Majesty into this? Why do they send Shen Yishi to purchase farmland in the name of the Textile Bureau?"

"They're desperate like cornered dogs," Tan Lun replied. "Zheng Bichang and Ho Maocai know that they're in big trouble, and they can't think straight."

"What is going on with Shen Yishi? The Textile Bureau has made him wealthy, but why is he getting mixed up with Zheng and Ho?"

"I don't understand that either," Tan Lun said. "Governor, it's important that we focus on Chun'an. If Hai Rui did not carry out the execution, it means that there is something wrong with the verdicts. At this critical juncture, if we pressure farmers to sell their land, they could rebel against the government. I don't think Hai Rui can handle all this alone."

"Let's approach this from a different angle," Governor Hu reminded Tan. "What would Zheng Bichang and Ho Maocai do if they find out that Hai Rui has postponed the execution?"

"Zheng and Ho might have schemed to fabricate the farmer-pirate collusion case," Tan replied. "Once they realise that their plot could be foiled, they would definitely send people to kill any potential witnesses. Governor, you need to go there immediately. You're the only one who can control the situation."

"No, I can't," Governor Hu shook his head vigorously. "Let's make a plan fast before we stop the boat nearby. I need to get off and take a land route to see General Qi Jiguang right away."

"Do you mean to say that the pirates could launch attacks any time soon?"

"Internal strife will inevitably lead to foreign aggression," Hu nodded with a worried look on his face.

"You bastard, I'm going to kill you," Ho Maocai cursed loudly at Jiang, the squad leader who had returned to the imperial inspector's office and reported to him about the botched execution in Chun'an. At one point, Ho lost his temper and kicked Jiang with his right foot. Fortunately, years of military training had given Jiang the agility to dodge Ho's kicks by quickly jumping to the side. Ho lost his balance and was about to fall when Jiang held him with both of his hands. Feeling humiliated, Ho slapped Jiang on the face.

Zheng, who sat there exasperated by the news, frowned at Ho's farcical outburst.

"I sent two squads with several hundred soldiers over to control the situation, and you couldn't even kill a few criminals," Ho yelled loudly, giving Jiang another slap on the face. "The Imperial Palace has raised a bunch of useless fools like you."

"But Hai Rui was supposed to take charge of the execution," Jiang argued with his signature stubbornness. "We didn't have your authorisation to execute the criminals. Your Honour never issued any papers for us."

Ho Maocai thought there was some truth in that. He softened his tone but remained furious. "Why didn't we ask Hai Rui to sign off on the execution papers."

Despite what had happened, Ho still saw Jiang as his confidant. Once they both calmed down, Jiang raised his head and ventured,

"Your Honour, Hai Rui is fearless, and it looks like he wants to fight the execution order at all cost. Before we left, he had a letter delivered to Governor Hu. I personally think we should act fast before the whole thing blows up."

"Why don't you leave us alone for a few minutes," Zheng interrupted.

"Yes, sir," Jiang saluted before exiting the hall.

Ho felt that his mind had gone blank. All he did was to stare at Zheng.

"What do you think we should do?' Zheng asked.

"The gloves are off," Ho replied. "There's nothing else we can do except to kill him."

"How?"

"Whatever works, hacking or poisoning him to death."

"How can we justify getting rid of him?"

"Collusion with the pirates, or disrupting the implementation of a national policy. We can come up with all sorts of excuses to get him executed."

"Those excuses sound too grand and abstract," Zheng sighed. "Please come up with something more specific."

"How specific do you need? We captured the pirates and their cohorts, and we sentenced them to death, but the new magistrate refused to carry out the execution. This alone could get Hai Rui the death penalty."

"This doesn't hold water," Zheng argued impatiently. "You people did not prepare any case files, and there have been no interrogations. You arrested those suspects at dawn, and the report reached my office in the morning. Wasn't that a bit too fast? Hai Rui doesn't believe it. You've been in the field of criminal justice for more than a decade. How could you be so reckless and make such errors?"

Frustrated and upset at Zheng's rebuke, Ho stood there, sweat streaming down his cheeks. Then, he grabbed a fan from a nearby table and started fanning vigorously.

"Have you released the dozen or so pirates from the provincial prison?" Zheng asked.

"Not yet," Ho replied.

"Good. Please suspend the operation. Also, didn't you promise to reward the pirates with silk if they cooperate with you? Stop it right away."

"We should immediately send people to the Chun'an County prison and get rid of Inoue Toushirou and those peasant instigators," Ho said with a fierce look in his eyes. "Then we'll detain Hai Rui."

"Who's going to do it?" Zheng questioned.

"I'll send Jiang back there," Ho said without thinking.

"What are we going to do about you?" Zheng sighed. "How do you expect two squad leaders to subdue and arrest a magistrate?"

Ho smacked his forehead and said, "Sorry, but you and I can't get involved in this, can we?"

"Send Gao Hanwen over," Zheng suggested.

Relief washed over his face, and his eyes lit up.

"Jiang and Xu can visit the county prison first and kill the pirates and the farmers," Zheng added. "Then, Gao will go there afterwards to arrest Hai Rui. We have to get everything done before Governor Hu arrives."

"This will allow us to kill two birds with one stone," Ho said. "While Gao Hanwen is there, he can help Shen Yishi acquire more farmland."

"We have to be really careful," Zheng warned. "This is our last resort. If anything goes wrong, you and I could end up inside a death cage."

明

To ease the awkwardness between him and Gao Hanwen, Zheng Bichang changed into casual clothing before visiting the Hangzhou mayor's yamen. Upon his arrival, Zheng was all smiles and looked unusually cordial.

Gao went along with Zheng's pretence. An idealistic and upright scholar, Gao knew that his literal and metaphorical fall had a lot to do with the person in front of him. So, deep down, he was filled with anger but tried to maintain his dignity despite his poor health.

"I've said everything that I need to tell you," Zheng said with a look of feigned concern. "I should have allowed you to rest up for a few more days, but the dire circumstances in Chun'an and Jiande need your presence. So I'm afraid you have to toughen it out and go. Fortunately, you are taking a boat, and I've asked a doctor to accompany you there. So, while work is important, you also need to take care of your health."

"I'll go, but I don't need a doctor," Gao replied promptly. The young man's sudden change of mind surprised Zheng, making him wonder what he was really thinking. But Gao's face remained cold and inscrutable.

"Brother Gao, you are required to use this trip to implement the land-conversion policy," Zheng warned. "Regardless of what happens, we have to make sure that farmers plant their mulberry trees in June."

"I was the one who came up with the policy proposal. I think I know what to do."

Gao's words made Zheng shudder with concern. "The South China Textile Bureau has shipped the grain to the two disaster regions," Zheng reminded Gao. "If we can't buy up the land and plant the mulberry trees on time, you could be held accountable."

Gao rose and said, "I understand. Is that all? I'm afraid I need to pack for tomorrow."

"All right," Zheng said, trying to contain his vexation. "By the way, I have sent soldiers to accompany you. Given the hot weather, I would advise that you set off early in the morning."

"Understood," Gao replied. "Since I'm not feeling well, I really am not able to walk you to the door."

Appalled at such a breach of courtesy, Zheng was ready to explode but quickly regained his composure.

"You can be excused," he said and headed towards the door.

After Zheng stepped into the darkness, Gao slowly sat down. "I need help," he called to a servant. "Get me a bucket of water."

"Your Honour, do you want warm water or cold water," the servant asked.

"Get a bucket of water from the well," Gao ordered. "Please scrub the floor where Mr Zheng stood."

"Understood," the servant replied with a quizzical look.

A few minutes later, Gao's personal aide rushed in. "Your Honour," he whispered to Gao. "Someone from the South China Textile Bureau wants to meet you."

Gao did not respond.

"It's kind of odd that this person came in from the side door," the aide continued. "It seemed to me that he deliberately avoided Mr Zheng. He said he has something urgent to discuss with you."

"Whatever the reason, please let him in," Gao finally replied.

Seeing that Gao looked somewhat ill, the aide quickly said, "If you're not feeling well, I can always tell him to come another time."

"Did I say I'm not feeling well?"

"All right then," said the aide before he hurried outside. A few minutes later, the servant came in with a bucket of water.

"Go and scrub that chair and the floor there," Gao instructed.

The servant ladled out some water and poured it out onto the chair, on which Zheng had sat. Water dripped off to the floor.

"Do you mind if I ask you to move into the other room," the servant asked. "I'm going to scrub the floor here."

"My side of the floor is clean," Gao explained. "Just scrub the spot near the chair."

The servant was about to bend over to scrub when the personal aide shouted. "Stop. Our guest is here."

Despite the heat, the guest was draped in a black cape with a hood.

Gao stared at him in surprise.

The person stepped over to a chair opposite Gao and removed the hood from his head. It was Yang Jinshui, director of the South China Textile Bureau.

Neither Gao nor his aides had met Yang before, but from the gold-rimmed official hat, they knew that he held an important position within the Imperial Palace.

"I have something important to discuss with Mayor Gao," Yang told the aide and the servant. "Please excuse us."

Yang's imposing manner spoke for itself. Without waiting for permission from Gao, the aide and servant quickly exited.

"Mayor Gao, it is nice to meet you. I'm Yang Jinshui."

Gao sprang to his feet.

"Oh, please sit down," Yang said.

Gao sat down hesitantly.

"I'm aware of what happened between you and Madam Yun," Yang said calmly. "Four of my subordinates who went to blackmail you have been punished. I've come here to tell you that nobody can blackmail you. The note that they forced you to draft won't be valid unless I give approval. In other words, they can't use that to threaten you."

Gao could not believe what he had heard. His eyes beamed.

"Do you know why they did that to you?"

"Yang Gonggong, please advise," Gao said, trying to control his emotions.

"They want to smear His Majesty," Yang said.

Gao's eyes widened.

"Did Zheng come to see you just now?"

Gao nodded.

"Did he urge you to purchase land in Chun'an and Jiande?"

"Yes."

"Did you agree to do it?'

"Death will pay all debts. I have nothing to fear."

"No, no, no," Yang said. "You won't die, and there is no need for you to die. They are the ones who deserve capital punishment."

Gao gazed at Yang in disbelief.

"Do you know how they manage to purchase land in the disaster areas?"

"I don't know."

"Let me tell you then. They are going to do it in the name of the Textile Bureau. They want to tell local folks that His Majesty and the Imperial Palace have sent them to buy up the land."

"They wouldn't dare, would they?" Gao said.

"I know you're a smart person and understand the implications. Since Zheng has asked you to leave tomorrow, you should go ahead. But, instead of purchasing land, I want you to do something else for me."

"Please tell me," Gao said earnestly.

"When you are there, go on the boats and remove all the Textile

Bureau's lanterns. Tell everyone that the Imperial Textile Bureau has nothing to do with the scheme."

Gao nodded, his eyes sparkled with hope.

明

The weather in May turned unusually hot and sultry. By the time Feng Bao approached the Prince of Yu's mansion, he was sweating. Inside the courtyard, he could hear the prince's angry voice. Pausing for a few seconds, Feng pricked his ears.

"Why isn't Feng Bao returning?" the prince shouted. "Please send someone to get him."

As the baby's wailing filled the room, Feng Bao dashed into the room and announced, "I'm back… Don't cry…"

"Amitabha! Glad you're back," Princess Li said with relief before handing the baby to Feng Bao. "He's been crying all afternoon."

"But Your Highness, I'm dripping with sweat," Feng Bao said, unsure if he should hold the baby.

"That's not a problem," the princess said. "We're all sweaty today. Stop his crying first."

With permission, Feng smiled and clapped his hands to get the baby's attention. The young boy stopped crying. Staring at Feng's smiley face, he giggled.

The prince also calmed down. He looked at Feng, waiting for a report from him. Feng bowed slightly, but the two palace maids made him hesitant.

"Why don't you two go and pick up two chunks of ice from the cellar," the prince said, using the excuse to send the maids away.

Now, Feng was alone with the prince and princess.

Feng walked close to the prince and whispered, "I just delivered the message to Lu Gonggong. He asked me to tell you that he's aware of what is happening in Zhejiang."

"Is that all?" the prince asked.

"Oh, Master, I'm not done yet," Feng quickly continued. "Lu Gonggong said the empire belongs to your family and he understands and appreciates the fact that you care deeply about your subjects. He's going to find an occasion to report what you have told him to His Majesty tonight."

The prince's face looked relaxed as he turned to his wife, who handed a towel to Feng for him to wipe his face.

"This is too much," Feng quickly dropped to his knees with the baby in his arm. "Your Highness, I can't take it."

"Just take it and wipe the sweat off your face," the Prince of Yu ordered.

"This is awfully kind of you," Feng said, stretching out a hand, with his palm up. Princess Li placed the towel that had been soaked in cold water in Feng's trembling hand. As he was wiping the beads of sweat from his head, the baby widened his eyes and watched quietly.

In June 1561, a heatwave hit Beijing, making it the hottest month in twenty years. In previous hot-weather days, people living and working inside the Forbidden City could always feel a fresh penetrating breeze blowing through the palaces, even though the rest of Beijing was shrouded in suffocating heat. Experts attributed the breeze, known as the royal wind, to the Forbidden City's majestic fengshui.

Unfortunately, the breeze seemed to have dried up this year. For ten consecutive days, the willow trees along the moat remained stagnant. While some concubines and senior eunuchs staffing the twenty-four yamens could access ice, the other one hundred thousand junior eunuchs and maids suffered tremendously in the unbearable heat. Since palace etiquette required that they wear long robes every day, many were struck with malaria and had itchy red rashes all over their bodies and faces. Meanwhile, the humidity inside the palace aggravated the malaria, turning the red rashes into inflamed boils. As a result, the absentee rates were high. Thanks to the imperial doctors who had shipped carts of herbs to prevent heatstroke, no heat-related deaths occurred inside the Forbidden City.

Oddly enough, inside the Yuxi Palace, Emperor Jiajing ordered all of his windows closed. One night, a eunuch on duty carrying a liquor jug and another holding a wooden basin quietly approached the palace. Perspiration streamed down their faces. At the entrance, they put down the wine jug and the wooden basin, and pricked their ears, trying to find out if His Majesty was ready to receive them.

They could hear Emperor Jiajing chanting poems. Knowing that it would be an inopportune and possibly unforgivable act to barge in, the eunuchs stepped away from the door and sat at the bottom of the stairs, fanning their faces with their long sleeves.

"The heavenly god is acting up again," said one eunuch. "Last winter, there was hardly any snow, and now we have this unbearable heat. I wonder if the heavenly god is about to come down and conscript more people into the heavenly army. "

"I have heard that many people outside are dying of heat," the second eunuch agreed. "The government is distributing free herbs to residents."

"But His Majesty has the body of an immortal," commented the first eunuch. "He leaves his windows open in the dead of winter, and on days like this he keeps his windows shut."

"Lu Gonggong is half an immortal," added the second eunuch. "He has the stamina to keep His Majesty company for hours inside. I think the chanting has stopped. Let's go and check."

They crept up to the door, and it was quiet inside.

"Lu Gonggong, we have brought you the liquor jug and the wooden basin," one eunuch announced softly.

A few moments later, the palace door opened, and Lu emerged. His head was perspiring.

The two eunuchs dropped to their knees. "The jug is quite heavy," one said. "Shall we carry it inside for you?"

"I'm not that old," said Lu. "I can do it myself."

"Of course you're not old," the eunuchs replied in unison. "You'll live up to at least ten thousand years because His Majesty needs your company."

The eunuchs lifted the liquor jug from the ground and handed it over to Lu. He carried it inside and then came back to fetch the wooden basin.

"Go and have a rest," Lu Fang dismissed them.

Since Emperor Jiajing refused to open the windows, smoke from the burning incense lingered inside the palace. A stack of hymns written by Grand Secretary Yan Song and his deputy, Xu Jie, were smouldering inside a brazier in front of an altar.

Dressed in a thick yellow cotton robe, with the front buttons open, Emperor Jiajing sat cross-legged on a bright yellow cushion. His feet were tucked inside a pair of comfortable black cotton shoes with silk vamp. As the eunuchs had described, the emperor seemed to have the body of an immortal because there was not a single bead of sweat on his body.

Lu placed the wooden basin in front of the emperor's feet. By then, he was perspiring profusely. When he opened the wine jug, an intoxicating smell of liquor assaulted his nostrils.

Even the emperor noticed the strong scent. "Is it Maotai?"

"Yes, it's sixty years old," Lu Fang said. "We just found it in the wine and vinegar cellar."

"The liquor is a few years older than I am," said the emperor.

"The aged Maotai was distilled from the best grain, which combined all five basic elements of earth – gold, wood, water, fire and earth," explained Lu, who lifted the jar to the edge of the wooden basin and slowly poured out the liquor. "Only stuff like this can nurture your heavenly body."

The emperor watched appreciatively as Lu sat down on a stool next to him and slowly rolled up his trouser legs, revealing two long thin legs, which were covered with red rashes. Lu carefully soaked the emperor's left foot in the wooden basin. "Master, does it hurt?"

The emperor winced with pain but quickly gained his composure. "Please go ahead," he encouraged.

Slowly, Lu washed the emperor's left shin and foot with the liquor.

When he finished the left foot, Lu cupped it with both hands and let it rest on the edge of the wooden basin. Then, he moved his stool closer to work on his right foot. The emperor glanced at his left foot, and he was pleased to see that the rashes looked less conspicuous and the swelling seemed to have gone down a bit.

"My good old Lu Fang," the emperor said with gratitude. "Where in the world did you find this concoction? It seems to be working."

"Your humble servant knows nothing about concoction," Lu said, gently wiping the emperor's right foot. "I heard about this prescription from Dr Li Shizhen while he was here years ago."

"Do you mean the Dr Li who was recommended to me by the King of Chu?"

"Your Majesty certainly has an accurate memory."

"That person was a good doctor, but, unfortunately, he just didn't get it most of the time. He needed to cultivate his Tao."

"It's not something that ordinary people can achieve easily," Lu complimented as he rolled down the emperor's trouser legs and put on his black cotton shoes. "My Master has been cultivating the Tao for several life cycles. How could anyone compete with that?"

The emperor looked surprised when Lu lifted the wooden basin and poured the used liquor back into the liquor jug. "What's that for?" he asked.

"Many folks believe that Your Majesty possesses the body of an immortal," Lu explained. "They are eager to drink up the liquor that has washed your feet. Besides, this is good stuff, and it'll be a waste if we throw it away. Why don't we just gift it to your subordinates."

Seeing that Lu was putting the lid on the jug, the emperor quickly stopped him with a serious look. "They're lying to you," he said dismissively. "One can only achieve nirvana through one's own cultivation. It is pure nonsense to claim that one can attain good luck by touching the things that I have used. If you give away this jug of liquor, people could get sick after drinking it. We have plenty of gifts in the palace to give away, not this liquor."

"All right then," Lu answered in a choked voice. The emperor glanced at him, but Lu quickly looked aside. Walking over to a jade basin on top of a rosewood table, Lu pretended to wash his face, but he was actually wiping his tears. Before turning around, he picked up a string of prayer beads. "Master, I'm going to dump the liquor," he promised the emperor when he handed over his prayer beads.

Noticing his tears, Emperor Jiajing enquired, "Why are you crying?"

Lu dropped to his knees beside the emperor. "It is truly touching that you instructed your humble servant not to gift the tainted liquor to your subjects," Lu said, trying to contain his emotions. "It shows your Buddha-like compassion. The thought that so many people, big and small, rely on you for protection really tugs at my heartstrings."

"You're quite emotional today," the emperor asked. "Any bad news? Is there a natural disaster happening somewhere?"

"There's been a drought in some northern provinces, but I heard that it's not that severe. So that was not why I felt a bit sad. I'm just afraid that some evil officials at the local level could take advantage of your compassion and benevolence to tarnish your reputation."

"Have you heard anything?" the emperor probed, looking alarmed.

"An express report from Yang Jinshui arrived this evening," Lu replied.

"What is it? The land-conversion programme has encountered problems?" the emperor pressed.

"Your Majesty, you should first promise me not to be upset if I show you this," Lu said while pulling out an express letter with three chicken feathers. "You're still recovering from the rashes."

The emperor grabbed the letter and started reading it. Lu held up a silk lantern and stood behind the emperor to provide light.

"Call Yan Song over," the emperor shouted after reading the letter and tossing it onto the floor.

明

Standing in front of Emperor Jiajing, Yan Song felt old and frail. The sweat that dripped down from his long eyebrows fogged up his eyes. The image of the emperor, who sat opposite him, became blurry.

"We had no snow last December, and since summer there's been hardly any breeze," Emperor Jiajing lectured. "Didn't I ask you to check with the astronomer? What did he say?"

To Yan Song, the emperor's voice sounded so distant and vague, and he could not make out every single word.

Except for formal occasions, such as a worshipping ceremony or exorcising ritual, Yan Song could enjoy the privilege of sitting on a stool when talking to His Majesty. But it was different this time. Emperor Jiajing not only summoned him to the palace in the middle of a hot and sultry night but also refused to let him take a seat. Even though Yan Song hadn't figured out the reason for such a change, he could astutely feel that the years of trust and respect he had built with the emperor were being eroded. Regardless, Yan Song, an experienced politician, remained calm, trying to direct his thoughts quickly from the current abnormalities to the emperor's question.

"Your Majesty, I did not make the enquiry," he replied slowly.

"Why?"

"I did not feel it appropriate for an ordinary official like me to discuss astronomy with anyone. Your Majesty is the son of heaven and should summon the imperial astronomer to personally enquire about any heavenly phenomenon."

"So are you implying that the lack of snow and the current heat-wave are my own doings?"

The emperor's accusation hit his partially deaf ears like a clap of thunder rumbling towards him from afar. Even though he was eighty, Yan Song had sharp mental faculties. Lifting his robe, he slowly dropped to his knees. "In Shangshu,[1] the author stated, *Three years of bumper harvests will be followed by three years of shortages; while a minor disaster strikes every six years and a catastrophe descends every twelve years.* This has been the case since the times of Emperors Yao and Shun. That's why we save during the good years and use the savings to tide us over during the bad years."

Seeing that the old man was soaked with sweat, Emperor Jiajing softened his tone. For more than two decades, his grand secretary ruled on his behalf, and, even when reprimanded, Yan Song was still attempting to defend the emperor's reputation. Touched by Yan Song's loyalty, the emperor was at a loss for words.

"Grand Secretary Yan, please rise," Lu jumped in, trying to help him up. "His Majesty did not order you to kneel."

Seizing Lu's hand, Yan Song managed to get to his feet. Lu looked to Emperor Jiajing for directions, and the emperor eyed the stool next to him.

"His Majesty asks you to sit down," urged Lu.

"I'm grateful for Your Majesty's kindness," Yan Song took the stool that Lu handed him, tears welling up in his eyes.

The emperor resumed his questioning. "You just mentioned the need to store up leftover grain and save it for the bad years. At the moment, two counties in Zhejiang have been flooded. What have we done to help the victims there?"

"We are in the process of implementing the strategy of combining the land-conversion policy with our disaster-rescue efforts. That is, we offer subsidies to farmers while urging them to sell their farmland so we can convert it into mulberry fields."

Emperor Jiajing shot Lu a knowing glance, and Lu shook his head slightly.

"Please go home and check with your son," Emperor Jiajing continued. "When you come back later, give me an update on the latest situation there."

"Yes, Your Majesty," Yan Song rose and kowtowed before Lu led him out.

Emperor Jiajing watched as Yan wobbled away. He looked lost.

"Yan Song is getting too old to manage our national affairs," the emperor sighed when Lu returned.

"He's in a tough spot," Lu replied sympathetically.

"Let's see what he has to say tomorrow. If his son, Yan Shifan, neglects his filial duties, I doubt he can be loyal to me. It is outrageous that the merchants would buy up the farmland in the name of the Imperial Textile Bureau. If it's Yan Shifan's idea, I assume that Yan Song would come in and seek forgiveness tomorrow."

"I think so too," Lu Fang said. "Once Yan Song admits guilt, we'll send a notice immediately to the provinces."

"One more thing – please keep a close eye on your own people," Emperor Jiajing reminded, his tone becoming stern. "They're no longer as well-informed and capable as they used to be. You talked about how Yang Jinshui has figured out a way to remove all the lanterns that bore the names of the Imperial Textile Bureau. But it was already too late, wasn't it? My reputation has already been tarnished. How do we manage to salvage that? Tell that servant of yours that if he continues to let such things happen I'm going to have him beheaded and hang his head on the grain boats."

"I will send someone to deliver the message right now," Lu replied.

"Send a few Imperial Secret Police officers over to Zhejiang. They can wear civilian clothing and monitor the situation closely. It looks like we need to arrest and kill a few this time."

"Understood."

10

ALTHOUGH THEY VARIED IN SIZE, ALL THE PRISONS IN ZHEJIANG Province, whether at provincial, city or county level, were built with a similar layout that included a long passageway, sturdy iron bars, and stone walls and floors. In every prison, an office for the warden on duty stood near the entrance to the passageway.

Upon his arrival, Hai Rui upgraded the warden's office at the Chun'an County prison, turning it into a magistrate's makeshift yamen.

Soldiers occupied the yard outside the temporary office, but Hai forbade them from swarming in. Instead, he posted a group of sword-bearing prison guards at the entrance and within his eyesight. Sitting at a rickety desk, Hai carefully reviewed a stack of prison files left by his predecessor.

Two prison guards carrying two buckets of food and a basket of bowls and chopsticks came in and requested permission to enter the prison. "Your Honour," said one of them, "we're here to deliver lunch for the new inmates."

"Can you divide up the food here?" Hai enquired.

The two guards eyed each other, looking baffled, but they complied and filled up a dozen bowls with rice. Although they had begun to carefully stack up the rice bowls inside the buckets, Hai stopped them.

"Why don't you two try the food first?"

"But, Your Honour, this is prison food."

"Just take one bite," Hai demanded.

After a few hesitant moments, the two guards tucked into the food with chopsticks. One guard stuck a piece of sticky rice into his mouth and gave a grimace of sincere and unrestrained disgust.

As the saying goes, one loses the right to be treated like a human once he's in prison. In every dynasty, the Imperial Government allocated money to cover food and other expenses for prisoners, but corrupt prison officials often embezzled the government funds. They would either feed inmates with cheap stale rice or mix the stale rice with husks. In some extreme cases, dishonest and brutal officials added sand and dirt into the rice to make up for the quantity of food that should have been served. Therefore, the food was hardly edible. The two guards could have never imagined that they would encounter such an overly demanding boss who insisted they try the inmate food first. Even though they cried foul, they wouldn't dare disobey Hai's order.

After the two guards sampled the food in each of the twelve bowls, Hai issued a warning. "Please tell the cook not to tamper with this food," he said. "If an inmate dies of poisoning, I'm going to force you and the cook to swallow all of the poisoned food."

"We wouldn't dare," the two guards promised in unison.

"All right then, you can go in now."

The two guards picked up their buckets and disappeared into the passageway.

Tian Youlu, Hai's deputy, stepped in and sat on a seat opposite Hai.

"Do you have anything to report?" Hai asked.

"Your Honour, I met several rice merchants today," Tian said while wiping sweat from his forehead. "I begged them, pleaded and almost dropped to my knees, but I've only been able to borrow two days' worth of grain subsidies."

"Have you started distributing it yet?" Hai asked.

"We're doing that now."

"I told you to borrow three days' worth of rice," Hai said

without looking at him. "You're still one day short. Go out and try harder this time."

"Your Honour, I don't think I can," Tian said with a determined and stubborn look.

Hai did not respond and continued his reading – he was now examining the county ledgers.

"I threw myself at your mercy, so feel free to put me in custody," Tian said.

"I'm not going to put you behind bars because of this," Hai said. "When the subsidy issue is all done, I'm going to look into something else that you might be involved in. By the way, how did the dams along the Xin'an River break?"

"Your Honour, that question has long been settled – Chang Boxi, your predecessor, was found liable. The Imperial Palace had him executed," Tian said, his face turning ashen. "You can't dredge it up again and blame everything on me."

"Get out and borrow more grain."

Tian rose from his chair and whined, "Your Honour, what's done is done. New owners don't dredge up old debts. If you try to settle old scores, you'll meet the same end after you leave here someday."

"I don't have a son, and I have no intention of walking out of here alive," Hai said, shooting him a stern glance. "Go and do your job now."

"All right, all right," Tian said before exiting the office.

A few minutes later, Tian returned with sweat dripping down his cheeks.

"Your Honour, they're finally here," he shouted excitedly.

"Who are here?" Hai asked.

"The grain boats from the South China Textile Bureau," Tian said.

"Which agency?"

"The South China Textile Bureau!"

"Are you sure?" Hai asked.

"A messenger just came back with the news," Tian replied. "He said he had seen the Textile Bureau's lanterns on the boats. I'm also told that a Textile Bureau official is waiting for us at the county yamen."

"Why don't you go and meet with him?" Hai suggested. "Try to find out who he represents and if those boats belong to the South China Textile Bureau."

"If those boats carry lanterns that bear the name of the South China Textile Bureau, I'm sure it's them," Tian reassured Hai.

"Go and check it out," Hai said, his eyes sparkling. "It would be wonderful if they have truly come to purchase farmland in the name of the South China Textile Bureau."

Tian failed to understand the sarcasm in Hai's remarks. "You're right," he quickly responded. "If the Imperial Palace comes out to purchase farmland, we can be spared of lots of work."

Hai shot him an impatient side glance.

"Did I say anything wrong?" Tian asked quizzically.

"No, what you said is right on target. Once you confirm their identities, ask them to wait for me at the pier. I'll meet with them there."

"All right then," Tian uttered a sigh of relief. "Your Honour, now that the imperial grain boats are here, can we return the rice that we have borrowed from the local merchants tomorrow?"

"Did the merchants demand it?" Hai asked, his eyes boring into Tian.

"No, not yet," Tian stammered.

Hai turned his back on Tian. The news relating to the grain boats bearing the name of the South China Textile Bureau threw his mind into turmoil.

Realising that Hai had become preoccupied with something else, Tian crept out.

The sails on the boats had dropped, but the South China Textile Bureau lanterns remained on the masts that were lined up neatly in a straight line, like a forest of spars on the river. The white silk lanterns with red characters glowed prominently, and people could see them clearly from a distance.

The elaborately decorated big boat that carried Shen Yishi was anchored at the pier while the smaller plain grain boats, linked by metal chains, floated along the river approximately twelve metres away. In times of natural catastrophes, grain boats always kept a safe distance from the pier to prevent looting by starving farmers. The local government also tightened security at the pier, and there was a heavy presence of guards.

Shen changed into a set of quasi-official robes. Given his decades-long contractual relations with the South China Textile Bureau, Yang Jinshui had requested the Imperial Palace bestow an honorary six-level official title on him a few years before. As far as uniform was concerned, Shen's robe differed slightly than those of officials who had been appointed by the Imperial Personnel Ministry. His had no mandarin square,[1] and his hat carried no wings. While a government official could easily tell the difference, the public had no clue. They would automatically assume that he was a de facto member of the officialdom.

A diligent businessman, Shen always kept a low profile and seldom showed off his honorary official title. Thus, when he appeared in his government uniform, his aides were taken aback. They had no idea that their boss was part of the officialdom.

Quietly, Shen sat on a chair that his aides had placed at the bow of the boat. The pier was packed with farmers; their hungry eyes locked on Shen and the bags of rice on the boats.

In the distance, Shen could see that his personal aide, escorted by four fully armed soldiers, rushing over on his horse from the north side of Chun'an County. Upon approaching, the aide dismounted and jumped on the walkway that connected to Shen's boat.

"Sir, I'm able to confirm with a prison official that the convicted pirates and their collaborators are still alive," the aide whispered to Shen. "The execution did not happen as scheduled. The criminals are being locked up in the county prison. I'm told that the new magistrate is waiting for the governor's office and the Justice Department to re-examine their cases."

"What else did the new magistrate say?" Shen asked without taking his eyes off the flowing river.

"I didn't get to meet with the new magistrate," the aide explained. "His deputy passed on a message to me, saying that Magistrate Hai Rui would find time to come and meet you today."

"The county is running out of grain subsidies today, and the magistrate doesn't seem to be concerned," Shen wondered aloud.

"I think they have managed to borrow three days' worth of grain from the county's big rice merchants," the aide said.

"If that's the case, I do want to meet with this new magistrate."

"Let me go and urge him to come sooner."

Shen stopped him. "There's no rush. Besides, I don't think he'll listen to you."

The aide stood there, looking lost.

"Take a few of our folks with you and hang out near the county yamen," Shen ordered. "Let me know quickly if you hear anything."

"Yes, sir!"

After his aide left, Shen yelled at the people inside the cabin, "Anyone there?"

Two male servants emerged.

"Yes, sir?"

Shen removed the official hat from his head and handed it over to a servant. "Please help me change into my civilian clothes," Shen said, walking inside bareheaded.

The servants followed him. From the back, they could tell that Shen looked stiff and uneasy in his official robe, which probably didn't feel as solid as his usual cloth-and-linen outfits, or as smooth and light as his silk pyjamas.

明

Shen Yishi was right. Hai Rui refused to leave his office, regardless of who pressured him. When he single-handedly postponed the execution two days before, he had been left with one option – waiting. There was no way of knowing what would await him and if Zheng Bichang and Ho Maocai would show up. If the two of them refused to come, what orders would they issue to Officer Jiang? He had no clue. His only hope was that the messenger who carried his letter could reach Hu in Suzhou on time. If Hu received his message on time, Tan Lun would definitely persuade him to come to his rescue. He was certain of it.

However, Suzhou was further away from Chun'an than

Hangzhou. If Governor Hu happened to be travelling elsewhere, he would have missed the letter and there would be no way to know when he and Tan Lun would be briefed on the latest situation in Chun'an.

When Hai arrived in Chun'an a few days before, the county government had nearly run out of grain subsidies. He had pressured Tian Youlu to borrow rice from local merchants, and the loan would enable the local government to extend the subsidies for four more days. By then, Hai figured that Zheng Bichang's grain-carrying junks would have arrived. His strategy was to intercept the grain boats on the grounds that the pirate collusion case required further review by Governor Hu and the Imperial Palace. In this way, he could stop Zheng's people from taking advantage of flood victims and offering to purchase their farmland at a cheap price. Once he obtained the grain, Hai would "borrow" it in the name of the county government and then distribute it to flood victims as a form of loan to tide them over. If peasants could plant crops in June or July, they could harvest the rice in September or October. After the harvest, peasants could pay back the loans to the county government. If this worked, he could effectively stop the land-acquisition scheme. Of course, that was just a plan, and he was certain that his superiors would never approve of it. But Hai was determined and ready to report it to the Imperial Palace, even though it meant that he could face prison or execution. Once the emperor knew about the truth, political changes would take place. Besides, as long as he could force the Imperial Palace to modify its rice-to-mulberry conversion policy and fulfil the promise he had made to Tan Lun, who had brought him out from his native village, it would be worth the sacrifice.

When news came that the Textile Bureau's grain junks had reached Chun'an, Hai immediately felt that an opportunity presented itself. Based on rules established by the founder of the Ming dynasty, the Imperial Palace could not usurp land from farmers or civilian landowners. The emperor's daily expenses were covered by income from his royal estate. If the emperor's expenses exceeded income, the Department of Treasury would set aside money to cover the deficit. Given the emperor's vast wealth – in theory, the emperor owned his empire, and the whole kingdom belonged to him – there was no reason for him to rob his subjects of their livelihood. It was obvious that those who came to purchase farmland in the name of the South China Textile Bureau, which was affiliated with the Imperial Palace, had violated an ancestral rule and broke the Ming Law. Why would they do such a thing? Even though Hai had no way of knowing their motives, he was certain of one thing – Zheng Bichang and Ho Maocai would not want to come to Chun'an, where their involvement in the deal could be exposed. In fact, all of the provincial agencies would probably stay away from this puddle of murky water.

Without the interference of Zheng and Ho, Hai felt that he could very well intercept the grain boats on charges that the buyer had "tarnished the sacred reputation of the Imperial Palace". The challenge was that he had no trusted officials to help him. Besides, without any soldiers at his disposal, he could not leave the county prison and entrust the guards with the care of the prisoners. If the guards murdered the peasants, Hai would lose the critical witnesses. The consequences would be unthinkable.

When darkness fell, the two guards who delivered food the previous day brought in a candle lamp with a silk shade for Hai. After placing it on his desk, they went on to hang two kerosene lamps on the walls of the passageway. The faint glow from the two tiny lamps made the passage seem even darker.

"Why is it that you only lit up two tiny kerosene lamps today?" Hai questioned. "I want you to hang a large lamp at the entrance of each prison cell."

"Your Honour, the county government rations kerosene oil," one of the guards said. "We nearly ran out of it today, and we had to bring the kerosene oil from home so the place wouldn't be in complete darkness."

"What month is it?" Hai asked.

"Your Honour, it's June."

"Do you mean to say that we are running out of our rations for the year?"

"No, sir. There's a daily ration, and we pick it up every evening," replied one of the guards.

"Where do you pick it up?"

"At the warden's."

"Where is he now?" Hai asked.

"Your Honour, he's probably taking a break now since he's worked for two nights in a row."

"Please bring him over here," Hai ordered.

"Yes, sir," the guards complied.

At that very moment, Warden Wang and Deputy Tian were sitting inside the county yamen with Officers Jiang and Xu, who had just returned from Hangzhou with a verbal order to pre-emptively kill the farmers and the Japanese pirates.

When Wang and Tian were briefed on the killing order, they stood there stiffly and stared at each other in silence. Officers Jiang and Xu fixed their eyes on the warden and the deputy magistrate, waiting for their answers.

Tian finally stirred and said, "Oh, by the way, I have to go now. Magistrate Hai asked me to arrange a meeting between him and the official in charge of the Textile Bureau's grain boats. That person is waiting for me."

Before Officers Jiang and Xu could stop him, Tian bolted towards the door. He looked like he was fleeing hell. But as he was about to cross the threshold, two policemen guarding the entrance pointed their swords at him. He froze, with one foot in the door and the other outside.

"Go back in," one police officer barked.

By then, Tian realised that provincial police officers had taken over the county yamen. Appearing too afraid to go inside, Tian remained where he was. "Wha-what is going on here?" he asked, his voice shaking.

Someone came up from behind and patted him on the shoulder. Tian turned around, pulling the other foot into the door.

"You've held this position for many years," said Officer Jiang sarcastically. "What are you afraid of?"

"I... I am going to meet with an official at the Textile Bureau," Tian replied, his body continued trembling.

"We've just shared our secret order with you, and now you want to run away," said Jiang with a ferocious look.

Tian's legs trembled. "Please have mercy," he begged, falling down on his knees. "I have young children and elderly parents at home. For the sake of my family, I promise I won't divulge the plan to anyone. As for killing the prisoners, I'm really incapable of doing that..."

"Shut up," Officer Jiang shouted. "Sign your name on this agreement."

"Please, I'm the lowest-ranking official in the government," Tian continued. "You can do this assignment without me. It wouldn't make much of a difference if I get involved or not. Please, please have mercy."

"Are you signing the document or not?" Officer Xu banged his fist on a desk.

Tian sprang to his feet. Warden Wang looked startled as well.

"Both of you need to sign your name here," Officer Xu ordered.

"Sir, I don't know how to read and write," said Warden Wang.

"Oh really?" Officer Jiang said. "I understand that you come to the county yamen every day to procure supplies. Who is signing the receipts for you? If both of you refuse to sign your name, that's fine with us. We'll just have to kill you instead. Let me get some help from my police officers."

Two officers walked in with knives in their hands.

"All right, all right, I'll sign," Warden Wang shouted.

Picking up a calligraphy brush from the desk, Warden Wang acted like a true illiterate by toying with it clumsily in his trembling hand. It took him a while before he managed to hold it in the right way and scribble down his name. The characters looked awful.

"It's your turn now," Officer Xu turned to Tian.

Tian slowly walked towards the desk. When Warden Wang handed him the calligraphy brush, Tian tried to hold it steadily, but his legs were giving out. He felt his body wobbling.

"You can sit down," Officer Jiang said impatiently.

Tian took a chair and sat by the desk. When he looked at the agreement, he suddenly felt hopeful. "There's no space here," he pointed out.

Officers Xu and Jiang rushed over to examine the agreement. It turned out that Warden Wang had written his name in such big characters that they occupied the whole signature section.

"What the hell did you do?" Officer Jiang glared at Warden Wang.

"I told you that I don't know how to write," Warden Wang lowered his head and blabbered.

"You can sign your name at the top of the page," Officer Xu told Tian.

"But nobody signs a document like this," Tian argued.

"Just do it," Officer Xu banged his fist on the desk again.

Tian complied and put his name in a blank spot at the top of the page.

明

The big lamps made a very noticeable difference, and the passageway inside the Chun'an County prison was lit up nicely. Tian and Warden Wang returned to the prison duty room. At the entrance, they paused distractedly when they saw Hai Rui sitting at his desk with his eyes almost closed.

Reluctantly, Tian and Warden Wang crossed the threshold and walked in. Four police officers followed them inside.

By the time Hai opened his eyes, Tian and the warden, with four police officers behind them, stood right in front of him.

From their looks, Hai could sense that something had gone awry. Tian forced out a smile while the warden cast his eyes downward. The police officers stared stonily at the wall.

"What happened?" Hai asked, looking slightly alarmed.

"Your Honour, the Textile Bureau has sent someone here to take you to the meeting at the pier," Tian stammered, his eyes cast downward. "I think you should get prepared to go."

"Where is that Textile Bureau official?" Hai asked.

"I saw him at the pier… on a boat…"

"Didn't they promise to send someone over to fetch me? Where is that person? Bring him in then."

"He's... he's actually waiting for you at the county yamen..." Tian said, looking startled.

"Well, if he wants to see me, why didn't you bring him over here?"

Tian's mind went blank. "I... I have no idea... Your Honour, it's not the right time for such questions."

Hai turned to the warden, who stood there silently with his head down. By then, he appeared to have understood what Tian had been trying to hint.

"I made it very clear two days ago that nobody is allowed to enter my office without my permission," he yelled at the four provincial police officers. "How did you get in here?"

The police officers looked at each other without answering.

"Get out of here," Hai barked.

The officers did not move.

"Could you bring Officer Xu in here?" Hai asked Tian, his deputy.

"Wh-why don't you wait outside then?" Tian signalled for the provincial police officers to leave. The soldiers looked lost but complied with Tian's suggestion.

"Where is Magistrate Hai?" Officer Xu questioned the four police officers as he stood in a dark corner outside the county prison. "How dare you leave there without getting him out?"

"Magistrate Hai threatened to summon you if we didn't leave," one soldier reported.

"When we told Magistrate Hai that a Textile Bureau official wants to see him right away, he insisted on seeing the person at his temporary office inside," another guard added.

"He's a pain in the arse," Officer Jiang cursed in the darkness.

As they were talking, Officer Xu noticed that the door to the warden's office clanked shut.

"Why did they shut the door?' Officer Jiang wondered aloud.

"Magistrate Hai is probably afraid that we might barge in again, I guess," one soldier pitched in.

"Go over to the door and wait for my order. I'll let you know what to do next."

The four police officers rushed over to the prison entrance. Officers Xu and Jiang stayed in the dark corner.

"We think Inspector General Zheng and Director Ho have met their nemesis," Officer Jiang muttered through his teeth. "Magistrate Hai is bad news."

"Why don't we set the place on fire and get rid of him, along with the other prisoners?" Xu suggested.

"If only we could," Jiang replied. "That would save us lots of trouble. But the boss told us that the new magistrate was appointed by the Prince of Yu. The only thing we could do to stop him is to secretly kill the pirate and the farmers and then lay the blame on him. This is the only way to gag and silence the Prince of Yu and implement the rice-to-mulberry conversion plan."

"But if he's not coming out, there's nothing we could do," Officer Xu complained. "We can't just wait like this."

"Let's stay here for a few more minutes and see what Deputy Tian has to report," Jiang said.

"I don't think we can afford to wait that long," Xu insisted. "Mayor Gao Hanwen is scheduled to get here at the crack of dawn. Once Mayor Gao is here, we won't be able to do anything."

"I have a backup plan," Jiang whispered. "We'll stay here until midnight. If the new magistrate still refuses to come out, we'll have someone dress up like a pirate, break into his office and kill the farmers and the pirates."

"What about Magistrate Hai?"

"We'll kill the others and keep him alive," Jiang said. "Since he refused to allow any police officers to enter the prison and guard the prisoners, we'll withdraw. Once all the prisoners are killed, people will inevitably blame him for negligence of duty."

Inside the prison office, Deputy Tian and Warden Wang shut the door at Hai's order and then sat down, facing Hai across the table.

"Now that we have plenty of time to kill, why don't we chat about your families?" Hai said in a leisurely tone. "Let's start with Deputy Tian. You have three sons, and I was told that you tutor and supervise their studies every day. What an exemplary father!"

"Thanks for your compliment," Tian said without raising his head.

"I'm not finished yet," Hai added, raising his voice. "You might be a good parent, but you're a lousy son. Your mother passed away, but you refuse to take care of your father. I'm told that you, your wife and sons reside in a comfortable house near the county yamen. How could you let your father live alone in a small hut on the south side of town?"

"Yes, I deserve the reprimand," Tian murmured almost inaudibly.

"You're even worse," Hai turned to Warden Wang with a fierce look. "You were raised by your widowed mother, but when you grew up and managed to get ahead, you abandoned her, leaving her with your poverty-stricken brother. For a low-level warden, you have a wife and a concubine. Aren't you ashamed of yourself for deserting your mother?"

Startled by the scolding, Warden Wang raised his head to face Hai. "Your Honour is truly a mirror, and nothing escapes your notice," he said.

"I'm shouldering a huge responsibility at the moment," Hai said with a piercing gleam. "Unfortunately, neither the imperial inspector nor the director of justice is willing to help me. But regardless, I'm going to persist and find out who has violated laws and conspired against the Imperial Palace. In this way, when His Majesty and the Imperial Palace decide to investigate the matter, I will have an explanation and answer."

Deputy Tian and Warden Wang had been feeling apprehensive upon their return from the county yamen. Hai's remarks sent shivers down their spines. Despite the cold dampness in the prison duty room, they both sweated profusely.

"To tell you the truth, no matter how high our rankings are

within the Imperial Government, we all crave the same thing – a settled family life," said Hai, who softened his tone and suddenly switched gears. "Nobody wants to ruin himself and bring disaster to his family. I have a widowed mother to support. She's turning seventy this year. I have a daughter, but not a son. You two are more blessed than I am."

Hai's words warmed Deputy Tian's heart. Just a few minutes before, he saw Hai as his nemesis, but now his hostilities towards Hai had dissipated. Hai seemed more like his saviour or friend. "Your Honour, you're a rising political star and an immortal who has descended to earth. Our situations are incomparable," he said, sounding almost emotional.

"Don't say that," Hai replied. "In comparison, I do have one advantage over you. All my family members reside in Fujian Province. The Imperial Palace has promised to support them if I die on my job here in Chun'an."

Deputy Tian locked eyes with Warden Wang, who glanced back briefly.

"Your Honour, we're told that the Prince of Yu has appointed you to this post," Tian whispered.

"Does it matter?" Hai asked.

"Of course it does," Tian replied. "The whole world knows that the Prince of Yu will take over the throne someday."

Warden Wang nodded in agreement and gave Hai an earnest look.

Knowing that the two would open their hearts and loosen their tongues, Hai decided to confront them directly. "I want to be straight with you – are you willing to keep your family safe and leave Chun'an peacefully after your tenure is over or are you setting up yourself for trouble?"

Tian stood up. So did Warden Wang.

Tian fell on his knees and pleaded, "Please help us."

Warden Wang followed. "Even though you are the magistrate of your county, many people see you as our local god," he said. "Only you can save us."

"If you listen to what I say and help me overcome this hurdle today, I promise that I'll forgive all of your past transgressions and protect you."

明

The four police officers dispatched by the Provincial Justice Department waited outside the prison entrance, monitoring closely who was coming and going. When Deputy Tian emerged from inside, they immediately went up to him.

"Where is Officer Jiang?" Tian whispered. "Where is Officer Xu?"

"They're waiting for you there," one officer pointed to two dark figures in a shadowy corner under the eaves on the left side of the prison courtyard. Deputy Tian looked in that direction, and it took a while for his eyes to adjust to the darkness outside.

Tian walked over to the dark corner and reported, "It's hopeless. Magistrate Hai said he won't leave the prison until he sees the Textile Bureau official here."

Officer Xu lost his patience. He was about to barge in when Officer Jiang pulled him back. "Let's try to get Mr Shen's personal aide here. Where is he?"

"He and several bodyguards are waiting at the county yamen," Tian replied.

"Bring him over here," Officer Jiang ordered. "Tell him to lure Magistrate Hai out of the prison and take him to see Mr Shen at the pier."

"I doubt he's going to listen to what I say…" Tian said.

"Tell him that you have seen Mr Shen and it is Mr Shen's idea…"

"All right, let me try then," Tian said, looking hesitant.

"It's not a matter of whether you try or not," Xu yelled. "You have to get him out. Full stop."

"All right, I'll go now," Tian promised.

明

The moon lay shrouded in the clouds, and a few lone stars were twinkling. In previous years, the rice seedlings would have grown into lush green plants, and frogs in the field would have croaked non-stop. With the flooding this year, farmers were not able to plant any rice seedlings this season. Wild grass ran rampant. The chirping of insects choked out the croaking sounds of frogs.

Loud rumbling sounds of a horse-drawn carriage came from the distance, scaring some insects into silence. As the vehicle entered the horizon, the wobbling lantern lights turned broader.

A contingent of cavalrymen escorted Mayor Gao Hanwen as his carriage headed towards Chun'an. Four soldiers led the way, and another four followed behind. A captain's horse galloped along the carriage to take orders from Gao and protect his personal safety.

Before Gao left, Zheng had arranged for him to take a boat, but Gao insisted on travelling by land. So Zheng changed his plan at the last minute and assigned the captain and eight cavalrymen to keep Gao company and, more importantly, to control his itinerary. He was scheduled to arrive in Chun'an the next morning. So far, the timing had been perfect. With about one hour before sunlight, Gao and his entourage planned to take a short break after reaching the foot of Five Lion Mountain. Once they passed through the mountain, Chun'an would be right there.

Gao sat inside the carriage, with his eyes closed. Even though his body was still weak following his collapse at the conference, he felt more invigorated. Yang Jinshui's secret visit gave him a glimmer of hope, enabling him to breathe again and vent his frustrations and grievances. Gao was well aware of the dangers and uncertainties that lay before him, but with the guidance of the Confucian philosophy that he had mastered, he was confident that he could handle the challenges. At the same time, he was also eager to see Hai Rui. During the second conference at the inspector general's yamen, Gao felt deeply touched by Hai's fearlessness and his awe-inspiring statement – *I would turn myself into a river or a mountain to nurture the earth and become the moon or a star to decorate the sky.* To Gao, Hai was the living embodiment of righteousness, and he long admired him. The moment he embarked on his journey to Chun'an, Hai had been on his mind. The thought that Hai was fighting the evil forces by himself in Chun'an further enhanced his admiration. Gao grew excited at the idea that the two of them would soon join forces there, and it energised him. Opening his eyes, he lifted the curtains, trying to find out about their exact time of arrival.

Suddenly, the carriage came to a halt.

"Where are we now?"

"Mayor Gao, we are at the foot of Five Lion Mountain," the captain replied.

Having read the Chun'an Almanac, Gao was familiar with the local topography. "This means that we'll be in Chun'an after we climb over the mountain," he said.

"Your Honour, that's correct," said the captain.

"Let's keep going then," Gao urged. "In this way, we can reach Chun'an before daylight."

To Gao's surprise, the captain dismounted his horse and ignored his order. The other cavalrymen followed suit.

"Did you hear what I just said?" Gao asked.

"We're exhausted, and so are the horses," answered the captain. "We need a break."

"All right then," Gao said. "But let's make it brief. We need to leave soon."

"I doubt we can get there before daylight," the captain said. "Why don't we rest up and start after daylight?"

Before Gao had the chance to reply, the captain ordered his cavalrymen to feed the horses and lie down to take a good night's sleep.

Gao immediately understood the situation – the delay was deliberate and part of Zheng Bichang's scheme. In a fit of rage, he jumped down from the carriage and walked up to the captain. "Please hand me your horse," he ordered.

"Your Honour, what are you trying to do?" The captain held the reins tightly.

"You can take your break, and I'm going to Chun'an by myself."

The captain pulled the reins and said firmly, "I'm afraid you can't do that, Your Honour. The inspector general has assigned us to protect you, and we can't let you go alone. It's not safe."

Gao raised his head. Heavy clouds covered the moon, and the

stars twinkled silently. Under the dark sky, Gao felt lonely and powerless. Suddenly, he heard the captain yelling. "Who's there?"

Gao turned around and saw a dozen men on horses coming out of a forest nearby.

Gao's bodyguards pulled their daggers out, waiting for combat. As the strangers were approaching, Gao could make out a man pulling a horse. Two others carrying lanterns walked beside him.

"Freeze," the captain shouted at the strangers.

"Are you blind?" the stranger in the middle yelled back. "Can't you see the big characters on the lanterns?"

Gao looked closer and realised the stranger was Tan Lun. The characters on the lantern read *Governor's Yamen*.

The cavalrymen, looking timid and deflated, put their daggers back into their scabbards and made way for Tan Lun.

Gao, who had met Tan at the Xinyang hotel, went up to greet him. When Tan Lun held his hands, Gao appeared choked up with emotion.

Tan pulled Gao aside and whispered. "Let's go somewhere else to talk."

Seeing the two officials walking away into the forest, the captain beckoned two of his cavalrymen, instructing them to follow them.

Tan paused and asked, "What're you doing?"

"Your Honour, we have been tasked to protect Mayor Gao," the captain answered.

"I overheard your conversation just now," Tan said. "Mayor Gao intended to go on with his journey, but you tried to sabotage his schedule and refused to leave. As his escort, that's not the right thing to do, is it?"

The captain remained silent.

"The Ming Law stipulates clearly that military personnel are subservient to civil officials," Tan chastised. "You are a low-level Justice Department officer – how dare you threaten the Mayor of Hangzhou and Imperial Emissary?"

The captain saw a group of guards from the governor's yamen swarming out of the forest.

"Remove their daggers and put them away," Tan ordered.

The guards rushed over, wrestled down the captain and the cavalrymen, then disarmed them.

"Move over there," Tan yelled.

The captain and his men crouched down on the side of a pathway.

"This way please," Tan said, leading Gao towards the forest.

明

Deputy Tian managed to bring Shen's personal aide and four provincial police officers to the prison courtyard. Officers Jiang and Xu, who crouched down in the dark corner, nodded at the group as they headed towards the entrance.

Deputy Tian knocked on the door. Someone inside asked a few questions before the door opened. Tian led the way, and Shen's personal aide followed him in. The four police officers, however, were prevented from entering.

"Come on over," Officer Jiang called out to the policemen. They dashed over. "Do you know if our men outside have changed into civilian clothes yet?"

"Yes, they changed clothes quite a while ago," said one policeman.

"As soon as Magistrate Hai leaves here with Mr Shen's personal aide, we'll break in and kill all the criminals in custody," said Jiang.

"Understood," the four provincial policemen replied in unison.

明

Inside Hai's temporary office, Shen's personal aide was taken aback when the thick door clanked shut behind him.

"Please take a seat," Hai greeted him, pointing to a chair in front of the desk.

The aide, looking nervous, sat down slowly.

"Are you with the Textile Bureau?" Hai asked.

"We're contractors for the Textile Bureau."

"I was supposed to meet with your boss earlier," Hai explained. "But we have a major criminal investigation going here. The case involves collusion with the pirates. So I can't leave. I appreciate your coming over to see me here."

"We have about one hundred grain boats anchored at the pier," the aide said quickly. "My boss can't abandon the grain boats and come over," the aide said.

"I'm not asking him to come over," Hai said. "I'll go and see him there."

The aide stood up and said, "That's perfect. Let's go now, and I'll take you there."

"There's no rush," Hai said, signalling him to sit down. "We have another hour before daylight. If you don't mind, I would like you to wait here with me. I'll go with you in the morning."

"I was told that you have promised to go there now," the aide said, turning to Deputy Tian to confirm.

"No, you must have misunderstood me," Tian explained. "I didn't promise that."

"Then why did you bring me over here then?" the aide asked, looking visibly annoyed.

"You're here on behalf of the Textile Bureau. Under normal circumstances, I would need to entertain you as the routine courtesy of a host. But since I can't do that at the county yamen, I thought I would entertain you here."

"There's really no need," the aide rose and pushed the chair out of his way. "I'll go back to the county yamen and wait for you there. I'll see you when you're back there."

"You can't leave now," Hai said and then asked Warden Wang to lock the door from the inside.

"What are you trying to do?" the aide asked, looking alarmed.

"As I said, I want you to be here with me until daylight," Hai reassured him. "Then, we'll go and check out the grain boats at the pier. Please sit down and relax."

Officers Jiang and Xu were becoming impatient.

"What do you think is happening inside?" Officer Xu asked his colleague. "Why aren't they coming out?"

Sensing that something had gone wrong, Officer Jiang ordered a policeman to find out.

Officers Jiang and Xu watched as the policeman knocked on the prison door. He appeared to be talking with someone from the inside. They engaged in a long conversation, but the door never opened.

"What is going on in there?" Officer Jiang asked when the policeman came back, looking dejected.

"A person inside told me that Magistrate Hai is talking business with Mr Shen's personal aide," replied the policeman. "Magistrate Hai will go and visit the grain boats after daylight."

"Did you have the chance to talk with Deputy Tian and Warden Wang?" Officer Jiang asked.

"No, but the person at the door told me that he was passing on the message that came from Deputy Tian and Warden Wang."

"Damn it," Officer Jiang stomped on the ground and cursed. "Those two bastards have betrayed us."

"I don't think it's a good idea for us to wait here," Officer Xu suggested. "Why don't we bring some of our people over and break into the office. But first, we need to get the Textile Bureau rep out."

"Sir, the door is locked from the inside," a policeman reported.

"Go and strike at the door, hard," Officer Xu, whose face became livid with anger, ordered.

"But what if we harm the textile bureau rep?" Officer Jiang reminded. "We could be in big trouble."

"It's getting late," Officer Xu argued. "Let's strike the door open first."

After giving it some thought, Officer Jiang said, "Why don't we set the house on fire first? Then, we can claim that we are part of the fire brigade and need to break the door open. Once we get in, we'll rescue the Textile Bureau rep and abduct Magistrate Hai. Then, we can kill the rest."

"What a good idea," Officer Xu agreed. He asked the provincial policemen if they understood the plan.

"Yes, sir," the policemen responded.

"Let's divide up into two groups," Officer Xu instructed his men. "One group will start the fire. Once the place is in flames, the other group can break in and snatch Magistrate Hai and the Textile Bureau rep."

As the policemen went about gathering dry cigarettes for the fire, more people joined them. The small courtyard suddenly became chaotic.

As Officers Xu and Jiang were directing traffic in the courtyard, another policeman ran up to them for help.

"What's wrong?" Officer Jiang asked.

"Sir, the door's so thick, and we don't have the tools to knock it open."

"Go and find a wood column," ordered Xu, who looked visibly upset.

"But there's no wood column in this courtyard," the policeman argued.

"Run outside and see if you can get one," Officer Xu yelled. "If you can't, knock down the porch at the end of the street, and take one from there."

"Yes, sir," the policeman said before dashing outside with his colleagues.

Officer Xu was right. The policemen spotted a store not far from the prison at the end of a small street. The storefront was supported by a thick wooden column. "That's it," one policeman shouted with excitement.

The group hacked away at the bottom of the wood column with knives. Very soon, two deep cuts appeared.

"Let's push it," one policeman suggested.

"When it collapses, people inside could get hurt," the other said hesitantly.

"I don't think it will kill them." The first one shrugged off the concern and began kicking at the column. The wood became wobbly but did not collapse. A few tiles fell from the roof and smashed onto the ground. The commotion woke up the people inside the store.

"Burglars," someone shouted from the inside.

"Shut up," two policemen walked up to the window and yelled. "If you keep yelling, I'm going to kill your whole family."

Silence ensued.

"Let's keep going," said the policeman who was kicking at the wood column.

When another policeman tried to shove it with his shoulder, the structure vibrated but remained unmoved. Soon, he hit the ground bouncing on his backside.

A third policeman came up with the idea of forming a human chain. First, he stretched out his hand against the wood column, and a second policeman pushed against the first one's back, and the third one pushed against the second's back, and the fourth pushed against the third… When the line was ready, the policeman at the front shouted, "I'll count to three, and then we'll all push together… one, two, three, push…"

The storefront crashed to the ground, and tiles scattered everywhere. Fortunately, the policemen had enough time to run away from it. Before the dust settled, they pulled the wood column from the debris and carried it on their shoulders.

Before the policemen reached the prison courtyard, they heard the urgent clattering of stallions' hooves. Startled, they paused. An entourage of cavalrymen emerged from a side street and stopped. Their horses galloped around, braying.

The official was Mayor Gao Hanwen. "What are you doing?" he asked the policemen, who stood there, stunned at the sudden appearance of a dozen cavalrymen. "Which yamen do you work for?"

"Your Honour, the county prison is on fire," one policeman stammered. "We're trying to knock the door open and save the people inside."

"The prison is on fire?" Gao asked, looking shocked. "Please take us there."

The policemen did not move.

"Let's go!" Gao shouted.

Seeing that the cavalrymen pulled their daggers out, the policemen backed down and led Gao's entourage to the prison courtyard, where fire torches were lit and a group of provincial policemen had set up a big pile of dry cigarettes next to the prison building. All they needed was the big wood column to knock the door open.

Since light now illuminated the courtyard, Officers Jiang and Xu retreated to a small vacant room and hid behind the door. The commotion and clattering hooves outside caught their attention.

"It doesn't look good," Officer Xu speculated aloud. "Why don't we set the building on fire first?"

"Wait, don't do it," Officer Jiang stopped him.

As Officers Jiang and Xu were discussing their next move, the policemen carrying the wood column hurried into the yard, followed by a dozen cavalrymen.

Officer Jiang slammed the door shut. Through a small window, he and Officer Xu spotted Mayor Gao on his horse, which was circling the courtyard.

"Where is the fire?" Mayor Gao asked.

The policemen holding the fire torches quickly tossed them onto the ground, trying to stamp them out with their feet.

"Stand still there," Mayor Gao ordered. "If anyone moves, I'm going to have you arrested on the spot."

"Stand in a line," shouted the head of the cavalrymen, all of whom bore the badges issued by the governor's office.

The two dozen policemen, who had been dispatched by the Provincial Justice Department, quickly followed orders and formed two straight lines on both sides of the courtyard.

"Where is Magistrate Hai?" Mayor Gao asked.

"Your Honour, he's... he's inside the prison duty room," reported the policeman who was responsible for getting the wood column.

Gao dismounted his horse and said, "Take me inside."

When Hai Rui saw Gao Hanwen at the door, he rose from his chair slowly. Nearby, a steep flight of stairs led down to the duty room. Tian quickly rushed over to lend Gao a hand. "Careful with the stairs," Tian warned. Gao pushed Tian's hands away and strode down, his eyes sparkling with excitement.

Across from the desk, the two men stared at each other, speechless.

"Your Honour, did you see Governor Hu?" Hai asked in a soft voice.

"No," Gao shook his head. "But he sent someone over to help us."

"You talked with Mr Tan?"

Gao nodded.

Hai uttered a sigh of relief. Suddenly, he was overtaken by exhaustion and plopped down on his chair.

"Please take Magistrate Hai to the yamen so he can have some rest," Gao told Deputy Tian and Warden Wang, who rushed over to assist Hai. But Hai struggled to stand up.

"I apologise," he said to Gao. "But, Your Honour, I can't rest yet."

"Do you think you can hold up a bit longer?"

"Your Honour, if you can hold up well, so can I."

For the first time in a week, a faint smile flashed across Gao's face. "Can you all step out for a few minutes," he said to the people in the room. "I need to discuss something with Magistrate Hai."

Deputy Tian and Warden Wang exited the room. At the entrance, Tian pulled a cavalryman aside and whispered, "Officers Jiang and Xu are hiding inside one of those rooms in the courtyard. If you do a thorough search, you can catch them."

The cavalryman shrugged off his suggestion. "We only take orders from Mayor Gao," he said. "You have no authority here."

Deputy Tian swallowed his pride and turned to Warden Wang.

"No need to worry," Warden Wang steadfastly consoled Deputy Tian. "We're going to get back the signed paper, regardless."

Inside the prison office, Gao and Hai sat across the table. "As long as I'm here, I don't think anybody would dare make trouble for you," Gao said. "Based on Mr Tan's suggestion, you should go to the pier directly and remove the lanterns that bear the South China Textile Bureau's name. Then, take over the grain boats by force. I wouldn't be able to do it. You'll be perfect for the task because you have the backing of the Prince of Yu, who recommended you to the Personnel Department."

"How many troops do I have?" Hai asked.

"How many do you need?"

"What are you saying?" Hai asked, looking baffled.

"This is a signed document from the governor's office," Gao pulled out a piece of paper from his breast pocket and handed it over to Hai. "With this paper, you can have as many troops as you need."

Hai reached out both of his hands, but Gao did not release it at first. "Brother Hai, do whatever is needed to help the people here," Gao promised. "Regardless of what happens, I'll be with you here."

Light streamed into the room from the windows. The day was breaking.

It had been a sultry and windless summer, but a gentle breeze suddenly rose at daybreak. Emperor Jiajing immediately instructed his eunuchs to open his palace doors. As the silk curtains that separated different halls danced in the breeze, the emperor sat with his legs crossed on his bright yellow meditation mat and watched the invisible wind with fascination. The eunuchs noticed that the emperor, dressed in a thick Songjiang cotton robe, looked calmer and more refreshed than he did the night before.

Grand Secretary Yan Song was granted an audience this morning. Panic covered his face as he stared ahead, with his aged eyes seemingly absorbing nothing. Everything on the other side of the silk curtain seemed hazy and blurry. Meanwhile, his son, Yan Shifan, knelt in the outer chamber.

Lu Fang went about his routine. First, he replaced the incense on the altar and picked up a fan before moving over to stand next to Emperor Jiajing. The open palace doors had allowed some bugs and insects to fly in. Lu held the fan to ward off any such attacks.

"His Majesty's sincerity paid off handsomely," he murmured as he slowly swayed the fan. "We finally have a nice breeze. I bet the rain will arrive in a couple of days."

"Why don't you stop the chatter now," Emperor Jiajing interrupted. "Let them do the talking today."

"Yes, Your Majesty."

Yan Song turned to his son and started the session. "Yan Shifan, please give us an update on the rice-to-mulberry conversion programme in Zhejiang Province. Have the flood victims received government subsidies? Please state truthfully any new development to His Majesty."

Yan Shifan's voice could be heard distinctly outside the hanging curtains. "I received a report from Zhejiang last night. The report says that some local farmers have allegedly conspired with pirates and intended to start a riot. The provincial government has assigned Hai Rui, the newly appointed magistrate for Chun'an County, to handle the case. Once this is settled, we're going to implement the land-conversion strategy to help with the disaster relief effort. We're certain that the new mulberry trees will be planted by June."

"How is your strategy going to work?" Emperor Jiajing asked. "How do you use conversion to help with the disaster relief effort?"

There was a moment of silence.

"Your Majesty," Yan Shifan's voice sounded again. "We encourage large silk merchants to step up and purchase farmland from farmers. Then, they can convert what they have bought into mulberry fields. We have also made arrangements to help farmers who have lost their land during the flood. After they sell their farmland to silk merchants, they can still continue farming on the land they owned before."

"Who are those big silk merchants?"

"Your Majesty, I'm referring to those merchants who own large-scale silk mills in Zhejiang Province."

Emperor Jiajing glanced at Lu Fang, who looked back knowingly and spoke up. "You're talking about the South China Textile Bureau, aren't you?"

The question sent Yan Song reeling. He made a quick eye contact with Lu Fang.

Yan Shifan's voice, full of panic, came from the outer chamber. "Your Majesty, I... I... don't know what Lu Gonggong meant by that?"

Emperor Jiajing peered at Lu Fang.

"Heaven knows whether you're aware of it or not," Lu Fang continued in his high-pitched voice.

Yan Song rose from his mat and dropped to his knees.

A strong howling wind rose, attacking the palace from all sides.

The windows clanked. When the hanging silk curtains flew up in the air, the audience could see Yan Shifan kneeling in the outer chamber.

Lu Fang rushed over to Emperor Jiajing's side to grab a flying curtain. When he firmly held it in his hands, another one on the opposite side began floating, passing over Yan Song's head.

The clanking palace doors caught the attention of two young eunuchs, who ran to the entrance to constrain them.

"Close them!" Lu Fang shrieked. "Close the palace doors."

The roaring wind made it almost impossible to push the doors shut.

"Leave them open then," Emperor Jiajing ordered.

"Your Majesty..." Lu Fang looked at the emperor while clutching the curtains.

"I just said it – do not shut the doors," Emperor Jiajing repeated.

"All right then," Lu Fang told the eunuchs. "Leave them open. Come over and help me tie up the curtains."

The eunuchs who were holding the doors wouldn't dare release them for fear that they could slam and damage the frames. "We need help inside," one eunuch shouted to his co-workers outside the palace. Two more eunuchs immediately rushed in, as if they had been blown in by the wind. They ran over to where Lu Fang was standing and took the curtains from Lu's hands. For the first few minutes, the eunuchs had to kneel down to restrain the flying curtains.

Once he let go of the curtains, Lu stepped in front of the emperor, trying to shield his master from the blast that was blowing onto his face.

Emperor Jiajing brushed him aside and said, "There's no need to protect me from the wind."

Reluctantly, Lu moved to the side and turned to the emperor nervously, trying to figure out what he wanted to do next.

The wind that assaulted his face became so fierce that Emperor Jiajing had to close his eyes. "Yan Shifan," he said. "Before the heavenly god and me, please respond to me truthfully."

Yan Shifan knelt there, his back against the wind. He widened his eyes and answered nervously, "Your Majesty is the son of heaven, and I would never dare lie about it."

Oddly enough, the minute Yan Shifan uttered those words, the wind died down, but the sky darkened. A rainstorm was on the horizon.

Emperor Jiajing waved his hands slightly, and Lu Fang got the signal. Turning towards the two eunuchs who were trying to tame the curtains, he said, "We are all right without your help. Please exit. On your way out, tell the same thing to those two at the entrance."

"Yes, sir." The two eunuchs tied the curtains to a column, and then they rose and retreated. At that very moment, a bolt of lightning struck, followed by waves of rumbling thunder.

"Can you hear the thunder?" Emperor Jiajing asked Yan Shifan.

"Before heaven, and before Your Majesty, I swear that I did not lie. If I did, let the lightning strike me dead."

As if scripted, a bolt of lightning flashed as thunder roared in the sky. More thunder exploded, and lightning struck the ground outside the palace.

As the heavy rain cascaded down, Emperor Jiajing looked beyond the meditation room and through the big palace windows. A water curtain of rain looked like a canopy of heaven. "The heavenly god has handed me this vast country," he lamented. "As his son and the parent of my people, how could I rob my farmers of their livelihood by taking advantage of the flood and buying up farmland at a cheap price? If I'm an ungrateful son, the heavenly god would reject me. If I'm a heartless parent and ruler, my subjects would overthrow me."

Yan Shifan's pale face turned whiter.

Yan Song summoned enough strength and urged his son in a stern tone, "Respond to His Majesty."

"If the rumours prove to be true, I deserve to die," Yan Shifan replied. "If any officials in Zhejiang are buying up farmers' land in the flooded areas in the name of the Textile Bureau, I'll launch a thorough investigation immediately."

"Is it really worth investigating?" Lu Fang interjected. "It's quite obvious, isn't it? Officials in Zhejiang had decided to purchase farmland in the name of the Textile Bureau even before Yang Jinshui returned to Hangzhou. When the grain boats departed, Inspector General Zheng Bichang and Justice Department Director Ho Maocai were spotted at the pier supervising the operation. They would have reported this to the Privy Council, wouldn't they?"

"The council never received any report on what you just mentioned," Yan Shifan insisted. "If it's true that Zheng Bichang and Ho Maocai have orchestrated this scheme, I will have them executed on the spot on behalf of His Majesty. Personally, I'm also willing to take the blame and receive whatever punishment Your Majesty deems appropriate."

"I like what you just pledged," Emperor Jiajing continued. "Given what you have just said, I feel obligated to accept your promise and apology. But, on the other hand, I doubt my subjects will accept my flimsy explanation."

Then, the emperor moved to Yan Song. "I put you in charge of the Privy Council, but you have ended up with this huge hole in the budget," he rebuked. "To help you resolve the budget crisis, I agreed to your land-conversion plan. If you shift the blame of the current budget crisis to me, I think I should give up the throne and let you two take over."

There was a Chinese saying that goes, *Being in the company of an emperor is tantamount to living with a tiger.* Deep down, that was how Yan Song and his son felt at that very moment. Yan Song removed his official hat and placed it on the floor. So did Yan Shifan.

Yan Song raised his head and said with tears running down his cheeks, "Whatever the transgressions are, no matter how grave, I should be held accountable. Yan Shifan will also take responsibility. If our resignation can help cleanse the stains from your sacred name, we would like to do it now and seek your forgiveness."

"We're neck-deep in this mess, and now you want to quit?" the emperor said sarcastically.

Another round of thunderstorms rumbled outside, but inside the palace there was an awkward silence. The emperor and his ministers sat there, quietly.

"Why don't we give him another chance?" Emperor Jiajing said to Lu Fang. "We'll allow Yan Shifan to launch an investigation. What I said today was meant for the four of us. I hope you keep it to yourself."

"Understood," Lu Fang replied.

Yan Song and Yan Shifan lifted their teary faces and looked at the emperor with relief.

"I'm giving the Privy Council back to you," the emperor said. "Go and do whatever you need to do."

The father and son dropped to their knees in unison and expressed their gratitude before picking up their official hats from the floor. Yan Shifan rose quickly, but his father was struggling to get up.

"Give your father a hand," Emperor Jiajing ordered.

Yan Shifan stepped up and helped the old man up by his arm. Emperor Jiajing watched as the father and son disappeared in the passageway. Then, he looked out of the window. There was no let-up in the rainstorm. It felt as if the whole country was soaked in an overwhelming rain.

"Have the Embroidered Uniform Guards[2] arrived in Zhejiang?" Emperor Jiajing suddenly asked Lu Fang.

Lu Fang tiptoed to his side and whispered, "Your Majesty, they just left last night."

"We should select a few more capable ones and send them over," said Emperor Jiajing, who was suddenly seized with disgust

"Yes, Your Majesty."

Had it been on a sunny day, Yan Song's double-seat sedan would have waited in front of the stone steps that led to the Yuxi Palace. According to Imperial Palace rules, the prince or a senior/ailing minister could enjoy the privilege of riding on a double-seat sedan. As the grand secretary, Yan Song was granted this special treatment after he had turned seventy. However, due to foul stormy weather, the eunuchs carried the sedan all the way up to the front gate of the palace. While waiting patiently under the eaves, the eunuchs sheltered the sedan with a rainproof canopy and put up the curtains.

Since Yan Shifan was too young to enjoy such a privilege, a eunuch standing next to the sedan chair prepared him a big umbrella.

At this very moment, Yan Shifan held his father by the arm, and the duo tottered on the long passageway – in fact, they were literally dragging their feet. The passageway linking the emperor's meditation room to the outer chamber ran fifteen metres long, but Yan Song felt that he was trekking one thousand metres.

Since he took over the Privy Council twenty years before, Yan Song had weathered many political storms. Would the canopy over his sedan and the large-sized umbrella shelter him and his son from the current one? The old man could not fathom it. He felt as dark and gloomy as the weather.

The father and son finally reached the main entrance. Before the high threshold, Yan Shifan attempted to assist his father, but the old man paused and pushed his hands away. Instead, Yan Song lifted the bottom of his robe. Slowly, he put his right foot over the threshold and then the left one.

Having endured a gruesome meeting with Emperor Jiajing and then the cold shoulder from his father, Yan Shifan found it hard to hold his anger. Moving to the side of the entrance, he watched silently as his father wobbled out of the door in silent rage.

The eunuchs waiting next to the sedan quickly jumped into action. One person tilted the sedan from the back to make it easier for the old man to board while another one held the curtain open. However, Yan Song ignored them and walked away into the pouring rain.

The eunuchs stood there, stunned. So did Yan Shifan. Forgetting about his anger, he grabbed the umbrella from a young eunuch, caught up with his father and held the umbrella over him.

Yan Song paused on a stone step, staring at the cascading rain. "I don't need the umbrella," he said without looking at his son. "Move it away."

"Father," Yan Shifan yelled, his voice filled with heroic generosity. "All your life, you have sheltered His Majesty from wind and rain. Your son has done the same thing for you. If anything happens, I'll take all the blame, and I'm willing to die on your behalf. There's no need to worry. I will not drag you through the mud."

Yan Song turned around to face his son. Tears mixing with raindrops flew down his cheeks. "Let me tell you something, Son," he sobbed. "In this country, there is only one person who has the power to summon rain and call for wind. That is His Majesty. There's only one person who has the ability to shelter our family from rain and storm – that is me, not you. I have weathered storms under His Majesty for twenty years. Nobody can protect you from the wind and rain that you have incurred upon yourself. Throughout history, a minister's fall could implicate nine branches and generations of his family. But the laws of the Ming dynasty call for the death of ten branches! Throw away your umbrella. It can neither protect you nor our Yan family."

Yan Shifan stood alone in the white rain as his father tottered away. The wind and rain pelted the old man's face and body.

Meanwhile, Yan Shifan let go of the umbrella, which quickly rolled away in the flowing water. Like a marionette, Yan Shifan followed the misty figure as it tumbled in the distance.

ABOUT THE AUTHOR

Liu Heping was born in Hunan Province, southern China in 1953. He spent his childhood in the theatre and went on to become an acclaimed screenwriter, novelist and historian known for his deep insights into the events of Chinese history. His pioneering historical drama about the Ming dynasty, *Da Ming Wang Chao 1566*, was first published as a novel in 2006 and sold nearly a million copies. The following year, it was broadcast as a 46-episode TV series that garnered popular and critical acclaim in China. His Chinese Civil War TV drama, *All Quiet in Peking*, gained a cumulative 400 million online views in the month following its first broadcast in October 2014. The series made waves among China's intellectual circles and was picked up for international distribution by Netflix. Liu's realist approach to the historical and contemporary transformation of China has been hugely influential and well received in the Chinese-speaking world.

ABOUT THE TRANSLATOR

Wen Huang is a Chicago-based writer and translator. His memoir about growing up in Xi'an in the 1970s, *The Little Red Guard*, was a *Washington Post* Best of 2012 pick. He started translating Chinese non-fiction works in 2005, and since then his translations have been published by Pantheon, Harper Collins and Amazon. In 2007, he was the recipient of a PEN Translation Fund Award. His writings have appeared in *The Paris Review*, *Harper's Magazine*, *The Asia Literary Review* and *Words Without Borders*.

Carolyn Alessio, Michael Bradley and Bill Brown provided Wen with insightful feedback and valuable editorial assistance while he was translating this book.

ABOUT THE SERIES

In 2007, *Da Ming Wang Chao 1566* captivated Chinese readers and TV audiences with the true story of a humble scholar-official named Hai Rui who stood up to the rampant corruption within the court of the Jiajing Emperor.

The Taoist Emperor is the first in a series of four English-language novels that have been translated from the original Chinese. The remaining three volumes – *The Imperial Governor*, *The Chief Eunuch* and *The Defiant Magistrate* – are works in progress and will be published by Sinoist Books soon.

NOTES

CHAPTER 1

1. Gonggong: a respectful way to address a senior eunuch
2. Yuanxiao: sticky rice balls
3. Li Shizhen: a legendary herbal doctor in the central province of Hubei

CHAPTER 3

1. Wang Yangming: a philosopher and military strategist

CHAPTER 5

1. Mi Nangong: a calligrapher, painter and poet during the Song dynasty
2. Huang Tingjian: a calligrapher, painter and poet during the Song dynasty
3. Li Qingzhao: a poet and essayist during the Song dynasty

CHAPTER 6

1. Ji Kang: a writer, philosopher, musician and alchemist from the Three Kingdoms period
2. From a love poem in the ancient *Book of Songs:* "Across the bank, a deer bleats, in the wilds where it eats."

CHAPTER 7

1. Yu, the Great: a legendary Chinese ruler who introduced flood control
2. Sheji: a Chinese deity of soil and harvest

CHAPTER 9

1. Shangshu: one of the Five Classics of ancient Chinese literature

CHAPTER 10

1. Mandarin square: a badge that was sewn onto the suitcoat of an imperial official
2. Embroidered Uniform Guards: the imperial secret police